JUSTIFY MY SINS

A Hollywood Novel

in Three Acts

Felice Picano

Beautiful Dreamer Press

Beautiful Dreamer Press
309 Cross St.
Nevada City, CA 95959
U.S.A.
www.BeautifulDreamerPress.com
info@BeautifulDreamerPress.com
Publicaton date: March 31, 2019

Paperback Edition
10 9 8 7 6 5 4 3 2 1
Printed in the United States of America

ISBN: 978-0-9981262-8-9
Library of Congress Control Number: 2018964066

Cover Design by Kei.
Cover Layout by Tom Schmidt.

**Selected works
by Felice Picano**

The Lure

Eyes

Like People in History

The Book of Lies

True Stories

Nights at Rizzoli's

Justify My Sins

A Hollywood Novel
in Three Acts

ACT ONE

1977: THE PITCH

Her mind is Tiffany-twisted,
She's got the Mercedes-Bends.
She's got a lot of pretty, pretty boys
That she calls friends.

                    --The Eagles, "Hotel California"

CHAPTER ONE

"Mon-ey!" the chorus sang out. "It's a gas!" they added ecstatically.

"*What?*" Vic yelled into the receiver.

When the woman answering—Maggie it sounded like—yelled back and he still couldn't make out what she was saying, he shouted, "I can't hear you. Hold on. Let me shut this off."

He slid over the desk, pressed the button that lifted the arm off the LP, and returned to the phone.

"That's better. Now what were you saying?"

"We had a bet, " Maggie said. "I say it's *Atom Heart Mother*. Justine says it's *Dark Side of the Moon*."

The music Vic was playing in the background, she meant.

"Hope you didn't bet a lot," he said, "because Justine's right."

"Rats! Well it was your literary agent, Marcie, who called just before you got into the apartment. She said it was very important." And in a lower voice. "She said it was from Hollywood."

"O-kay!" he cheered.

"Please don't tell me you're going to Hollywood, Mister R.," Maggie said.

"Jus, He's going to Hollywood," Vic heard her say to her colleague at the phone answering service in an aggrieved voice.

"I thought you would be happy for me," he complained.

"We are, Mister R. Well, *I* am," she modified. "But you know it's always sorta' been a long-distance dream of mine."

He hadn't known that.

"Maggie!" he said, "Planes leave twice a day outta Kennedy headed for El Lay."

"You know what I mean, Mister R.! Being invited! Having someone *else* pay!"

She sighed.

"That's what's happening with you, right? Someone's inviting you out there and paying your way and your stay at where? the Beverly Hills Hotel, I'll bet?"

"If you put me through to Marcie, I'll find out where I'm staying and I'll be able to tell you all the lurid details," he tempted.

"Oh, sure. Sorry, Mister R. Hold on. Here goes."

He heard it her starting to dial.

Maggie broke in to add, "You'll make sure and call us back, won't you, Mister R.?"

"Maggie! Dial! Dial my literary agent."

She dialed and her heard it ring once, twice. Dane, his agent's most recent—and most wildly irreverent—gay male assistant answered.

"She's in a good mood, for once," Dane giggled. "Better get her while she's hot."

Dane put through the connection and Marcie answered with a resonance as though she were deep within someone's toilet.

"Why do you sound as though you're in Antarctica?" Victor had to ask.

"I'm—can you hold on a sec, Vic?—Ooops! There goes the fuck—" A crash followed, followed in turn by a much chastened Marcie, completing her sentence, "—ing table with the lamp my tight assed mother gave me last Chanukah."

Before he could ask, Marcie explained:

"I was attempting to stand on my head, against the wall. Yoga," she added lamely. "It was your idea, Victor."

"For your two hundred year old spine? You never did any yoga when I suggested it before. Has Mick finally talked you into doing some postures?"

"Rick," she corrected, "did, in fact, show me a few postures."

He could hear her shushing Rick and getting him out of her office.

"Rick," he stood corrected. "I'll just bet Rick was showing you 'some postures.' What was he doing while you were standing on your head and answering the phone? Jerking off? Or was it something a smidgen more oral in nature?"

"God, you've got a filthy mind" she said, then chuckled. "Thank God for that. Or you'd be just another client instead of my favorite ever client."

Rick was Marcie's twenty-four year old lover, literally an actor model waiter, almost a decade younger, whom Vic and she had chanced upon together six months before in the Vampire Diner over Denver omelets that looked as though they might contain bits of some of the afternoon's pudgier customers, along with Black Russians of a most suspicious frothiness. The place was of course packed at 3:41 on a very early Sunday morning from local clubs debouching when they'd finally fled the ghastly *turistas* and a very stoned, octopus-like, groping Liza-Minelli-and-Friends mass at Studio Fifty Four. Marcie had instantly declared the boyishly cute waiter with a nice bod to be gay. But Victor had taken one look at his flat-footed stance and dreadful sneakers—black and white high top canvas with red white and blue laces—and had as immediately intuited that no one even vaguely homo could be that color-challenged. So they'd done as usual when interested in someone and both made a play for him, taking turns while the other one was in the john. Result: the past fall and now winter, Rick was living in Marcie's townhouse-cum-office uptown. He sometimes acted, sometimes modeled, and sometimes waited tables, this time at the neighborhood Country Cousin, where he smiled pretty and acted clumsy and "kinda dumb," so naturally the over-intelligent and older faggola clientele that predominated were charmed and gave him phone numbers which he bunched up and ditched nightly and sizable tips which went right into the tight band of his BVDs without, alas, altering his taste in wardrobe.

As Marcie was, in her own blunt if not exactly accurate terminology, "past her prime" at thirty(ish?), and already married and divorced once (that she'd admit to; Vic had qualms and questions, questions and qualms), the Rickster was a definite find. Even when pouting, which meant whenever Marcie was calling the shots and paying (that is, always), he was admittedly arm-candy-supremo. Not that Marcie was in any way unattractive. Her face was amazingly pretty and still quite young, in that good-complexion-despite-light-freckling, lose-your-baby-fat-later southern Russian manner, with twinkling black eyes and loads of curly jet hair. Recently, she'd managed to locate two seamstresses whose talent was to wrap her zaftig torso in fashionable rags so she appeared even stylish going out to the Met's First Night of the Season or whatever benefit Vic had been comped tix for. Marcie had no trouble at all being every-day voluptuous, but it was her misfortune that she couldn't abide the guys (and there were plenty) who whistled at her crossing First Avenue over-quickly on tottery heels, guys Vic thought were hotter than hot. No, instead it was the more epigone she desired: men with very white skin and very fine blond-like hair, with sharp ridged noses, and obvious shoulder blades, sporting first names like Bryce and Connor and pedigrees yea long. Luckily the Rickster had something else yea long to compensate and his Fallen Angel demeanor fitted nicely into Marcie's official, let's-not-be-too-recognizably-anything-at-all ethnic category.

Vic said, "I'm going to be even more of your favorite client when you tell me about our big motion picture coup."

"Well, to be honest, Vic, I don't know who these people are. They aren't the top major players in town, Trent admits." (Trent was Marcie's agency's lawyer.) "Although this one guy, Ed Trefethern, seems to have invented the 'Made for TV Movie of the Week.' That's not so shabby!"

"Yesssssssssss. Go on."

She said the magic words: "They're making an offer on *Justify My Sins*."

"Meaning what? They want to do it as a TV Movie of the Week?"

"From what we can figure."

"Vagueness from Marcie Stein Whittaker? The sharpest gal agent in the New York biz?"

"The thing is, Vic, they're all out there in El Lay, and they're all men, even the assistants." (*Two counts against them*, Vic thought.) "And they don't really communicate all that well by phone." (*Third and most cruel count against them.*)

Vic knew these problems were deeply confounding to Marcie, if not downright insulting in their foreignness. Had she been born in Chechnya, Palau, or along the Rio Quadalquivir, locales without reliable telephone service, someone of Marcie's smarts, ambition, and seriousness of intent would probably have ended up a jailworthy street huckster, a Sister of Mercy Mother Superior, a dictator's string-pulling courtesan, or something equally discreditable. Instead, she'd become one of the hottest literary agents, not only by virtue of her instinct for what would sell, but also by consciously chatting up the most senior editors and, more crucially, their often ignored assistants and Gal Fridays. She would arrange to meet the latter on the sly at Bloomie's "blush" counter to try some new samples, and commiserate with them about nondescript beaus from Fort Lee, New Jersey over half-gallon Capuccinos at pokey delis next to vest pocket parks. As a result, her agency's manuscripts found themselves subtly moved to the top of whatever pile, her phone calls somehow always got through, and she could actually get multiple bids on books those rare times she "threw an auction." But what could Marcie possibly schmooze about? How could she possibly "get to know" a SoCal assistant named Moby or Harv who lived in The Blue Pacific Arms in Torrance Beach sharing four pieces of furniture in a five room flat with another guy and an Iguana named Bogart (because it smoked unfiltered Camels)? Especially if said assistant drove a raked GTO and possessed a Dopp kit containing nada but Baby Oil, Prell, and Lava soap—if he even had one. What could they possibly discuss? Where to find a superior board wax for his new cherry-wood Shorty? The built-in flaws of dual carburetors? Did mai tais get you bombed deeper, or just faster, than Planters Punches?

"Have Dane talk to them. He's sure to find the one 'sister' among them all." Victor suggested. "Even if it were a tribe in the Amazon, Dane would locate the 'sister'."

"I have, and Dane has, but he says even that guy's not much help. Dane actually dubbed him 'faux gay.'" She audibly pouted. "So Trent asked the company to Telex over the deal. He's just gotten all nine pages of it, his secretary told me. He's got to go over it inch by inch. If it looks at all good you're going to have to go out there and see them and the situation for yourself."

"Meaning?" Vic prompted.

"I don't know, Vic. It doesn't look all that great to me. They're telling us it's too late for them to rent you a cottage at the Beverly Hills Hotel. You'd have to settle for a suite, although I insisted that if so, it must overlook the pool."

"I see. So I can step over the railing and commit suicide at a moment's notice. Well, that's not too much of a disaster," he admitted. "And transportation?"

"Well, I told them you'd been in a four car accident while performing multiple cunnilingus on a girl scout troupe, so your driver's license has been revoked."

"You didn't happen to mention that the girls were all little people with muscular dystrophy?" Vic asked.

"I withheld that detail. As well as the fact that they were all actually males in girl scout drag. And so they agreed to spring for a car and driver for you for the week."

"A week will be nice," he mused.

"First class air tix of course. Driver meets you at the airport, naturally, et cetera," she was reading off a list. "Room service—within limits of course. Oh, here! You'll have one meet-and-greet with them, after arrival, and then a minimum of four work meetings."

Vic loudly groaned, his body's autonomic reflex to any sentence containing the letters *w, o, r* and *k* strung together like that.

"The option is for one year and isn't terrible." She reeled off the figures Trent had given her. "So you get to keep twenty grand less my cut even if it goes nowhere."

"Not bad for a week's work," Vic concluded.

"More, of course, if it goes forward. The scenario, the script, et cetera, each raise it further up on a sliding scale. Trent will messenger you all the gories. It could add up. Call him with any questions and we'll conference-call about it. In fact, call anyway and we'll conference-call, okay?"

"Okay. Marcie? Now for a totally unrelated question. Did this recent crash that I overheard when calling at all involve the antique lamp from Czar Nicholas' court that your Mother gave you for your wedding?"

"Tell me you didn't like that lamp, did you, Vic?"

"Why? Is it totally trashed?"

"It's fireplace chunks soon to be ashes," she admitted.

"I absolutely . . . hated it!"

"Well, then you're lucky. I was about to give it to you as a birthday gift."

"Going to have to thank Rick, no matter what it was he did to you to make you topple over."

"If you must know, he was tickling me behind the knees."

"What?"

"You heard me."

"Marcie, you must be the only person on the planet who is ticklish behind the knees."

"That's exactly what Rick said. He didn't believe me ether."

"Suddenly all this has fallen into the realm of Too Much and Far Too Bizarre Information. Ciao-sers!"

"We're still all going to the Black Party at Flamingo, yes?" Marcie asked.

"Sure, but that's not for at least another month."

"I know but I just found the most fabulous jodhpurs. Black rubber. Almost up to my armpits!"

"Stellar! And you'll be carrying the riding crop too, right?"

"And I've got the black micro-skirt."

"Sounds great. What about Rick?"

"Well, he's finally agreed that it might do his career good to go." She didn't spell out which career. Flamingo being a private gay club, it could be any of the three: actor, model, or waiter. "So he's agreed. However, he absolutely refuses to wear the black leather jock strap."

"Crapola! It would look great."

"He said his inner thighs are too hairy."

"You mean his buns are too hairy! That's what he's afraid of! Showing his crack."

"That I don't for a second doubt, knowing what kind of preverts will be all around him at Flamingo. But his ass isn't hairy. It's smoother than my boobs. At any rate, we've settled on these great black leather short-shorts I found down in that Ess'n'Em shop on Christopher Street. And on top, we've gotten him a smart criss-crossed leather and chain mail vest."

"The jockstrap would have been sensational. But I still get to lead him into the club on a leash, correct? That was our deal."

"Correct. And you have him for the first hour, yes. After that he reverts to me. He's even agreed to talk dirty to you."

"Cool beans."

"When I told Marcel I was going to the Black Party, he's my hair burner and queerer than three Mondays in a row, well, he nearly had a fit."

"I told you it was a more difficult ticket to get than *A Chorus Line.*"

"Who knew?"

"I did. Ummm, Marcie?"

"Ummm, what, Vic?"

"I'm going to Hollywood aren't I?'

"Looks like it."

He jumped into the air and almost touched the ceiling.

Get that cash with both hands!—And make a stash!

CHAPTER TWO

"Turn that up, would you?" Vic asked, tapping the Limo's glass partition to get the driver's attention. The song was from The Eagles, a group he'd only recently heard of, and it was catchy and twangy, definitely rock and yet kinda folksy-country sounding too, and it must be a hit, as it was being played on every AM station in the country this late February in 1977.

The plane trip had been calmly, luxuriously exciting. Even better, the woman sitting next to Vic was a well-known late-night TV host's wife. She couldn't have been leggier, prettier, or more literate. She'd even heard of Vic, she said, from "haunting bookstores." Not saying she actually bought or read a volume; but the word out—and she confirmed it—was that her short, cute, and very intellectual husband actually did read, rather than relying on show producers or assistants to read and then (badly) précis the guest's writing for him.

That revelation occurred at twenty-nine thousand feet over Ohio. By Missouri, the sun had set out his left hand window, and they'd gotten tipsy on the free martinis and had managed to wolf down three orders between them of the not-bad Tournedos Rossini. At Kansas City, the lights dimmed for nappies, but they kept drinking and were each given second plates of dessert—New York cheesecake with a blackberry center. By then they were on a first name basis, and she was telling him in gross detail (which he encouraged) about her first two fiancées. The first was the heir to an international hotel fortune with a propensity for mutual anal shenanigans and a substantial "tool kit" for said fetish custom manufactured in Finland. The second had been a Dallas Cowboys linebacker who "screwed like a quarter horse" but whom she later discovered had made identical outfits to her own, which he then wore while masturbating privately in front of a mirror.

But if all that weren't great enough to begin a Hollywood flight with, a world famous comedienne had been in the row in back of them, all by herself, having bought both seats so she could spread out, and she had whined and demanded so much, that approximately somewhere over Denver in the flight the First Class steward, "a well-put-together queen of a certain age" as Vic's pal Gilbert would describe him, had had just about enough of her, and had loudly replied to her umpteenth-hundred demand, "You're not the only passenger on board, you know, Mizz ____. Maybe these passengers," pointing to him and the famous guy's wife, "would like some extra service too." The steward had then turned around and done what Gilbert would have agreed was "flouncing off in a huff." He'd later reappeared and very loudly offered them more martinis and a third plate of cheesecake.

Tipsy, already cake-stuffed, and very surprised, they had accepted and then giggled and giggled like naughty children until they'd landed.

They kissed each other's cheeks in the VIP lounge upstairs at LAX as their luggage was being gathered by various uniformed people, making promises Victor was sure they'd never fulfill to see each other soon. Meanwhile, her husband—looking shorter, more muscular, and a lot more butch than he'd ever seemed on the tube—and Vic's newly arrived and self-announced chauffeur—tall, dark-haired, uncute and rather distressed facially—had looked on without comment.

And now here he was, all by himself, in the spacious backseat of the powder blue Fleetwood six-door, zipping along Sepulveda Boulevard, headed north toward the hotel. The night was cool and balmy, utterly blissful after a Manhattan winter that seemingly refused to end. When he'd left, there had still been six foot high ridges of filthy frozen and refrozen snow banks hard as steel all around the airport and defining the runways. Here, it was like being on another planet—or at least another hemisphere. He could smell night-blooming jasmine and orange blossoms, and was that frangipane too? It was Highway Heaven and if he weren't so intent on looking around, he would have settled back into the deep tufted leather seat with his eyes closed and just listened to the perfectly reproduced sounds of Tchaikovsky's Mozartiana from the three built-into-the-sky-blue-satin-ceiling speakers and simply inhaled the night.

Of course arriving so late—11:45 at night—there would be no one but the night staff in the hotel lobby. But Vic checked in easily, attempting not to gape at the immense, celebrated lobby. The very stiff-backed and somewhat puckered-mouth fellow who presided behind the desk at this hour explained extremely carefully to Victor's driver, as if English were his second language, where he might park every day. He then produced a plastic-like placard for the driver to place at a very particular spot in the front right area of the Caddy's windshield (not an inch to the left or right, he warned) whenever he parked outside or was awaiting Victor.

That was when Vic discovered that the driver would not be there at all hours and times but would instead come for him for any meetings. He needn't call for the driver for anything having to do with the production company, although Vic could also prearrange the driver for other trips, day or night. Oh, and the guy had one night a week off.

The driver took Vic aside as he was leaving, "All the staff here will look at you like they expect a tip. Don't do it. Only tip the bellman and the waiters. And not too much!"

"What about you?" Vic asked. "Do I tip you?"

"Only if I do something special." He laughed insinuatingly, making his face even uglier. Then he added, "I'll tell you when."

The fireplace was huge and in full flame despite it being more than sixty-five degrees outside, but the Cyclopean armchairs and sofas facing it in upholstered versions of the famous Bird of Paradise wallpaper were bereft. The thin bellman scrambled directly up the long staircase to his room and Vic followed. But once settled in the two large rooms with their own version of the famous wallpaper, he immediately decided he was far too excited and came back downstairs to look around.

He heard laughter from a doorway that turned out to lead into the Polo Lounge, but he was too timid to enter, although there were groups of twos and threes at tables and at the bar.

Another hotel person, shorter, more ethnically raven-haired, passed by, and seeing his bewilderment said, "Kitchen's closed for food, sir. But if you want a bite, try the Coffee Shoppe," and he led him circuitously around to it.

As they passed an older couple, he distinctly heard her say, "No. I don't know him. Do you know him? Maybe he's in music. They're all young in music these days!"

The Coffee Shoppe was closed too, and wouldn't reopen till six a.m. but the hotel guy went into a doorway and found a chef there who did room-service and he came out, very friendly, also ethnic looking, and took Vic's order for a nighttime snack. "If you like grilled cheese, sir, I can make you one. Or, you might want to try our version of it. It's called a kay-sa-dee-ya." Okay, Vic would have that, he said. And beer.

He signed something, then walked out to the pool, deserted this late but with voices filtering out from the Polo Lounge, and it all seemed so strangely different: the palm trees high above, the soft slurring of flowering bushes with wind, and the stars beyond the encircling mist.

By the time Vic returned to his suite, there was the food, all laid out in covered salvers with vanilla napery, smelling great. He'd just begun to eat when the hotel phone rang.

Surely not the people from Silver Screen Films? They weren't watching him this closely, were they? And it couldn't possibly be Marcie?

"Hel-lo! Beverly Hills Hotel, Suite Thirteen! I have always wanted to answer the phone like that."

"Tell me you are absolutely quivering with room service, and that you have a champagne flute in one hand and jam sauce dribbling down your chin from a Charlotte Russe in the other

Gilbert Onager, his closest friend in Manhattan.

"Gilbert, snookuns! No gentiles ever eat desserts with French names anymore."

"Not even Peche Melba?"

"Nope. What ungodly time must it be there? Like sunrise?"

"Close. I put the alarm on to wake me, so that I could get all the dish, the impressions, the feelings, the thoughts, *momento por momento*, as it is happening to luckly little *toi*!"

"Dearest Gilberto. Dearest, utterly demented, Gilberto. No one in their right mind would ever drea . . . Well, if I must. The napkins here could swaddle a grown man as a diaper with room to spare and are softer than cashmere. Ironed with creases, they stand up by themselves."

"Ooooh!" Gilbert cried.

"The grilled cheese sandwich whipped up *especiallymente* pour moi by the overnight room service chef, Manuel, is actually some Spanish concoction and is just runny with three cheeses, the name of only one of which I actually recognized, placed atop dots of *jalapeños*—hot little green peppers to you—and perfectly barbecued chicken breast strips, between two white cornmeal *tortillas* that would swathe even your enormous ass."

"He's there nine minutes and he's already speaking the lingo! My ass is a lovely size. Or so Jeffrey says."

"Jeffrey is blind as a bat. On the tray alongside it," Victor continued, "is carefully placed half of a perfectly ripened avocado, sliced finger wide, and two Valencia oranges also sliced. Several springs of curled parsley and a scattering of a black bean, toe-mah-toe, and corn salad grace the side of the enormous plate. A Pentel-thin wavey line of *tomatillo salsa verde* encircles it all, for a visual effect."

"Stop, I beg you."

"The beer, ice cold, is imported from Mexico, natch. A brand I've never heard of. Tres somethings or others. And has a slice of lime squashed into the top, past which one pours it into a glass."

"I die. I die."

"Shall I stop?"

A very offended, "Of course not!"

"Some elderly people in the lobby thought I was a rock star. I did not disabuse them. She was wearing a gold lame top of such vintage I suspect it was possibly the first one ever fashioned by man."

"Be still my heart."

"The car I have for the week met me at the airport and is the largest Caddy made in Detroit, painted that same shade as your sainted grandmother's hair, with burled wood inside the doors and surrounding a small bar. My driver's name is Anthony Cecil

Meade and he is plug-ugly and six feet six with a bizarre scar from above one eye along the sideburn line and around the lower part of the ear. Doubtless picked up in Alcatraz when he was doing a dime on manslaughter because, Gilbert, he resembles nothing so much as an underpaid, and definitely under-utilized, but nevertheless quite trigger-happy assassin."

"Gasperooni. Basket size? And do not say you didn't notice."

"Sizable." Victor admitted. "Could be tube socks."

"Or tube steak!"

Gilbert was by his own admission "on the modest side, genitally speaking"—seldom a fault in a bottom with a perfect bubble butt—and from what Vic had seen of Jeff, getting blown in the Everhard Baths, he was nothing special either. Yet both of them were constantly pretending to be size queens.

"As for the flight here. Hold on to your oversized Fellini picture hat with too many ribbons, Gilbert. This one was for the books."

"You met someone famous?"

"Try, I sat next to _____ _____'s wife the entire way."

"You must stop now, Victor. I'm close to cardiac arrest."

"And in the row behind us," Victor continued unfazed, "Was _____."

"And now I'm experiencing a complete panic attack. She's my all time fave—"

"Who turned out to be a to-tal, de-mand-ing, ut-ter bitch on wheels!"

"No! I've just passed out," Gilbert announced. "The next sound you shall hear is my death-from-too-much-dish rattle."

"Are you sitting down? Are you in the big living room chair obliquely looking down into Needle Park?"

"How did you guess?"

Then Vic told him everything that had happened.

As he spoke, finishing off the beer and spitting out the lime wedge, twirling avocado and orange slices at the end of his fork in salsa verde, then nibbling on them, he could so precisely picture his closest friend that it was as though he were looking through a wall-mounted camera.

Gilbert would be clad in his Barney the Dinosaur grape-juice-purple flannel pajamas with the double cloth sole-stockinged feet and button-up front and back flaps. The largest size available in Macy's Boys Department, because while Gilbert was petite, he was also a man of thirty-two. The pre-war ten foot ceilinged West Side apartment would be heatless and thus ice-box cold this early in the day, so he'd also be wrapped in the eiderdown federbed Jeff had bought for them in Dusseldorf last year and seldom used himself because he was one of those heat-manufacturing sleepers. Gilbert's green-as-a-Coke-bottle eyes would still have a slight film on them, since it physiologically required a minimum of two hours for him to fully awaken, and for much of that time he resembled a four month old infant: glistening pupils, dewy cheeks, bruised-looking lips, squonched earlobes. His unfashionably short, Gund-bear-brown hair, with its natural cedar highlights and hint of a widows peak would manage to look rumpled until it met one pass of a flexible comb, at which point it lay down as though painted on. His upturned nose and long vulnerable looking nostrils made him look years younger. ("Don't you drown in the rain?" had been nine-year-old Victor's introductory question to him when they'd first bumped into each other and gotten Anorak arms and pinned-on gloves tangled up in a fourth grade wardrobe.)

Utterly unathletic Gilbert, whose closest approach to a sport had been "jazz dancing" in his early teens, had, like most guys Vic considered to be "homunculi" (that is, under five-feet-two) a near-flawless body, as perfectly proportioned as a Da Vinci drawing, and featuring those gorgeous and dynamic buttocks. This commanding evidence of apparent masculinity was almost always promptly overshadowed by Gilbert's nearly unstoppable femminess of attitude and gesture. Over the years, Vic had himself become far more macho, indeed downright butch, had worked out and exercised way past the norm, because of the need to constantly and usually instantly rescue Gilbert from one form of unjustified assault or another. These had ranged from the not unexpected school yard bullies and always volatile street ball toughs to otherwise colorless college profs with a yen for nude spanking, and normally sane boyfriends who just couldn't resist slapping him around a little during sex.

Gilbert possessed a solid sense of self esteem and a pleasant, not unmanly tenor voice. Under Vic's careful and iterated tutelage over the decades, Gilbert had come to understand that in any new or even marginally dubious situation, he must deeply tamp down his inner Lorelei Lee until the last possible moment, when it would invariably erupt, complete with silver balloons, champagne bubbles, and platinum curls.

When Vic was done talking, Gilbert audibly sighed. "I'm *bouche baie* from a surfeit of glamor, even at second hand. The sun is up. Nothing better could possibly happen to me today than this wondrous phone call, so I'm calling in sick and staying home."

"Mister Mitch will have a heart attack, if you do."

A reference to Gilbert's employer, a just-off Park Avenue florist. "Em-Em," as Gilbert usually called him, despite his unruly toupee, too obvious maquillage, and High Society pretensions, had a client list and delivery address book that The Heart Association would commit mayhem for.

"He'll probably also develop hives by noon. Uggh. That's an unattractive picture! Well then! It'll be the morning off! Who cares? After all, it's your very first night in Aitch-Wood!"

Pleased that someone else was sharing it all, Victor hung up, brushed his teeth, changed into his new sapphire-blue silk boxers and fell asleep reading John Fowles' latest, most impenetrable yet book that he'd begun on the plane, then forgotten because the TV guy's wife had been so much fun.

Just before he dozed off, Victor thought, *Welcome to El Lay. Welcome to the Ho-tel Ca-lee-for-nya!*

CHAPTER THREE

Jim was speaking into the phone now, at one end of the huge conference room, gesticulating at no one in particular as he spoke facing the floor-high glass windows that gave a sweeping view down, down, deeply down off this plateau of Sunset Boulevard into a vast bowl of Los Angeles—or West Hollywood, or South Hollywood, Victor couldn't be sure, though he'd looked over a map at the hotel earlier in the day. Because the weather was unnaturally crystal clear—where was the famous smog everyone talked about?—just beyond the bowl of unending two and three story buildings, and a single, lonely, horizontal line of skyscrapers, he could make out a ridge of hard brown hills, and beyond those to the left what looked like downtown, backed by picturesque gray mountains with snow on them. A cluster of skyscrapers, and, to the right, another sharply angled cluster of much less altitudinous structures—apartments? hotels?—fronting the glittering-in-the-early-afternoon-sun Pacific Ocean. He already knew that was Santa Monica.

"Ellen," said Stan, the not uncute heavy-set guy in the tan shirt and sharply creased brown trousers, identifying the caller. Thinking he'd been addressed, Vic turned to say something in response only to see Sam, the youngest of them all, standing at the side table fixing himself a mug of half coffee, half hot chocolate. Sam had been addressed, not Vic. Whiplash thin, his frame accentuated by his black slacks and deep blue shirt, Sam now turned and asked, "His wife? You know her, Stan? Do you believe it?"

"I met her a half dozen times," Stan clarified, out of the side of his mouth, so that Victor faced aside again, feeling he was intruding, and he even edged slightly away from them although he clearly would be in hearing distance unless he left the room altogether, not a real option. "And, I don't know if she is." Adding, "He thinks she is."

"What's he going to do about it anyway? . . . If she is. She's got the trust fund, right?"

"I say let her. You know, keep her out his hair a bit."

"Yeah," Sam sniggered. "They are a little bit too close, if you know what I mean." He uttered a little snort of a laugh. "It's not natural."

"Wives!" Stan concluded, dismissively, as though he'd never even consider one.

Jim was now saying into the phone: "No. I don't know exactly when. After this. Well, but I've changed my mind and I'll be home early. No, I don't know exactly when! After this meeting! When this meeting is over! I'm at a meeting, you know."

There was one more exchange too quiet for Vic or any of them to hear since Jim faced away, his forehead against the window. Then he hung up, or rather stopped talking, still holding the phone, with its forty foot long cord, still staring out the window.

Stan and Sam sat down at the opposite side of the big pale green glass and matte metal German conference table that filled yet failed to dominate the oversized room. Taking that as a cue, Victor sat opposite them.

Stan had a much-thumbed looking copy of the paperback of *Justify My Sins* which he was tapping with two fingers as he sipped his coffee. Vic had spotted another half dozen fresh copies of the book outside on the receptionist's desk, and three more piled next to the Danish and croissants on the matching glass and matte metal German side table. Vic wondered if he ought to take one and pretend to read it. He wished he'd brought his Sony Personal CD player to the meeting.

"He's here!" Jim announced from the window.

The others stood up and went to the window. So did Vic, joining them in looking down at the street, where a canary yellow Rolls Corniche convertible pulled slowly up to the garage entry. From two floors up, and because it had its canvas top down, one could make out the top of the head of the driver, which was reddish, and the exposed shining marbled wood and blood red leather interior (surely it couldn't be Corinthian, could it?).

They all returned to the table and from out of nowhere attaché cases were produced, colored paper folders were removed, scattered on the table, and opened, and two more battered copies of his second novel were suddenly, magically, also presented.

"So, Victor, may I call you Victor?" Stan announced as though they were all on radio. Vic nodded: *Sure. What else? Adolf?* "Well, Victor, we were all incredibly impressed by *Justify*. Just an amazing piece of work, we all thought. Right, guys? And utterly unprecedented, really."

Vic wondered suddenly if they were being audio-taped.

"Thanks."

"I'm ashamed to admit that I came to the book kind of late. All the women in the office had passed around a copy and read it when it caught my eye. And when I mentioned it to someone I sometimes see, well, she said everyone at her yoga class was talking about it."

"A real page turner," Jim allowed. "And that ending. Just stunning."

"Breathtaking ending," Sam agreed. "Believable, but it just . . . knocked . . . the breath . . . outta me."

Which, Vic thought, *was the same thing as saying breathtaking.* Oh-kay!

That was when they all heard, and even more so, felt Ed Trefethern come into the outer office. He made some kind of low greeting to the receptionist, and then sidled directly into the conference room, signaling to them to stay seated and continue the "discussion" while he all but tiptoed behind Vic, whose shoulder he touched lightly, and went to sit at the far end of the table.

"When my niece from Wisconsin visited a month back," Sam was saying, "Cindy, she's eighteen, and well she was reading it too, well, I knew Stan was onto something."

"It's a national bestseller, Sam," Vic attempted to say it with no overtones at all in his voice (such as, "Hey stupid! wake up!"). "That means that many people all over different parts of the country are reading it."

"Right!" Sam said in a way that strongly suggested that he'd never really thought the term through to reach that particular conclusion before.

"It also just came out in Spanish, titled *La Justificacion*!" (Vic said in his superb, Madrid-accent.) "Or simply, *The Justification*.

Published in Buenos Aires, Argentina, and for sale all over the Hispanic world, and in one of those big paperbacks from Germany, with a title I won't even attempt to pronounce." (Little laughs from the others.) "So those, along of course with the British Commonwealth hard-soft and book club editions that came out twelve, ten, and four months ago, means that it's also an international bestseller." Would he have to spell out what areas were covered by the Commonwealth market? He hoped not.

"In fact," Vic decided to take a chance at chipping away at a few of the remaining Alaska-sized ice-fields remaining around the table, "last week I got on an IND subway in Manhattan, going uptown, and there were four people on that one subway car reading the book. Mostly the paperback."

In short, guys, in case you didn't get the hint, it's a best seller.

"Right," Jim now jumped in, looking at Ed for approval, "But it's not only that excellent commercial element, terrific as that is, that attracted Silver Screen Films to your book, Victor." He paused, dramatically. "It was the human element of the story you told."

Oy! Gott! Victor thought. *Don't! Please! Do not open your mouth and continue!*

Alas, Jim did continue, managing to spout four in a row, count 'em, of the most mealy-mouthed, say-nothing statements Victor had ever heard from a single person in a single room at a single time.

Worse yet, Sam and Stan agreed, loudly and vociferously reiterating and weaving in even more ghastly variations upon these supposedly complimentary effusions.

Vic felt as though he'd been afflicted by the most virulent case of crotch-itch and hot-foot ever, only all over his entire body while wearing white coat and tails, attending a chamber recital as part of a memorial service for a very beloved older person at someone's penthouse, and thus completely unable to scratch anything.

"I thought the novel was mean!" Ed Trefethern suddenly said.

Finally! A mind in this room had been exposed in the process of actually thinking!

"It was pretty mean." Victor looked at Ed now.

Ed faced him off. "I thought the author had a really bad experience in romantic love and he wanted to get revenge with this book."

"Could be. Maybe." Victor admitted, eye to eye with Ed. "I wouldn't totally deny that. In fact, down with love! Romance doesn't work! It never did! It never will!"

"It's a crapshoot," Ed modulated.

"And the house, not you, always has the best odds," Victor concluded.

"It's downright brilliant," Ed said. "And hearing you now, Victor, I see that much of the book's strength is due not only to its great plot and believable characters and terrific writing, but also to its author's honesty."

Jim all but wailed, "But Theo and Anna-Marie are made for each other!"

Victor faced him now and ruthlessly declared, "And that's why it works—for a while!"

Jim couldn't see, but Vic sure could, one of Stan's eyebrows go up, and Sam's face tilt down.

"They're each other's soul mates," Jim argued.

"And that is why Theo alone is privileged enough to see Anna-Marie out of her flawed and miserable existence!" Victor punched the lesson home.

"And poor Theo is left . . . With his whole life ahead of him, except now. . . . it's totally emptied out!" Jim sputtered on. "Knowing that . . . "

"Theo was weak!" Victor stated. "And Theo was foolish! Theo deserves nothing better!"

Jim's face got a near-purple red, his eyes bulged. Little veins stood up along his temples. Even his hair seemed electrified, flying away from his scalp. But he was speechless.

Stan, meanwhile, coughed the fakest cough Vic ever heard, and Sam was looking down in his lap with an intensity that suggested he might have located the fabled Northwest Passage there.

"So we're all on the same page here!" Ed asserted. "This will be a coup for Silver Screen, a very classy project, Book of the Month Club, yet popular too, a real feather in our cap. But—and there's always a but, Victor—but finding the best possible form for your wonderful story is essential." He turned to Vic and stretched a big hand (not that of an artist) sprinkled with combed red hairs, to tap Vic's outstretched fingers. "And that's where we all come into the picture. Fellows!" he addressed the others. "Victor here has done all the work so far. What do we have for him?"

Sam began talking about his preliminary conversations with some of the television network execs and program people, which sounded hopeful, and then it was Stan saying something about amortization figures, which was completely boring to Vic but which they all seemed to comprehend, then Ed, who was what, the executive producer? is that what Marcie had called him? was saying, "Tim, why don't you tell us some of your ideas for locations, sets, and costuming for this." So *oops!* it was Tim not Jim, and as Tim began talking, Vic listened, interested in what he had to say, but also thinking, *Listen to them, so into themselves! And me, I'm a Johnny come lately, the new kid in town.*

Finally at the end of Tim's discussion, Ed, apparently the boss, turned to Vic and asked if he had any questions.

"Yeah, I kinda of do, although they'll probably sound stupid. From what all of you were saying just now, I gather that what's the next real step is that you all want me to go back to the hotel and write out a five or six page precis of my novel stressing the characters and dramatic elements, right? So someone will buy this as a television movie of the week."

"That's exactly right," Ed said, with a fatherly smile. "We don't even have to tell him what to do, Victor's so brilliant. So . . . Where's the problem?"

"Well, to begin with, I've never written anything like that before." Leaving hanging the rest of the sentence *and I don't have a clue how to do it.*

"Look, Victor. You know this story inside out. No one knows it better than you," Stan said. "You can do it easily."

Tim added, "And of course, once that's done, you show it to us, we give you notes on it, and then join us three in pitching it."

"Notes? Meaning what? Queries? Edits? Ideas?"

"Exactly," Ed said. "Simple as can be."

"And then we pitch it?" Vic added, repeating a word he'd heard the others already use, and which he also didn't completely understand.

"At the networks," Jim said. "Actually we're focusing in on one network. But of course the other two, also."

Vic had a single instant and complete thought: *This is totally doomed to failure. Totally. I've written stories, novels, even bad little one-act plays, but I've never done anything like this before.*

One major problem was that not only was he the newbie here, sitting in on something they all knew everything about, but also he didn't really give a shit. Yeah the money, the fame, all that crap. Now if one of the four were even vaguely, remotely fuckable. . . . Maybe the younger big guy, Stan. He was kind of a teddy bear, and those big guys had a way of lying back and just letting you do whatever you wanted, and that could be fun—sort of—for a limited while. But this other one, this Tim, tennis-playing-slim with his layer-cut hair combed over his ears and three hundred dollar sunglasses, with the heiress wife who was cheating on him with her pool boy, or Sam with his shiny I. Magnin shirts and pimped out trousers and his shoes in colors only otherwise seen in velvet sofa paintings—no, no, no, afraid not.

And then they all supported each others' last statements and Vic died inside yet again thinking *How did I let myself get into this mess? And how can I possibly get myself out?*

CHAPTER FOUR

Leaving the office, Ed held Vic back, and clapped a hand over his shoulder: The Older Guy being nice to the Newbie.

"Let's have a drink. Just us two."

He let the others go talking away down the elevator (it was two floors for Chrissakes—who needed an elevator?). Then as they reached the vast underground garage, Ed gestured to Vic's driver, Meade, who had just awakened, hearing other car ignitions being turned on: He was to follow the Corniche. Ed and Vic would drive together.

The separate leather seats were deeply tufted, like those sofas in the Harvard Club Vic's publisher had taken him to after *Justify*'s tenth week on the *Times* list. The car's stereo system, he happened to notice, was MacIntosh, with Klipsch speakers. The telephone next to the transmission lever was the same over-polished burled walnut as the dashboard and door interiors.

Victor thought, *I'm riding in a car that's more finely appointed and more expensive than my parent's last house.*

"A phone in the car is a great idea," Vic commented.

"There's one in your limo too."

"Really?"

"They're usually behind that little door right next to the bar."

"I'll look for it."

"I'm in the car so much, I'd be lost without it," Ed said.

Gilbert was simply going to up and die when he told him about cars with phones!

Ed did something, and a panel moved and a Nakamichi double cassette deck was revealed. "You know this singer named Midler?" Ed asked. "My wife got me some of her records. I like her."

"Bette's great! I play her all the time," Vic said.

Skylark came on, and they listened as Ed steered left suddenly and they dropped down the steepest road that Victor had ever experienced outside of San Francisco. Luckily, in the Corniche, they merely floated down.

In between songs, Ed mentioned the name of the place they were going to. "Kind of my hang-out. Hope you don't mind too much."

"What kind of food do they have?"

Ed looked confused then explained, "Everything! Anything! The chef will make anything you want."

Vic had never heard of that kind of a restaurant before, although now that Ed repeated the name, it seemed familiar: hadn't Marcie hoped in their latest phone conversation that someone would take Vic there so he could report back?

They were on Melrose Avenue headed west, when suddenly Ed veered directly into what looked like a little forest of enormous ginger and banana plants. He pulled up onto a graveled sidewalk and stopped. A Hispanic guy in a maroon uniform ran up to them and Ed tossed him the keys and stepped out.

Suddenly they were within some sort of Mayan temple with knee-high carved-block canals featuring lily pads and birds of paradise. Netting swung from the quarter mile high ceiling, holding yet more flora. Vic scanned the roof for Mynah birds, prepared to duck. Could a blow-gun dart be far behind?

A handsome woman with long chestnut hair and severe makeup wearing the same deep red color as the Roll's seats and the valet's uniform, greeted Ed, looking downcast.

"I gave away your table," she groaned. "No one from your office called. So I was sure you wouldn't be coming."

"See what I get when I surprise you," Ed pouted. "Don't you have anything, Rina?"

Victor saw at least a half dozen unoccupied tables. What was wrong with . . . ?

A waiter in the same uniform glided up to Rina, whispered in her ear, and slid away again.

"Eric says that Stacey and Jill at number fourteen are getting up right now. We'll bus it in an instant."

"Fourteen?" Ed moaned. "It's Antarctica! Victor here," he took Victor's hand and put it into Rina's warm one, "is the best selling novelist in the country." (Total lie!) "Vic's from New York City for Chrissakes. The Big Apple. Fourteen is where you're going to put him? Fourteen?!"

She twisted her mouth repentantly, as though she'd suggested they should plotz on the floor between the outer kitchen door and the trash bins. Then she looked at her list.

"Hold on a sec, Mr. Trefethern."

She vanished. Ed turned around looking smug and satisfied. He'd been putting on an act.

Good thing, because for the briefest of seconds Victor thought he should say he didn't really care where they sat. Then some instinct told him to hold that thought. Clearly something here at no name restaurant was, as Sherlock Holmes would say, afoot.

Another waiter, short, sandy haired, muscular, yet recognizably tres gai, came by, greeted Ed and appreciatively checked Victor over. "Don't tell me you're waiting?" he asked Ed, as though an imminent execution were planned for them both.

"I surprised her, Joel," Ed said, little boy guilty. "What can I expect? I've got a big Macher from out of town. And Rina wants me to take fourteen."

All too apparent alarm twitched the waiter's snub nose and dimmed his lightly freckled upper cheeks. "Fourteen? No way!" He looked at Victor once more, then, "A secret, Mister Tee? I've got total nobodies at thirty-one. They're staying at the Bel Air and we did it as a favor for the concierge. I'll get them out the door before you can say Tina Louise!"

Ed and the Joel turned to look at another area of the restaurant deep inside some kind of bower.

"Is that Laddie, there at thirty two?" Ed asked.

"Laddie and Goldwyn Junior," the waiter's voice descended to unsuspected baritonal depths.

"I guess that'll do," Ed admitted.

"Momen-tee-no!" the waiter trilled and sailed off.

"He's a fruit, but a sweetheart, and he treats me well," Ed explained.

Hustled out of their seats, two well-put-together women in their thirties came up to say hello to Ed and be introduced to Victor. Jill turned out to be Clayburgh, even taller and more soigne in person. Stacey, Vic would later find out, was a talent agent with a famous mouth and a disputatious reputation.

"You're so young to be so cynical," La Clayburgh said upon hearing his name, swanning an endless arm and ultralimp hand for him to touch. Her clever way of saying she'd read *Justify*.

"No!" Stacey cried when she too heard the news from Ed. "How can that be?" She stared at Victor as though he had a minimum of three heads, none matching. "I was sure that author's name was pseudonymous and that you were really a woman!" Now her eyes went gimlet. "I sure wouldn't wanna' date you! You know us gals far too well. I could never put anything over on you."

All four laughed politely.

"So, Ed," Stacey changed the subject with the adroitness of a walrus bedding down, "you never call me with roles for Jill." Stacey pretended to be much aggrieved.

"I'm mostly doing the little screen these days," he admitted.

"We're not closed to the Tube," Stacey looked to Jill for confirmation. "Right?"

"Soon as something comes up, I'll call. I'll call."

"Too bad Anna-Marie is so young," Jill said to them all. Vic wondered if she would ask him to rewrite the part right there in the foyer.

"Not to mention kinda ethnic, too," Stacey pointed out. The two of them kissed the air around the men and left.

"Praise from Caesar," Ed said, then, "as though you'd date her."

The maitresse d' reappeared, "Table thirty-one" she announced in a voice so triumphant Vic expected trumpets and dancing girls to precede them, "is ready!" She acted as though she'd pulled two rabbits and a small locomotive out of a napkin before their very eyes.

"Laddie," whom Ed clasped upper arms with, looked similar to some old time movie star and in fact turned out to be the son of one, and was himself a film producer. As was his dinner companion, the son of a legendary producer. Later on, hearing this line up, Gilbert would sigh, "My God, they're like major major major!"

At the third table in the gardenia-drenched little dining enclosure sat Red Buttons and Carol Bruce schmoozing, she having to step outside periodically beyond the red rubber siding and wave in at Red through see-through plastic while smoking brown ciga-rillos. Victor was astonished they didn't let you smoke at your table. These Angelenos were strict!

Ed ordered them appetizers Vic had never heard of, and dry Rob Roys which he explained were Scotch Martinis.

"Yum! So! You're satisfied with the table?" Victor felt com-pelled to ask.

Panic on Ed's kindly face. "Why? Aren't you?"

"I don't know any better, Ed. I would have just sat any-where. . . . Is it okay if I order off the menu?"

"Sure anything."

After they had ordered, with Ed dictating various additions to the waiter—Eric not Joel—Trefethern turned and looked Victor over. "You're thirty-three? Nah, I don't believe it. You look much younger. At most twenty-five."

"I still get carded in some places," Vic confessed. "Of course that's usually because they're so depraved no one's willing to take chances with the law."

Ed momentarily looked as though Vic were joking. "Not Plato's Retreat?"

"Well, that's the one place I can publicly admit going to."

Ed narrowed one eye, still not sure if he was being toyed with. Then he laughed. "Believe me, looking younger isn't terrible out here. You're going to fit right in."

Vic wanted to disabuse Ed instantly, to tell Ed that he felt to-tally out of his element. Elements, rather: Grime. Filth. Noise. Rudeness. He couldn't find any here. His own kitchen had never been as clean as any public men's room he'd seen so far this trip, and on top of it, they were citrus-scented: every ten seconds puffs of orange came through a vent. The sidewalks looked bleached, what, every week? twice a month? Where were they anyway? Was this still Beverly Hills?

"We're in West Hollywood," Ed explained. "About a mile from your hotel. The truth is," Ed said, "everyone lives in Beverly Hills, in Bel Air, Brentwood, Encino Hills, Pacific Palisades, Toluca Lake, but everyone eats, talks, drinks, does business, and definitely eve-ryone screws around in West Hollywood. It's been this way since I got to this town during the war, 1942, to make movies about the

Pacific Theater for the War Department. And from what I heard back then, it was true even before the Forties."

This was a lot more interesting than the doomed precis or scenario or whatever they were calling it based on his novel. So Vic asked Ed more questions.

"Maybe I don't look like much at sixty-three," Ed told him, "but back then I was taller and slimmer. In uniform I looked the part." He winked. "When Capra brought me around this place back then, they all came humming around. Gals—a few guys too. Howard Hughes tried to get me to come live in one of his West Hollywood apartment houses. He used one building to keep starlets who he used to get regularly blown. And another building for the guys he used to regularly blow."

As he spoke, Vic could see Ed at twenty-eight. Slender, twinkly blue eyes, strawberry blond hair: blowable.

Vic had to ask. "Well, did you take up his offer?"

"Nah! I was stuck over at the barracks, where the Veterans Hospital is now, off Wilshire and the Four Oh Five. That wasn't there either, back then. Nor the One Oh One. And to answer your other, politely unasked, question, sure I would have let him. Coupla' guys from his building he made into movie stars." He named three actors and Vic had to whistle in recognition. "Seemed like a fair trade to me at the time."

He laughed and looked at his lap, then up again. "You're a talented kid. And it's rarer than we all pretend. By the way, I saw what you were up to with the fellows at the office." He wagged a finger at Vic, who now sat perfectly still. "Naughty, naughty, Victor! Just because you've got as much I.Q. as any two of them added together doesn't mean you can let them know it. They're good kids anyway. Came to El Lay to make movies. Stars in their eyes, and they're all slowly working their way up."

"Up to what? Your job?"

"If they're smart and lucky. Maybe one will make it."

"Stan," Vic guessed.

"That's my bet too. The others will end up in some agency, or doing something in an office at a studio. Or maybe end up running some crafts alliance to the industry. Truth is, Vic, only money and talent really shoots straight up out here."

"I promise in future I'll be much, much kinder," Vic said.

"Good. Except," Ed gulped his drink down, "Tim had that coming to him anyway. The others will probably thank you. They're so sick of hearing about it."

People kept drifting by and saying hello. Once Ed got up to say hello to someone else leaving. In a half hour everyone in the place knew who Victor was.

Ed told him, "Even if this doesn't work out, this project? You ought to come out here and live. I'll find you work in an instant. Smart guy like you? Maybe script polishing or stuff like that at first. Higher pay than you can imagine. Then some script partnerships. Coupla' years you're on your way. Find you a nice little place, maybe up in Coldwater Canyon. Get you some kind of cute new jalopy: those new Corvettes are cute . . ."

How could Ed have such nutso great expectations? And why did Vic feel that everybody in the restaurant was watching him?

"You just met me," he told Ed. "How do you know I'm any good?"

"I got your agent, what's her name? Marcie? She's a piece of work, huh? Got her to send me the proposal and chapters you did for the third book that you're publishing. It's terrific. You're the real thing, kid. The real thing doesn't grow on trees."

The rest of the lunch went like that and lasted two hours, with entrée, salad, and a dessert, a meal which could have fed a small Michoacan neighborhood. Vic ended up taking half of his back to the hotel.

Outside the restaurant afterwards, they bumped into Richard Chamberlain and Irving Wallace, waiting amid the gravel near the street for their cars. The actor wore the thinnest leather slip-on loafers Vic had ever laid eyes on: but then they were for walking nine feet, from the car to the door. They'd never actually touch sidewalk, not to mention the dreaded tarmac! Dark haired car valets in uniforms sprinted into action whenever they sighted anyone even vaguely customer-like. Ed introduced Vic to the actor and author. Both, gratifingly, had heard of Vic. Chamberlain looked better on screen, a little too angular this close up. And each one of them ended up having a valet drive up a Corniche convertible. The actor's was maroon. The writer's was silver.

Joel, the helpful waiter, rushed out for Vic's autograph. For a minute Vic thought he'd slipped a phone number in, then saw it was only the restaurant's matchbox.

"Hundred thousand dollar cars!" Ed commented, after the others had driven off. Getting into his own car, he concluded, "They're like anuses out here!" gesturing at the banana trees. "Everyone's got one!"

Victor sank into the back of his limo and easily located the phone just where Ed had said it would be. It even had a number, which he copied down.

Back at the hotel, there was a message from Paul Gibbons, the black-haired Angeleno guy he'd met last summer at Fire Island Pines. They had exchanged phone numbers and Vic called him when he got into town. Paul said that he was free tomorrow night and definitely wanted to see Vic.

All right!

Gilbert called from New York, whining about the unceasingly icy weather and D'Agostino continually raising its prices on baby lamb chops which Gil snacked on like an ogre on four-year-olds.

He listened to Vic's "Tales from Lunch," providing more oohs and aahs than a third grade class at Ringling Brothers. But once he was done, he put on his serious voice.

"Listen, Victor, when you get around to opening your travel gift—and don't say you did already open it because I would have heard about it if you had—you will find alongside it a printed invitation."

"What kind of invitation?"

"Smart of you not to prevaricate and pretend you opened it. There's a new leather bar opening there in L.A. this weekend. The hottest man I ever did it with—B. J. natch" (his term for "Before Jeff," his boyfriend) "—sent that invite to me. He will be there. His tricks will be there. His buddies will be there. Guys in chaps without underwear will be there. People with large, uncircumcised penises will be there. You must go."

Vic gave Gilbert five excuses why he couldn't possibly go.

"All overridden!" Gilbert commanded, "You shall go because I cannot go and dearly wish to go and furthermore I want to hear all about it. No excuses."

And Gilbert hung up.

Proving that in the end, he was just another Pushy Bottom.

CHAPTER FIVE

"Don't look now, but I think that's the guy I have a date with tomorrow."

His friend turned and looked. "Perfect Paul?" Andy asked, astonished. "You have a date with Perfect Paul!?"

"I told you not to turn and look, and yes, Paul Gibbons." Vic had to laugh. The nick name fit Paul so . . . well, so perfectly. "Why's he called that?"

"Dar-*linnngggg*!" Andy pushed him between two stacks of wooden beer cases where they could have some privacy. "Isn't it obvious. He's the most perfectly beautiful human male in the universe! Is your movie company paying for him, too?"

"Is my what?"

"Perfect Paul has been on the cover of *Data Boy* every three months. No one else has ever come close."

Paul was with some other guys, but he was looking around while he held his Miller Hi-Life all but untasted. He was six-two with wide shoulders, slim torso, even slimmer hips, and long, sturdy legs. On the beach at Fire Island last year he'd revealed perfectly shaped feet and admitted he'd made extra dough being a foot model (who knew such a distinction existed?) over the years. He could have easily been a fashion model, period, except that Paul had this problem: he couldn't for the life of him believe he photographed differently than the way he saw himself: as some geeky, gawky fifteen-year-old. How he actually turned out in photos constantly freaked him out as "some other guy." So, for example, in group shots, he tended to hide behind people, always explaining that he was too tall and would block them, and then he'd make a goofy face at the camera, thus proving his point about looking odd.

Despite this, he had an Apollonian stature and figure. Add to that his nearly blue black hair, usually found only in comic book heroes: "Hollywood Hair," Gilbert had called it for its thickness, heft, length, and luster, and he'd only seen Paul twenty-five feet away from the deck of Halston's house on the ocean.

Since then, Paul had added an inky black closely-trimmed mustache and beard that perfectly outlined his solid lower face, highlighting his utterly kissable lips. Check out his long straight nose and small ears, his slightly high cheekbones, his perfectly sized, utterly symmetrical ice-water blue eyes nestled in a luxuriant valley of eyelashes and thick jet eyebrows. The left brow was divided three quarters down its length by a tiny scar—from a swing hitting him face-on as a child, Paul reported—providing that minuscule flaw that Confucians and Taoists believe anything natural must possess to be truly beautiful. Paul's face culminated in a perfectly rectangular, unlined forehead and almost equally flat flanking temples. He sported three sets of dimples, two on either side of his lower lips, and another cleaving his chin, making for an especially ebony detail that drew eyes to his beard.

What was intriguing was how Paul managed to dress so ordinarily. That t-shirt looked like one Vic had owned at age nine and probably came from an irregulars bin at Penney's. His jeans were white, costing perhaps ten dollars down the street; the cowboy boots, doubtless some unexceptional brand or, better yet, used. Yet he always looked amazing! To Vic, Paul seemed even more handsome with the beard than when they'd met at The Pines. He also seemed fairly bored tonight, although the guys he was with were quite busily trying to entertain him or involve him in their conversation—if they weren't actually coming on to him, separately or together. Vic's instinct told him should take advantage of the situation soon and go say hello.

"He's on the cover of what?" he asked Andy.

Andy squelched over to the bar, rummaged rapidly, and came back with a five-by-four inch stapled pamphlet.

"See!" He held it out, and there on the cover was a black and white photo of Paul Gibbons, beardless, looking gorgeous, and, Vic couldn't help but notice, obviously taken when he'd been looking away then suddenly turned back to the camera.

"Three hundred an hour," Andy said, pointing to the small print.

"For a massage?"

That's what the cover read. "Paul Gee. Masseur."

"Massage? *Mass*-age? Dar-*linngggggg*. It's the kind of massage in which the fin-al-ee is ev-ery-thing!"

I am so naïve, Vic thought. *Such a child. It's embarrassing.* No wonder Paul had called back so quickly. It was business. He couldn't possibly go over to Paul now. In fact, he now had to talk Andy into covering for him as he tried sneaking out of the bar and into the back alley where they had parked. Vaseline Alley, Andy had called it, because guys who met each other in the bars along Santa Monica Boulevard stepped into the oleander bushes here to check each other out—and sometimes didn't emerge until they were done. This, Vic thought, was one of the best inventions of West Hollywood and had it all over Chelsea, where the best you could do was go into a doorway where everyone could see you making out.

"Block me," Vic said. "I'm leaving."

"Don't make a move," Andy said, then reported. "He's looking over here. Looking . . . looking . . . looking. Looking away."

"Now!?" Paul asked.

"No sudden movements of any kind or you'll draw his attention. I'll tell you when."

"Really?"

"Do you have any reason not to trust me?" Andy asked.

Well, yeah, kinda, Vic thought. *I sure do.*

Andy Grant, like Gilbert, was another of Vic's childhood friends and in fact he predated any other. At six years old, Andy had been utterly obsessed by dogs. He had two himself: his parents' stately Italian boxer and a dim-witted, over-friendly, German Shepherd. Even so, he went after virtually any dog anywhere near his path, despite the fact that some leaped on him to play while others leaped on him to tear his throat out. Andy subdued them all, eventually, with sloppy kisses and unceasing affection. Andy had been a cute lad then, with his huge mop of unruly dark blond hair and his elfin little face with its soft, caramel-colored rather houndlike eyes.

His passion for dogs slowly subsided, to all their relief, but it was suddenly replaced at age ten by his weird new bent—for girls. Well, not girls so much as more specifically whatever breasts any girl might possess. One time, Gilbert and Vic counted the words in a ten minute Andy Grant monologue, ranging in variety from the sci-entific-sounding "mammaries" to the expected "titties" to the vulgar "bazongas" at two hundred and fifty four hits. For the next three years, he and Gilbert kept their distance from him as Andy tended to hang out only with girls of all colors, stripes, attitude, and even age, and he'd apparently gained enough confidence with some local females to be constantly touching, fondling, exposing, or dis-cussing the multifarious aspects of what he called their "frontal beauties." During that era, Andy had changed his look from an all-purpose Munchkin into a Rock-God Wannabe, who dressed like one of Journey's more stoned out amp-roadies and whose sanitary habits equaled that of a street person.

By the beginning of high school, another metamorphosis had taken place, and suddenly Andy Grant was not only cleaner, but *obviously* cleaner, since he exposed as much skin as possible via his new passion: swimming and diving. This he did alone, in duos, and on teams. Constantly. He was taller and more slender now, virtually hairless, his page boy light brown locks mown to a buzz cut. If Vic and Gilbert had seen little of him before, they now saw a lot more, whether they planned to or not, since Andy was everywhere: at least everywhere even vaguely maritime and competition-oriented that a townlet on the upper mid-Long Island Sound might offer.

It was only after a year or so had passed that Andy again ap-proached Vic and revealed the true nature of his new obsession. One stormy day when his parents were out of town, Andy brought Vic into a carefully multi-locked inner room, where he displayed for his old pal how his "hobby" had metamorphized from breasts to—penises. Naturally Andy's explorations proved to be as prob-ing and thorough with teenage boys as those with preteen girls had been. Down had come the dozens of cut-out photos of various breasts in his huge bedroom closet, replaced by scores of male members in as many shapes, sizes, and colors as Vic assumed possible. And when Andy took up a secondary, if related, avoca-tion of photography, they became predominantly pix of lads he knew, taken with or without their permission, before or after he'd had his way with them, and of course invariably erect.

It was around this time that Andy's father had decided to leave

Big Blue where he'd reached his own glass ceiling and go to work as a partner for another computer start-up on the West Coast. In his junior year in high school, his family had moved to the Bay Area, and now, as the Grant fortune slowly amassed, Andy had moved to his own spread in Topanga Canyon with a *pied a terre* in West Hollywood, of course, far closer to the action. He was no longer daily photo-diarying dicks, but he continued to catalogue guys' schlongs with his usual thoroughness—and in his own inimitably passionate manner. His hair longer, his face still young, his body still quite acceptable, Andy had transformed himself into the youngest and most attractive "dirty old man" Vic had ever met. Every action, every gesture, every word, and even his tone of voice said, "I'm getting you whether you want me to or not."

All this Gilbert had warned Vic of, having seen and barely fended off Andy at a funeral back East a year previous. But what could Victor do? Andy was his oldest friend: he couldn't not see him out here, could he? All he could really do was strongly limit the times and places he did see him.

"Okay, I think . . . "

Andy did something with his body which looked to Vic like blocking. He dashed left and a second later Paul Gibbons had him by the shoulder. "Vic? Is that you, Vic?"

Caught.

"Hi Paul." Behind Paul, Andy stuck his tongue out and went up and down as though licking Paul from head to toe, then, momentarily sated, he slunk off.

"Were you leaving?" Paul asked. "'Cause I was thinking of going."

"Oh, sure." Thinking, *How do I tell him I don't have any more than forty-six bucks on me? Maybe he'll take a check?*

Once out in the alley, Paul instantly pushed him against the wall and began kissing him. Paul's tongue was down his throat so long and so intensively that Vic began to lose his breath. At the moment he was about to black out, Paul withdrew.

"Gosh! That was nice," Paul said, "I just knew, first time we met, that you'd be a firecracker."

Vic had forgotten what a sweet tenor voice and nice, All-American Boy temperament Paul had. Must help the comfort zones of out of towners dying for a "massage."

Paul grabbed him by the arm and briskly pulled him along. They were headed for the bushes for sure.

But no, instead they stopped at a low silver car. Wasn't that one of those Mercedes-Benz coupes with the—

"Watch this!" Paul said, hitting a little remote-key-thing in his hand, and the two doors came straight up over the top of the car.

—gull wing doors? Yep!

"Cute! Huh?"

A sixty-five grand Mercedes. "This your car?" Vic asked.

"Yep. Gift from an admirer," Paul he explained. "Get in."

They drove out of the alley, startling two guys when the Benz's headlights flashed their undressed lower torsos in the bushes.

"Ooops!" Paul said, "I usually dim it here, to be courteous. But I'm so excited seeing you!"

When they drove past the bar and stopped at the light, Andy was outside, talking up a guy with a walrus mustache and a substantial basket whom he'd all but pinned to the wall. He seemed to be moving in for the kill when he noticed Paul, smiled his dirty old man smile, and then made a low Peace sign at Vic.

"This your first time in Wee Whore?" Paul asked. Then laughed. "My little joke!" He kissed Vic once again while swinging around a corner onto another main street headed uphill. "How about a little tour of El Lay."

At every light, he kissed Vic longer and longer, until Vic began to feel light-headed. The feeling only increased as they were now on a wildly curving road, headed through high surroundings. "Laurel Canyon," Paul announced, then shifted into third. There was no traffic ahead of them and they swung around the esses and half curves going about fifty. Once when Vic all but fell into Paul's lap, Paul held his head there and laughed. But Vic thought, *Oh what the fuck*, and at each new curve he nuzzled his head there again until there was a substantial boner beneath the white denims.

They crested a hilltop. Trees, stars. "Mulholland Drive. We'll come back and do it from another end," Paul announced, then drove down the hill, which curved less but which opened out to an enormous view of another light-filled city ahead. "The Valley!" Paul announced. He reached into his t-shirt pocket and pulled out a little glassine envelope.

At the longish red light at Ventura Boulevard Paul opened the envelope and spread it out on the little console area beneath the radio and temperature controls. He rolled up a twenty and sucked up a line.

"Your turn." He handed the rolled bill to Vic.

"Cocaine going 'round my brain." Vic thought of Jelly Roll Morton's song as it hit.

Then they were moving forward again toward a ramp twisting left onto an elevated highway.

"The One-Oh-One," Paul announced, and looking past his silhouette, Vic could make out the Hollywood Hills, clear in the night with some houses way high-up, lighted.

He'd never felt better. But he could feel better yet. He made a decision, and bent down again, over Paul, who'd not lost his hard on. He unzipped him and pulled it out and began to work on it. Paul kept driving, and he kept sucking, then lifted his head for another hit of coke, then sucked again, back and forth, until Paul changed lanes rapidly and Vic hit something with his ear and suddenly the doors were going up, and Paul was hooting, laughing, and Vic went back down on him with the doors open and the cool night air rushing past his face and touseling his hair.

Just before Paul came, Vic noticed a carload of teenagers passing by on Paul's side. Someone in the car saw him and they remained alongside the Benz, tooting their horn repeatedly, and yelling encouragement out the open window.

"You fit right into life in the fast lane!" Paul commented as they got off the freeway.

They parked at an overlook on Mulholland Drive, with the basin of Los Angeles spread out in front of them like an electrified road map for square miles on end. There, they exchanged saliva seemingly forever while a teen couple in the next car watched for a while, then got into their own thing.

"You are one dirty boy, Vic! One naughty, dirty boy!" Paul shook his finger at him. "So. We're still on tomorrow, right?"

"Don't you have a massage tomorrow?"

"I only work in the afternoon," Paul said, after more necking. Then Paul returned Vic's favor, but this time with the gull wings firmly shut.

He dropped Vic off at the hotel and kissed him again, right in front of the doorman, then spun out of the gravel porte-cochere, doing forty.

Vic all but staggered as he walked into the lobby and very, very slowly up the stairs to his room.

The doorman must have said something because since he'd checked in, no one on the staff had paid Vic any attention, but suddenly thereafter, everyone at the desk knew and used his name.

Hmm! Vic thought. *So it is true. There is no such thing as bad publicity!*

CHAPTER SIX

"To write this scenario or outline or precis or whatever it is, I was forced to use a typewriter from the hotel that I swear was last used by Kim Novak to write a thank you note to Mrs. Darryl F. Zanuck," he told Marcie on the phone. "It's aqua and cream colored. With Atoll-blue ink!"

No comment.

"Six pages. And their so-called notes were of a stupidity that even I, with my newly, and much lowered expectations, found appallingly jejune."

Still no comment.

"Tim, the jerk, asked why Anna-Marie had to be killed at all! Can you believe it? It's only the crux of the whole fucking book, and he—"

Still not a hint of a comment.

"We've had another meeting since that *matin degoutant*! And they actually expect me to walk into some stranger's office and tell him I am willing and able to write an entire television movie based on this . . ." he shook the pages at the phone ". . . abortion!"

His agent hadn't said a word. Was she even there?

"Marcie? Are you still alive?"

"Barely. All I know is their check cleared," she said. "I've deposited the money minus my commission into your account." A pause, then, "Ed telexed to extend your stay at the Bee Aitch Aitch for another week. He says they all like you."

"*Like* me? How could they possibly like me!?"

"Don't ask me, I'm only your literary agent," she replied.

"I mean they don't know me. They haven't talked to me. Not a one, except of course Ed himself. But then it turned out that despite his show of great sincerity, even he had a hidden motive. He actually thinks I'd jump at a chance to move out here and become a junior screenwriter under his tutelage."

The minute it left his mouth he knew he shouldn't have said a word.

He heard what was surely the most loathsome ever combination of outrage and sinus clearing: Marcie at her haughtiest.

"May I remind you, Victor, before you toss all your eggs into the Hollywood basket, that you have a new contract for a new novel, to be titled, *Nights in Black Leather*, with your current publisher, who has already put a great deal of time, money, and effort into promoting your first and second book, the latter a current bestseller. Which, by the way, may I also remind you, is the cause of your being out there in sunny California in the first place. And if you think for one moment, I'm going to base for you . . ."

He let her rant on for a while. Then:

"Marse, I'm not even vaguely considering his offer. Despite the fact that I was offered more money than God!"

"How much?" the financial agent in her instantly bypassed the offended agent of two minutes before.

"You don't want to know. It was obscenely high. For a rewrite!"

"Don't do it! I'll get another advance from Laetitia."

His editor. "I'm not doing it. I already told you that, Marcie. These people and this business or whatever scrap of an iota of it I've seen so far is completely beyond me."

She didn't hear.

"I'll talk to Laetitia right away, just as soon as you and I are done." Marcie said. "I always thought they underpaid for your next book. This is a good way to get them to raise the price. They really want one book from you every summer for several years in a row. That's the plan."

Whoever knew "they" had "a plan"?

"Can you really get more beyond what they agreed to pay?" he asked.

"Upfront, as a second advance, sure."

"Well, sure then, try to get more and I'll keep Ed dangling. But I tell you the way all this is going, it's going nowhere anyway."

"That's not what Silver Screen Films thinks," Marcie said.

It suddenly struck him. "I've got to stay here another week? Even though this is a total disaster?"

"Vic, look on the bright side. It might still happen."

"And I might still grow a very attractive vagina, but in the way things usually work, I doubt it."

She laughed. "I might even go lesbo for you if you did."

"Rick being more of a shit than usual?" he asked.

"This doesn't leave the phone, Vic, or you'll find your cute ass in such a sling." She took a deep breath to add, "He's auditioned for this movie."

"Auditions mean noth—"

"He's been called back twice and his agent, who has done and when I say 'nothing' I mean 'less than nothing,' I mean 'actual negative amounts of work on Rick's behalf.' Well this jerk says they really do want Rick for the part."

"A movie? A feature film? That's great!"

"It is a movie," she was speaking carefully. "And it will be feature length. All resemblance to anything even vaguely cinematic suddenly goes out the door from there, Vic. It's set in the Serengeti Plains and it's"—she hesitated, then spit it out as though it were all one word, "Some kind of out of jungle-space-slasher-flick. I mean Rick has been on Broadway, for Chrissakes, although in smaller roles, I admit."

"Does it have a title yet?" Vic had to ask.

"I swear, Vic. I'll come out there and personally kick your butt down every stair of that hotel and across the width of Sunset Boulevard if you reveal a single word of this conversation."

"Who am I going to tell out here? Sam with the layered hair? Tim with the cuffed jeans and questionable rhinoplasty?"

"Lucy. Lowell. Herb. They're all just a phone call away."

That is, people they both knew in publishing in Manhattan. "I swear on . . . well, on my unmet lover's foreskin or something equally valuable, I'll never reveal it."

"It's titled . . . *High-Savannah Holocaust*."

He laughed despite himself, but managed to cover it up so she couldn't hear. "That's not so terrible."

"Come on, it's ghastly. Can you just see Rick explaining it on his resume when he goes up before Joe Papp for Shakespeare in the Park?"

"He can always say he's experienced to play the lion in *Midsummer's Night Dream*."

"You're a real help, Vic. Thanks." She began a lengthy coughing fit.

"When does Rick leave?"

"Next Thursday, if you can believe it. I guess they're afraid he'll come to his senses and back out of the contract. He'll be in Tanganyika, which, he's been told, is mountainous and thus dry and sunny by day, with temps no higher than seventy-five degrees and . . . and . . . you'll still be out there in summertime L.A. Meanwhile I'm on my third, count 'em three, head cold of the winter, I am wrapped in a wool sweater with a wool jacket and wool hat looking like some extremely minor character out of *Heidi*, the heat's on full blast and I'm still freezing here."

"The sacrifices you make for your clients. One question more. Will he be back in time for the Black Party?"

"I don't know. And I don't need your sarcasm. I'm now hanging up."

"Wait. Marcie. What do I do?" Vic asked. "I mean this is already totally wasted time."

He could almost hear her shrug.

"Let me remind you: you are getting paid . . . Oh! I don't know. Take some time off today. Go sight-seeing!"

"I have been taking time off. I'm walnut-colored from the poolside and I've been out every night screwing my brains out. I work maybe two hours a day, tops! Which is more than they do. They work maybe an hour every day. Silver Screen, I mean. They take a half hour meeting. Break for lunch. Come back another half hour and leave for the day."

"You never know what might happen," she said and followed it up with five more clichés, then added, "Victor, please. Do it for me."

He hung up, but five minutes later, the phone rang again, and he picked it up sure it was Marcie with a sensible plan for salvaging this operation, but it was only the desk downstairs: his driver was waiting, and he was reminding him that Vic had a meeting with the guys at Silver Screen in twenty minutes.

Arrrgggghhhh!

The humpiest room-service waiter of them all, and there definitely was a grouping of truly certifiable cuties, chose right then to come pick up the remnants of Vic's lunch. The guy looked like a younger more muscular Bjoern Borg without the beard.

When he asked, as usual (they all asked, incessantly), how he was, Vic said, "I'm deeply depressed! You wouldn't care for a blow job, would you?" Figuring what could the guy do, report him to the manager?

"Gosh! Well! That sure is a great offer. I mean . . . "

He hemmed and hawed so cutely that Vic said, "Never mind. Oh, you forgot this," and Vic put a napkin on the tray and exited into the bathroom to brush his teeth. When he came out again, mercifully, the room service waiter was gone.

CHAPTER SEVEN

"Gotta remind you," Vic's driver began, "it's my night off."

"*No problema.* I'll get someone at the party to take me back to the hotel."

Given the driver's sour look at that, Vic asked, "Bad idea?"

"Let me put it this way: you'll all be drinking. Remember what the drive up here was like?"

Fifteen hairpin curves in a row with two streetlights spaced a mile apart and invisibly overhung by bougainvillea—and they'd gotten lost twice.

"Got it. I'll call a taxi."

Meade had a card ready for Beverly Hills Cab.

The house was 1930s Stock Broker's Tudor, not very different from some of the heaps Vic and Gilbert used to bike past daily on their way to middle school. But this one had a deep, curvy driveway and various extensions that he'd later discover included a substantial guest house, a pool cabana, and even a little awning-covered "viewers box" for watching whomever was playing tennis on the regulation-sized court. Inside, it was a bit more updated than the few ancient piles back home he and Gil had stepped into with their Elizabethan-era cupboards and frayed Turkey carpets brought over on the ship that had closely tailed the Mayflower. Here it was all modern and bright. Hell, they even had electric lighting!

Vic was the guest of honor, and as he arrived relatively late, they sat down almost immediately. People out here ate dinner early, went to sleep early, and alas, Vic fretted, awakened awfully early too. When he'd commented on that, one of Silver Screen's secretaries offered, "It's so beautiful every morning! Who'd want to stay in bed?" after which she sashayed out the room humming like Snow White before he could rip the metal pencil sharpener off a desk and hurl it at her. Less Polyanna, another suggested, "We've got to do business with the East Coast, which is three hours earlier. Maybe that's why we're here by eight a.m? So we can catch them before they're debilitated by cocktails at lunch."

Ed Trefethern didn't only know movie people. Present was a woman with a quite consciously shaved head who was a new underground "dance-artist." Also a playwright Vic had vaguely heard of, and an aging Sci-Fi novelist, who turned out to look like nothing less than your standard, wacko-scientist from any 1950s Giant-Ant movie. He immediately took Vic aside and said, "You're fresh from New York?"

And when he admitted it was less than a week, the writer said, "Please, say something Yiddish."

"I'm not Jewish," Vic protested.

"You're a New Yorker." He argued. "Please!" he begged. "It's been so long. Anything!" he prompted.

Just then a stout Mexican cook passed by.

"A *schoene maedel* she's not," Vic commented.

The writer's hand went to his heart. "Lovely. More! More!"

"What do you want me to say? That I find this burg completely feydreit? Because I do. Welshmen, like our charming host, schmooze like alte kockers from Kiev. While guys who should be Black Panther killers chomp on bialy's smeared with grieves and schmaltz and wish me a maazel as though they were moils. What gives?"

"Thank you. Thank you," the Sci Fi writer said, his eyes spinning with pleasure, and once more uttering "Thank you!" he meandered off.

Two major movie stars flanked Vic at the big dinner table. She was the only woman he'd ever seriously consider going straight for. A few years older than Vic, a star at seventeen, now a major actress whose every film got her more award nominations than Cecil B. De Mille could purchase; British, naturally; intellectual as they came; salty; tart-tongued; and if not a political Anarchist, then at least pretty darn close. To his surprise, the dark haired young-looking slender fellow across the table from her and to whom she addressed her most lacerating critiques and revolutionary concepts, was, although known as an infamous ladies man in the Hollywood Press, evidently her devoted lover, as who wouldn't be. He would sit there quietly, listening to her vituperation about the U.S. Government, the CIA, the Pentagon, IBM, and General Motors, until his cute little nose would twitch like a bunny rabbit's and suddenly he'd erupt with, "Now that's just plain utter nonsense. Right, Vic? Tell her!" And Vic would have to mediate, looking first into Her scrumptious face and gorgeous, if angry, blue eyes, and then into His scrumptious face and gorgeous, if pissed off, brown eyes. At least twice he wondered which one he'd kiss first, given the chance.

Ed's wife Jennifer only became a clear individual among all the weirdos and strong personalities after dinner, when she offered him a "tour of the place," evidently an expected part of any visit in this city where the private and public blurred so seamlessly. Case in point: the feuding actors were now smooching in a not very hidden bower in the terrace off the study.

As there were photos of older children and an older wife, clearly Jennifer was spouse number two or perhaps number three.

"It's so funny," she said as she led him up the twenty-foot wide stairs that led, not to a throne room, but merely to the second floor, "but I only dated guys my age till Ed came along. And I was never satisfied with them. What can a young guy know? No offense, since from your books, you're obviously maturer than your years. Ed kept pestering me to go out. Finally I said okay. Well he ran me off my feet. He's unstoppable. The energy. The wide interests. So now I'm spoiled. He'd better stick around a while," she shook her fist in Ed's general direction, her cute face bunched up in a theatrical threat, "so I can try to wear *him* down. Now this is my sewing room. I do sew, in fact I'm an amateur clothing designer. I made this dress and also what J____ (the female movie star) is wearing tonight. Whaddya think?"

Vic thought, now at last he could gawp at her very large breasts without seeming to ogle, and that the outfits were great and Jennifer was kind of a hoot: a buxom starlet who read, thought and sewed?

As they were wandering through the outside grounds, she took his arm and said, "He likes you." Ed, she meant. "He wants you around more. He's bored with the people around him these days. They're no . . . challenge."

"I like him too," Vic admitted. "And you too, Jennifer. But I don't think Ed realizes that I'm not exactly a free agent. I've got a new book out in two months that I must, by contract, publicize, and I'm supposed to hand in another novel by next September. A big one."

She made a face, then brightened up. "Well, then—after!" She hugged his arm closer and he enjoyed her lemon verbena scent and her pillowly softness. "We get to New York a lot. Always for the holidays because of Ed's kids. We've got a place in Midtown. You won't escape us that easily."

They made a tentative date for months in the future, by which time Vic expected to be safely brain-dead from novel-writing overwork, and she went to the kitchen to look over dessert as he wandered back into the house.

He found Ed alone in a library that looked as though it had to have been taken right out of a movie-set in a single piece, complete with vast stone fireplace and shelves of picturesquely dropped and angled-as-though-just-skimmed-through books. Ed was reading *The New Yorker* and simultaneously watching a football game on TV with the sound off.

"I do the same thing," Vic admitted. "Two things at once. But what team is playing at this time of the year? Oh, it's a film?"

"Videotape." Ed shook the long rectangular box at him. "Some guys at the sports desk at the networks kinescope them for me. You know what videotape is, right?"

"Oh sure. I did an article for a magazine about it, maybe six years ago. I'm waiting for it to get cheap enough to buy myself," Vic added, realizing as he said it that after his last two advances he could easily afford a video player. Weird how he still thought like someone with a fifth of his new annual income.

"I like Jennifer," Vic said. "She and I made a dinner date for your place in Manhattan for sometime this coming summer."

"You may come to your senses yet. I tell you, Vic," Ed's arms waved to take in the study, "the life here is unbeatable!"

"From what I can see. But maybe I still need a little more punishment."

Ed laughed, nodding outside. "Stick around with the love birds.

They'll provide all the punishment you can take. I can only say that because we're good friends, you understand."

"I do. Tell me, they're not publicly together, are they?" Vic asked. "I mean I know they make movies together and all, but . . ."

"I wouldn't say anything, no. And as a rule, I find it best to wait until a couple announces something," Ed said. "Which in my opinion, those two never will do . . . You know, Vic, not everyone wants to be a Burton and Taylor."

With champagne and Irish coffee was a homemade strawberry rhubarb pie with whipped cream, which someone must have discovered and then told the producer was Vic's very favorite sweet.

He turned to Ed. "You're trying to seduce me, Mrs. Robinson . . . Aren't you?"

Everyone laughed.

CHAPTER EIGHT

"How good a party can it possibly be at four o'clock on a Sunday afternoon?"

"It's an El Lay party. You'll see," Andy responded. They were talking car to car, Andy of course having a car phone, too. Didn't everyone?

"The only reason I would even dream of going," Vic admitted, "is that hot guy from New York who works for Long Meadow Records left a message at the hotel saying he'd be there. For him it's a work assignment."

"What guy? Is he cute?"

"You think I'd go all this way for a for a schmuck?"

"Speaking of schmucks—" Andy interrupted.

"Haven't seen his. Nope."

"Possibly you will today, since I expect this soiree is going to quickly devolve into an Oh Arr Gee Why."

"At four in the afternoon? At tea and crumpets time?"

"It's a Hollywood Hills party, Vic."

"You 'expect' or you plan to incite an orgy?"

"Don't have to. The B____ brothers will be there," naming actors he'd heard of, "all three of them. One B____ brother among good looking gay men is a certifiable orgy flint. Three of them? Well, it might get out of hand."

"Good thing I wore clean underwear," Vic murmured then realized in an orgy it wouldn't stay on long. Maybe he should ink his name into the back label when he disrobed, like kindergartners did with gloves and hats.

"It's not that far now," Andy insisted. "On Mount Olympus."

"Isn't that Northern Greece?"

"Try southern Laurel Canyon. Is that you in the pale blue Caddy?"

"Why? Where are you?"

"Directly ahead. In the '63 charcoal Lincoln Continental."

"You mean the one that looks like the Kennedy assassination vehicle?"

"La meme exactement! Okay, that is you, I can see your lip gloss reflected in my mirror."

"Liar! Bitch!"

"Have your driver follow me," Andy hung up.

"Meade, follow this guy ahead of us. The dark gray job," Vic specified. "He'll take us right up to the house."

The phone rang again two minutes later: this time, Gilbert.

Vic reported the near-incident with the super good looking room service waiter.

"The waiter was probably just surprised by your openness," Gilbert opined. "He might be available. Just be ready for him."

"Ready? What do I do if he says yes? What do I tip him when he arrives at five and comes at five fifteen?"

"Depends how big his tip is!" Gilbert chortled. "Never mind: a twenty. Unless he reciprocates. Then at least fifty."

"Gilbert, you see it now, don't you? It's all in some kind of perverted inverse ratio. The more disastrous the film angle gets, the more sex I seem to get."

"Inverse ratio? Oh you mean like, 'the angle of the dangle is equal to the heat of the meat'?"

Vic chose to ignore that. "I go into any fern bar here on Santa Monica Bee and they're lined up, these amazing pretty boys in a row. Each of them ripe for the plucking by guess who? At this moment Andy is taking me to a Mount Olympus party he assures me will be a stupendous, star-studded orgy."

"You're never coming back, are you?" Gilbert asked.

"So last night, before I'm to see Perfect Paul fourth night in a row, there's this dinner party that Ed, the executive producer, is giving in his humongus, half-timbered castle somewhere in the Hills above the Sunset Strip. My driver is off for the latter part of the night, so I have them call me a taxi to take me back to the Bee Aitch Aitch. Who shows up? Some twenty-four year old unemployed actor. Muscled. Darkly handsome. Green eyes. Thick, chestnut hair that falls like it's been ironed. Ratty surfer tee shirt that looks glued on with perspiration and jizz. Ditto for the ripped surfer shorts. Shorts, and flip flops, for chrissake, Gil! At night! Left nothing to the imagination."

"And we know that as an author you've got a great imagination. But you were about to see Perfect Paul?" Gilbert reminded him.

"Exactly, so I am shut-mouth quiet until we are two streets from the hotel on Sunset when he suddenly pulls over to the curb, stops, and turns around and says could he ask me a question."

"No!"

"Honest to Diana Ross truth, Gilberto. So I say ask away. Seems that a nice looking middle aged fellow the night before gave Surfer-Dude a Cuban cigar as a tip and said he'd been thinking about what that cigar would look like in the driver's mouth the entire ride home."

"Shut! Up!"

"This is what The Surfing Cabbie tells me. He says he stripped off the cellophane and put the Cubano cigar in his mouth for the guy, who tipped him and got out."

"Uh-huh?" Even clever Gilbert couldn't see where this was going.

"So the driver asks me, 'What do you think that was really about'?"

"You mean," Gilbert asked, "because Freud said sometimes a cigar is just a cigar?"

"Looking at this guy, Gillo, and how he was more and mostly less dressed, Freud does not apply. So I was bored and a little 'stunada from dinner's fourteen wines and I said the first thing that came into my mind. Which was 'Your fare wanted you to blow him.'"

"You didn't?!"

"I did. I was bored. I was high. What would you think?"

"I'd *think* it; I wouldn't *say* it."

"Well, I said it. 'Really?' Driver Googie asks, not at all offended. And I said 'Really!' and then for verisimilitude, I added, 'Your fare probably was holding some other twenties in his hand, like this,' I splayed out my hand with three of them, one for the ride and two others."

"Oy! The writer and his verisimilitude," Gilbert groaned.

"And the Surfer-Dude says, 'He *was* holding them out. Just like that!'"

"Saints alive, Miss Sofonsiba!"

Vic went on, "Then I added, 'Which he wanted you to have. Or, I might be wrong, and instead, you being cute and all, maybe he wanted to blow you.'"

"Tell me you didn't actually say that, in the back of a cab on Sunset Boulevard and . . . where were you?"

"I don't know. Foothill. Alpine. One of them. It was fascinating, Gilbert, watching all the counters tumbling around behind that perfect face like in one of those slot machines. I kept holding out the twenties at Sir Gidget the Hunky Cabbie and suddenly all the counters fell into place going blink blink blink in those money-colored eyes and I swear I all but heard them go ka-ching! He snatched the twenties, stuffed them in his tee shirt pocket and said, 'But understand, I gotta stay in the car in case I get a dis-patch call.' So he drove up a block or two behind the hotel and came into the back seat and I had a big steak for the second time that night."

"All because . . . ?" Gilbert hadn't quite gotten the 'moral' and he now needed one for closure.

"All because . . . I was about to meet Perfect Paul and didn't care if I sucked off this handsome, unemployed surfing actor's eight incher. Ergo I was casual enough about it for him not to be threatened in the least."

"You . . . are . . . the master of the hetero pick-up, Vic-tor-ee-a."

"I'm now hanging up, Zhil-berte."

"Go to the leather bar premiere!"

"I said no, Gilbert! No!" and hung up.

At which moment Vic realized he'd not completely shut the window between the front and back, and the tall, ugly driver had heard every single word.

After another minute or so they stopped and there was a tap on his side window. Andy. They'd arrived.

By his seventh day in town, Victor had ceased to be amazed by the interior decor of the Los Angeles homes he saw. Their sheer nuttiness was only outdone by their expense and by the fact that given the chance, he'd move in to any of them in a second.

This one, contemporary stone, steel, and glass, was set in woods, making it totally private; only the roof deck had a view. The house sported what El Lay people referred to as "various water features": brooks, rills, little cascades, larger water falls, and several pools, including the first infinity version he'd ever seen up close, as well as a lap pool, two hot tubs, and several foot baths. They were all over the house on every level. Filled with hot guys frolicking—either naked or in speedos.

Since it actually was a publicity event for some new Disco Diva discovery for Long Meadow Records, the entry and main rooms had the appurtenances of such, at least as Vic had come to know them: a long table set up with copies of her "fabulous new single," as well as an eight minute, longer version for club deejays to spin, along with photos, bios, and such-like. The Diva herself had already been there and was expected to return and sing a number after she had made a surprise appearance at some club on The Strip.

And there at the table was Mark Chastain, dressed in dark slacks, tan and black silk moire shirt, and brown penny loafers. He looked professional. They'd only met once before. Vic had forgotten how manly, but not how handsome, he was.

As Vic and Andy arrived and were greeted by their host and Long Meadow Records' owner, a feisty little bulldog of a hot Jewish New Yorker named Hal Dern. Their host was wet but not quite dripping, wrapped in a rainbow colored bathrobe; Dern was dripping, clad only in a speedo with a two-sizes-too-small A-shirt on top.

Andy took one look at Mark and said, "Honey, get those clothes off so we can see all your muscles. All of them, I say, child!" He soon enough vanished, arm in arm with the host, while Hal recognized Vic and gave him a hug.

"The big man!" he announced as though there were two hundred and not six other people in the room. "The famous writer! Out in Hollywood making deals!"

"The big record producer!" Vic declaimed back. "The famous Star Maker! Out in Hollywood launching a Diva."

Having failed to embarrass Vic, Hal left muttering something.

"What'd he say?" Vic had to ask Mark.

"He's got some single-cut coke back in his bedroom."

"I'll pass. Did you have any?"

"One line. Hours ago. So!" Mark looked pleased. "You showed up."

"You doubted?"

"I'd heard you were very busy."

With Perfect Paul, he means, Vic thought. *Wonder who...?*

"Working for some film company," Mark completed his thought.

"If you call that work. But it looks like you really are working!"

"Well, I've got to stand here and greet everyone and offer them a disc and this material," he handed them to Vic in a shiny plastic bag.

"And you can't go into the water and show all those muscles, child!" Vic added.

"Not until six. Our plane is at 7:30. That gives me about..."

"Three minutes in the water."

"That's what I figured," Mark looked unhappy. "And I arrived yesterday morning on a red-eye. With Her in tow, and I mean in tow given her size and heft. And I was with her or setting this up all the rest of the time."

"And now you've got to go home. Doesn't sound like much fun."

"It's a job," Mark admitted.

"Where's Will?" Vic asked.

"Will?"

"Will Traylor?

"I guess back in New York. Why?"

Wlll had introduced them. Actually, Will had brought Vic to meet Mark one day at the offices of Long Meadow Records, talking about Mark in detailed adoring length before and after said meeting.

"Nothing. I just got the impression he was...you two were..."

"Did Will tell you that?" Very sincere and concerned.

"Not in so many words. Maybe I just assumed it."

"Oh?"

Maybe because Will wanted me to assume it? Vic thought. *Because Will knows I'd never bird-dog anyone he was dating.*

"Look, it's not important," Vic said.

"But you came anyway?" Mark asked.

"I thought you'd want support . . . you know, a familiar face in a strange town . . ." Vic trailed off.

"You came out of loyalty?"

"I suppose."

"Not because of 'the guys'?"

"I just heard about 'the guys' while driving over here . . . It's not true, is it? What my pal told me?" Vic asked.

"How could I tell, stuck here in the foyer?"

Andy chose that moment to reappear. He was in small square Nautica boating shorts and nothing else. He took Vic aside and said, "It's insane. In five minutes I've ingested two sizable loads of man-juice. When are you coming?"

"In a minute. I'm busy."

Andy looked over Mark. "You've got the eye, my pal. He's a beaut." He sized up Mark, who was now talking to two new arrivals, and said, "Not quite a beer-can dick, but almost. You may not be able to handle it."

Vic laughed. "How could you possibly tell that through Dockers?"

"All the cock I've seen in my life, Honey? Please! I'm a professional. Little secret: the give-away is the guy's ass. The size, shape, but mostly the angle of the ass. See, his is good sized and firm looking, which already is an important indicator for size given his waist is only about thirty inches. Mmmmm mmm! But see how his ass angles up, not down? That's because those upper glute muscles are needed to hold a larger male member than normal in front."

"Oh, please." Vic was blushing. "Even so, how do you know it's not long instead of thick?"

"Now that's where *experience,* and even more, *instinct* come into play," Andy lectured.

"I'll bet."

"You'll see that I'm right."

Vic changed the topic. "Are the B____ brothers here?"

"I thought I saw one. Maybe not." Andy then named three music stars whom he'd already encountered around the house in "embarrassing positions." Vic would grant him two, but of the third:

"Isn't he married to a famous bikini model?"

"All I know is he pushed me away from the two, I said *two*, large, tubular, fleshen objects he was taking turns having his way with. I'm going to have to let ____ ____ (naming a British singer known to be fey), who's holding court in the foot baths, do me. Just to tell everyone he did. Although he's done everyone else here too. Toodles!"

Vic went into the other room and came back with a Vodka Tonic for himself and a Gerolsteiner bottled water for Mark.

"Thanks, I am supposed to stay here."

"I'll take over if you need a men's room run. I've almost learned your *spiel* by heart."

"Very funny." Mark looked at Vic more seriously and began, "Look I know that you're famous and all. But I've never read any of your books."

"The whippings begin at nine on the dot," Vic said darkly. "Of course if you read one of my books before then and can pass a simple, hundred-question true or false quiz, you're safe."

"I'm not seeing Will," Mark added. "Nothing against him. I'm just not."

"Cool. Okay," Victor replied and suddenly felt that a door had just wedged open. "My next book is out in three months. Read that one. It's my best. Based on a historical incident in the midwest around the turn of the centry."

"I see people reading your books all the time. I'm just into other stuff. The *Ballets Russes.* I'm reading about Diaghilev now."

"The Russian impresario?"

"There's this new book out on him and Nijinsky. And another on Nazimova, the '20s Russian film star."

"Rudolf Valentino's beard," Vic said. "I saw her film, *Salome.*"

"Wasn't that great!" Mark enthused. "Those art deco costumes. Even when she was at rest, the feathered points of her crown were in wavelike motion all the time!"

And so between new arrivals, they talked about Stravinsky and Ida Rubenstein, Debusssy and Rimsky-Korsakov, Ravel and Lotte Lehmann.

Andy would reappear at intervals of fifteen minutes, with news flashes from the infinity pool or lower spa, saying, "Took two more loads. While I was busy rimming this hot, shaved-head Brazilian named Emilio, one of the B___ brothers suddenly began porking me! Without even asking my permission! Of course, once I saw who it was halfway up my anal canal, I let him." And at a later check-in, Andy reported "___ ___," naming the married musician, "is really going to hell. Coking, tripping, *and* sucking. Super slut!"

By four-thirty the new arrivals were down to a trickle. By four forty-five, they were non-existent. Mark and Vic got chairs and fresh bottled water. They were comparing Beecham versus Toscanini's conducting style, and whether Gieseking or Michelangeli was *the* Beethoven pianist of the century, when the host came out in quickly thrown-on street clothes, distress apparent in at least one small, relatively undrugged region of his face.

"Had to phone an E.M.T. unit. Let me know when they arrive!"

"Someone almost drown?" Vic asked.

He named the rock star. "He's got killer cramps and is vomiting."

Five minutes later the emergency vehicle arrived. Hal Dern appeared and gave minute-by-minute updates from the bedroom hallway as they pumped out the guy's stomach and installed a five minute drip against dehydration then left.

One of the E.M.T. guys came back and called for the host to sign some papers. Mark went to get him, leaving Vic alone with the med worker, a tall, red-bearded fellow.

"You seem pretty blasé about a near drowning?" Vic said.

"Near drowning *in semen,* you mean!"

"No?" Vic asked.

"I'm blasé because it happens once a month."

"You're kidding."

"At least. Hetero amateurs!" The med worker sneered. "They all want to take a walk on the wild side. Think it's so cool. Tomorrow night they'll surprise their friends in public telling the whole dinner table how they starred at a homo bash. What they don't realize is that a guy's jizz is chock full of amino acids. Mix that with drugs, and whammo!"

Luckily, Andy *was* used to them, given the rate he was going today.

When Mark returned, the Med worker said, in a voice only they could hear, "Look, the home owner and that other guy are pretty busy partying. You two look sober and responsible. You ought to get this guy," meaning the rock star, "back to where he lives. Drive him. Give him these if he gets woozy in the car," he handed Vic some Dramamine. "Can I count on you?"

"Don't worry," Mark assured him.

"I've got a car and driver," Vic said.

"Good men! Go in half an hour at the latest," the med worker said. "I put sedative in his drip. He'll be going under."

"There goes your three minutes in the pool," Vic said when the E.M.T. guy left. Then, "Why not get your bags and all, and we'll drive this guy home, and then I'll have my driver take you right to the airport?"

Andy came out to report that the Gay Brit tenor gave passable head, but "nothing to sing about." And that it was rumored that someone famous had overdosed.

"Everyone's fine," Mark said, trying to dampen the rumor.

Meade helped them with the singer, getting him out to the Caddy without anyone else seeing. He looked short, thin and craggy, exhausted, pale, and already very drowsy. Vic's driver surprised them by saying, "I know where he lives. Took them home from an event once," emphasizing the word "them."

In the back seat of the car, the rock star fell asleep sloppily, first on Vic's shoulder, and then when he moved him gently to the seat, onto Mark's chest. Mark let him lean against him. What a nice guy.

Mark and the driver half carried the rock star up the few stairs and into the foyer, their ring had been answered by a blonde in yoga togs and a Mexican housekeeper, both of whom seemed concerned.

After Mark came back to the limo, Meade remained talking with the wife a moment and wrote something down on a piece of paper for her.

"I left your name and your hotel number," he reported to Vic back in the driver's seat. "Just in case he's a good guy and wants to give you something."

"Come on! He'll be too embarrassed."

"Well, I did it anyway," Meade said.

Traffic was easy going west, and Mark relaxed for the first time and shut his eyes. Vic let him lean on his shoulder, not minding the pressure one bit. He thought Mark was dead asleep until Meade announced they were at L.A.X. and asked what airline they needed. That's when Mark took Vic's hand in his and answered the driver. Vic couldn't believe how oddly exciting that was, suddenly feeling his hand clasped so . . . affectionately? proprietarily? in Mark's. And Mark held it until the car stopped for him to get out.

"See! You're on time! As promised," Vic said when they were getting out Mark's luggage.

Mark kept looking at him. So Vic asked, "What?"

"In New York? Two weeks from now—you'll be back by then, right? There's a performance at Lincoln Center. A double bill of Stravinsky's *Rossignol* and *L'Histoire du Soldat,* in English. They're very seldom done." He named a well known English actor who would narrate the latter chamber opera.

"Okay. Sure, I'll go with you."

Vic wrote his phone number down for Mark, who put it into his shirt pocket, by his heart.

Meade went to park the limo. Vic walked Mark to his plane and waited with him in the departure lounge. When his seating section was called, Mark hugged him quickly, hard, so that Vic was suddenly enfolded within the strong solidity of his arms, shoulders, and upper back. Vic felt the oddest little flutter in his chest.

Mark stepped away without another word and without looking back.

Still unhinged by that little flutter, Vic waited until, watching from the floor to ceiling departure lounge glass, he could see Mark's 707 taxi along and then ascend safely into the air and stash itself inside L.A.X's perpetual clouds.

I'm just a hopeless romantic, Vic told himself. *Here I go again!*

In the car, Meade commented, "He seemed like a together guy."

"He did, didn't he?" Vic responded, amazed in retrospect by the entire afternoon.

CHAPTER NINE

Vic had no idea why they were having this meeting at Silver Screen Films. Only that it was planned for in his schedule and Meade called for him at the hotel. So he'd gotten dressed, gotten his little scenario kit together, and was driven here.

He arrived second. Tim was already at the conference table, and he quickly got up, confidently strode over to Vic, grabbed his hand, and, shaking it, dragged him over to the window.

"Gotta thank you, Vic. You were *totally* on the ball."

"Thanks!" *About what*, he wondered.

"It was harsh when you said it. But you laid it on the line and even though it was like being socked in the kisser at the time, the way the other guys were silent and all, even at the moment it happened, I knew you were dead-on right."

Vic fumbled toward the side table to get coffee and try to figure out what in hell Tim was nattering on about.

"Stan backed you up a hundred percent. So, soon as I got home, I faced her right away. Told her that it was my fault, and that I'd been a weakling and a fool. But I also said it was her fault and that she was a bitch because she was taking advantage of the situation. I told her I'd pack my bags and get out right then. We could have our lawyers do the rest."

Oh shit! What Vic had said about Theo. In *Justify My Sins*! Tim had taken that to mean himself, with his erring wife, instead of Vic's blanket condemnation of straight romance.

"She broke down and asked me not to leave. Fell apart totally. She admitted she'd acted like a spoiled brat. We talked for, I don't know, maybe three hours. Everything came out. Her side of it. My side of it. She said I was finally acting like the man she thought she'd married. We're fine now. God, you are *good!* You know women inside out, don't you?"

Vic tried not to keep from sputtering his coffee onto his shirt front. He could see the headline: *Queer Saves Shaky Marriage.*

Luckily, Sam came in at that moment, got his coffe and sat down. Tim quickly moved to his usual place at the conference table, but the receptionist buzzed him and he left to take a call in his own office.

Sam looked around and in a most conspiratorial tone of voice said, "Not a word to anyone, right?"

Vic crossed his heart, wondering what Sam could—

"This girl I'm seeing? Two days ago I get home and I catch her in the sack with another girl. She say's they're just fooling around. I was like, stunned. Had. No. Idea. What. To. Do."

Vic almost laughed: Queer Abby was more like it.

"What *did* you do?" he asked.

"Well, nothing. The other one got dressed and left and she and I had a dinner to go to, so . . ."

"Was she hot? The other girl?"

"Hot enough." Sam's eyes danced a little.

"Why not bring it up sometime. Wait till it's a good positive situation, when you're both having fun. Then say something like, 'Oh, you know that Christina, or whatever her name is, is really cute. Why not ask her to join us for after-dinner drinks some time?'"

Sam blinked a half dozen times.

"You mean and have, like, a . . . three way?"

"Or whatever, Sam. It *is* the 1970s!"

Sam laughed oddly and Vic could guess that behind his eyes all kinds of scenarios were rushing past. One scenario evidently scared Sam and he suddenly asked, "Well what if, like, we do that. And then my girl wants to do it with me and another guy?"

Ah, the ultimate fear: two dicks in one bed.

"Well, Sam, turnabout *is* fair play," Vic said.

"So, I'm guessing that kind of stuff happens all the time in that Plato's Retreat? Right? That sex club you've got in New York? I just *know* you've been there. You maybe even have a membership."

Vic admitted he had been there, recalling but not saying that it had been with his agent Marcie, of all people, pre-Rick. But he didn't have a membership.

Vic added, "I prefer things to happen a little more naturally, myself. That way no one gets embarrassed and no one has to explain anything to themselves or each other later on. I mean, Sam, *that's* the problem. *Not* what you're *doing*. But how to *square it* later on. Because it's just like electricity otherwise. Know what I mean? All a matter of plugs and sockets."

"Oh, wow!" Sam enthused, and he might have added, Leaping Metaphors, Batman! "Like, our plugs are made to go into a lot of different sockets. The *plugs* don't know the difference. They just know that they're in a *socket!*"

Vic couldn't leave it alone. "Right. And, Sam, we've *all* got sockets for those plugs. Because they're all pretty much the same size and the plugs fit anywhere."

"Wow!" Sam recognized it with a little edge of thrill in his voice. "Oh, man!"

Vic thought, *Fuck Your Mind For a Nickel!*

Stan and Ed came in then and Sam quieted down. Tim joined them, still in a good mood, and Trefethern took a phone call.

Stan held out an envelope with Vic's name on it. "This just arrived for you at the front desk."

Vic opened and found three pairs of tickets to the rock star at the orgy's next Los Angeles concert, a month from now. No note, natch.

"Who likes ____ ____?" he asked the table, adding, "I'll be back in *Nueva Jorck* when this happens," and when Ed, Sam, and Stan all said they did, he handed around the tickets.

"You make friends fast, don't you?" Sam asked. He looked at Vic with a new respect. "Interesting friends!"

Stan and Ed told them that they had just come in from a 'pitch session' at one of the networks, and Ed confessed, "I think we made a real hash of your book there, Vic. Although the truth is, it was the only project of ours they were interested enough in to ask to hear about in any detail. There's no question that you've got to come to the Network with us when we present it. If not, there's no saying how we'll junk it up."

It was at that point that, as they no doubt had carefully planned it not ten minutes previously, Stan brought up the "question of the to-some-folks downer ending" of Vic's novel. He and Ed began introducing what they termed "a few vague possibilities" for how "the story might be less of a downer," and were joined by the others, allowing Vic to know that this had been planned by all of them together. Maybe if there was a moral, or a lesson learned, or something really hopeful for Theo's future that Vic might emphasize while he discussed the story at the network?

Having been with them long enough to figure out how this table-talk game was played, Vic said sure, he'd definitely think about all the "great ideas" they had suggested, not one of which he thought was of any relevance to his book, and not one of which he planned to give any credence at all, never mind present to anyone else.

Despite that, he was still tickled about being the romantic advisor for these loser guys just because he'd written a novel. And on top of that, Mr. Generous in giving them third row seats at the Coliseum

As the meeting was breaking up, Ed took Vic aside and told him that the British movie star from dinner had "liked Vic a lot," and had suggested that he join her and her b.f. sometime. Another British actress, a friend of theirs, was in town and J____ would like her and Vic to meet—and doubtless argue, Ed added. "This lady is also, quote, fiercely intelligent, unquote," Ed said. "Which doesn't seem to bother you one bit in women. She'd probably spit out these guys," looking at the office where they'd gathered, "in four seconds flat."

CHAPTER TEN

"Officially, it's *Will* Rogers State Beach. But of course, *we* all call it *Ginger* Rogers."

So saith Andy as he parked the Assassination Vehicle in the parking lot. The trunk held the enormous assemblage of Surf'n'Sand requirements Andy had: way beyond chairs, towels, and umbrellas, but fortunately just short of tubular surf-horsies. Vic let himself be heaped with half of it until he was blinded by too many towels and garments and had to be led forward to the spot Andy stopped him at, close enough to the water.

It was a perfect day. No clouds. Seventy-six degrees Fahrenheit. Tiny breezes everywhere. Little wavelets in the ocean. Hot guys in ones, twos, and threes on blankets all around. The sweep of the beach to his left, over to the amusement park on the big public pier; to his right, miles further across the multihued blue bay waters, past Malibu, and up to Point Zuma. Behind their heads, picturesque little Santa Monica Canyon breaking for a moment into the regularity of the scenic cliffs, topped with residences barely visible within so much green, and then the formal majesty of an avenue of huge, Washingtonia palm trees along the tippy top of the Ocean Avenue Promenade.

What more could anyone want?

Well, for one, Mark Chastain would be nice, Vic thought. Right here, with his clothing off, holding Vic's hand, talking to him about the intricacies of Ravel's *L'Enfant et le Sortileges*, and looking right into Vic's eyes with his own dark brown eyes, eyes Vic had decided resembled nothing less than Teuscher's Champagne-truffle chocolates. He sighed.

"See? You should have undressed and joined me at the orgy." Andy admonished. "But would you listen? New Yorkers!" he scoffed at the wind.

Not a clue, Vic thought.

He mooned on a bit, then they went for a dip in the freezing cold water, frolicking as though they were Tony and Jack being girl-band members in *Some Like It Hot*. They lay on the beach, then Andy got antsy and went blanket-hopping while Vic reattacked the John Fowles novel in which he'd advanced an entire three pages since his plane left LaGuardia airport over a week before.

Still believing that Vic was groaning over his wasted opportunity, Andy dragged him over to be introduced to 1) Jason, strawberry blond, muscles for weeks, fabulous face; 2) Scott, slender and abdomen-pretty, with auburn locks; 3) Darryl, cocoa au lait, bass-baritone sweet, golden-green eyes, and . . .

"Wait!" Vic all but flattened Darryl of the creamy thighs while he rudely stared: "Isn't that Christopher Isherwood?"

They also rudely stared and replied in one voice, "That *old* guy?"

Andy added, "Why? Do you know him?"

Darryl fled such perversity. Andy groaned. But Vic steeled himself, saying *It's not for me, it's for him, it's not for me, it's for him*, and went over to where this rectangular looking man with a square-looking head, long, striking, carefully combed silver-gold hair and milky blue eyes was busily annoying innocent shells on the strand with some kind of ferrule.

Out of the corner of his eye Vic could see Andy abandoning their set up so as not to be contaminated by Victor's all too apparently bizarre taste in men.

"Mr. Isherwood," he began in a rush, and the tan, abstracted face looked up at him. "I'm very sorry, but I once promised a very dear friend that if I ever came to the West Coast I'd look you up, and I never would have had to nerve to do so, but since you're right in front of me, I have to do it or I'll never forgive myself."

Well, *that* got the famous writer's attention.

"Now be very careful young man how you answer next," was the reply, "or I shall turn 'round and leave you alone, holding your pud. What was the name of the friend that you made this rash promise to?"

"Wystan."

"Oh, my God! And who are you?"

Vic told him his name.

"You're that successful young novelist, no?"

"Now I am, but Wystan never even knew I planned to be a writer."

"That's why I recognized your name. Wystan must have talked about you. *Justify My Sins*, yes? What are doing out here? Business or pleasure?"

"It's supposed to be the first but is turning into the second, and since the first appears totally doomed I'm just totally going for the second."

The author laughed.

"He seldom would come, Wystan," the famous man added. "Told me any place s that could so utterly seduce an old Round-head like myself would snag him instantly, as he was so very vulnerable to impressions. We went *there* of course, Don and I, to Brooklyn and then to St. Mark's Place. Not that anyone besides Wystan could actually reside in that flat. You must recall it. I see from your look of remembered appall that you do recall it. But still, I was always a little bit offended that Wystan seldom visited."

"And then, just before the end he went back to England," Vic said. "I got almost a letter a week once he was in England. He hated Oxford!"

"Ah, but he loved the attention."

"His flat was robbed after a few weeks there. He said no one would speak to him. Why did he go back? I think going back is what killed him," Vic said. "I never could understand it. None of his New York friends ever did."

"But he died in Austria. He loved Austria," Isherwood said. "You're still angry with him. But that's why we have funerals and memorial services. To shake off that lingering anger."

"I wasn't even invited to the shindig up at Riverside Cathedral," Vic confessed. "I was only a book clerk. Why bother inviting me? In fact, not Orlan Fox, no one, even bothered to call and tell me Wystan had died. I heard about it in a supermarket aisle. Over frozen minute steaks. I was talking with a friend, and as he wheeled his cart in the other direction, he tossed over his shoulder, 'You've heard that Auden's gone, right?' It was so cold, hearing it like that."

"How very sad. You were very fond of him, weren't you? I believe he was fond of you."

Vic felt suddenly bereft all over again, as though reliving that awful moment in D'Agostinos. He thought he might burst into tears.

Isherwood pointed at the blankets. "Is that where you are? Why don't we go sit a minute?"

That was kind, and so they did and Vic gave him some iced tea and immediately wondered if Andy had laced it with anything, then said, "I'm sorry to drop all this on you, first meeting and all."

"No matter. No matter. This is what friends do: talk about their departed. Ask the hard questions. Can't do it with strangers, can we?

"He was so happy in New York with the new editions of the poems and the essays coming out and with *The New Yorker* stipend and *The New York Review* stipend, all of which he richly deserved. I'm sorry. I'm being a big baby. And rude."

"I believe Wystan was seduced. I suppose we all have our price. And they were so angry at us back in Britain," Isher-wood said. "Never forgave me for leaving, and for then coming *here* to live, of all places, like a beach bum. That's what they wrote, each foolish one of them. As though I subsisted on meadow clover and sea-bracken. You mustn't forget: they'd won the big war but in reality had lost everything. The first half of the century, their chief poet was an American. He stayed. He changed citizenship. Still. He was American-born. Then they simply dismissed the lot of us coming after Eliot as second-raters, politicos, anarchists. Poor Stephen and Wystan! No wonder we fled. But then there Wystan was, at the *end* of the century, the star poet in the language, despite everything, and he'd been living in America since thirty-nine. They couldn't accept that, losing out their official poet to the United States on *both* ends of the Twentieth Century. Dreadful concept! So they offered him the sky. He cut some sort of bargain that would keep him near his house in Bergesetten, which he loved so much, and close enough to Greece, to be able to step in, in case 'Blondie' got into trouble again. And Wystan took them up on it."

The great man then asked Vic how he liked Los Angeles and Santa Monica. He pointed to where his own house stood, just visible, window glass winking in the sun through the canyon cleft. He went on to name and describe the various areas and points of interest within their view, making it all seem even more interesting.

"That edifice Aly Khan built for Rita Haworth. And see there, at the junction of Sunset Boulevard and the Pacific Coast Road, it only became a highway later, is Castelmare. You can see the spot from here. That's where Marion Davies had her house, built into the cliff. Three stories high. Several guest bedrooms for those who drove in from Hollywood or Hancock Park to stay the night. It was considered such a distance then, to come here to the ocean, and cars drove so much more slowly too. She threw parties there, away from William Randolph Hearst who was such a prude. Of course, these were all just villages back then! It was all very small potatoes indeed out here on the strand in those days. All over Pacific Palisades there were orchards and nurseries and flower farms, only a score or so actual homes."

Vic asked about the big holes in the cliffs he'd noticed all about them, upon what appeared to be concrete abutments. "They look just like bunkers for cannon emplacements," Vic opined.

"That's precisely what they were. From Eurkea down past San Diego, they were built all along the coast. We were very fearful of Hirohito, you know. There were always rumors of Rising Sun submarines coming into the bay here and showing up at Huntington Beach and Palos Verdes, although what they expected to see beyond the naval installations I can't for the life of me think. It was all fairly primitive otherwise. But it was a fearful time that you're happy to have missed, the Pacific War, even if the preponderance of young sailors nearly compensated."

Explaining the history of the area, he lifted Vic's spirits so much that when Andy returned to the blanket and offered Isherwood grass, the writer smelled the smoke in the air and said, "Hemp? No thank you. I've had it before, of course."

He might have remained for more than that hour if they hadn't suddenly heard shouting from behind them. It turned out to come from a slender man on a bicycle with a mustache, beard, and jagged shock of dark hair.

"That's Don. He's a marvel of an artist. Come meet him."

Don wouldn't step onto the sand, so they walked all the way to where he waited, all but beating one toe in annoyance, wearing run-down plimsolls and never-ironed slacks. It turned out that there was some kind of urgent phone call, so Isherwood had to leave.

"Despite his youth, Vic was a good friend of our Wystan, from his palmier, later years," Isherwood explained to Bachardy.

Don said he'd like to draw Vic sometime.

They parted with clasped shoulders all round, and promises to stay in touch. This sounded sincere. And Victor promised himself he would definitely do so.

In the Assassination Vehicle driving back to the hotel, Andy looked Vic over, up and down.

"What?" Vic said. "Spit it out!"

"Little Victor is all grown up. Everything about your life is so . . . complicated. Just like a real grown up."

Meaning that Andy's was anything but.

"Andy, you have no idea *how* complicated."

"But we're still going to Studio One tonight. Do not dare say no.

"Sure, let's go. I'm up for it."

"See! That's what I mean! You're completely impossible to predict."

Because the Studio One crowd at Robertson Boulevard was so thick, and the front door staff was so disorganized or deliberately holding folks back, Andy suggested they go in through the VIP lounge to which he, of course, had a pass. There was even a small queue on Lapeer at that special entry and stairway up. But everyone knew Andy, so they were soon upstairs at the long bar, then they were overlooking the airplane hangar length and height of Studio One's dance floor.

Andy had drink coupons *naturelement,* and he had to greet or exchange information or introduce Victor to a score of guys. Meanwhile it had been far too long since Vic had heard such good dance music so well played. He was eager to get down onto the dance floor.

He'd just managed to pull Andy away from Contestant Number Seven to go downstairs when Perfect Paul showed up in the VIP doorway, so they had to hug and kiss and talk. They were just about to catch up, and Paul was apologizing for having to leave a message at the hotel canceling their date tonight, when a man who looked like he might be Paul's grandad emerged from the upstairs restroom, spotted them and came over.

His name was Otto something or other, Vic didn't catch it over the music, which was getting louder by degrees even way up here in the lounge. He worked in neoprene and other plastics back in Racine, Wisconsin, Paul said. When Otto began talking to some other folks, Paul took Vic aside and said, "Otto's only here for a few days. Would you mind it a lot if I didn't see you for a few nights? He's a great old guy. but he doesn't know anyone here in El Lay, so whenever he shows up, I kind of take him around."

This came as both a surprise and a relief to Vic. Since the afternoon with Mark Chastain, he had been trying to figure out a way to tell Paul that he wanted to cool it off between them without hurting Paul's feelings. Now Paul was doing it for him.

"That's great. I've gotten really busy myself and this is sort of my last party night out before I have to buckle down this week."

Otto rejoined them and they dropped downstairs to the dance floor where after a while Jason from earlier on the beach (strawberry blond, muscles for weeks, fabulous face) joined them, and then when Otto and Paul seemed to wander off, Jason and Vic were joined by Scott (slender and abdomen-pretty, with auburn locks) who brought in his train Andy Grant, but not, alas, Darryl of the cocoa au lait complexion.

Paul and Otto said goodbye after an hour or so, Paul kissing Vic's ear and shouting over the din of "Ring My Bell" that Victor was a "dear man and so very understanding."

Some two hours later when he was pretty well danced out, Victor went looking for Andy. He only located him after half an hour, two blocks away, parked in the WeHo library parking lot in the backseat of the Assassination Vehicle, top up and window fogged, furiously sixty-nining someone Vic had never met.

"We'll be done in a second!" Andy looked up to call out. After assorted climactic noises, they both were.

As he was driving Vic and the other guy (Mick? Mike?) home, Andy suggested that Perfect Paul's elderly companion was undoubtedly the person who had undoubtedly gifted him with the gull-wing Mercedes, so *of course* Paul had to be with him while he visited.

No, Mike butted in (it was Mike after all). He'd met Otto last summer. He came to El Lay every year. He was Paul's gay grandfather. No one else in the family knew about his sexual orientation. Paul took him around and made sure he enjoyed himself and met guys. Wasn't that cute?

Cute and typical of Perfect Paul, Vic thought, *who was a d.o.l.l.*

As he dropped Vic off at the hotel, Andy said, "You understand now why I drive this old heap? If we're both under six feet tall, the backseat is perfect for 'The Act.'"

"I'll remember that next time I'm in the market for a convertible."

"Now that you're free again nights," Andy opened the glove compartment at a traffic light and handed Vic two double-sized postcards.

One was a V.I.P. pass to the Club 8709. The other a duplicate of the invitation to the new leather bar that Gilbert had been urging him to go to in Silver Lake. There seemed to be no escape from that place, did there?

"It's supposed to be aitch-oh-tee," Andy said of the new club. "The Detour, as it is named, is being opened by people I know and it is guaranteed to be *de trop*. While *this*," letting the pass flutter in his fingers, "is your entrée to what is simply the pickiest bathhouse in the universe. *Avez vous* fun, *mon ami!*"

"What are you talking about?" Marcie demanded. "I *never* ask you to do *anything* for me. So just this once, and because it is so very easy for you, I can't understand why you would want to *refuse me.* I mean this is all about *your book,* Victor!"

"What do you mean you *never* ask me to do anything for you? What about the boring awful Random House party?" he asked.

"That was for your career," she retorted quickly. "Remember? We were thinking of leaving Laetitia. Random House would have been a good place to hop to."

"What *I* remember was that *you* were pissed off at Laetitia over something having nothing whatsoever to with me or my books, and you decided to go suck up to some Random House editors you didn't know, and since I'd just gotten that Pee-Double-U starred review, you were using me as bait."

"Lord, how you distort everything. No wonder you're a novelist."

Vic continued, unfazed. "Item number two: What about that dinner with Brian DePalma where you knew in advance he wanted to turn my—and I'm quoting from the *Hartford Courant*—subtly chilling, utterly engrossing, first novel into some kind of psycho slasher flick?"

"Victor? How could you possibly turn down a meeting with a film director, even a newish one like Brian de Palma? A first time novelist like yourself."

"Who, I repeat, said he wanted to turn my first novel into some kind of psycho slasher flick, which it was merely the complete fucking opposite of."

"Well, anyway you found that lady friend of yours and went off with her, what was her name, Pat Louse?"

"*Loud*! Pat Loud. Yes, she and I did reconnect outside the restrooms, where by the way I went to barf repeatedly as a result not of dinner, which was over priced but not inedible, but of your so-called 'negotiating' with Mr. De Palma, which resembled as closely as I could make out a rim-job, and I don't mean on your aging Toronado coupe's tires. But thanks to Pat I was able to escape and let you and Brian discuss having *apres-dinner* sex, which I believe was the main reason we were having that dinner in the first place, Marcie, since you very well knew I would never in a zillion years agree to him, or Hitchcock for that matter, mutilating my novel like—"

"We did not have sex," she interrupted to declare primly.

"You did not have sex because his wife checked into the hotel a half day early and unexpectedly. At, I believe, about the same time that you had his wienie well in hand under the table."

"You couldn't you have seen that!"

"X-ray eyes," Victor said. "Item number three: What about the time you and whatever that guy's name was—Bryce or Bryck or somesuch—came by my Pines summer rental house from Davis Park via the Botel Sunday Tea Dance, not only *not* invited, but *specifically* not invited, and in full knowledge of that, because I'd told you beforehand that I had a house guest of *mucho importancia* that weekend. And, let me add, you not only invited yourselves to dinner, but crashed there overnight?"

"We brought cheese and crackers for starters, didn't we?" Marcie argued. "And your so-called guest was just another trick."

"Yeah well, f.y.i. he felt so constrained by other people in the house, especially straight people, and so he wasn't *even* another trick! Plus before you woke up the next morning, that guy you brought kept waving his meat in front of my face through his skimpy BVDs while pretending to read the cereal box, as though I couldn't live without any."

Marcie changed the subject. "You've already met Jim Anthonys. He's a nice guy. Once you remember, you'll see. He'll take you to dinner and talk to you about the new book which he's seen the proposal to and which Laetitia has spoken to him about. How can that kill you?"

"I'm busy tonight." Which was partly true. He had at last given in and agreed to go to The Detour's opening.

"So's Jim Anthonys. This is for *tomorrow* night."

There was silence from both ends, which Vic broke first.

"Tell me who this guy is again?"

Marcie named the film company which Jim and his business partner had started as a subsidiary of one of the studios allegedly to produce a small number per annum of quality, small budget films.

"I'll owe you big time, Vic " Marcie said. "We'll go to the Terrace on your birthday."

The upper-class place in the penthouse of that building over-looking Columbia University's quad.

"Jim Anthonys knows that the book is a thinking man's western, right? Based on a true crime in Dakota Territory?"

"He got the proposal. He thinks it's great."

"And—details—Where? When? And for how long?"

"Joe Allen's."

"Broadway and forty-seventh street's a little far to go even for you, Marcie."

"It seems there's a Joe Allen's near you in La La on Third Street, off," reading something, "is it Saint Vincent?"

"No, dear that's a hospital in Greenwich Village where they either ignore or try to convert gay men. Could it be San Vee-cen-tay?" he corrected. "Hold on, Marce. What's the address?"

"Eight Seven Fourteen Third Street."

Victor checked the bath house pass Andy gave him. And . . . Yes! Joe Allen's was across the street.

Vic *would* have dinner with this Jim Anthonys (why the plural? how many personalities did he have, anyway?) then drop across the street to the bath house. Knowing he would be fucking his brains out later would make the dinner fun, even if Jim Anthonys turned out to be multi-hemisphere lobotomized.

"Well, if I must. Do it just this *once!*"

"Now you know why you're my *favorite* client."

"Enough about me. What word from the world traveling film star?"

"Don't get me started. There's an actress in the film!"

"To everyone's astonishment!" Vic replied.

"To *mine.*"

"Oh, please. *High Chapparal Barbecue*? Doubtless she's petite, blond, with a forty-inch rack, and constant need of protection."

"Rick declares it's only thirty-eight."

"And your lover Rick knows this rather personal statistic how, exactly?"

"They all do. Because her tops keep getting ripped off by branches and stuff in the running scenes. Or so he says, and they have to be replaced."

"Every six minutes? Picturesquely?"

"Something like that." She sounded very gloomy.

"Well, Alain Resnais this film director is not! But I'll bet the guys are going to line up for it somewhere. C'mon, he's in the jungle. Rick's probably having a hell of a time. And the last thing he's thinking about is that blonde."

"He says he's having a terrible time and he's sorry he went," She began sniveling, "And he wishes he could break the contract and come home."

"Pobrecito, Rick! I'll light a candle for him."

"Maybe I should go."

"Have you been invited?"

"No, but . . ."

"Let's see. Not invited to the closed set of a film in progress six thousand miles away. Yes, That's smart. I'd do that." Vic said, then shouted, "Right after I *castrated myself!*"

"That's about what my mother said."

"You must be depressed if you're actually talking with your mother."

"She's impressed Rick's in a film."

"Correction, Marcie, she's impressed by Rick's *paycheck* from the film."

"You're right. She's a witch and I think my cold is coming back."

"I heard it's seventy degrees there. Freak heat wave."

"Be nice to Jim Anthonys. I'll call you afterward. Oh by the way, do you know some guy named Mark Chastain?"

"Met him out here Sunday. Why?"

"He called and told my *tres gai* assistant, Dane, that you left something with him?"

Left something? It must have been my heart, Vic thought.

"Want his number?" she asked.

Mark called with a lame excuse to call back?!!! Insert bells lights and whistles!!! Then repeat: Mark called?!!!

"Sure, let me get a pen," Vic said as tonelessly as he could.

Ed and the others were waiting out on the street in front of Silver Screen's offices when Meade pulled the limo up and Ed signalled Vic's driver not to park but instead to follow his canary yellow Corniche. They went west along Sunset but dropped down Doheny to Beverly Hills. They turned onto Santa Monica and looked headed toward Century City. Ed called from his car to Vic's.

"We're going to the Network. Brandon will see us now. Now all *you* have to do is tell him about the book. Tell him the story, just the way you wrote it for us."

Omigod, it's showtime!

"I don't remember *how* I wrote it for you."

"Don't be nervous. You'll do fine," Ed assured him.

Fifteen minutes later they arrived and Meade drove down into another vast, cool underground parking lot, and the others gathered at the elevators up except for Ed who was schmoozing with someone he'd met. He arrived five minutes later in the three story-high glass-ceiling lobby. Stan or Tim had given their names to the centrally located receptionist and they'd been sent to cool off in one of the seven living rooms within this airport of a waiting lounge.

Now that they were here, suddenly Vic was a blank wall.

The other guys were nervous too. Probably his blankness projected not only to them, but to the entire cortege dancing attendance in this vast room.

A few minutes later Ed sauntered over and they were called and escorted by a pretty efficient-looking Sorority-Sister type secretary whose thin lips boded no good. They went through double doors and into a huge office with gargantuan windows facing in two directions. Through one Vic could look directly west past miles of flat residential development to the ocean and what must have been Santa Monica beach where he and Andy had played the previous day. Only this was from a height of twenty stories. The other direction looked north to Beverly Hills, Bel Air, and the mountains beyond and was equally breathtaking.

The man they were introduced to was a few years older than Vic, and it took Vic a few minutes to realize who he was: Brandon Tartikoff, the network's Boy Wonder, with a dozen hit shows and advertising revenues up the wazoo. He was the network's savior, leading the previously hang-dog third-place network into the very top tier, which the other two biggies were now trying to catch up to.

"Cool views, aren't they?" Brandon asked.

"Most cool," Vic agreed.

"It's kind of like the best tree-house in L.A."

Yes, it was. Even cooler, Vic detected an East Coast, in fact New York suburban accent. Brandon had a pleasant squarish face, cute mouth, very large, very dark, soulful eyes, and he reminded Vic of some of the cuter Jewish guys he'd gone to college with. He instantly heard Gilbert's voice asking "Never mind business, the real question is, would you *do* him?" Vic answered silently, "For sure, I'd do him."

They all sat down and coffee mugs were brought and filled and everyone shuffled around a bit, trying not to act like there were too many people even in this oversized office. After some introductory remarks by Ed and Stan, they all glared at Vic as though he was wearing clown's makeup.

Brandon said, "So Ed tells me you've got a story to tell me?"

At first, Vic was baffled. *Story? What story?* Then he thought, *Oh! the* novel's *story!*

But did Tartikoff not already know the story of the novel? Hadn't Ed Trefethern said, Well, we've got this book, a psychological thriller about a strange yet utterly contemporary boy-girl romance, set in the singles scene of East Side Manhattan and . . . Let me send it over by messenger. Surely he . . . ?

Or not.

Vic suddenly had to assume not. So he began speaking and it actually all came back to him: the character's names, the relevant settings, their various relationships, the story itself, dramatic crest by dramatic crest, leading to the plot's tangled but inevitable climax, the denouement, and at last the tragic ending.

When Vic was done, the Silver Screen crew all sighed in audible relief behind him, signifying that he'd not too apparently screwed up.

The Boy Wonder asked Vic six questions about what he'd just told him. At first Vic though they were details, which meant that Brandon had listened carefully. Vic answered them as best he could, but his reasoning changed as he did so. Maybe this guy did not care a bit. It might just show that he was being courteous.

Ed began speaking about other, similar stories, and how Vic's was fresh and different. Tim followed Ed, talking about how they'd done demographics with the publisher and how the story "slanted" male forty, female sixty, and heavily to ages eighteen to thirty-five—in other words, the most desirable advertiser demo of all, perfect for the network's proposed time slot. Stan then spoke and said how they'd done some "initial basic expense analysis and cost differentials," and then he began to spout various percentages which would mean, as he concluded that "the numbers are workable for the network." Vic assumed he meant to produce the film without losing money, and of course for ABC and Silver Screen to work together. Sam, the youngest, just sat there, trying not to look impressed by the decor.

After all that, Brandon allowed that, "It's a terrific story. I can see why it's so popular. And I can easily see why you folks are so high on it. I think it would make a heck of a production. Who were you thinking of for the leads, Ed?"

"Anna-Marie's role is the one we need to settle first."

Ed then named several actresses whom he thought would be good for the role, then added, "You and I were both happy with Dee Wallace in that last project we did together. She read and knows Victor's book and even though it might be a very different role for her . . ."

The next five minutes were all about Dee versus several other actresses, most of whom Vic had no idea of. Meanwhile Vic kept thinking, *Wasn't Dee Wallace cute and pert and blond? Very blond all-American Midwest-looking?* Anna-Marie was supposed to be slender, dark haired, and kind of ethnic-looking. Wasn't that, after all, the attraction for Theo, who was himself (at least in the book) cute and strawberry blond and all-American and Midwest-looking? If Anna-Marie was all-American, whom would they suggest to play Theo?

Ed was speaking, however, and since Vic was The New Kid he wouldn't barge in, even with something as basic as this.

When Ed was done, Sam spoke up and mentioned someone else to play Theo who came from daytime television and who Vic didn't know but who they said would bring in "the ratings" (that is, that show's female audience) with him.

Brandon stood up, signaling the end to the meeting. Handshakes all around, wishes for Vic's further success, and for his new book too, of course.

They all got up and turned to exit.

Vic followed the other guys. Behind him, he could just make out Ed trying to get some word from Brandon, and Brandon saying something vague that ended with the words, "but you know, Ed, it's edgy stuff!"

Vic stopped and heard Ed reply, "How edgy can it be? It was six months on *The New York Times* paperback bestseller list. Selling in Spanish and German too! What used to be edgy isn't any more. You know that. Young people, our targeted audience, want a bit of an edge. Your own surveys tell you that."

"You're absolutely right, Ed."

At which point Vic knew with a total certainty that it was a dead deal, and at last, for the first time since he'd arrived in California, he could relax.

He heard Brandon tell Ed that he'd think it over.

Vic joined the other guys who had trooped over to the elevators and were getting in when Brandon had his assistant tap Vic's shoulder and ask him back, alone.

The Boy Wonder stood there just inside his doorway, a big boy after all, looking at Vic without saying anything, but holding Vic's outstretched hand.

"You and I come from the same place. Maybe a couple of towns away," he began. "Few years apart."

They began talking about what schools they'd gone to. The parks and beaches and lakes they'd played at. Neighbors, really, growing up just a few miles apart.

Brandon smiled. "I feel like we know each other already!" he said, and held Vic's hand. *People you meet out here*, Vic thought, *they all seem to know you*. "I just know we're going to see each other again." Brandon added. "But right now? . . . this project? . . . I just don't know."

"I know." Vic said. "You love it. But the story is too subversive."

"Something like that."

"It *is* an anti Romeo and Juliet story," Vic admitted. "That *is* how I sold it to my publisher That *is* how I wrote it. That *is* why it's a best seller!"

"You're still here a few days more?" Brandon seemed to change the subject.

"I leave this Sunday evening."

"Don't leave earlier. Promise me."

"Why?" Vic felt he had to ask.

"You know . . . In case I want to reach you. To talk things over."

"Sure. Fine. I'll be here until Sunday evening."

This time Brandon gave him a warm clasp on the shoulder, almost a hug, and a firm handshake.

The others were all still congratulating each other when Vic got down to the garage. Ebullient, except for Ed.

"Comparing where we grew up and all," Vic said for the others, to explain what the return chat was all about.

When no one else was looking, Vic raked a fingernail across his throat and Ed choked out a small laugh—he knew too they'd bombed.

CHAPTER ELEVEN

"I can't let you off here," Meade said.

"This is the address I was given," Vic replied.

"Maybe so," the driver argued, "but look! We're in the middle of nowhere!"

Where they were actually wasn't so much "nowhere" as it was the corner of Virgil and Santa Monica Boulevard, about a block before it met Sunset Boulevard, in an area known as Silver Lake. And it was dead, dead, dead. Yes, there were street lights, spaced out widely on the empty streets filled with wind-blown trash. And it was true that on either side were houses and even a few two-story apartment buildings with a few solitary lights on. But there were no storefronts. No street life. No activity at all. At least not by night. In fact, the area looked warehousey. It looked light in-dustrial. It looked, Vic thought, exactly like the kind of area where a hot leather bar *ought* to be.

"I have it on the best of word that there is a rocking party be-hind those three windows." Vic pointed.

"I'd better wait for you."

Right, and cramp my style totally in case I meet someone hot?

"Go home." Vic said. "If I need a ride I'll call a cab."

He got out purposefully, in full confidence that behind the win-dows with those little red votive candles was actually the world's hottest leather bar premiere, as he'd been promised on numerous occasions by Gilbert and Andy.

Meade continued to sit there until Victor waved him on, and only when the limo vanished around the corner did Vic cross the street and go inside. He'd dressed specifically Village-Chelsea: tight 501 jeans with the top button open, cowboy boots with thick heels, black fitted t-shirt that didn't quite meet the belt, one size too small jacket that wouldn't ever zip up. This is as hot as Vic would ever look—and it usually got someone-or-other's interest.

He strolled into the bar, which was indeed open, and indeed lighted with red votive candles, and indeed had rock music playing. It possessed two bartenders and two customers dressed much like Vic huddled at the far corner of the bar, half necking with each other—that is, when they were not talking to one of the bartenders. The other barkeep was at the other end mostly talking on the phone. That was the entire population of the Detour.

I know this is laid-back California. But, even so, is this it?

The two customers at the bar ignored him. Two more came in and spoke with the other bartender. Vic drank a beer and was ignored. Once, he got up and looked behind a leather curtain which led to a tiny patio supposedly devoted to outdoor sex—by raccoons, he assumed, since no people were present. He returned to the bar, finished a second beer, then asked the less dreary bartender of the two to call him a cab.

He went outside to wait. As before, the street was empty in every direction. A very long block away, there was extremely sporadic traffic on Sunset Boulevard mostly headed downtown.

On the one hand, he was amused and secretly pleased: after all the urgings and goadings to come tonight, Gilbert would be utterly crushed and humiliated. Vic would hang this alleged premiere in front of Gilbert as a indication of how completely off Gilbert's supposed gay party radar was. It would be such great fun to harp on it month after month.

The wind rose, and what might have been a car's headlights turned toward him, but then turned all the way around in a U-ey and were gone.

While Vic was irritated, he was also strangely satisfied. After all, it was now three days that he'd gone without sex in Los Angeles. Given how much sex he'd had, how often and how unavoidably he'd had sex the previous week, this was something of a streak. Perhaps with the TV film deal officially a corpse, he didn't have to worry any longer and could return to his usual being hit on once every few weeks while he concentrated upon getting into bed with the handsome, the warm, the affectionate, husband potential Mark Chastain. Maybe in fact this was the clearest sign yet that Vic's fooling around days were officially over and it was time to settle down, and who better with than with Mark?

It all made great sense, and if he'd had to journey three thousand miles to "get it," well, he'd just "gotten it."

This thought had just been fully assessed, concluded, and somewhat ratified, when a single headlight did turn onto the empty road and head toward him. A second later a motorcycle roared up and stopped not two feet from where Victor stood.

Perched on the large, handsomely decked-out black Harley Davidson with yellow trim was a tall, well-built blond with a crew-cut not quite at the fly away stage, a brushy blond mustache, and no shirt to cover his hairless, evidently oiled torso and heavily muscled arms and shoulders. He wore black leather bike gloves, tight black leather trousers, black engineer boots, a jauntily worn black leather peaked cap, and—the final touch—one black leather eye-patch.

The eye that was exhibited was hazel, lavishly lashed and twinkling. A half smoked cigarello dangled from the thick, bottom lip.

I don't believe this even for one second, Vic thought. *Is there someone here with a camera? Because if this isn't a "Kodak moment" I don't know what is!*

"Party over?" Eyepatch asked, a steady baritone.

"Never got started," Vic replied and looked at his watch.

"That bad?"

"It's 11:45, two customers inside, and I'm outta here," Vic assured him.

"Waiting for someone?"

"A taxi."

"Want a ride home?"

"What's in it for me?"

Eyepatch played with his crotch.

Vic thought, *If I say no to him, the universe will instantly shatter into a skillion shards.* Instead he said, "I'm not really into the pain thing."

"Vanilla's okay," Eyepatch allowed.

"Okay. Sure. Why not?"

Victor hopped onto the back of the motorcycle, got his hands into the leather belt and yelled into Eyepatch's ear, "Take Sunset all the way to Beverly Hills."

Instead, Eyepatch took side streets Vic didn't know until around West Hollywood when he leaped onto Sunset. This allowed him to roar around corners, speed mightily, show off, and even pop a few wheelies. By then his perspiration and light, slightly lemon- and coconut-flavored body odor had totally permeated Vic's face, and Vic was, as a result, rock hard.

Only at the entrance to the Beverly Hills Hotel did Eyepatch falter and turn to look back at Vic. After all his stunt-work, this gave Vic an edge up. He yelled, "What are you waiting for?

"Are you sure about this?"

"You can park over there!" Vic pointed to the space where Meade's Caddy usually sat. "That's my spot."

The doorman over-dramatically fell back two feet to let them through the wide entry. Vic hooked two fingers through the belt loops of Eyepatch's black leather pants as he walked him into the lobby, past whoever was there and up the very long and public staircase to the second floor corridor.

Outside the room door as he fumbled with the key, Eyepatch started nibbling his nape and laughed low and dirty.

Let's see: he's shirtless and wearing an eyepatch, so of course walking through the Beverly Hills Hotel lobby as an obvious sex trick would excite him.

"I have to admit," Eyepatch allowed, "this is a first for me."

"Well, if it's going into your diary," Vic responded, flinging open the door and dragging him into the suite by his now open zipper, "let's make sure you need more than one page."

They ravaged each other's bodies like starving lunatics who hadn't had sex in a month for an hour and forty-four minutes.

They slept for another hour out of sheer exhaustion before Eyepatch got up got dressed and took off. Vic didn't even hear the motorcycle roaring off.

The next day, showering, Vic discovered hickeys where they couldn't possibly exist, as well as one thick gray sock that he was certain wasn't his, and as he was getting dressed, he came upon a pencil-scrawled note stuffed in his underpants that read, "Fuck you!—next time! Burt."

When he descended to the main lobby at noon, Vic could swear that every member of the hotel staff he passed, from pool towel-boy to shoeshine man, looked at him then very rapidly looked away. They all treated him very carefully and called him "Sir." He guessed that unspoken fear and respect would rule the staff's every action toward him until he checked out. Even the usually surly cavernous-cheeked desk clerk cringed when Vic bitched about receiving the wrong hometown paper and promised it wouldn't happen again. Three rags from New York appeared at his door fifteen minutes later.

He waited hours before telling Gilbert what had occurred, and only did so because Gilbert had begun ringing every half hour, evidently avid to hear about the Detour premiere.

When Victor told him what a disaster the debut was, Gilbert could be clearly heard choking back tears. When Victor then mentioned how and with whom he'd gotten back to the hotel, Gilbert was silent for such a long time Vic wondered if he'd fallen out the window and onto Verdi Square below.

His friend suddenly uttered in hushed tones, "I think I can die now, knowing that fantasies *do* come true."

"It wasn't *my* fantasy."

"I realize that fully and that is why you are so very close to be-atification, Blessed Victor of the Many Hickeys, because it *was* the fantasy of possibly ever other sane gay man in America, and you selflessly and seminally fulfilled it."

Later, on the phone with Marcie, Victor said, "Listen, we have to get a leather eyepatch for the Rickster for the Black Party."

"Won't he look . . . *lacking?*" she asked.

"Marce, *croi moi,* until you see Rick in a black leather eye patch, you can have no idea how aitch-oh-tee he can look."

"If he ever returns from Africa," she sniffed; cold number four had settled in for the duration.

Fresh from the coffee shoppe and the longest and possibly largest breakfast of his life (three courses: meat, fish and dessert; after all, he'd burned about twelve thousand calories the night before), Vic brushed his teeth and thought, *Now that the staff is in line, I really could live at this place. I really could!*

The phone rang and it was, of all people, the unmelodious Melanie, the TV Boy Wonder's ice-bound assistant, asking Vic if he could hold for Brandon. Before he could say yes or no, she was gone.

Well, Brandon had promised he'd call, and here it was Thursday afternoon, and he was calling. He'd remembered. How nice.

"So, listen, my East Coast friend," he began promisingly enough, "how about you come over here tomorrow afternoon."

And Victor thought, *No, please, do* not *say what I think you're going to say.*

But he did, saying, "And pitch me some ideas for television series." Just as Vic was about to let out a very audible moan, Brandon made it worse, adding, "I don't want you to think about it too much and I don't want you to talk to Ed Trefethern or any of the other guys about it first."

Geez, Louise, Vic thought, *give me a break, will you?* But Brandon would not be stopped. "I just want to hear what you have to say, right off the top off your clever and completely with-it head."

"You're kidding," Vic said.

"Why would I be kidding? You're the smartest person I met all month. In three months, possibly."

"Thanks for the compliment, but Brandon, think about this for a minute. I live in the *far west* of Greenwich Village. I only got a television two years ago. Because someone left it to me in his will. And because it was delivered."

"That's why whatever you'll come up with will be fresh. Unlike all the people I see and hear from all day, week after week."

"Perhaps so, but aside from *Star Trek* reruns, I haven't watched anything but Public Broadcasting specials in over a decade!"

"I watched *Star Trek* religiously. Look, Vic, I know you don't like offices and all the crap here and neither do I. The people staring. The expectations. Let me sweeten the deal. I'll buy lunch at ____'s," naming what Sam and Stan at Silver Screen had mentioned earlier that week was the most talked about West Hollywood restaurant of the minute. Utterly impossible to get in.

"Well . . ." He wavered for an instant and Brandon stepped into the tiny caesura as though it were the Gulf of Mexico:

"Everyone will see you with me and want to know who you are. I know you don't give a shit about any of this, but we'll have some fun, and make them wonder what we're up to, and who knows maybe come up with something really new and different."

Brandon was unquestionably seducing him in the only way he knew how. Not as a lover, not even really as a business guy, but as a potential friend, or at least as one smart guy to another who probably didn't want anything else from him but company. Vic guessed that was rare enough with all the wheeler-dealers around him, and that Brandon may have just been throwing in the pitch session because it would give him an excuse. Maybe he was just trying to honestly connect with someone without all the brouhaha and trinkets?

"Okay, Brandon, I'll come to lunch so long as you understand I've got a new book out in the Fall, better than the last, and a fourth, even more phenomenal, already in the works, and I'm going back to Manhattan in three days to finish them."

"You are hotter than hot," Brandon said. "I know that."

Ah, you have no idea how *hot*, Vic wanted to say. *But the staff here at The Beverly Hills knows.*

Aloud, he said, "That wasn't exactly my point. What I meant was that I just don't have *time* for anything else, if by some wild chance something I happened to say to you should develop into anything. I didn't have time for Silver Screen, either. I know this sounds weird to you—and I don't mean to demean you or your work or any of it in any way—but really I was coerced by my agent and others whom I couldn't let down into coming out here. And I really only did it for the weather." *And*, he added to himself, *I stayed for the men!*

"Look, I do understand. And that's great. In fact, Vic, I wouldn't come to you if you weren't already busy . . ."

"Up to my neck, Brandon. Under contract. Up. To. My. Neck."

"I wouldn't come to you if you weren't already 'up to your neck.'"

"Okay," Vic said. "Then we *absolutely* understand each other."

"We *absolutely* understand each other," Brandon parroted. "See? This is the best meeting proposal I've had in years! Someone who won't give me the time of day. Except for tomorrow, for an hour or so at one or two or whenever. Lunchtime. And just a few ideas off the top of your head. Great. Let me turn you over to my assistant. She'll set you up. Ciao."

As soon as he heard the Vivaldi *adagio* aural wallpaper in the background, Victor wondered, *How did I just let this happen?*

"You understand of course that you are superseding some very important people who will be very difficult to reschedule," Melanie of the Antarctic had the nerve to say to him. "I'll be re-shuffling his schedule for the next fourteen days."

"Look, this was not *my* idea!" he defended himself. "I was the person who *didn't* want lunch with Brandon at ____'s."

"I understand," she said in a tone of voice that clearly signified that she didn't believe him for a second. Because, he realized, Melanie's entire existence depended upon *not* believing him, and instead believing that any person plucked off any point on the planet—a subsistence barley farmer from Srinigar, say, or a Lapland reindeer herder, or even a Xiang Xiang hunter-gatherer in Namibia—would kill for exactly this lunch experience with her boss—rather than, say, passing an entire harvest without a trace of locusts, or having two does whelp at one time, or happening upon a large, undefended honeycomb.

They settled on two o'clock and Victor felt as though his day, which had begun in a screwed-out haze but had been coming around into semi-demi-normal, was now all but ruined.

Only one thing to do: call his agent and complain.

Her instant, badly snurfled response: "Do you have room in your luggage for fresh oranges? If not, buy another bag and I'll pay you back. Bring as many as you can. You're only checking one bag, right?"

"Sure. Fine, I'll bring an entire case of Valencias with me. But what do I do tomorrow, meeting with this guy?"

"Is he cute?"

"He's cute. He's hetero. But so what? I'm already so fucked out I doubt if I'll get it up again in the coming decade."

"Then why did you agree to meet with him?"

"What if I'd just called you and told you I'd said no to meeting Brandon Tartikoff, the man in charge of programming for the hottest network on TV?"

"I'd murder you as soon as I got my hands on those oranges."

"*Et voila!* My point exactly."

"Well, Vic, you've got to tell him *something*. Think about it. What excites you to look at?"

"Marcie, you know very well my idea of exciting visuals is stumbling around the long-abandoned piers on the Hudson River while I'm high on MDA, watching semi-clothed queers and assorted river-rats attempt at mating."

"I think that's just a *tad* too louche for Prime Time. What about some actor or actress you like? Maybe you can make up some program about him or her? Remember . . . who was that one you were going on about last month?"

"Last month?"

"She was in some Off-Broadway prison movie take-off play you were raving about."

"You don't mean *Divine?*"

"She the one with all the eyebrows and the plunging neckline? The fat girl who ate poop in that awful film?"

"That 'fat girl' is a guy named Glenn Milstead."

"But you told me Divine was nominated for some best actress award."

"An Obie for *Women Behind Bars*? He's still Glenn. He's an actor, remember?"

And as Vic himself said those words aloud, an idea of the utmost swillishness gurgled slowly up toward the pathetic, nearly liquid surface of his overheated, overhumid, and severely sexed-out brain.

"Thank you, Marcie. You are a very brilliant agent and the most stunningly loyal friend a writer could have and I must thank you once again."

Marcie didn't like the sound of that response, not one bit. Hard experience had taught her that excessive compliments from authorial clients meant one of two things, neither good: either she was about to be dumped for a larger agency, or she was about to receive a summons to civil court and be soundly sued for malfeasance.

"Vic-tor!?" she warned. "What are you thinking about?"

"Nothing. At least not yet. But you're right. I'll *go* to that meeting. And I'll have an idea fresher than fresh. So fresh, it'll leap off the lunch table and scurry onto the pavement."

"*Vic-tor?*" she warned, even more fearfully, but he quickly said: "Gotta get dressed for dinner with your pal at Joe Allens. Ta!"

CHAPTER TWELVE

"So," Jim Anthonys interrupted his interminable monologue long enough to recognize another likely source of consciousness in the room, "this place must seem terrifically familiar to you, coming from New York and all."

It was in fact about as close to a duplicate of the Manhattan eatery as could be accomplished this adjacent to the Pacific Ocean, right down to the fake brick walls. Victor was certain that if the management could have trained Collie-sized IND subway rats to slither past without anyone tipping off the health authorities, they would have attempted it.

His first foray into the men's room—anything to escape—had delivered the admittedly mixed thrill of that acridly-reeking, fizzily-dissolving soap in the two urinals instead of the mint julep-flavored ice cubes like most other WeHo eateries. In another words, a real touch of Lower East Side Pirogi Palaces. The second dash in had revealed two tiny specks of blood on the otherwise pristine sink counter—either someone mainlining or, more likely, someone trying and failing to.

Luckily, the Manhattan food was duplicated too.

"I could live on Joe Allen's cheeseburgers and giant onion rings," Victor responded, thinking, *When will this dinner be over?*

"Now, did I mention the upcoming slate we have in post production?" Anthonys went on, and Victor thought, *Only seven times already. Please, stop me before I kill again.*

It wasn't that there was anything intrinsically wrong with Jim Anthonys, aside from his last name, so badly in need of a trim. The problem was that he possessed one topic: his work. Any attempt Victor made to alter that topic went immediately absolutely nowhere. As for his so-called "upcoming slate," the two films Jim mentioned, they were surely calculated to induce instant and terminal ennui in even the lowest I.Q. First, a diplomatic spy story set in World War Two Paris. (I believe we *all* know how *that* turned out!) Second, a light romantic comedy among unattached teachers at a Gifted Ed school in Greenwich, Connecticut. (Hetero W.A.S.P.s in love, young Gentile geniuses being smarty pants—Oy! Quick! A hundred Tuinals!) These weren't exactly calculated to set off fireworks in Victor's mind or britches. Nor did the stories emanate potential for anyone even half as perverted. (What if the spy plot failed and the Germans won the war, invaded the States, and converted the residents of Lake Ronkonkoma into Hitler Youth Zombies? Victor might go for that!)

At some point, maybe around the twelfth rephrased retelling of the allegedly romantic so-called comedy, after Vic had said he thought both ideas had great market possibility (allowable under the axiom "there's a sucker born every day"), Victor asked why it was that, given this "super slate," Jim Anthonys believed Vic or his work held any interest whatsoever for his company?

Had Anthonys replied, "They don't, I just like to hear myself talk," or, "They don't, I'm just interested in your agent's tits," or indeed any of a half dozen other possible responses, Vic would have settled into the chair and listened a bit longer.

What Anthony's said however was, "Well, something in your line may come along the pike some day for us."

Rather than torture himself parsing that sentence for either grammatical correctness or deeper meaning, Vic thought, *Yes, I agree: something in my line may come along the pike some day for you—in the event of my death and your transfiguration, neither one of which I am ready for or at all intrigued by.*

Perhaps Victor put up with him so long because Anthonys appeared to be content with what he was: a thirty-and-some-year-old Westerner, probably from Wyoming or Idaho, based on the not too subtle cowboy accessorizing of his dress: authentic-looking brass belt buckle of a dramatically head-on longhorn steer, a speckle of braided thread on the cuffs and collar of his open-throated, light-checked cotton shirt, a "Rockies" twang distinguishable after his third Bourbon and water.

And still he droned on, and still Vic tried to drown it out with just one more beer and yet another onion ring the size of a hubcap. Jim had made the Big Time and was determined that every-one not only know it but say they knew it.

Wait, was that fair? Look at the guy! He's in hog heaven. He'll go home to Pocatello Falls and tell everyone how he'd dined with this unstoppably brilliant best-selling novelist. What else could he say? He wouldn't stop talking long enough for Victor to be boring.

Then too, look at Jim's past, evident upon his visage. His upper neck and lower face were bumpy and hard-skinned, uneven and just sufficiently pitted for Vic to recognize what must have been stupendously amok teenage hormones and their banner: super-duper acne. That couldn't have been pleasant to experience and must have been a bitch to deal with. Jim's clear, pale gray eyes with their wedge of blue each, like a clouded lake with a patch of sunlit sky peeking through, were nice enough. His Anglo-Scots features were acceptable enough, though his mouth was a bit wide. But look at his ears! Why, they were perfectly sized and shaped. Let the guy drone on, he's obviously had his bad times, and now he's enjoying himself.

Stop being such a critic, Victor!

"So thanks for your time, and it's been terrific, but I've got to take off," Vic heard and so became aware that Anthonys was say-ing it and standing up. "Don't worry about the dinner check. I took care of it last time you were in the washroom. That beer goes right through one, doesn't it? I always say you only borrow suds. See ya around now!"

A hurried handshake through the hoary adages and he was gone.

Vic remained seated, and slowly nibbled on another vast, vaguely vegetable frisbee and nursed along his Miller High Life, figuring it might be another ten, fifteen minutes before Jim's car was valeted out and he could take off.

A half hour later, Vic was standing on the surprisingly long line to get into the 8709 Baths just across the street and down the block.

He'd just gotten into the glass fronted entryway and was about number six in line when he managed to find his pass. He looked about himself and immediately felt something of a piker. He was in casual street clothes, holding a card. The other five ahead of him each carried little gym bags filled with who knew what amazing little sexy uniforms and erotic toys, and they were already dressed in "hot" outfits.

In fact, they were all extremely good looking with great physiques, including the light-skinned African-American preppie (number three in line) in tan khakis, crimson and silver stadium jacket, and bone white Converse Hi-Tops with his light mustache, sketch of a beard, basketball defense biceps and pale blue eyes. *Yum*, Vic thought.

Behind Vic, just wedging into what space there was off Third Street and into the wind-shielded portal, were two great looking guys, one of whom was already a member, the other his guest—at least from their conversation.

"So I was telling you about this Max who is in my opinion sexy, although a bit sloppy in the abdomen area," the bathhouse member was narrating. "Max was directly ahead of me and raring to get in here coupla weeks ago. Max's secret weapon is his very large and, just from waiting on this line, already very hard boner. So the Twinkie at the counter starts giving him a hard time about coming inside. He might be overlooked and he might not feel comfortable, and all this bullshit. A not so subtle put down on his imperfect body. Max finally says 'Don't worry Sonny boy!' He opens his fly and slaps his enormous salami onto the counter. 'Wherever I go with my pal here, I'm usually welcome.' Of course they let him in."

They laughed and so did Vic. He was number three now.

Seeing Vic's pass in his hand, the member behind him said, "Now this guy is a V.I.P."

"How many inches do you have to have to be a V.I.P?" the guest asked.

"If I showed you," Vic said, "I'd have to blind you right afterward."

The guy at the counter was now giving the very hot black guy a hard time—busily "carding" him. Vic could already see the guy's college I.D. and driver's license on the counter, and he was being asked for more proof. What more did they need? Ancestral emancipation papers? A certificate of Good-Standing from the Daughters of the American Revolution?

"Racist pig!" the member said in a low voice behind Vic.

"I'd like that guy to be in here tonight," his guest muttered.

"Me too," Vic said, and fueled by a half keg of beer and half a field of onion rings, he decided to do something about it.

He bustled past the two guys between and up a few steps to the entry counter where he put his arms around the black guy, grabbed him by his amazed head and planted a fat kiss on his lips. At the same time Vic looked at the cards on the counter, saw his name was Darryl, and slapped his own big V.I.P. pass atop them all.

"Darryl, honey! You said you were going to meet me at Joe Allen's. Not here. Are you that horny?"

Darryl and the guy at the counter both looked surprised.

"He's with me," Vic said to the Counter-Twink, then grabbed all Darryl's cards and his entrance fee money off the counter, shoved them deep in Darryl's pants pocket, and began to pull him into the doorway. "My honey! *And* my guest tonight!"

"Your rrrrroom kkkkey!" the baffled Twink stuttered.

"Oh, and a locker room key, too. He's got so much crap with him tonight because, well, just take a look at that body! We are going turn this place *upside down*! C'mon honey." Vic pulled Darryl along and inside, enjoying the looks on all the onlooker's faces.

Once in, Vic let Darryl go and moved on ahead. But Darryl caught up to him and, still not having fully grasped what had just gone down, said, "I don't . . . I mean, thanks . . . but I don't . . . Did you want me or . . . ?" he tried.

Vic gave him the room key and said, "Darryl, you are a doll, but the simple truth is I just really hate prejudice in all of its many, tacky forms. However! Should our paths cross later on . . ." He raised both eyebrows and Darryl let out a laugh.

He did see Darryl later on, but that was somewhat after his not quite life-changing encounters with Extreme Annoyance and Great Astonishment.

Extreme Annoyance arrived within a half hour in the guise of Joel, the insinuating waiter at Ed Trefethern's favorite WeHo restaurant. Joel appeared on the scene just as Vic decided to take a shower and see what everyone else in the huge shower room was putting on display. Similarly unclad, Joel had a natural-looking tight little body indeed, probably a combo of criminal genes and growing up on some truck farm where he obtained great deltoids from shoveling manure and great glutes being bent over a rail by an elder brother. Even though Vic was practicing his I'm-an-Algonquin-in-the-Pennsylvania-woods silent walk, where he would see all and no one would focus on him, Joel did focus, and worse, Joel began following Vic, stopping him repeatedly and pleading for sex. This ended less than an hour later with Vic cornered in the mirrored labyrinth between the two buildings that comprised the 8709 with Joel on his knees barring Vic's way saying, "Please! Please. Tell you what? I'll just hold it in my mouth and count to fifty."

Vic said okay just to get rid of him, but in less than a minute a scene developed right there when the two guys who'd been behind him on line happened upon them. Then another hottie joined them. Followed by Perfect Paul. Not too many days ago Victor wouldn't have believed he would be the center of a group of men so astonishingly hot and so astonishingly into him and each other. Paul was no longer a paragon here. He was one of the guys, as hungry and avid as anyone else. The end result was that Vic was so otherwise engaged and multiply pleased that Joel remained a great deal longer than the brief time he'd asked for, long enough to receive Vic's climax before stealthily taking off while Vic was still being erotically manhandled.

A short nap in the not inactive steam room was required before Vic was ready to move about again. And that was when, while cruising by a certain line of open-door roomettes, Great Astonishment reared its head, in the form of—of all people, let's be frank—Jim Anthonys.

Anthonys was clad in a Palomino-hued ten-gallon hat, split open sheepskin chaps, and mid-calf cowboy boots with ruby-tipped spurs. Otherwise he was naked with various hurtful-looking instruments close at hand: braided whips, branding irons, etc. He was so busily being serviced front, aft, and on each nipple that although Vic watched for a good five minutes, Anthonys never once recognized him.

Vic didn't need a sign from heaven: it was clearly Time To Go.

The cabbie that the Twinkette at the door called for him was another absolute number, this one a recent Persian émigré named Dariush with huge dark eyes and a voice like silk being rubbed over bare flesh.

Victor shut his eyes the minute he sat in the back and didn't open them until he had to pay the fare.

CHAPTER THIRTEEN

"So, it's a comedy and a drama, both?" Brandon asked.

"That's right," Victor answered with a completely straight face, into which he inserted a succulent, perfectly french-fried zucchini stick.

Mmmm! This was as good as the *Mozzarella in Carozza* earlier. Just finding that particular appetizer on any menu outside of real *paisan* neighborhoods like Sheepshead's Bay, Brooklyn, or Federal Hill, Providence was amazing, never mind one so perfectly cooked. Maybe there *was* something after all to these Hollywood restaurants!

"And the stories are all to be based on your years as a caseworker for the New York Welfare Department?" Brandon needed to know.

"Every one of them! You see, Brandon, there were three units of five social workers along with their unit supervisors. Three units, each housed in largish former high school classrooms. So that's a potential seventeen minor characters beside our main character."

"But you would focus on the other four people in our heroine's unit and her supervisor?" Brandon asked, concerned. "So as to give it a tighter feel?"

"Absolutely, and based on the make-up of my own unit of several years, the breakdown will be totally New York City melting pot. One guy, we'll call him Ganesh, is a middle aged, elegant, perfectly groomed Indian national with that perfect diction and British accent, but slightly off, because he's from Dehli, right? And he won't admit it but he's a racist. Not so cool in Spanish Harlem."

"Go on," Brandon was enjoying this.

"Another case worker is Shannon, a tall, very pretty Afro-American. She becomes our heroine's best pal and buddy. The thing about Shannon is that while black, she's a Princess who grew up in a gated all-Negro community in Eastern Queens called Cambria Heights, where celebrities like Rochester from *The Jack Benny Show*, Jackie Robinson, and Nat King Cole all live. She's got no clue at all about ghetto life and is constantly horrified."

"Good. Different."

"The third person in the unit is Mrs. Sterling, a petite white woman, close to sixty, not quite incompetent, but this close. Very good-hearted and concerned, but ineffectual. Picture her as once beautiful, now over-cosmetized, wearing old satin bolero jackets over a skirt, utterly out of her element in 1967 Upper Manhattan. She's been married and divorced for decades, living on gin and olives until she ran out of suckers to pay her way."

"Our tragicomic nostalgia gal." Brandon said. "For the older set. Terrif."

"Number four is a tall, slender, fair haired guy from Tennessee who's come to the city to become a film *artiste*. He's William Ashley Brent and everyone calls him Ash. He's far more interested in his arty little sixteen-millimeter movies which he looks at continually by the daylight of the men's room airshaft. By night he hangs out with the Warhol crowd at the Union Square Factory. So he comes in late, hung over, sometimes not at all, and can be a real screw up. The rest of the unit covers for him, takes over his cases, and protects him."

"He's for the young, male, hipster set. Don't stop! The supervisor?"

"She's a little busy-body of a Puerto-Rican named Conchita-Anita Sensale. Once a hot *tamale* who men fought over with knives and machetes beneath the 110th Street on-ramp to the Triboro Bridge, she's now a wise, somewhat controlling great grandmama. But she hasn't lost one bit of her fire or her fun."

"Wonderful! And our heroine? The one who'll interact with these great characters and with another problem case week after week?"

"She's unusual to look at. Not your garden variety attractive,"

Vic said, toying around the edge of his mouth with an especially fat zucchini stick. "But there's something about her looks that draws you in. A certain lust for living and indifference to life's worst blows. She's utterly compassionate one minute," Vic said, "but then harder than Barbara Stanwyck the next minute. Hard to like. But impossible not to be fascinated by. Down to earth but intensely . . . Zen!"

"Yes!" Brandon said.

Vic let the zucchini stick enter his mouth and swizzled it around, making little buccal noises while Brandon went on. "And each week, she'll face one more difficult and improbable problem of The Human Condition after another!" He took a sip of his until now untouched Kir and declared, "A name! It needs a name!"

Vic bit into the zucchni stick and swallowed the tip, then put the rest of it athwart his plate. "Well, I was thinking of calling the show after the name of the actress."

"And so," Brandon wavered, "It would be . . . ?"

"I thought of calling the program, *It's Divine!*"

"People won't think it's religious?"

"What if they do, at the beginning? After the first few episodes, they definitely won't make that mistake."

Brandon had already ordered them both the same dessert, a hazelnut flavored *crème Inglese.* It now arrived and like everything that preceded it, it was scrumptious.

"Good. Good," Brandon was pleased.

Fifteen minutes later, as the valets ran for his Corniche and Meade idled the limo's engine for Vic, Brandon said, "See? And you thought this lunch would be awful. Come on. Admit it. You were totally pessimistic!"

"I admit it," Vic said, huge-heartedly.

"And I should have no trouble locating this Underground star? What was her name? Divine?"

"She's in a long-running Off-Broadway hit as we speak. *Women Behind Bars.*"

Handshakes and slaps on Vic's shoulder. Brandon took off.

Victor got into the car, holding a little doggie bag packet of zucchini sticks, but the driver didn't take off immediately and instead stared in the rear vew mirror.

"Are we going any time today?" Vic asked.

Meade revved the engine but didn't move. "In a sec. I just wanted to see that look a little longer."

"What look?"

"The look that says I just screwed someone something fierce and he doesn't have a clue it even happened."

"Who? Me?" Vic asked all innocence.

He burst into laughter as the Caddy shot forward and he fell back against the seat.

When they got to the hotel, Victor asked, "By the way, is Silver Screen Films paying you well for this job?"

"Very well. But you know what, even if they weren't, this job has been fun. Totally different than what I expected, and different than any driving I've ever done before. In fact, you took me to places I didn't even know existed in my own city. So don't even think of tipping me."

The two bigger bags were packed and at the door. Vic's and the newly purchased hotel-insignia duffelbag containing a case of juice oranges for Marcie. Vic was just stepping out of the shower, wrapped in a towel, when the door bell rang.

He briefly thought of trying to get dressed before answering, but someone knocked and yelled, "Room Service," so instead he lowered the towel to sit jauntily on his hips and opened the door.

And the Goddess Venus, who had shone with unwavering attention throughout all of this journey, outdid Herself. Before Vic stood the blonde, bearded, stellar young room service waiter he'd lusted after the most. Today he was dressed in white shorts, a pale yellow Izod shirt, and tennis shoes, and he said:

"I was done for the day, but when I saw this package was for you . . ."

Thinking, *Now Victor, don't panic*, he asked, "Can you come in?"

"Sure, thanks." Noticing the bags, "You're leaving soon?"

"The car's coming in about an hour and a half."

"Maybe I should go?"

"Absolutely not. I've been hoping you'd drop by. A drink?"

"Coke is fine. By the way I'm Rainer."

"*Deutsche*?" Vic asked.

"My Dad was. It's a family name."

Rainer sat. He sipped some of Vic's soft drink. He told Vic how he was trying to become the tennis instructor for the hotel, subbing for the official one on his days off and vacation weeks, really working one-and-a-half jobs. Explaining the cute outfit.

When Rainer was done talking about himself, Vic thought, *It's now or never*. He'd already moved over to the little sofa where the young man had settled. Rainer had legs like tree trunks and fuzzed blonde hair all over. He was the most desirable person Victor had been this close to in a week. Vic was suddenly aware that he was physically trembling, and he realized with surprise that it was something he'd read about often enough in novels but had never himself experienced. At the same time, he recognized it must be a purely physiological result of a combination of anxiety, tension, and lust—pure lust.

"Your towel," Rainer said as he leaned forward, "is coming off . . ."

Meade was travelling along Sunset, headed toward the airport, and Victor was thinking that for once, following his exhausting play-date with Rainer, he'd probably be able to sleep on the airplane, when he remembered he still hadn't opened the package that had been delivered.

Inside was a revolver. Or rather a fake revolver, looking real enough except that it was too lightweight. Vic handled it, looking it over, trying to figure out what it did or meant. Only when he pulled the trigger, did he understand: it emitted a flame. It was a cute and funny cigarette lighter!

It also seemed to come wrapped in two pages, a Telexed mimeo of Divine's resume from the Manhattan talent agency that handled the actor, which of course included several photos—most famously the one from *Pink Flamingos* with a gun outstretched in Divine's pudgy hand, pointed directly at the camera.

Along with it was a note on the network's stationery, "from the office of Brandon Tartikoff."

It had one line and read, "Bang! Bang! You got me!"

ACT TWO

1986: NOTES ON A
REVISED REWRITE

"ASA NISI MASA! ASA NISI MASA!"

> --Federico Fellino & Enzo Flaianao
> Children's Spell from <u>Eight & A Half</u>

CHAPTER FOURTEEN

Frank Perry was a smaller man than Vic had expected. But then so had been those two movie stars he'd met at dinner and so was Liza Minnelli at Studio 54 and of course Truman Capote—and just about every other allegedly famous person Vic had met in New York, except maybe for Tommy Tune, who was almost ostentatiously tall and thin and bubbly: far too bubbly for any single human person.

Perry was small and thinnish, with one of those nebbishy bodies all too common in middle-aged straight men: bodies that looked utterly unattended to, seldom if ever remarked upon for any reason either by themselves or their women. Maybe a barber once a month looked closely, if in a limited area. Perhaps a tailor or medico bothered once a year to probe or measure for repair or refitting, so why should Frank bother with it? Unlike Vic and his friends, who, being gay, knew that every other gay man on the planet looked at them with an inborn interior combination telescope, microscope, and ocular slide-rule marked to the millimeter, checking the overgrowth of a sideburn or mustache, the hang of an overbite, any potential excrescence of neck hair, noticing to the decimeter the flesh of any future love handle or past foreskin. Clearly this man was far less looked at than listened to, as Perry was, after all, a film director.

Small, unprepossessingly unphysical, with straight dark brown hair, shorn as though by any haircutter anywhere in the country, with no distinguishing facial hair, facial features from Donegal, Ireland a generation or so ago, not one of which stood out in any particular manner—neither eyes nor mouth nor nose. He could fade into the background of Grand Central Terminal during rush hour, a hydrogen bomb weighing down his valise, and never once be noted by the Hispanic security guards overstuffed in their gray uniforms, or by the cool-dude, chatty, shoeshine Blacks, until they all blew apart into a billion tiny carbon atoms.

Now, for Victor, arriving at his appointment with Perry, there were other surprises. His agent had given him the address on 47th Street off Seventh Avenue, the infamous Brill Building, which had been during the 60's and 70's a famous rival of Tin Pan Alley for producers, agents, and arrangers of rock and folk music. The actual office door read "Paul Schrader," the writer director of sexy Richard Gere's Armani-fest film, *American Gigolo*. Perhaps he was a friend or colleague, Victor thought, letting Frank use his office for this visit and interview.

The bigger surprise however was who answered Vic's ring. Of all people, it was young Sam Alan Haddad, the bottom guy on the rung at Silver Screen Films years before in West Hollywood. Sam still wore his peanut-butter hued hair long if more stylishly cut than before, but gone were the narrow sharkskin slacks and midnight blue faux-silk shirts, his Oil Sheik/Rodeo Drive Pimp-look replaced by a more ordinary, even kinda *'gayische* casual wear of the day: well fitted khaki slacks, pastel Tommy Hilfiger cotton sweater, just like those Victor wore, with penny loafers.

"Bet you're surprised," Sam said, shaking Victor's hand.

"Are you behind all this?" he had time to ask just as Frank Perry, smaller than imagined, entered from another office, still on the phone. "I'll be there in a minute. The Coast," Frank added, referring to the phone call. "Sit. Sit. Get comfy. Sam'll get you coffee. Sam?"

Sam fled and returned some minutes later with the coffee—one cream, one-and-a-half sugar—just as Victor took it. Sam had remembered that just from getting it for Victor three times several years ago. He was good.

Victor had a half a minute to ask, "You're what here?"

"I'm Frank's assistant. Production Assistant, I guess."

Victor had to ask, "You brought *Justify My Sins* to him?"

"No. Not at all. Funny thing is Frank was *reading* your novel when he hired me. He had it right out there on the desk, a marker about twenty pages from the end. We began talking about it. I think that conversation got me the job, if you really want to know, since I knew the book inside out by then, and he liked it so much." A laugh which allowed Victor to notice that Sam had gotten new caps on his front teeth, top and bottom. Then in a quieter, more serious tone of voice, he added: "You know that he and Eleanor had this humongous split up. That was a business as well as a personal divorce. Right after that is when I came on board."

Victor *had* kind of known that. At least about the marital divorce. But of course it must have been doubly disorienting for both, possibly a real horror, splitting up *everything*. They'd been a writing-directing team for what, over twenty years, since the early sixties, right? *David and Lisa*, cute Keir Dullea's debut before he went on to star in the *The Fox* and, most famously, in *2001: A Space Odyssey*. Had that been the two Perrys first movie together? No, Perry had done those TV films based on Capote's holiday novellas. And there had been *Diary of a Mad Housewife*, and that movie on the beach with the dead seagull, and the one from the Joan Didion novel, too, *Play It As It Lays*. Maybe *David and Lisa* was the first to be nominated for an Oscar. Eleanor and Frank had been a writing/directing team up till—when? She'd died of cancer a few years back, hadn't she? Before he did *Mommie Dearest*, no?

Suddenly Frank was there, gently moving Sam aside. "Done," he said and Sam slid to a seat in the back of the room, while Frank replaced him. "Glad to meet you!" Frank looked at Victor closely. "Now what is all this Merry said about you not wanting to sell me the film rights?"

"Marcie. And I only came here, Mr. Perry, out of deep respect for you and the films you've made. Really and truly. Because I'm sorry to say that my book is unfilmable."

Perry looked amused. "You base this on what?"

"I'm sure Sam told you about the experience with Silver Screen in 1977. What he may not know is that since then the book has been under film option every year until, I believe, last month, by one person or another. Mostly film stars. Sissy Spacek had it for a while. That television star, Lindsay Wagner, for a time. And then another TV actress, whose name I don't recall. Producer Renee Missal at Universal Pictures also took an option on it. In the last few years, I usually just take the option money and rent a summer place on Long Island with it, knowing it will be free again soon. And other than that, I've stopped thinking about it."

"The book is still in print!" Sam said. "I saw it on a revolving rack in Woolworths on Broadway among current bestsellers."

"True fact," Victor admitted. "The book's been reissued once more by the paperback house, as it sells so well. A different color background for the cover art, and all the rest is the same. It's our little money engine."

"So it must be still relevant, what is it, six, seven years later?" Sam argued.

"It's relevant *period*," Frank said. "Because of its characters and story. I like it. Victor. I want to do it."

"The book is unfilmable, Mr. Perry," Vic said. "You'll be wasting your time and money. Honestly, you will. It's got traps and pitfalls all over the place. I don't want to sell it to you or even *option* it to you. I'm saying this as if I were a friend."

There was a half-minute of silence, then:

"You know what I'm thinking right now," Frank asked.

"You're thinking you can do it, because you're better than all those people who optioned it. And you are. You're a pro, you're among the best in the business. Despite that . . ."

"Sam will tell you how I work. I collaborate. That's how I've worked for years. I collaborate with the novelist, the biographer, the screenwriter. We work closely together. During that collaboration, we reach the heart of the book or play or script. We discover it together—*and* we conquer it."

"I understand that. Now hear me out, Mr Perry. *Justify* has two main problems keeping it from being a successful Hollywood movie. First, even though it's told from both Theo and Anna-Marie's alternating points of view, *Theo* is *always* the desired object. Anna-Marie never is. It's Theo's mostly nude body, not hers, after all, that's on the book jacket, four hundred and ninety thousand paperback copies later. And even though I know that you're unusual in that you treat and exhibit your male and female leads equally, I believe this male sex object in the story is a real problem. Hollywood makes movies where women are the desired object, not men."

Perry was about to say something, but Vic held up a hand to forestall him. "Second, equally crucial, no happy ending to *Justify My Sins* is possible without making the rest of the book nonsense. That's what stymied it the first time."

"You've thought this out carefully, haven't you?" Perry asked.

"Obviously! I've been trying to figure out why it hasn't worked as a film, year after year. Not worked for one person after another. Now if we were in France, say, or Sweden, *maybe* it could be done."

"So you do think it *is* possible," Perry said.

"It's possible. Not in our patriarchal time. Not in our sexist society. And *not,* I'm sorry to say, in your *particularly* patriarchal and sexist business, Mr. Perry."

Frank turned to Sam. "You were right. He's tough as nails, this one. He looks like a little sweetheart, but once he opens his mouth he's a real street fighter."

Victor laughed. *I'm almost forty years old*, he thought. *Do I really still look so much younger?*

There was another much longer silence in the room.

"That's a big compliment Frank just paid you, Vic," Sam said from his seat ten feet away.

"Now Vic, here's my deal," Perry said. "You and I will meet once a week at my office from 1:00 p.m. to closing, and even later if need be. We'll first do the scenario together. Then we'll write the script together. You'll take it home and polish it, working at least one day of the week on new material alone, and then bringing in your new stuff which we'll then go over. We'll be writing the script *together.* I can't give you more time than that as my company is in the midst of preproduction on another film and in actual production on another, and we'll soon be going into postproduction on that. But it shouldn't take more than four to five months for us to get something together. We'll work out the money business with Merry or whatever her name is. It will be Writers Guild of America scale, plus steps and bonuses."

"I'm not a member of the Guild."

"You have to be to write this script. We'll include the WGA sign up fees in the contract. Sam?"

"Got it," Sam noted it down.

"The long and short of it is I want this book, Victor."

"But how? By which I mean *logistically* how? If your offices are in L.A.?"

"My production company has a lease with—what is it, five? six months, Sam?—left on a house off Benedict Canyon up near Mulholland Drive. Three bedrooms. Big decks. Views. No pool, so it'll be basic. But nice. We've got a car for you under lease. Merry—Marcie—whoever, said you just had a show close Off Broadway that Sam saw on his last trip here. Your second produced play. Sneaky, aren't we? That's how we know you'll do fine mixing dialogue and action for the script. She also said you're *not* signed up for any new book at the moment so you can't use that as an excuse. I told you we're sneaky. You told Sam you liked El Lay. So it'll be four, five months out there in the sun, at pretty good pay. Having to put up with me for half a day a week! What have you got to lose?"

Nothing was said about a wife and kids or girlfriend having to be brought along. Had Marcie also discussed that angle? No. Come on, let's be honest, Vic, after *Nights in Black Leather*'s sensational reviews and sales, everyone on six continents not hiding in an underground shelter had to know by now that Victor Regina was gay.

"And so . . . Victor . . . why not?"

He wanted to say, "This is so sudden, Mr. Perry!" the way the pretty young thing always did in those movies when she is asked to go onstage for the diva, the featured player becoming the lead overnight. Instead he asked, "This would be beginning approximately when?"

"Did you hear that, Sam?" Perry looked back as his P.A. "A real writer! Suddenly all of his words are tentative and 'approximate.'"

Facing Victor, he said, "It would be as soon as possible. I don't suppose you can come back with us to L.A. in three days? Look at him panic, Sam." A laugh and then, "No? Then how about we play it by ear? But pretty soon, after all the contracts are signed."

"You're sure you want me to do this, even though I don't believe we'll succeed in working out the story?" Vic asked.

That, he knew was the tougher question.

"Sam said you're a hard worker. You've published what, five books and put on two plays in seven, eight years? Sounds like hard work to me. So as long as you work as though you believe in our script, I don't care whether you *really* believe or not."

"Working with you would of course be a great, an amazing honor, really."

Before he could say anything more, Frank stood up. "You better believe it! Think it over and get back to me or Sam tomorrow. He'll tell Marcie exactly when our flight leaves. I want this book, Victor. And I very much want you to write it with me. And now if you'll excuse me, I've got to get back on that stupid phone and find out why daily rushes aren't arriving here for us to check. It's the Fox screening room, right?" he asked Sam, "Or are they going to Rizzoli?"

"Fox," Sam said and Frank half shambled into his office again. Sam joined him and they confabbed a minute before Sam came out again and the door was closed and he came up to Victor.

"A house. A car. You'll still have time for your own work. And whatever else you may need out there. All you have to do is contact me and I'll try to get it."

"I know, Sam. But . . . does this work? You've done this before?"

"That house? That car? The last co-writer had the same house and the same car. She loved it. And that's the film being prepped right now. Go home and think it over. But say yes or he'll be impossible for me to work with."

Sam picked up Victor's jacket and walked him out of the office. As they walked, Victor said, "I wasn't kidding. It really is an honor. Anyone else—I wouldn't have even shown *up* today. And Mr. Perry? Frank? He's not like a psycho once you know him? Screaming in uncontrollable rages? Hiding out in the toilet? Phoning at 4:00 a.m.? Be honest, Sam, for old times sake."

"Not a bit. Frank's the best boss I've ever had. A little disorganized. But that's my job. I'd lose a hand for him."

"Oh fuck, Sam! Don't say that."

The elevator doors opened, and two men about Victor's age stepped out, and Sam held the door for them but didn't get in.

"This the novelist?" the fellow with dark hair and a wiry frame asked with dancing eyes and a wry, familiar grin comma'ed by a dangling toothpick. Vic recognized him as Robert de Niro, Jr.

Sam introduced all three of them. The other, cuter, slightly more solidly built guy with light brown hair and rimless glasses turned out to be Paul Schrader. Given the time, early afternoon, and the toothpick, they were probably coming back from lunch.

"I'll see *you* later!" De Niro said as they walked off, pointing his finger pistol style at Vic, his trademark farewell from *Taxi Driver*.

119

"And the others?" Victor asked. "From Silver Screen?"

"Ed Trefethern retired," Sam said, as though only he counted. "Say yes, Vic," he urged, then turned and went into the men's room.

When he was gone, Victor could still hear Schrader talking, doubtless thinking that Victor was already in the elevator and gone, clearly saying to De Niro, "He wrote that infamous cult thriller. The black leather book?" The final word blurred as they entered the office.

That was four years ago! Victor Regina thought. *But if* he *knows about it, then they* all *must!*

Thus do we discover our reputation.

Maybe it was time to change it?

CHAPTER FIFTEEN

From the moment he awoke he became a detective. The place next to him in their double sleigh-style bed was slightly wrinkled, meaning Mark had indeed slept there. Touching it with his cheek, Victor still detected a hint of lingering warmth. It was 8:14 a.m., but Mark would have been up and out the door at least an hour ago. And yes, he'd been here last night, his furnace of a body chugging away, keeping them warm this mid-Spring morning in 1983 long after the building furnace had shut off for the night. Victor had one quarter awakened in transition from one dream to another, and had seen, even felt with his hand, Mark there.

Hadn't he? Or had he dreamt it?

Unlike Victor, Mark was all neatness and order, so what would be a clue? A tiny bit less girth in the toothpaste tube? An iota less heft to the shared can of lather? A humid towel?

The problem was that for the past three years Mark had been a "poor student," as he reminded Victor at sundry, increasingly inappropriate moments. He'd left his usual line of more or less commercially lucrative employment and, at the advanced age of thirty-two years, gone to law school, of all things, a decision that Victor had actually supported—no, actually championed, the more fool he.

And the first few years had gone pretty well. Sure, they were suddenly one income less, but it just so happened that Victor was suddenly earning enough for two with his third book, the historical Western *Heartache Canyon*, which was doing nicely, thank you very much, with amazing reviews and book club sales and several translations. Meanwhile, *Justify* continued to chug along like the little engine that could. Then *Nights in Black Leather* came out, and that had moved Victor onto another plane altogether, into the pages of the Sunday *New York Times*, onto the full front page of the Sunday *Long Island Press* Arts section with photos. It was re-viewed everywhere thereafter, shocking everyone, critics lining up pro and con, as it became the first openly gay title to be a book club alternate selection, a best seller in hardcover *and* in paper-back, making him so famous that within months he couldn't step out to the local deli for a midnight snack without someone recog-nizing him as in, "Hey! You're that . . . *leather guy*! Right?"

Right.

So who needed Mark's income?

Even so, Mark was attempting to be "utterly ethical about money," which meant they would only spend equal amounts: a clear impossibility. Victor put up with this for Mark's sake, even though it meant far less theater, concerts, movies, and virtually *no* dinners out, never mind operas, not to mention no vacations to-gether—not for two years. Unless, of course, it meant they wouldn't be able to take a trip to the Caribbean in the dead of winter between law school terms, where Vic had friends who had a big empty house just waiting for them. When that came up, Vic fliply declared, "We're going. I'll shell out now, you'll pay me later—when you're a rich lawyer. And you are going to be a rich one, since I surely don't intend to work the rest of my life."

That's pretty much how they'd more or less teeter-tottered in balance until Mark's final year at The New York School of Law and everything upended suddenly, horribly, and immediately fell to pieces.

First, because Mark was so smart, he was a top scholar, and so he'd been appointed to some kind of honor called "editing notes" at a place called *The Law Review*. And whatever his work there might be, of course it was on top of his already heavy because-it-was-the-last-year-of-law-school legal courses. Add onto that was added Mark's brand new, part-time employment after school and weekends clerk-ing in a six-person law office that was interested in hiring Mark when he got out of school. Another honor that couldn't possibly be turned down, nor cut back, no, not in any way, Mark assured him.

However, that onslaught ended not only the infrequent vaca-tions but also *any* concerts, operas, movies, theater, or even going out together. It was as though Victor were suddenly impoverished again. And bad as that was, once the third difficult year of classes was over in January, Mark's work load, which should have lessened a bit, suddenly seemed to double, because of course he had to study for the New York State Law Boards day and night—that is, whenever he wasn't at the law office near Lincoln Center or at *The Law Review*!

All Mark's friends assured Victor that next to these hoary, hairy exams, walking the plank and even SS torture chambers were April larks and the merest of fashion runway piffles.

So Vic had become a detective, having to now daily prove to himself that his lover of six years, the person he felt he'd been waiting for the first thirty-three years of his life, the man that cynical old Victor Regina unstintingly adored, actually still resided with him, by which he meant slept nights in their shared duplex in the chic West Village.

The dead-giveaway, of course, was that Mark unquestionably still *ate* there. Food vanished from the refrigerator at an alarmingly steady rate. Sometimes—like fruit or yoghurt cups—it was replaced. More often it wasn't, and instead new food-bearing objects appeared on the second shelf in their place: stark white take-out boxes, colorful packets, dynamically tinted sandwich wrappings. Only to vanish within hours, as though Mark could reach across Manhattan and teleport them from behind a shut GE door without himself being present.

Vic had never been anything more than a serviceable cook, relying on minute steaks, burgers, chicken breasts, an occasional pork or veal chop with one accompanying carb and veggie. But some months before, and under what felt to him like the same kind of intense pressure that metamorphoses coal into diamonds, he'd found himself on the slippery slopes of that suburban culinary purgatory known as The Wonderful World of Casseroles.

He eschewed tuna-noodle on the firmest of principles, but soon enough anything else would do. One of Mark's closest study partners ate no meat, but despite her size 1 clothing and her weight of about eighty-eight pounds, she did put away surprisingly oceanic quantities of macaroni and cheese, bulgur wheat with chickpeas and walnuts, spinach fettucini with pesto, and virtually anything containing cheese or eggs. Besides vegetarian, there was Victor's Spanish and Italiano casseroles, even his Greek and eventually

German and Russian ones. Love pizza? Vic figured out how to make a casserole taste just like slices of Ray's Famous on 6th Avenue. Go for Moussaka? Well a semi-mousse is what you'd get. Pork chops and sauerkraut? Red cabbage with apples and wieners? He'd discovered a chuck-wagon special from Utah funnily called "poke in the hole" and something British with cabbage and potatoes more oddly called "toad in the hole."

They were the perfect solution. Mark was seldom home to appear for the first eating of any dish, but a casserole he could eat cold or heated up later, tomorrow, or the next day. Vic even began making two of each dish per night, one for himself, Gilbert, and his b.f. Jeff, say; another, often larger version for Mark to eat at 2:20 a.m. or tomorrow—and tomorrow and tomorrow.

Visits to Balducci ended. Vic couldn't bear looking at those prices and that quality only to acknowledge that it would be chopped up tiny, gummed up with some kind of binder, and thrust in the oven for forty-five minutes at three hundred and seventy-five degrees.

But he did make other discoveries: cauliflower and broccoli married nicely with all sorts of weird foodstuffs if you put crust on and called it a pot-pie. Potatoes and red peppers had their own secret lives as ingredients. Tofu went with all kinds of Chinese-esque vegetables the recently sprung up Korean delis all over Manhattan had begun to feature.

Naturally, Vic realized in his heart of hearts that what he was cooking was, in sophistication, about two steps above pureed infant food in small jars. But with casseroles, he would at least have ocular proof that his lover was receiving samples of all the food groups—at rare times, all of them at once. He'd also be able to gauge the depth of his studying (or at least the *length* of his studying) by how many refrigerated casserole dishes were emptied and left soaking in sudsy water in the sink when Victor woke up the next morning.

"And so," he'd reflected while speaking to his best friend, Gilbert Onager on the phone, "I have descended rapidly from Authorial God to Beleaguered *Hausfrau*. And it ain't over yet. He's got three more months of this madness to go!"

"Sacrifice is good for the soul" was the usual response Vic received to these complaints.

"Unfortunately, Bertie, as I was certain you knew by now, I don't *believe* in the soul. Meaning that sacrifice does nothing but really suck!"

It was the morning after the meeting with Frank Perry, and Vic still hadn't told his best friend that had happened. Possibly because Vic had another (chronic) sinus headache, and despite three cups of java (the caffeine helped) and three Excedrin Super Strength tablets, he knew he simply could not possibly abide the high pitched screams sure to greet his news.

So he waited and waited, and it ended up being someone named Angelica Mangotti whom he spoke to for the first time that day who uttered the magic words that tipped his life. She innocently enough phoned looking for Mark to check some page numbers in a legal text. Vic looked at the scribbled schedule Mark had left a month or two before on the refrigerator door, hoping to locate him, and read it to her: "'Specialized Torts—Morgan's place.' I'm assuming you know what all that means," Vic added.

She'd replied, "Oh, shit! I was supposed to be at that study group."

Which was how Vic discovered that a new burden had emerged to further muck up his life: heavily structured, scheduled-to-an-inch-of-their-lives study groups for the dreaded Law Boards. Four to sixteen students were now meeting at various places around the city at various times—check the schedule, Victor—some lasting until 4:00 a.m. Meaning he would probably not see Mark again until it was all over months from now, in mid-June.

He gave Angelica the address and phone number she required from the schedule, hung up, and instantly phoned his literary agent.

"Has Trent gotten the Frank Perry contracts yet?" Vic asked.

"Hello. You look lovely today. You sound like shit. My god, Marce, was that really you on the front page of *The Post*? Those, Victor, are all *acceptable* ways to open a phone conversation with Marcie Stein Whittaker. 'Has Trent gotten the Frank Perry contracts yet?' is not, you may notice, among those choices."

"I'm desperate. I haven't laid actual eyes on my lover for about a month, He's been stolen by Law Board gypsies and exists in some legal Twilight Zone beyond time and space."

"So you want to give it all up and go to El Lay?"

"In a nutshell, yes."

"Well, I for one do not blame you one iota. And right after we hang up, I'm calling Laeticia Thwackbottom at Norton and telling her she loses, I win."

Victor was baffled—and when he understood, furious. "Do you mean to tell me you two had *bets* on when I'd *crack?*"

"*Bets? We two?* Honey, wake up. Half the Manhattan publishing world has put money on the odds. I don't know if I get the jackpot. All I know was that I did predict it would go down sometime this week."

He was silent in response. This was beyond callous.

"And so, to answer your question," Marcie went on, unfazed, "yes, Trent got the papers, and after a first look through the contract seems fine: house and car and WGA Membership included. Those were nice touches. It seems that you've finally learned how to ask for what you want."

"I asked nothing, Marce. I told Perry he was a fool wasting his time and money."

"I see!" she said. "You told him 'No go' and he salivated all the more and offered inducements." Then: "And now you're going?"

"He said for you to call and get their travel schedule. He wanted me to go back to California with him and Sam. I said I wouldn't, I couldn't possibly. But now I'm not so sure. Keep in mind, Marce, I still think doing this will be a waste of time and money. All I know is that I cannot remain in this duplex, in this city, in this situation with or actually *without* Mark, for one week more."

"You loved El Lay the last time, remember?"

"I was single, remember? I got laid twice a day, sometimes more. And I bonded with Mark out there, remember? All reasons why I loved El Lay the last time. Not one in any way applicable this time around."

"Is it a nice car?" Marcie asked.

"It's okay. A Datsun Z sport coupe. The house is on Benedict Canyon near Mulholland Drive. Is that nice?"

"God, yes!"

"No pool."

"You'll have to go to the Bee-Aitch-Aitch, that's about a mile away, and use theirs," Marcie said. "Oh, wait! You couldn't *possibly* do that! Since last time you stayed there, you brought back Mister Torture and Maim on a Silver Hog, and now everyone's sure you've got a major case of cooties, the clap, and who knows what other kinds of weird festering wounds."

"Is that last meant to be a crack about You Know What That's Going Around in an Epidemic Form?"

"Hell, no. Sorry." She was suddenly contrite.

"You're forgiven. But you're not completely wrong. I might have gotten a bit carried away at the Beverly Hills Hotel. Even so, I still get postcards from that Room Service Waiter I sixty-nined. Seems he's still there and wondering when I'm coming back."

"See! It won't be utterly horrible. Why don't I call Perry's assistant and find out when their plane leaves."

"It's Sam. Sam Alan Haddad. Does the name sound at all familiar?"

"Should it?"

"He was low man on the totem-pole at Silver Screen Films. Remember them? And no, he *didn't* bring the book to Frank."

"Then it sounds terribly fortuitous to me," Marcie said.

"Marce, you realize that I'm only saying and doing this out of sheer utter unmitigated panic. You're supposed to stop me. That's what agents are supposed to do."

"No, Victor, that's your *analyst's* job. You would know that if you weren't so pigheaded that you don't *have* an analyst like all the rest of us neurotics. Agents, by contrast, are supposed to make financially lucrative deals with all kinds of ridiculous perks included. And it seems you've already very nicely done that all by yourself."

"I know. I know. So what is this cold shoulder I've been getting? It's been a week since we talked. You have a new favorite client?" Vic asked.

"Never. But I do have some younger new clients who require a lot of my attention. Unlike yourself, Victor, whom, if I may remind you, are a quote, successfully arrived author, unquote and who doesn't need so much anymore."

"I don't feel successfully arrived, with or without quotes," he whined.

"What you feel doesn't count as reality, hon. If I've learned *any-thing* after five years with *my* analyst, that's it. My advice? Get out of this town as fast as your feets can move you. You should already be half packed."

"How much are you winning from predicting my crack up?"

"From predicting your cracking up *week*," she corrected. "I don't know yet. And when I do know, I'm certainly not telling you. If it's a lot, I'll buy you a cute gift with some of it. *If* you don't wait but instead leave *right away* with the director man."

"I'm packing as soon as I hang up."

She called back twenty minutes later with the time the following evening that Sam and Frank would come by in a limo to pick him up and drive him to JFK.

"Sam was surprised. I did not of course tell him what a crybaby and basket case you are, which is why you're joining them,"

"You're a saint, Marcie."

"I believe Jewish women can aspire to become martyrs, but never saints," she replied. "By the way Janet Shell was just here in the office. That's Janet, your fan? From your publisher's publicity department? Peg here had lunch with her and Janet stopped by to say hello. When she heard you were going to El Lay she reminded me that several big book shops out on the West Coast have repeatedly asked for you to appear for signings. Why don't I have her call you out there and arrange those?" Marcie said. "If nothing, at least it'll take your mind off what's his face."

"Okay. Fine. Sure."

"Vic?" Marcie was using her waif-in-distress voice.

"Yes?"

"I'm going to miss you!"

"I may be back sooner than you think."

"Do not come back till the damn Law Boards are finished."

"I know. I know."

After they were done talking, Victor looked around his bedroom.

Packing wouldn't be all that difficult. In fact, he was probably still three-quarters packed from the last two Caribbean vacations that he and Mark had planned in detail and then ended up not taking. It was all summer stuff in those bags, shorts, bathing suits, guinea tees, light shoes, windbreakers: things he'd use in California.

What *would be* a problem, he suddenly realized, would be figuring out exactly how many casseroles he could possibly cook and freeze for Mark in the less than twenty-four hours he had remaining.

CHAPTER SIXTEEN

"So! You've settled in?" Frank asked Vic when he entered the Canon Drive office.

"Kind of. Sort of. A little."

Which was all true. He'd gotten all his bags unpacked three days before. But while the house was nicely furnished, it lacked something. Call it culture for lack of another word. Three paperback popular bestsellers and a slew of oversized hard cover titles filled the three bookshelves and various single-shelf book-nooks strategically placed at points all over the very modern two floors of the rented sun-filled house.

Based on the titles of the books he saw laying around, whoever had stayed there previously had feasted on all-protein Lupercalias, become her own best friend, then seen the light and turned vegetarian, taken up power-running, gone on weekend fasts initiated by vegetable juice engorgements and ended with all fruit feasts, turned to "Dream Work," given up veggies for something called the "super carb-load diet," gone over to "Shiva-Enlightenment" (whatever that was; something trendily Hindu, he guessed) and at long last had found total comfort in "Financial Freedom."

Luckily, this morning the box of real books and cassettes Vic sent himself from Manhattan had arrived via UPS. He opened the cardboard carton he'd packed in about eight minutes between doing everything else he'd had to do last week, and then left it for Gilbert to actually send off, not at all remembering what he'd so recently put in.

The cassettes ranged from Glenn Gould's humming Bach to the Beach Boys' *Smile*, with everything in between from *Evergreen*, *Elton John's Greatest Hits*, and *Merrily We Roll Along* to Sibelius' tone poems and Solomon playing Mozart. The books were an even more eclectic selection: a Faulkner novel from that college seminar which he'd never gotten around to reading at the time— *Sartoris*; a Henry Green trilogy Mark swore by and had given him for his last birthday, doubtless saving up weeks to shell out the $4.95; Capote's *Music For Chameleons*; Stanislaw Lem's weirdly intellectual sci-fi in two mass market paperbacks with aptly mysterious and lurid covers—*The Invincible* and *Solaris*; Goethe's *Wilhelm Meister* in five slim volumes from England; an equally compact hardcover of ten Balzac novellas; Ackerly's *Hindoo Holiday*, which he'd already begun months before; and a fat paperback of all of E.F. Benson's gothic stories.

Once the cassettes were put out on display and the books spread around the house, and the other previously displayed volumes carefully boxed up and placed under the kitchen sink next to other preventatives and detergents, Victor did indeed begin to feel settled in. But it still looked bare. He needed to find a used book store and get a few more titles and maybe even some *National Geographics* or *Art Forums* for color.

"Good. Real settling in will take a while," Frank said. "Now get comfortable. Here." He held out a handful of what looked like popcorn to Victor who asked, "Is that what I think it is?"

"You bet. I need to nosh all the time and my wife says this is healthy for me. At least this way it is: without salt or butter."

Victor hadn't known Frank had remarried. He'd have to ask Sam who the new wife was.

Frank showed Victor the cannister that the popcorn came in which was about five feet high and two and a half feet around, with circus motifs brightly all over it, as though it was meant for some eight-year-old's birthday party.

"You buy it wholesale?" Victor asked.

"Have to. I go through maybe five of these a month. A truck delivers them," Frank said without a hint of embarrassment.

He began talking about a cardiac health scare he'd had a few months back, and also about many of his friends and partners who had gone downhill rapidly because of neglecting simple things like what not to eat or drink. He interrupted a long story about a friend's heart transplant to ask, "So the house is okay. How's the car?"

"Fine. Nice, in fact. Kind of sporty. A Datsun Zee. I just got my driver's license back again last year. Growing up in the suburbs, I've been driving since I was a kid, of course," Victor explained. "But after a few scatty years of totally weird not to mention unexpected vehicle accidents, mostly in Europe, I'd allowed my license to lapse. Especially as I didn't use a car at all in Manhattan and seldom on trips."

Victor found himself telling Frank about his most spectacular near-death turn, at the Georgia/Florida state line, thanks to a viciously temperamental Ducati Scrambler motorcycle, and Frank, in turn, began telling Victor about some of the people around him who'd died in various vehicle accidents. "Stunts, most of them," Frank clarified, "both onscreen and off. Written in a script, and more often not written but impromptu. More like the scripts were written in their own minds," he added, which was a telling if odd statement. Did Frank and all his movie friends constantly write and rewrite scripts for their lives and then live them out?

They discussed cars they'd liked and hated; European roads they'd driven upon; European (read French) inn and hotel meals they never forgotten; what books and magazines they were reading; what they hated about theater; what they liked about television. A hour went by and Victor wondered, *Is this work we're doing? Or are we just getting to know each other? And is that as important as doing some kind of specific work?*

He'd come prepared and wanted to show it. "I had a few thoughts on the plane," Victor said out of nowhere.

"You mean while me and Sam were dead to the world?"

In fact Frank had been dead asleep when he'd emplaned, and Sam not long after, so he'd had plenty of time to read. They'd both been snoring happily along before the plane had begun to taxi along the runway toward Jamaica Bay for take-off, slept through the first four hours or so of the trip, Frank awakening only to groggily eat, and stumble to the restroom before he stumbled back and fell asleep again. Sam hadn't even wakened for food, but the stewardess either knew or liked him because she saved it and he wolfed it down in the few minutes before they landed at LAX.

"Lucky you," Victor said, "I wish I could sleep on planes."

"You will. Take my word for it," Frank predicted. "One trip to come, you'll be so tired, you'll sleep through take-off and landing both, noisy as they are."

"So I was thinking," Victor went on, "on the plane: the book is already pretty streamlined as far as characters go: Theo and Anna-Marie, Theo's friend Bill, and the man she free lances art for; then Theo's nosy downstairs neighbor and the old lady across the street below Anna-Marie's flat. So, and I'm not sure how to say this, don't each of them gain extra in the script by how few of them there are?"

"They definitely do. Not only that, but I'd like you to streamline it a little further. If that doesn't offend you too much," Frank added, a real diplomat. "Theo's friend isn't really needed for the plot. Wouldn't you agree? He doesn't advance anything crucial."

"No. You're right. I put him there in the book to give Theo a friend and more or less to give Theo a sounding board. Bill's the normal guy. He'd never get into any kind of screwy situation with Anna-Marie."

"The viewer will do that normalizing work for us. Bill's not needed. Let's ditch him," Frank said. "Also, that guy Anna-Marie does art for—what's his name?"

"Alton Higgs."

"Great name. He's such a prig. Prig-Higgs. But Alton can be done totally off-screen. We don't need to use an actor at all. Understand, Victor, this isn't about saving money, although it does. It puts less people up there for the viewer to deal with."

"I get that. It focuses the concentration."

"Right," Frank added, then, "Who was it who said that facing execution had a way of focusing the concentration? Matthew Arnold?"

"Earlier than him. Samuel Johnson," Victor replied.

"You *would* know that. I'd lay money that no one else in this building of, what, twenty five offices? three people minimum per office? would have a clue."

"I'm a writer. It's my job to know useless information," Victor admitted.

"It's useless until you use it. And even then, you've got it at hand. All the good writers I've known are like that."

And Eleanor too? Victor wondered. *Your thirteen-years-older wife?*

133

"Back to the script: Anna-Marie's building super, while minor, *is* needed. He does advance the action. But he's only walk-on. Just has the one scene. As does the nosy neighbor. Except she may have two scenes. Would you want to play the super?" Frank asked.

"Mr. Nagy? In the movie?" Victor would have been less astonished if Frank asked him to play the lead.

"It's nothing, One scene. No more than one, two lines. It'll be a snap to learn the dialogue. It'll be fun. You'll see."

"Sure, okay." Victor said, being as casual as possible. Frank was full of surprises, wasn't he? "But my point is emphasized. Each of those remaining characters now take on a bigger role, don't they?"

"Victor, you absolutely get it. Yes, they're all bigger roles now, especially the nosy neighbor and the old woman who escaped the Nazis who lives downstairs."

Frank began talking about several actresses who might play those roles: clearly the old woman would be a much expanded part, given some of the stellar names Frank was putting forth as possibilities: Ellen Burstyn and Jessica Tandy, for example. Would they even take such a small role? If it meant working for Perry, Victor guessed, they just might.

"By condensing like that," Frank concluded, "you force the viewers to pay more attention to the characters you have.

"Condensing the places we'll see on screen also strengthens the importance of the scenes we retain," he added. "It's an intuitive thing. The viewer doesn't realize what's happening until he's deep inside the particular world of your movie. A world unlike any other."

Hey! I just got Film Writing Lesson Number One, Victor thought.

Sam knocked on then opened the office door and mentioned that someone was on the phone for Frank. He said the name, which meant nothing to Victor.

"I need to take this alone," Frank apologized.

Victor took his coffee out to the main office, but after ten minutes, Sam got a call from Frank, then Frank himself came out apologizing again. "Got a problem with some rushes. Me and Sam have got to go in earlier than we'd planned. In fact, right now!

Look, Vic, I know I owe you an hour or more for today. You'll come in earlier next time. That work for you?"

They all left the building together.

Victor followed Frank's stately charcoal gray XJ sedan out of the parking garage set deep beneath the building. The Jag headed south, toward Wilshire Boulevard, into a surprisingly colorful, cloud-filled sky that had been clear and sunny an hour earlier. As Victor exited, he aimed the sleek sports car in the opposite direction, toward Sunset Boulevard, heading toward the Pacific Highway and ultimately Topanga Canyon. Northward, the skies were still cloudless and blue. Victor would be earlier than he'd planned, but so what? Andy Grant didn't work (had he ever, since graduating college?). He was bound to be home.

"So?" Andy asked, hands on hips, "Whaddya' think of my place?" He stood high on a huge rock that looked like it might tumble at any second amid the nastiest looking little she-goats Victor had ever laid eyes on

"Andy, I think your place looks like a cross between Taliesin West and Tobacco Road."

Andy Grant threw back his leonine head and laughed loudly. This great noise frightened the five or six goatlets closest to him, who all looked up from their persistent foraging of what seemed to be an unending, unreclaimed, utterly wild landscape and they whinnied or hooted, or at any rate made that noise that little goats make when they're in agreement. Obviously they were less frightened of Andy Grant's barking laugh and his appearance than was Victor, who'd not seen his old friend since his last visit.

The house, or rather, the compound lay below them on a more or less brush-cleared if not all that earthquake-proofed looking patch of level earth. All around them was low scrub wood— flourishing despite the goats' appetite—riddled with stands of quite tall and even picturesque ancient-looking live-oak trees. The surrounding light must have floated in from the ocean, which was a few miles south, and so it all looked like "spacious skies"—with odd, marine-like colorations and hints of the seaside.

The low buildings composing the compound had been put up by some follower of Frank Lloyd Wright and resembled that architect's less successful attempts at small, domestic "Usonian" residences. There was a guest house immediately at the hewn half-tree-trunk gate to the property, a single room and bath made of lots of horizontal brickwork with deep inset tinted windows winking in the strong sunlight. Maybe a hundred feet away lay another edifice of a few more rooms, scads more blond, horizontal brickwork, and strong wooden beam supports and roofing covering rows of windows, some narrow and high-set close to the roof, others much bigger and angled open to the breezes. Then another few hundred feet away from there sat some wooden and brick sheds or shacks where the goats were housed, as well as a roofless jeep-like vehicle painted a putrid rust orange, and—under handcrafted covers—a nearly iridescent silver Jaguar XKE convertible with a real ragtop. Vic wondered what had happened to the Assassination Vehicle to which Andy had sworn such fealty.

The real surprise for Victor of course was how rural the area was. Only twenty minutes or so off the major highway bisecting Southern California's most populous valley, he felt like he might at any moment come upon a pair of idiot children playing with paper mâché dolls and cat skeletons in the dirt.

He had followed the careful directions given on the phone, but had anyway almost missed the "town" because it was a mere ninety foot twist of Topanga Canyon Road fronted by a grocery, a feed and grain shop, and a little white wooden mall-ette of maybe five other stores, including a "breakfast boutique," a combo florist and head shop, and what must be several art and crafts galleries.

Andy's road lay beyond that particular bit of urban splendor and before reaching another stretch of "town," consisting of another, arty, dinner-only, restaurant and what seemed to be the entrance to a tiny theater in the round, around which three middle aged riders on horses had gathered to chat.

Luckily enough it was daylight, and even luckier, property numbers were painted on the paved roads, wherever those existed.

Less lucky was Victor's first sight of his old pal and buddy.

Victor had heard that in certain areas of the country gay men were doing anything they could to avoid the "Auschwitz" thinness so symbolic of being afflicted with the illness only recently identified and named as the Human Immunodeficiency Virus. Even so, he'd put a greeting hand on the well-padded bent-over shoulder of some fat guy with long reddish blond hair and full beard, thinking it was the gardener or some local helper, and he was about to ask if Tubby knew where the owner was, when the oversized head looked up at him and the inimitably Andy-ish chocolate-candy-center eyes stared hard at him.

"Help me up, wouldya'?" Andy said, the voice all too familiar. When he was on his feet, all two hundred and fifty-five pounds of him, stuffed into Farmer Gray blue jeans and a too-small t-shirt, he added, "Vic! Boy! You are so fucking skinny, I could lose you between my legs and not miss you for a week."

"You wish," Victor rejoined, and was then greeted by a bear hug from which he extricated himself only with difficulty.

Andy showed him around the place and then inside for a beer, then said, "Come take a better look."

That's how they ended up on the big unsteady rock, which indeed gave a partial view of the Pacific Ocean, as well as in the other direction roll after roll of hill and dale, up and down, just like in a kid's coloring book.

Next had come Victor's Taliesin/Tobacco Road quip, which Andy took good naturedly, and then they returned and jumped up and into the open-top vehicle which Andy called his "'Ford Exploder." "You know what F.O.R.D. stands for? 'Found on road dead,'" Andy guffawed.

"Or is it 'Fix or repair daily'?" Victor replied. "My favorite was our neighbor back east who had a Fiat Berline coupe. Prettiest thing on the road, but it spent more time in the shop than at home. He told me F.I.A.T stood for 'Fix It Again, Tony!'"

He'd just gotten around to asking where they were going—back onto Topanga Canyon Road in the direction opposite of how he'd come, then onto a bunch of connecting dirt roads—when Andy said, "Wouldya rather see actor boys or soldiers?"

"Where? What?"

"Just up ahead. You can see 'em both. But we gotta hike a bit."

Andy drove upon a high curving paved road upon which a half dozen older houses were visible through big old trees, and they stopped and got out and headed down what Andy said was a trail. It just looked like grass patted down to Victor.

Twenty minutes or so later it was a real trail, with horseshoe prints and tire marks. They stopped and Andy listened. "They're still here, probably packing up for the day, unless they're working nights."

Andy went up between two huge rocks maybe twelve feet wide and eight high and shimmied up, belying his girth and weight, and then peered out through a wedge between them. A minute later he gestured for Victor to join him, putting a hand to his lips to keep him shushed.

The open space between the rocks was narrow and rectangular. Beneath them, maybe fifty feet away, lay a series of glens, all filled with an American Army encampment.

"Andy!" he whispered. "We can't be here."

"Hush. Look over there. Fourth tent on the left, some crew are taking showers."

"Crew?"

"It's a shooting set. A television show set. Look across at those hills and then picture a helicopter circling and then landing."

"You mean," and now Victor looked more closely, and sure enough there were the big medical tents, the surgery tent, the barracks, the H.Q., the period jeeps, "this is where they make *M*A*S*H*?"

"Why? You thought they shot it in Korea?"

"No, but . . . It's so close to you. And it's so far in off the road to have to come."

"For privacy, I suppose. I found it while hiking up to these rocks. There's a waterfall down below, too. These guys use those jeeps to come and go on the dirt path we took, and the stars and director use the helicopter to go to work."

"Oh, shit!" Victor whispered, despite himself. "Isn't that Klinger and Radar coming out of the H.Q.?"

Even from this far off, clearly one soldier wore pink petticoats and the other had his cap's visor turned up.

"This is too cool!" Victor declared.

But Andy was looking hard at another area. "Jeez! Look at the wanger on the black haired guy! I think he's just a grip. But so hot. And see that tall skinny reddish-haired guy with the long half stiff? He's an assistant cameraman."

"How often do you come here?"

"Every few days. Around this time they clean off, and I whack myself. Only safe thing to do anymore, you know."

At which point Victor became aware that's exactly what Andy was doing, inches from him, and suddenly the place became a lot less interesting and glamorous. He dropped away, down to the ground.

"Don't you want to see 'em?" Andy protested.

"Whoa! Wave that thing in another direction. No, think I'll go sit over *there* a while."

"Good idea. Stay outta sight," Andy commanded, and turned back. Twenty minutes later, as they entered the compound again, Victor felt he had to bring up the subject.

"You've got other things to masturbate to, right? Magazines? Picture books? Movies?"

"Sure but they're nothing like the real thing." Andy hugged him with one arm. "Why?"

"Because—when was the last time you read a newspaper?" Did he even have a television? No, there was no antenna up ahead.

"Gave that up a while ago," Andy said airily. "Papers too liberal and too opinionated. Television too fascistic and consumer driven. Why?"

"Well I hate to be the messenger of doom. But *M*A*S*H* is going off the air very soon. We may have been watching the last episode there today."

Andy flashed him a look composed of consternation, then suspicion followed by despair, and then suspicion again that once back inside the house, Victor suggested that Andy call someone he knew and find out for sure. It *had* been in all the papers.

His friend was so shell-shocked by the news that Victor decided that their previous plan for dinner would be too much to expect of him. He made up a story about having to talk to the East Coast before it got too late there, and took off a few minutes after.

The sight of Andy Grant among his busily chomping goats sadly waving goodbye, facing a future without naked guys to whack off to in the woods, might have been a tragic one if it weren't for a single detail. Unknown to Victor's friend, all the while they were departing one of the goats was happily chewing away at Andy's shirt bottom, hanging loose out the back of his denim jumper.

CHAPTER SEVENTEEN

"I told you before, he's in a meeting and he can't be bothered right now," Sam Haddad said and made a face as though he'd eaten something left in a restaurant fridge a day too long. "That's right. Uh-huh. Right. Well, no, he goes from one meeting to another, all day today. Uh-huh. No idea. I'd try another time." He listened, clearly wanting to be rid of the speaker on the other end. "Try tomorrow. Sure. Natch. Of course. I'll tell him you called."

He hung up the phone and looked up at Victor.

"Sor-ry. She is persistent."

"Actress looking for work?" Victor wondered.

"Worse," Sam said. "Far worse."

And before Victor could ask what that meant—bill collector? ex-fiancée? out of wedlock birth child?—Sam stood and ushered him into Frank Perry's office.

Frank was in his swivel chair, not at the desk but at a low table with his fully shod feet up, and he was reading some pages that Victor recognized as what he'd dropped by yesterday.

"Vic! my man! Have a seat. I'm just about to finish this."

"She called again," Sam told Frank.

"I don't see why you don't want to patch her through."

"Frank!"

"Okay. All right. You know best. Go now! I want to read this. Sit, Vic."

Victor sat opposite, opened the *New York Times* and began doing the crossword puzzle in ink. This wasn't as bold, impressive, or daunting a move as it might seem. Victor had been doing the *Times* crossword puzzle for decades, and it was only Thursday, so it wasn't as difficult as, say, Friday's puzzle or Saturday's. So he moved ahead, quickly filling in spaces.

Frank put down the few pages, got up out of the chair and began pacing around the big office. He would stop to scoop up pop-corn, he'd pause to look out the window—a nice view of the Hollywood Hills looking east—he would turn suddenly.

"What I don't get is how we believe, both in the book and in this little scenario you gave me, that this woman would just call this guy from out of the blue and begin speaking to him."

"Because it happened," Vic said. "Happened to me, in fact."

"Why did I never know it happened to you?"

"I thought my agent Marcie sent over all the supporting material? One would be the article I did for a men's magazine around the time the book came out in hardcover, about female voyeurs, telling the whole back story."

"That's right. I read that," Frank corrected himself.

"At least the first part of the novel happened to me. Unlike Theo, at a certain point I stopped talking to her on the phone and told her not to call again."

"And she really didn't call again?"

"Not while I was at home. Oh, and I also shut my blinds when-ever I *was* home so she couldn't look inside anymore."

Frank wheeled around, suddenly a prosecuting attorney in the courtroom. "And you did this *why?*"

"Because of what happened when a college friend of mine slept over."

"I don't remember any college friend sleeping over."

"You wouldn't. It's not in the book. Remember? Theo *doesn't* stop her from calling. Theo *doesn't* begin dropping his blinds to hide from Anne-Marie until almost the end."

"Tell me what happened," Frank said and sat back in the swivel chair and threw his feet upon the low table again.

"Well, in short, I freaked out," Victor said. "This friend from high school and college called suddenly saying she was back from Europe and looking for the little group we had belonged to at school. I gave her the phone numbers, but they'd all moved out of town and she was only around for a few nights. And anyway staying in the suburbs with her parents, where she was bored. We talked about some of the crazy places and crazy things we had experienced together when we were kids. She said she missed the city, so I said why not come in and have dinner, or catch a show together, and she did."

"What do you mean? Crazy places?" Frank asked, looking very stern. "What kind of so-called 'crazy things.'"

"Well, it began innocently enough," Victor recalled. "Out in the suburbs, we would go bowling, then to a Chinese restaurant that had just opened. Usually she and I went there alone. While our bowling buddies went for burgers next door. Now, I was sixteen when I graduated high school, so I must have been fourteen, fifteen at this time. She was a year older but she was a bit more mature looking." Vic illustrated with his hands arced over his chest. "So we ordered cocktails with dinner. Alcohol. Long before we were supposed to."

"They didn't ask for proof of age?" Frank asked.

"No. We began going there whenever we would go bowling, so we became regulars. One new waiter did ask if I was eighteen, and my friend said she was."

"What other crazy things?" Frank asked.

"We also went up to Tanglewood and Jacob's Pillow Summer Festivals with a teacher and a group from school, over summer weekends, and she and I would wander off by ourselves. Around the local town. Backstage. That kind of thing. We met John Cage and Merce Cunningham, Leonard Bernstein, a whole bunch of pianists and violinists, and of course a lot of dancers, as she was so interested in Modern Dance. We just pretended we belonged there. Or, we'd hang out in this pub in the town where they all congregated after performances, when we were supposed to be sleeping."

"At fifteen?"

"At fifteen. Oh, and at sixteen, after our senior prom, which was held in a hotel ballroom in midtown Manhattan, we all went to a nearby restaurant. She and I ordered liquor and got a little tanked. By then it must have been two-thirty in the morning, and while the others began arguing about where to go next in the limo we'd rented, the two of us danced down Broadway, right down through the nearly empty street, pretending we were Fred Astaire and Ginger Rogers. It was like a scene out of a movie. We were all dolled up in tuxedo and gown, right? The sanitation guys stopped work to watch us from their truck. The policeman on the corner stopped twirling his baton, the guy at the newsstand stopped unpacking newspapers. And they all applauded us. So we bowed, and casually strolled back to the limo."

"Down the middle of Broadway?" Frank was amazed.

"From 47th Street to 42nd Street. I was sixteen. She was seventeen." Victor laughed recalling it. "Another time, she wanted to hear the Beat Poets at the Metropole Café on the Lower East Side. Second Avenue and what? Eleventh Street? Around the corner from St. Mark's Church. So we took a bus and subway into the city and went there, dressed in black slacks with dark turtle neck sweaters, and berets on and all. Little baby beatniks."

"Did you hear Ginsberg?"

"We heard Ferlinghetti *and* Ginsberg, and then Ginsberg's boyfriend, Peter Orlovsky, began reciting a poem spontaneously as Allen sucked his dick."

Franks's popcorn sputtered out of his mouth.

"Onstage, about six feet away from us," Vic added, giggling. "He called it 'Blowjob Ode.'"

"What did your friend think of that?" Frank asked.

"I guess she knew about blow jobs. I certainly did, so we remained cool, dragging on our *Gitanes* cigarettes, sipping *Pernods*, occasionally snapping our fingers, like everyone else in the room."

"Okay! Okay! All that's pretty crazy for sixteen-year-olds. You use words accurately. Not everyone does. I was just checking. So, years later, your friend comes to dinner, and . . . ?" Frank prodded.

"And we meet in the Café Figaro in the Village, for old times' sake. We have dinner then wander through the Village to near where I'm living in the far West Village. We sit in Abingdon Square Park and she begins telling me about living in Paris and this bummer love triangle she's now in. Her best friend from when they were four years old. *And* the woman's husband, who my friend is passionately involved with.

"We talk till, I don't know, one, one-thirty, and she suddenly remembers the bus from the train to her parent's house stops at one o'clock. Can she stay at my place?

"So we walk there, and I give her a big old t-shirt as pajamas. She'll sleep on my single bed, while I sleep on the floor on the mattress. But we're up talking and finishing off my cheapo wine until maybe three or four. Then we go to sleep. Nothing happens—obviously. She's passionately involved with this Guillaume or whatever his name is. And we never had a sexual friendship anyway when we were kids.

"She leaves next day, all well and good, I walk her out to the subway since I'm also going there, headed to work, myself. But when I get home later that evening, the phone caller rings—my Anna-Marie—and she begins in on me and my friend, calling her a whore, and all kinds of names. This about a very nice young woman, and about this very sweet, friendly, completely chaste night that we two had catching up, sleeping ten feet apart. At this point I realize that my caller is obsessed with me to the point that anyone who stays overnight will come under attack, and that's when I end it."

"Just like that?" Frank asks.

"Absolutely. She's already acting like a psycho. I've got enough problems in my life. I don't need a psycho who won't even agree to show her face or meet me. So it's *arrivaderci, baby!*"

"Unlike Theo. And your woman friend?"

"I didn't see her nor even hear anything about her for years and years. Then I heard from mutual friends that she had moved to a Kibbutz in Israel. Sometime later on, I heard from a mutual woman friend that she married a Sabra and is raising a family there."

"So this really happened to you?" Frank asked, now holding up the paperback of *Justify My Sins*.

"Up to that point, yes. You have to understand, Frank, I was already somewhat kind of pissed off when I discovered she could *see* me, and was *watching* me! Although that was mixed, too, you know, because I didn't mind showing off for her and all. But this business with my friend, ruining a nice evening like we'd had, I guess that was my personal breaking point."

"You never found out who she was?"

"I had my theories. Directly across my street were several single-family townhouses. She could have been a servant, a nanny or nurse, who lived in the top floor of one of them. The top floors there would be slightly higher than my fourth story walk-up, and so would provide the right angle for her to see as far into my studio as she supposedly could. Either that or she lived above and behind those townhouses in the huge twenty-story high-rise, and she might be looking out from any of dozens of windows."

Frank asked Victor to clarify what he meant.

Instead, Victor grabbed a piece of paper and drew the parallel lines of the short Greenwich Village street. He dotted his apartment in the middle of one line. Dotted the townhouses opposite. Drew in the yards behind those buildings, and sketched the enormous apartment tower behind those fronting 12th Street.

As Frank asked more questions, Victor got another sheet of paper and began drawing the buildings in architectural elevation: the two rows facing each other, the taller apartment building behind the row of townhouses. This allowed Frank to see sight-lines between one set of windows to the others.

"This is great!" Frank said. "It's our set. At least our basic exterior set! *'Fade In. Act One. Scene One. Theo turns onto his street and advances toward his building. He can hear his phone ringing through an open window upstairs,'*" Frank said as though reading a film script. He stood up and pressed a phone button and a few seconds later Sam Haddad came in, surprised.

"You were so right, Sam. This guy's a genius. He just gave us the layout of our first and most needed set. Have copies made of this and send some out to . . . who's the guy we used on *Mommy Dearest?*"

"Bill Malley. He'd be perfect. He does intimate well. But he's up to his ears over at Paramount with several projects."

"What about Joe Chevalier, who we used for *Monsignor?*"

"I'll call and see if he's busy," Sam said and exited.

Frank was musing. "What you described? That night together? Sleeping ten feet apart? I don't know if it could have happened to guys of my generation."

Had Frank momentarily forgotten Victor's sexuality?

"She was very attractive, Frank. But we were *friends,* remember? Also, she *had* spent much of the night telling me how nuts she was for this other guy."

"No. No. You're right. You're right," Frank admitted

"When I was in school I was cute," Victor said. "No boast, point of fact. Girls were jumping on me all the time. But what I discovered in high school and college, especially through this young lady, was that sometimes a sexual relationship is the *least* interesting kind you can have with someone you really like."

"Tell me," Frank said, suddenly dispiritedly.

They went to work with the scenario, breaking it down into smaller and sometimes slightly different scenes than what Victor had laid out the previous morning.

Meanwhile, Frank paced. Meanwhile, Frank consumed a quart of unsalted, unbuttered popcorn. Meanwhile, Frank made phone calls upon suddenly remembering something or somebody.

Victor remained where he was all the time except once, when he used the washroom. In between Frank's phone calls, he would continue to methodically fill in the spaces of his *Times* puzzle. *It's so odd*, Victor thought, *here* I'm *the calm one. Me! The calm one! Mark would laugh at that.*

Frank had to take one phone call privately—his wife?—and so Victor went out to Sam's office.

"He's nuts about you," Sam commented.

"It's early," Victor disparaged. "Wait till he gets to know me."

"How's the house you're in?" Sam asked.

"The people next door went away while they're having the roof replaced. The first few days weren't bad, but now they're putting the new one on. Bang bang! Bang bang! From 8:00 a.m. on. Bang bang. You may have to come bail me out of the Beverly Hills jail. *Is* there a Beverly Hills jail?"

When Victor got home, there was a message on the answering machine. It was from a very perplexed and somewhat sleepy Mark Chastain back in New York, asking what Victor's note was all about. He didn't really understand it, and where *was* Victor anyway? Victor should stop fooling around and come home. Mark left an hour by hour schedule of places and names and phone numbers where he could be reached for the rest of the night.

"Guess the casseroles ran out sooner than I'd planned," Victor said, then laughed at himself, adding, "You've become such a hardened Hollywood bitch!"

CHAPTER EIGHTEEN

It took a while before Victor got up the nerve to call Mark. He knew he shouldn't feel guilty, but somehow he did, as though he'd abandoned ship, when in fact *he'd* been the one abandoned. Speaking with Jeff, Gilbert's b.f. and now a board-licensed psychologist, Victor had brought up his hesitation about talking with Mark and the guilt that he felt.

"Only natural," Jeff said. "You snuck out on him."

"Excuse me!" Victor corrected him. "He wasn't actually *there* long enough for me to sneak out on. And it is my apartment, which by the way I continue to pay rent on."

"True, true," Jeff mused. "But those are all *rational* points. When you feel guilty, it's always *irrational*."

That seemed true enough. But if Jeff were on the other end of the line right now, Victor would have to admit that it was because he was feeling extra-super-guilty that he was calling Mark at all. And the reason he was feeling extra-super-guilty was because of Jared Clapham.

Clapham was a roofer: in fact, one of two roofers working on Mopsy and Danny Porter's house next door. Bang-Bang. Bang-Bang. From 8:00 a.m. on, as he'd told Sam. *How* Victor and Jared had met was an intrinsic, indeed the crucial, element of the guilt Victor now felt. Victor had returned from a second visit to Andy Grant's place in Topanga Canyon and had been so dirty, sweaty, and dust-covered from yet another drive and on-foot trek to the hallowed television shooting spot, already mostly emptied of actors and humpy cameramen, and back, that once home at Mulholland Drive, he'd taken a second shower.

Victor's rented house was positioned high atop a ridge that ran through Los Angeles like a humped and distorted spinal chord. Given the unseasonable temperatures that had persisted all day, and with the sun still shining brilliantly, when Victor emerged into the twenty-by-ten foot patch of back garden still shaking off the shower water, he decided to plop down and obtain some rays. Unlike his previous trip, he'd not done much sun bathing since he'd arrived. He'd not gone to the beach, not even been near a pool. Now was the chance to make up for it. Somewhere on the surface of his mind was an idea that he might even get a head start on the tanning and so not burn when he began to go about it more seriously this summer.

One of the minor banes of Victor's life was how he could so easily be burned to a crisp. Because of his half-Mediterranean ancestry, he would still look like a feckless Greek sailor lad, exciting the envy of friends and strangers alike, who would ooh and aah over his golden skin, while he rushed home panicked to pour on another pint of pure aloe vera so he could even think through all the itching and pain. He could thank his mother's Scots ancestry for that particular dermal betrayal. She and his sister Cathy had at least received armsful of auburn hair and gray green eyes to compensate; all Victor had received was Mendellian-dominant and dull-near-to-death "br/br" ones, as his driver's license so accusingly read—and natch, the damned sun-skin sensitivity.

So he had been lying there on his tummy for close to an hour, eighty percent enthralled and twenty percent mystified by the Polish sci-fi writer's first novel. *The Invincible* was the story of an investigation from orbit and then on the ground of an alien planet's single life form. The Earth scientists could not for the lives of them figure out what anything on the unpeopled world really is or how it works, especially that primitive yet dangerous, possibly animal, possibly plant, possibly machine life-form that appears to have inexorably taken over everything else on land. Suddenly he felt a thump next to his *chaise longue* that was too quick and light to be an earth tremor.

He'd been listening through very good earphones to Bach's *Partita #1* with Glenn-boy's vocal accompaniment, and so he hadn't heard anyone approach. Now he took the phones off and was about to turn around, when he saw a pair of tan work boots before him.

Raising his head he made out sturdy if slender legs in well-worn jeans, diagonally defined at the hip by a work belt holding a variety of serious-looking implements. Above that, a shirtless, Apollonian torso and head, the latter capped by a yellow plastic construction hat. The eyes were hidden. What he could see of the face was tan, square-jawed, and kinda' lovely.

"I *said,*" Apollo shouted, "you're going to *burn like a mother!*"

He tipped back the hat brim and his brow was revealed to be equally rectangular and flat, the eyes pale, pale green, the mouth wide, amused and slightly open, the nose strong, flat, almost cat-like. Correction: the face was perfect—and godlike.

"I couldn't hear you," Victor said, "since I had to put on these earphones to block out all the *goddamn noise* you were making next door." He wasn't willing to give even an inch, not even to a newly-dropped-from-heaven construction-god.

"We're done now."

"For good?"

"For the day."

"Then go away! What's keeping you?" Victor put the earphones back on and returned to his book.

Instead the roofer hunkered down in front of Victor. When Victor looked up, the guy was still speaking.

Victor removed his headphones. "Explain why are you still here blocking my rays?"

"I was saying that if I don't 'block your rays,' you and especially that bare little ass of yours, is going to get good and burned."

Victor looked back over one shoulder at his ass. It didn't look in the least burned. Not even pink.

"I'm out in the sun all day," the roofer continued, "so I'm a professional on these matters. Oh, by the way, the name is Jared, Jared Clapham. Don't bother. I already know your name and who you are, and . . ." withdrawing a little bottle of some thick white, viscous-looking fluid that he opened and dripped onto one much work-cut and scarred but quite sturdy index finger, "this stuff has toasted me to an even light brown, and it can do the same for you, without any burning."

Before Victor could tell him to get lost again, Jared had dropped some of the goo, immediately cooling and wonderful, upon Victor's bare shoulder and then reached over him and began smearing it all over both his shoulders and his upper back.

Since Jared had to lean forward to do so, this placed his deni-med crotch and most particularly a long tubular object within it in sudden proximity to Victor.

Good lord, he thought, *is that thing for real?*

Jared was continuing to reach over, and as his transfixed victim made no move to get up, the roofer now slid around to one side (cleverly always keeping the boner in partial view) and now be-gan slathering down Victor's back.

"I can see your skin is thinner than most folks. I can tell by the blue shadow beneath." (It was.) "I'll bet you're the first one in any group to get mosquito bitten!" (He was.) "I've got a friend with a similar thin olive complexion and he burns like crazy, so I'm guessing you do too." (Of course, he did.) "Which is why you've really got to cover it all! Every inch!" (Go ahead! Do it!)

And so doing, he now went to work on Victor's baby smooth glutes. "Especially these darling little cheeks, which will bake to a high red if not properly attended to."

Victor turned to watch the boner in denim take on a life of its own, thumping slowly but steadily against the encasing material. He then turned to watch Jared's face and his concentration—that of a five-year-old tying his shoe—as he smeared on the lotion. He then noticed the guy wore a wedding ring, for Chrissakes, and so Victor dropped his head and thought, *You're just fantasizing, idiot.*

Until, that it is, one lotion-filled finger went right up against and then slowly slid into Victor's anus.

Victor jumped up, knocking the roofer aside, grabbing the towel he'd been reclining upon for front cover. "Okay, Mister Ja-red whatever your name is. That is *just about enough.*"

"You want a thorough covering don't you?"

He'd caught himself from falling over and now stood.

"How about going home and finger-fucking your wife?" Victor suggested, pointing to the ring.

"My wife is in Biloxi, Mississippi." (*Real big surprise that*, Victor thought.) "Many, many miles away. Listen, Victor, may I call you Victor? I had to break off work early today onaconna' I was so dis-tracted by your sweet little—"

"If I would have known that, I would have exposed it two days ago," Victor said. "If only to stop *all the fucking noise.*"

Jared dug into his pants pocket and came up with a little square plastic sealed package. It read, "Flents." Smaller print read, "40 Decibel Resistance."

"I got these for you."

Jared opened the packet and demonstrated how they would go into Victor's ears. "Best, least troublesome earplugs on the market."

Well! That was considerate of him.

"I know you're trying to concentrate in there, while we're hammering," Jared now said, a tad too seductively to be contrite.

"These going to work?" Victor asked.

"Sure they will," Jared cajoled. "Why don't you lay down again? I wasn't quite done. Your upper thighs need some too."

"I'll just bet they do."

"I looked you up," Jared said. Meaning he knew that Victor was gay—famously gay, *notoriously* gay. "Saw your books in Waldens."

"That doesn't mean I'll let just *anyone* . . ." Victor began, then stopped. Because *Nights in Black Leather* said exactly that. So, he rephrased it a bit: ". . . put just *anything* up my butt."

"Well once you get to know me, I won't be 'just *anyone*,'" Jared argued, then added, "and it won't be 'just *anything*,' either."

"Meaning what? You swing both ways?"

"Most definitely."

Jared's hands, thumbs hooked into each denim pocket, were spread open now, perfectly outlining the denim-bound Thumper.

Victor was thinking, *Wellllll, okay, come in. I'll do you, but I won't let you fuck me*, when they both heard the motor of a truck pull up next door.

"Hell! That's Mort. He must have come back for something. He'll see my Ram still parked and wonder where in hell I am."

"You'd better go," Victor said.

Jared turned and leaped five feet up onto the stone wall that defined the two back yards. As as he turned, Victor dropped the towel back on the chaise, preparing to lying down again.

"Man!" Jared whispered loudly, "I sure do want to come back and visit!"

As Victor began smiling, Jared said, "What say tomorrow I send him home early? You be out here again! You hear me?"

"Won't Mort notice me?"

"Naww. He's working on the other side of the house. And anyway he's . . ." Jared drew four sides of a square with his hands, meaning he was too dumb to pick up on anything. "C'mon. Whattya say?"

"We'll see," Victor said coyly and collapsed onto the chaise, deliberately lifting his rear as much as possible

"Hot damn!" was the last thing Jared uttered before another voice said, "There you are, Jay," and their voices went off together, out of earshot.

Well, nothing actually happened, Victor reminded himself. And possibly nothing *still* might happen, although that was pretty unlikely. Semi-intelligent Southern White Trash with big penises were, if not his number one physical type, then at least way up among his top three. It was about as perfect a set-up for marital unfaithfulness as Victor had ever experienced.

Ergo the guilt. Ergo his needing to work up his nerve before dialing *Nueva Jorck*. He could see by the schedule he had copied down that Mark would be at someone named Wayne Ralph's place, studying.

"House of Doom!" an unfamiliar baritone voice answered. "You have reached Doom Master Wayne. To what section of Hell may I direct your call?"

"How about putting Sacrificial Goddess Mark on the line."

"And this is?" the apparently amused and suddenly recognizably African American voice asked.

"This is Avenging Angel Victor."

"Ah, so!" Off the phone, "It's your lover boy."

"Vic! Hold on." Mark, sounding frantic. "I want to take this in another room."

A few minutes later, Mark was on the phone again. "You there?"

"Right here."

"Where is 'here' exactly?" Mark asked.

"'Here' is upper Benedict Canyon, just inside the Beverly Hills City Line . . . As I wrote in my note."

"Well . . . about that note . . . " Mark began.

Victor didn't like the way this was going at all. "Yessssss?"

"Well, well," Mark paused, clearly flummoxed. "What are you *doing* there, anyway?"

"If you'd *read* my note—"

"I *did* read your note."

"—you would *know*," Victor continued, "that I was coming out here to write a script with director Frank Perry based on my second novel. Did you get *that far* reading the note?"

"Of course I got that far," Mark said. "I just don't understand *why* you're there."

Oh, honey, Victor thought, *don't do this!*

"I mean, couldn't you write it *here?*" Mark asked.

"Neee-ooo. Because Frank Perry and I are writing the script *together*! Meanwhile, he's shooting one movie and finishing off another movie. Here! In Los Angeles! The place where people make movies! Is any of this becoming clearer?"

"Yeah sure. I mean I know all that. What I mean is why did you *go?*"

And here we are, Victor thought, *at the crunch*. Evidently Mark was doing well studying up on litigation techniques.

"Because, Mark, Frank Perry wanted me more than you did."

"*What*?!" Then, "You're not sleeping with him?"

"Don't be silly. He's older. He's straight. He's *definitely* not my type. There's no possibility of sex, never mind romance. It's all work related. And, Mark, *even so,* Frank clearly wanted me more than *you* did." Victor waited a beat. "I guess I was tired of not being wanted by anyone for *any* reason. So I came here to work with him for *his* reason."

He waited while all that sunk in. He could almost hear it all slither in, working its way around and through specialized torts and Ratchett vs. Minnesota, et al.

At last: "You're coming back, though, right?"

"Eventually."

"When?"

"Remind me when your Law Boards are?"

When Mark didn't answer:

"Sometime after that," Victor clarified. Then added. "And of course, when our script is written."

Now Mark sounded very sober. "I really screwed up, didn't I?"

"You're busy studying. Why even think about all this?"

"No, I mean I *really* messed up badly, didn't I?"

"You made a decision, Mark—or maybe you just let a decision be made for you—and now we're stuck with it. I don't know what would have happened if I'd stayed there. Maybe I would have bludgeoned you to death in your sleep and hung myself. This might be a *good* thing."

"Oh, man! I am such an asshole!" Mark despaired.

"Look, Mark. You don't need any of this right now. Why not just concentrate on what you're doing? Study hard. Pass the Law Boards. I'm here rooting for you."

"You're *there*, being the point. Oh, my God, I'm such an utter asshole," Mark's voice was beginning to crack. "I don't want to lose you, Vic. I don't know how I let this happen. Say you'll come back."

"Of course, I'll come back. It's my apartment, remember?"

Oops. That didn't help.

"Oh, God. I'll leave. I'll move in with someone else."

"I don't *need* the apartment, Mark. I've got a seven room house in Beverly Hills, rent free! Listen, Mark. Listen, okay? This. Is. What. Is. Happening! You are studying for your Law Boards in New York. I am writing a script to my novel in El Lay. These are both things we want to do! So we are doing them. How it happened, how we arrived at this point where we're three thousand miles apart, for several months, isn't really the point. It's not important. It's not useful. It's not worth going into. We are doing *these things*. Do you understand?"

Mark was almost in tears, "I was just telling the guys today how I've never been happier. I mean never, Vic. Never in my life."

Oy! Gott in Himmel! Now I've got to comfort him?

"Look, someone is at the door. I've got to go answer it. If you're still upset tomorrow, talk to Gilbert's boyfriend, Jeff. He's a therapist."

"Don't go!" Mark was shouting into the phone.

"This is the right thing for the two of us now, Mark. Take a few minutes and think it through and you'll see I'm right."

"I don't have any money or I'd fly out there," Mark moaned.

"You don't even know where I am!"

"I'll borrow it. Between all of us, surely we can—"

"Now I really *am* hanging up, Mark," Victor said. "Talk to Jeff!" and he hung up the phone, thinking, *Well that was about as bad as I envisioned it. Maybe even a little worse.*

Suddenly there *was* someone at the front door ringing the bell. Victor looked out the entry door's side glass and it was Sam Haddad standing there, a long thin white plastic bag in hand. Victor opened up.

"Look I know this is unexpected and all . . ." Sam began nervously. He looked inside. "You're not real busy or anything?"

"I just got off the phone," Victor said. "You look kind of . . . rattled. There a problem?"

He immediately thought: *Frank has changed his mind and wants to drop my project and he's sent Sam to do the dirty work.* And after all Victor had just told Mark!

"Not about you. No. God, no," Sam said. "That's all fine. Like I said before, Frank is nuts about you and you guys are making great headway and all. But I just have to talk to someone about something and I think you know enough and— Can I come in?" he interrupted himself.

As he asked, he held up the bag and pulled out an unopened quart of imported Vodka. "I thought this might grease the wheels a little."

"Yeah, sure." Victor was intrigued, and moved aside to let the younger man in. Was it his love life again? Had Sam finally gotten into that three-way with another guy?

"Something smells nice!" Sam sniffed the air within the entry.

"Me. New sun tan lotion," Victor explained.

"So! . . ." Victor said once the two of them were seated in the big top floor living room.

The February sun was setting quite splashily through the floor-to-ceiling windows through a scrim of eucalyptus and fir trees behind, making the valley below them look like a double page spread from a Thomas Guide map as it glimmered and glowed in horizontal grid-works of reds and oranges and golds and pale greens. "What's up, Sam?

"I'm pretty sure Frank's in love," Sam spurted out, then downed his Vodka neat and poured some more for himself. "Not with his wife."

"I see," Victor said, although he didn't at all "see" why it was any of Sam's or his business.

"Since she kind of works for the company, my gut tells me it's going to end badly—for all of us," Sam added. "Unless we do something about it."

"Meaning?"

"Meaning total disaster."

"That part I understood." Victor had, in fact, felt a sudden chill up his spine. "What I meant was, what you and I can do?"

"Well, one, it concerns a script. Two, I hold the checkbook," Sam said. "So, three, maybe I could hire you, perhaps under another name entirely, to help keep the disaster from happening. Or from happening quite so badly."

"How much are we talking about?"

Victor meant to be funny. But Sam was very serious indeed as he said, "If it works, my man, it is a *seller's market.*"

Meaning Victor could name his price.

"Well, now," Victor reached for more Vodka and more tonic for himself and then topped off Sam's drink, "You *definitely* have my attention. Tell me everything."

CHAPTER NINETEEN

The "problem script" had been with Victor for nearly week already as it turned out. Well, not the script itself, but the scenario for it. That first meeting at Black Hawk Films' Beverly Hills office, as they were leaving, Victor had asked: "By the way, is there a specific format you prefer to have your scenario written in? Since that's what I'm doing first?"

In response, and as he was putting on his jacket to step out of the office, Frank Perry had looked over his desk, moved some papers, and tossed Victor a twelve page scenario.

Two days later, when Victor had to type up his own work on the IBM electronic word processor thoughtfully set up in the sun-filled office just off the living room in the Benedict Canyon house, he scanned what Frank had given him. He set margins, type-size, type-face, and paragraphs to match it. He also followed the layout and underlining and when to use all caps.

But for the life of him, he'd never thought this was the scenario of a film they were about to begin production on a mere four weeks from now.

In fact, Victor had assumed it was a "throwaway," something that had come in from an agent or over the transom, and had been summarily turned down, but not yet tossed in the waste paper basket.

Why had he thought that? Well, the story was silly, the characters were ciphers, the dialogue was unrealistic and inane, and the plot had logic holes you could drive a twelve-wheeler truck through. That's why.

So, when Sam Alan Haddad told Victor the film Frank was about to make because he was infatuated with its female writer, and when it turned out to have the same name as the scenario Frank had given him, Victor unconsciously stood up, as though to put distance between himself and Sam. Only a moment later, when he noticed what he'd done, did Victor go back and re-seat himself in the chair facing the sofa, Sam, and the by-now completely set sun.

"I see," Sam said, "that you've read the script."

"Only the scenario. I'm sure once it's all fleshed out, it's a lot better than—"

Victor's belated attempt to be diplomatic failed.

"In fact, once it's fleshed out," Sam said, "it's a lot worse."

"How can that be possible?" Victor laughed nervously.

"I brought you a copy," and Sam drew it out of the plastic bag he'd walked in with. "So you can see for yourself."

Sam tossed it on the polished-to-a-spit-shine chunk of redwood between them where it sat, pink covered and vaguely radioactive with the potentiality of its sheer badness.

"Ideally," Victor began, "what you'd like is . . . what?"

"For her to die and for Frank to suddenly come down with just enough amnesia to forget the entire past few months."

Sam wasn't making a joke

"And, failing that unlikely eventuality?"

"She's gone back east. They speak daily. Well, they speak whenever I can't stop them from speaking. But she's—believe it or not—also married, and so she's got to be with hubby . . ."

"Who is an orthopedic surgeon?" Victor asked, since that's what the dim heroine's equally jejune ex-husband was in the dopey scenario.

"Exactly. She's got to be with hubby long enough for him to not suspect anything is going on."

"Which, anyway, it's not! Right?"

"Which anyway it's not, I strongly hope!" Sam clarified. "The upshot is that she will *not* be around for the next months at least of pre-production and few weeks of early shooting, although she did threaten a weekend with some local cousin's child's *Bat Mitzvah* in the period somewhere, as an excuse to spend a weekend here."

"You'd like me to rewrite it pretty much as they are shooting it? Change the pages every day?"

Sam nodded.

"But won't *someone* see the difference, even if Frank is too besotted not to? Won't, say, the lead actress see her part is slowly changing from the ridiculous to the, well, if not sublime, at least to the not totally awful?"

"Well . . ." Sam hesitated, then spat it out, "That's another, and equally large, problem."

"The lead actress is as big a problem as this script?"

"Perhaps bigger," Sam said and poured them both new drinks. "You see, this hot new agent, Joel Edison, has joined forces with Miss Hot Pants Script Writer to convince Frank Perry that this should be a vehicle for ____ ____," and he named a television actress who had just left the top-rated comedy of the past three years on the boob tube.

Victor was stunned. "Are we talking about the same Joel Edison who used to be a waiter at Ed Trefethern's favorite restaurant?"

"He became *maître 'd* there," Sam said, "but yes, him."

"The plot thickens," Victor thought, recalling how Joel had chased him around the Club 8709. "Joel used to be partial to me."

"Three years ago, he sucked me off at a screening, and I'm not even bi," Sam said. "He followed me into the john, cornered me in a booth urinal, begged, slobbered all over my pants-front. It was like being attacked by some kind of gay Alien. He doesn't understand the word 'no.' Finally, I just let him."

"Me three," Victor allowed.

"He's probably blown half The Biz by now," Sam added.

"Explaining his fancy new job."

"Not Frank however. He's old school and probably would run screaming from the john. At least I think he would. At any rate, Monster Girl Actress is Joel's client, as is Miss Hot Pants Script Writer, which is how the two met, and no doubt how he's foisting her onto Frank and onto the movie, which should never be begun anyway."

"Speaking of girls," Victor said. "You're not seeing that same young woman as when—"

"She left me for some old guy with lots of money."

"The woman writer convinced Frank to hire the Monster Girl Actress?" Victor asked for clarification.

"And both stink."

That was pretty clear.

"Maybe I should pay a visit to the her, in the capacity of . . . ? What?"

"Co-producer? Exec-producer?" Sam liked the idea.

"And say to her . . . ? What?"

"Anything. Tell her she has to kiss a gorilla. No. She might like that."

"She left you for some old guy with lots of money?"

"I was *so ready* for her to leave. I celebrated by buying a Porsche."

He got up and looked out the window. Victor joined him staring at the bright little Targa 46 sitting like a yellow and chrome insect that had just alighted on the driveway tarmac.

"Very Cute. Congratulations."

"To hell with women. I'll just whack off and pamper my Porsche. Look. I just bought it a black leather bra."

Victor couldn't miss the front bumper accessory.

"I'm not going to ask what you do with that machine exactly, Sam, nor comment on how sick a fucker you've become."

"I've no shame when it comes to 'Lotte." Sam all but drooled ogling his car.

Lotte: short for Charlotte, as in Goethe's *The Sorrows of Young Werther* or in Mann's *Lotte in Weimar*. Cute. Very *Deutsch.* Apt. Sick, but apt.

"About the Monster Girl Actress? Let me see what I can do," Victor suggested.

"If we can pull this off, I'll be forever in your debt," Sam said. Victor had to wonder how far that would actually extend.

CHAPTER TWENTY

"Stop right there!" she screamed. Then hushed herself and him while she carefully stage-whispered, "I. Think. They. Can. *Hear. Us.*"

Victor had just driven up to a split-level, wood-beamed suburban dwelling that looked identical to one he recalled from a Seventies TV series, either *The Brady Bunch* or *Eight Is Enough.* The residence was in that south-of-Ventura-Boulevard no-mans-land, not still Studio City, but surely not yet Sherman Oaks, so it might have been a house used for exteriors for either TV show.

More to the point, the huge front and side lawns were hummocked with many recently quite messily dug holes. Shovels and hoe-like instruments were sticking up out of a few with other, less easily identifiable, objects scattered close about.

The Monster Girl Actress (or MGA, as Sam and Victor were now calling her) was standing at the largest hole dug so far, right off the main paved walk to the entry. She was holding some kind of lengthy metal gadget Victor had never seen before, as well as what looked to be an enormous flashlight, and a thick wire-mesh enclosed lamp on a long extension cord. Scattered about her fishermen's thigh-high rubber boot-clad feet he could see small, deadly-looking barrels gaily decaled over with bright orange skulls, crossbones, and warnings—doubtless toxic killer.

Her boots were the least unexpected article of clothing the MGA had on. The rest of the outfit consisted of a bright scarlet closed-at-the-neck body stocking, long sleeved, and dropping down into her boots. That article of clothing was barely covered over with a tiny jumper patterned in a mucous green and drab yellow tartan, all of it accentuating how rail thin she was, with barely a boob to note. Her curly yellow hair was surprisingly Crayola yellow, and surely equally manufactured. Her face was pale, her eyes large, brown, and either determined or—and here Victor admitted to editorializing a smidgen—demented.

How she—a major television star about to embark upon a feature film career—could allow herself to be seen in that get-up amid this field of paraphernalia in broad daylight was what suggested that sanity had departed say about an hour earlier. This would prove to be not at all that far from the truth.

"Mole problem?" Victor asked.

"Is *that* what they are? Moles? I killed one at the beginning. And it looked like a big rat or a small beaver, but it had this mouth like a circular saw," she said, confidentially leaning on his arm. Her posture was not Miss Porter's School, instead resembling someone who had just been—unsurprisingly, given the surroundings—doing heavy digging.

"Sounds like moles," Victor admitted. "But wouldn't your neighbors know?"

He glanced around at the crinkled-up-in-the-middle café-curtained windows with little wedges of female faces peeering out, which, as he gazed, suddenly became flat and featureless and totally draped again.

"None of them have any. Only me!" the MGA confided. "See!" She grabbed him by a claw-like hand and dragged him around the house to one side, "There! Can you see?"

"You mean that stream bed?" he asked, innocently.

"*Stream bed?*" she accused. "It's the Highway to Mole Hamburger Hamlet!" she assured him. "They swim up it and land directly here and they burrow right in and, well, you can see what they've done to my gladiolas and rhododendra! Gone. My azaleas and dogwood. Eaten at the roots! My tulips and asters! Gobbled up like so many appetizers!"

"I've tried traps and toxins and they've worked sometimes. But insufficiently, so now," her eyes glittered as she spoke, still not letting go of his arm, "I've discovered another way." She dragged out the garden hose, which had a different nozzle than any he'd seen before on one end. "First I'm going to flood 'em with water. And if *that* doesn't work"—and here her voice lowered by degrees—"I'll gas the little mothas. Zyklon-14. You know what that is?"

Wasn't that, Victor wondered, *the formula SS Storm Troopers were accustomed to pipe into padlocked lorries overfilled with Jews?*

Before the horror could sink in, he tried changing the subject to the film.

She screwed up her face and looked at him clearly for the first time. "You're not," she hemmed and hawed, "what's his name?"

God? he wondered. *How could she tell?*

"Sam?" he asked.

"Sam!" she admitted, relieved. She clearly had only half a clue.

"No. But I'll be the guy who gives you script revisions on a daily basis," Victor said with more pure nerve than he ever thought he'd ever utilize with another human.

The claw hand came out again and her voice dropped even deeper and less easy to discern, "Well, just between us, it's a good thing. Because I love ____," she assured him, mispronouncing Miss Hot Pants Script Writer's first name, "and Joel swears up and down by her. But I did have a few ques-tee-ohns about the script myself. I'm not surprised they hired a Rewriter for it."

"Doctor," he corrected gently. "We're called script doctors!" he assured her, a fact that he'd only himself discovered yesterday.

"Well," she suddenly tossed her head, "more than once in the middle of a scene have I called out 'Is there a script doctor in the house!'"

She laughed inordinately at her joke, literally slapping one knee repeatedly.

"Right," Victor said as he kept subtly angling her toward the front door and, he hoped, privacy. She would allow herself to move a few steps before inevitably turning, as though inexorably drawn, to once again gaze upon the gutted miniature Gettysburg of her front yard.

"Then, you'll be okay with that?" Victor sounded to himself almost beseeching.

"Oh, sure!" she breezed back. "We used to get minute by minutes all the time."

Victor wasn't sure what that meant exactly but he could guess.

"Great. Then we'll be working together."

They spoke a few minutes more, and Victor now began edging

them back onto the street, toward where he'd parked the Z. The neighboring curtains, he noted, were once more wedged ajar with the trademark single eyes busily apeep.

He'd just made it into the car, had turned on the ignition, released the clutch and was caressing the gear stick into first when the MGA suddenly appeared at the passenger side window, fatal nozzle in hand pointed right at him, and yelled, "Make sure you call my agent and tell him all this. Because I get busy with other things and I forget. Do you hear?"

Joel Edison? Victor found himself thinking. *Must I—really?*

CHAPTER TWENTY-ONE

"But he's *gay*, so everything should be oh-*kay,*" Gilbert said when Victor found himself wondering what he should do about calling the *soi-disant* talent agent.

"Said Polyanna to the Ogre, just before it ate her whole and spat out hair, teeth, bones, and nails," Victor replied.

He was back at the house sitting at his desk, looking out the upper window facing east and thus at the Porter's roof, where Jared Clapham was lining up more roof tiles just prior to hammering them into place. The day had turned cloudy and gray early and remained so, postponing one of Victor's more pressing problems—that is, what to do about sexy, ass-deprived Jared.

The roofer wasn't making matters easy. Whenever his partner wasn't speaking to him or looking at him, he would rub himself as though he had crotch-itch, run his tongue all around his rather nice looking lips, and in general make obscene gestures in what he knew was Victor's general direction. As a rule this would have been a complete turn off. Unfortunately, as Victor was himself very horny and interested, it more resembled a menu of a la carte entrees, hopefully to soon arrive, and so proved most distracting.

"Listen Gilbert, Frank's P.A.," Victor explained, "a straight boy, and so not given to queenly exaggeration, compared this Joel guy to the Alien in the film of the same name. You remember *that* particular creature, I believe," Victor added. They both knew very well that Gilbert had picked his way out of a very crowded row in the Criterion Cinema on Broadway during a preview screening of the horror flick directly following John Hurt's stomach-exploding scene. Gilbert had dithered in the rear of the theater throughout the following hour or so, then Victor had rejoined him, unable to not notice that his friend still sported a skin tone midway between Russian and Camouflage Army Green.

"I still don't understand," Gilbert groaned, "how a restaurant waiter becomes a talent agent."

"Remember that story I told you years ago, about how Joel seated me and Ed Trefethern next to Alan Ladd, Jr.?"

"Yes, but . . . "

"Do that a hundred times to a hundred people and one is bound to hire you. It's Aitch-Wood, Gilly! Look at Frank's number two guy! At Silver Screen Films, Sam was the low man on the totem pole. He spoke last in any meeting. He was asked last to any gathering. He seldom said a word in public. He never offered an opinion. And now—well, now he's got command of Black Hawk's check book."

"Who is Black Hawk, again?" Gilbert asked.

"*What*, not *who*. It's the name of Frank's film production company. Remember?"

"Oh, right. You know I woke with this god-awful headache today. Still kind of have it. Whenever I get these headaches, they really run havoc with my memory."

This was the first Victor was hearing of Gilbert's "god-awful" headaches—in the plural. "What does Jeff say about the headaches?"

"Oh, I don't want to bother him with my little problems. You know that Jeff's like one of the tip top people at G.M.H.C. And you have to admit it's kind of complicated keeping up with all these nick names you have. Miss Hot Pants Script Writer and Monster Girl Actress and all. Maybe if . . ."

". . . if you met them?" Victor finished the sentence. "Why don't you? Why not come out here? The house has two entire bedroom *suites* and a spare I use as an office. You'd love it. You always say how you'd like to come here." As he was suggesting it, Victor became enthusiastic: it sounded so right. "Why not take some of that time off you've been saving forever from Mistress Mike the Flower Demon and fulfill your L.T.H.D. Surely, Gilberto, you remember what *that* stands for?"

"Of course I do, L.T.H.D. is my Long Time Hollywood Dream!" Gilbert said.

For years, Victor and Gilbert had an entire, semi-private, language composed of acronyms—just like *The Man From*

U.N.C.L.E.—that they used in public to comment upon friends, competitors, and passers-by.

"Remember the rest of them?" Victor probed. "O.T.L.?"

"That's easy. Out To Lunch."

"N.L.Y.?" Victor tried.

"No Longer Young."

"Now some harder ones. U.T.K.?"

"Under The Knife—i.e., *le surgery plastique!*"

"What about the ever popular T.C.T.L?"

"Too Cute To Live, of course."

"See? You're not losing your memory. It's just napping. And no wonder! If the only people you associate with are Jeff's glabulous old psychiatrist buddies."

"Some are women. Is 'glabulous' a real word?"

"Buddies and *biddies*," Victor amended. "If it isn't a word, it ought to be. I'm enshrining it in my next novel, titling it *The Fabulous and the. . . .* " dropping and over-modulating his voice, ". . . *Glabulous!*"

"It sounds like chronic kidney arrest," Gilbert said.

"What say I book a flight for you? How's Saturday morning? My treat."

"Can't," Gilbert said and explained precisely what already set-in-stone-engagement meant he couldn't fly to El Lay. They went through the entire two weeks to come, day by day, and Gilbert couldn't, for one reason or another, change, postpone, or cancel a single thing.

This, while inutterably sad, alas confirmed Victor's long-held theory that only famously important people could ever really do anything in life, because unfamous ones were so busy trying to make their lives seem important to themselves and others by insisting everything they did simply could not *not* be done.

Fiddling with a large paper clip with which he was scraping his teeth, Victor then had one of those Proustian moments recalling that evening a year ago at his dear old friend Joseph Mathewson's apartment in the Village. Earlier in the day when they'd spoken, Mathewson, who wrote as much as Victor but who, alas, was published maybe once every nine or ten years, had asked Victor to pick up half of their dinner on the way, claiming that he would be "at his desk all day." Later on, when Joe was in the kitchen cooking, Victor had gone to Joe's study to look for the phone number of a mutual friend. He'd opened several desk drawers, the last of which contained what proved to be the single longest paper clip chain in human history. Joe never lied, and evidently here was the proof that he had "been at his desk all day."

"You know, maybe I shouldn't—*ever*—come there?"

"Gilberto! What *ever* are you talking about?"

"Since it *is* a longtime dream, how can the reality equal it?"

"Well, it can't. Not actually. But the city is all so big and so chock-filled with places and people and things of interest, you really won't *notice* that you're disappointed because so much else will be so intriguing. Mulholland Drive and its enormous double views only a few feet apart, overlooking the city and the valley. The delicious scoops of perfect beaches at Santa Monica Bay. The Hollywood Hills from a hundred feet above the famous Observatory. Huntington Beach with all those sweet surfer boys out all day on their boards, as seen from the long old pier. In their black wetsuits they appear like little licorice canapés or nori wrapped sushi that you could just lift up and gulp down.

"Take regular, boring, old Rodeo Drive," Victor continued. "It's right around the corner from Frank's office, so at times I walk it to where I've parked the car. Yesterday, I peered into the windows of Bijan, that men's clothing store some Persian guy opened? You'll never guess what I saw in the window?"

"Was it worse than the worst excesses of the French Revolution?" Gilbert asked his voice edged with a thrill.

"No, but it could easily *lead* to a revolution. A floor length white ermine coat. For a guy!

"And, Gee-Aye-El," Victor went on temptingly, "I noticed, behind the fortunately furred mannequin, one of those enormous Range Rover vehicles, all fitted out for hunting elephants for some Maharajah. It was painted white and gilded bronze where there should be chrome trim. And you'll never guess what?"

"What?" Gilbert almost squealed.

"The side doors were open and the upholstery was all white ermine, *exactly* matching the coat!"

"Ohmigod!" Gilbert moaned.

"And get this, Guilty-by-Association, the sale sign read, 'For *him*—just because you care!' Price? Seven hundred and ninety thousand dollars for the—are you ready?—quote hunting outfit and mobile equipment unquote."

"I think I just jizzed my Calvins!"

Despite this and other word-driven excesses, Victor could not get Gilbert to commit to any air flight date, even though Victor offered to pay for the airfare, all other travel costs, and even to fake his own imminent death to Gilbert's employer on the phone, pretending to be Mr. Onager, senior.

His best friend changed the subject several times, most notably back to their own close friend growing up, Andy.

"So he's rich now. Does he live in Bel-Air?" Gilbert asked.

"Here is one place you *will* definitely be disappointed. He lives on some cleft in Topanga Canyon like Little Abner and Stupefying Jones, among goats and in architecture of questionable provenance."

"But he's still a dirty old young man, right?"

"Not quite. He's become a voyeur. A rather specialized kind of voyeur." Victor described his two visits.

"Gosh, what'll he do now that the show is over? Stalk Popeye?"

"*Hawkeye* is, I believe, the name you mean. And I have no idea."

"So he's another one."

"Another what?"

"Another Homo who's totally given up sex. Tell me you're not. I mean I know you're guy-married and all, but the way guys used to throw themselves at you out there, surely that's not *totally* stopped? I know you're being extremely circumspect and all because of my big mouth, but feed me one little crumb. Please, please, Victoria."

"Well, okay, but this does not get repeated in person or by phone or you agree to die the death of a million tiny paper cuts!"

"Agreed."

Victor told him about meeting Jared and it wasn't actually sex, only flirtation, or at the most, foreplay, and so didn't count. However, it totally satisfied Gilbert—leading Victor to wonder if Jeff was still putting out, or if theirs, like many relationships during this epidemic, had become yet another sexless *marriage blanche.*

When they finally hung up, Gilbert said he was much cheered and claimed he no longer had a headache. But Victor couldn't fail to notice that they'd not selected a date for a plane trip.

Ten minutes later, Mark called—he now called twice a day, one way of making amends—and Victor found himself ending this second call by saying—"I know you have no time, but I've just got to know if my best friend in all the world has *it*. Would you go see him? And report back."

"Won't he think me visiting him a bit strange?" Mark asked, sensibly enough.

"Of course he will. Clever you. Why don't I send you something for him and you bring it over? I've found a cinematographer's visor-cap from a movie set Sam took me on the other day at the Fox lots. It's got the name of some movie printed on it and is totally authentic."

"He'll love that," Mark agreed. "You are a good friend. But, Victor, do you really want to know if he's that sick?"

"Don't I?"

"There's no cure. There's no treatment. It's all downhill from the diagnosis. You'd better think about it. I'll go, if you want, but . . . *really*, think about it."

Victor was in fact thinking about all the implications of that advice when the phone rang again. He was sure it was Mark and was about to say he'd thought about it and had changed his mind when a seductive male voice came on and said, "Sweetheart hot guy! I understood from one of my darling divas that you were coming to visit lonely little *moi.*"

At first Victor couldn't place the voice; then he *did* place it.

"Joel? Joel Edison?"

"*La meme!* See you at say—five? Let's go have a friendly drink. Mischa will come on the line now and provide all the gories. Ta!"

Seconds later a Byelorussian-accented male assistant was giving him directions and Victor was scribbling them down, wondering what he could possibly say.

CHAPTER TWENTY-TWO

On the way there, Victor just happened to pass a shop with a sign that read "Personal Security" and dashed to a sidewalk parking place.

"Are you sure you don't sell Chastity Belts?" Victor pleaded a few minutes later. "What about metal underwear with locks in front?"

"For . . . .?" the sleek silver haired gentlemen asked, baffled if unfazed.

"Me."

He looked Victor up and down and said, "Afraid not."

"I'm meeting with a talent agent!" Victor groaned.

Instead of saying, "Aren't you a little old for the casting couch, buddy?" he said, "I'm most sympathetic. We do have Mace."

"By now, he probably sniffs Mace like Poppers."

At the huge agency's outer office, where more people by far were leaving for the day than arriving, Mischa slouched over to fetch Victor. He was about twenty and looked a lot more like Mike-From-Cleveland despite his Mark Antony ash blond bangs. His bulky, dull, multi-colored knitted sweater flattened over an umber leotard and elf boots, and even given his slightly swaying walk, his posture could easily have resulted from being flogged with a ferrule during his growing years as punishment for performing inelegant *plies*.

"Here he is." The assistant lounged half across his employer's overfilled desk, introducing Victor. "I must go now—to doctor."

"Go! See if I care," Joel said, from his big swivel chair where he was on the phone.

"I must go. Bad lungs." Mischa explained. Or at least that's what Victor finally figured out he'd said: Mischa's pronunciation of the last word would have defied even Noam Chomsky.

"Who asked?" Joel made shooing movements. "*Raus! Raus!*"

The waiter-turned-maitre'd-turned-talent agent had always had a not uncute face and a nicely tight body. Seated there, alternately talking low on the phone and making apologetic faces at Victor for having to do so, he looked great. He wore a skintight pale blue Oxford shirt that clung to his far more muscled and filled out torso and arms, and when he hung up the phone and stood to shake hands, his Armani trousers were equally filled out.

"Look at you! I told everyone that the most sensational novelist in America was coming to visit and they left copies of your books to be autographed. In fact, the Financial Officer—an ancient and extremely hard-nosed snob who's been here since, I believe, the days when they represented Ouida and Ida Tarbell—left a hardcover of your third book, which he said is the best Western-horror novel ever. Who would have dreamed that a cute kid like yourself would turn out to be so lit-a-rare-ree?"

Although it was clearly an agent's Aitch-Wood spiel, it wasn't exactly what Victor had expected. Where was the come-on, the dirty leers, the innuendoes? And look—there were in fact six paperbacks where he'd pointed to on the sideboard, most of them *Justify My Sins*, natch, but also a few newer titles, including *Nights in Black Leather*, and the British hardback of *Heartache Canyon*, all with little post-its declaring whom he should autograph the book to. Had he planned this visit for a week? Seemed like it.

"You really want me to sign them?"

"You're a famous author."

As Victor was doing that, he realized two things. First that the old Joel Edison appeared to no longer be present, or if present, then strictly held in abeyance and Victor's chastity was therefore safe. And second, that was kind of too bad. He wouldn't mind a Joel looking this good attacking him.

"Great! *Perfecto!* Cal, the CFO, said to me earlier, 'You sure now how to pick the talent when it's hot, Joel-o-boy.'"

"What are you *talking* about?"

"Please. We all know you're writing a script with Frank. And everyone is talking about *the* collaboration of the year."

No. Really. What was *Joel talking about?*

Seeing his befuddlement, Joel tossed three magazines at Victor, saying, "At least that's what it says here. The dailies. I marked the relevant pages."

Victor had to sit to read the tiny one-liners about him and Perry that appeared lost in thick verbiage and small typed paragraphs in *Variety*, *Billboard* and *The Hollywood Reporter*.

"These are like . . . totally *minor* mentions—" Victor began.

"Those lines, Li'l Buddy, will get you entrée into every agency in town."

"One even has the title of the book wrong."

"Totally unimportant! These broke a week ago, I'll bet your film agent is fielding offers like crazy."

"I don't have a film agent," Victor said, and at that second he suddenly felt the extreme squishiness of the ground beneath his feet as the abyss slowly opened up, all but making a gross, sucking noise.

"'Shirley, you jest!' to quote one of my favorite lines from one of my favorite movies," Joel exclaimed.

"*Airplane*. No jest. Marcie's lawyer, some guy named Trent in New York, looked over Black Hawk's contracts," Victor explained. "I actually did the deal myself. I got a house, a car, free plane trips. The first two on loan of course."

"Not bad. Not bad. Although some writers get them, period," Joel added with much eyebrows. "But I'm not going to pressure you. I called and said let's go have a friendly drink so let's go have a friendly drink." He grabbed a jacket and opened the office door. "It's just around the corner. We don't even have to drive. New Yorkers!" he explained to someone's assistant still at her desk as they passed her, "they hate to drive!"

If they'd been in Manhattan, they'd have probably ended up in an Irish bar with a half dozen booths, and maybe even a few free standing tables. Instead, two steps out, Joel had taken one look at Victor's sport coat and said, "You're dressed enough for The Bistro Garden."

Only a few blocks away, it was already filling up with early bird diners—although of an older and much fancier generation than the usual breed.

The maitre'd knew Joel—Victor had to assume every maitre'd in town knew Joel by now—and seated them in a booth near an excrescence of yellow onyx that passed for a bar. Victor ordered a Dry Rob Roy, which Joel glanced askance at over his own lovely-looking huge Martini.

Victor was still trying to come to grips with a sexless, non-assaultive Joel. He couldn't quite believe it.

"My partner, the beautiful Mark Chastain, an unofficial Living Legend of Fire Island, and myself last year decided only to imbibe cocktails ordered by Bette Davis or Joan Crawford in their movies."

"Singapore Slings and such?" Joel asked.

"Sidecars and such," Victor confirmed.

"Living Legend, huh? No wonder I'm dirt under your fingernails," Joel said and sipped demurely.

Fishing for compliments, too. Why the lad appeared nearly human.

"You'll do," Victor said. "In fact, success looks good on you."

"Praise from Caesar . . . " Joel allowed.

"So tell me about your client list—especially your 'darling divas'?" Victor said.

"Must I? So soon in the evening? We were getting along so nicely."

That was amusing, if not quite witty. "Humor me."

"Well, this is not to leave this table but frankly I was a bit agog when Frank called to say he was optioning, never mind buying, one of my darling diva's scripts."

"Because . . ." Victor said, "it what? Needed work?"

"Because—you've grown quite diplomatic—but yes, it needed work, work, and more work."

"Then you must have been even more surprised when Diva Number Two was brought on board? Or was that entirely your doing?"

"I knew Diva *Numero Uno* knew Diva *Numero Dos.* So I mentioned her to him. I scarcely thought I'd be taken up on it."

"Because Numero Dos has no record on the big screen?"

"That's not precisely true. After all, she supported ____ ____ two years ago in that comedy. And it grossed forty-nine mil and change, North American. Now I know you're going to say that a Girl Scout cookie could have supported ____ ____ two years ago and it would have grossed forty-nine mil and change."

"That was refreshingly honest and utterly unexpected," Victor declared. *And even a bit witty*, he thought. "From all this, I take it, you won't be totally unhappy should I decide to come along and sort of underpin the entire operation. That, after all, is what some people close to the project, whose names we shall not mention, are asking me to do, you understand?"

"Not totally unhappy?" Joel lowered his voice. "Victor Regina, if someone of your caliber *doesn't* come along to underpin the operation, we may well lose the patient, if you catch my drift."

So he'd bitten off more than he could chew—and admitted it. Victor wondered if this was a possible first for Joel. "That's what my unmentionable source also thinks."

"I mean I've got other clients. But having those two—any two, really—tank in one fell swoop in something that's bound to be highly publicized? It's not high on my desk calendar for 1986, you know what I mean?"

"We've met. She's not *always* that nuts, right?"

"Not always. And not so much *nuts* as she's given to—well, enthusiasms, shall we say. But they're usually quite—temporary. And usually harmless."

"Really? Well, I wouldn't want to be *any* kind of rodent in the San Fernando Valley these days! What about the Diva on the east coast?"

"Well, that's a lit-tle more com-plick-ated." Joel polished off his Martini and caught the eye of a waiter for a second one. "Being a writer and all, she possesses wrongheaded ideas, in addition to enthusiasms." He smiled. "A fatal combo at best."

"The current wrongheaded idea being . . . ?"

"The current wrongheaded idea being that Frank is her *soul mate!* It's partly his own fault," Joel was quick to point out. "They're in cahoots on it."

"So I heard. It sounds extremely icky."

"Icky doesn't begin. If one was a real guy, they'd fuck and have it over with. If they were both gay men, they'd fuck and have it over with. If they were Lesbians, they'd discuss fucking and have it over with. But unfortunately, they are sensitive, semi-intellectual heterosexuals . . ." Joel's eyes rolled as he accepted Martini #2 and began to bite the edge of the glass and sip. "They have to make a big *megilah* over what seems to me to be a few overly lubricated hormones, instead acting like they're Paolo and Francesca for Chrissakes and, yes, I do know who 'dem old *Italianos* are."

"Comp Lit One?" Victor asked.

"Comp Lit Two." Joel reached over and put a nice looking and very well manicured hand over Victor's in a nice, not grabby way.

"I'll be so very grateful no matter *what* you do to alter in any way this—mess!"

"How grateful?"

"I'll take on all your books and try my best to sell them."

"Even *Nights in Black leather*?"

"Maybe not that one. Honestly, Victor! Who in the world would option that for film?"

Saith the queer to the queer, Victor thought, *about a queer novel*. He answered, "Rainer Maria Fassbinder."

"Who? What?! *No!*"

"Kid you not, Joel. Fassbinder read the German translation which is the best selling gay book ever in that country, and he told me he was very, very interested. We had three international phone calls. He wanted to set the action-murder-opening in Hamburg's shipping yards. Described in detail how he'd do it."

"Brilliantly of course. But Fassbinder, alas, is history now."

"So find me another Fassbinder."

"Easiest thing in the world. Just kidding. But look, I'll certainly go to bat for the first and third novels."

"My little play just closing Off-Off Broadway? Is that too gay?" Victor tried.

"It's too *little!* And," Joel admitted, "probably too gay, too. I did see it. Two months back. I was on a flying trip there to see two clients, including one client from hell, and I saw it listed in the papers and went. It was cute."

As later diners began coming in, they filtered over to the area where Victor and Joel were sitting, and of course they knew Joel and so soon there were a half dozen at the table, all in "the Business," natch, and all treating Joel well, or at least as an equal, and all seemingly happy to make Victor's acquaintance, whether they'd read the one liners in the dailies or not.

The last pair of guys to show up were a few years older than Victor. One was a dissolutely handsome actor with hair falling over his pitted-skin face who had never fulfilled his earlier potential but whose baby sister was busy working all the time. The other was an actor/producer, equally good-looking, aristocratic. As Joel quickly became engaged with the other man, and as the topics Victor and Joel were interested in had been discussed and done with, Victor and the actor/producer became instant table buds.

Joel loudly decided to join them and some other people for dinner right there, and though invited, Victor demurred. He had phone calls to make and receive from back East.

As he was leaving, the actor/producer he'd just met said, "He's some guy, huh? He signing you up? Or is he tucking you in nights?"

"He's trying to sign me up." Then, "'He tucking you in'?"

"When I was between wives," the actor/producer laughed. "I used to leave my door unlocked and he'd come by very late at night and"—the guy looked around to see if anyone was nearby watching or listening, and when he determined they weren't, he made a closed fist hand to his mouth gesture a couple of times. "Joel would—you know!" He laughed. "No muss, no fuss! I slept like a baby!"

Victor laughed with him.

As Victor stood up to take off, Joel gestured something vague at him: perhaps see you later? Or was it tuck you in later? Who knew for sure.

As Victor drove away, he thought about it. He didn't always remember to lock the Mulholland Drive House. Odd fact but true. Back east he'd carefully lock every triple lock. Here, he seldom thought about it, missed locking up half the nights, and he didn't kick himself the next day when he found the deck doors open or even the front door unlocked.

Maybe Joel had become more subtle.

And maybe Victor would find himself tucked in soon himself.

CHAPTER TWENTY-THREE

"I'm a little confused by the ending of the scenario"

Frank said—pretty much out of nowhere.

They had been working on the script itself, the opening ten minutes, that initial set-up of Theo's life at his office, his solitary life at home in his studio apartment, the phone calls just as he got home nearly every day with no one on the other end or someone suddenly hanging up. And then that fateful phone call when the person on the other end *didn't* hang up but instead turned out to be a young woman with a seductive British voice asking if he was the same Theo that a friend of hers had dated briefly. Theo's guarded response, "No." But then their initial conversation, which went on for some time and would lead to everything else that happened, that would eventually change both their lives.

Victor had assumed the basics of this Perry scenario had been all worked out two weeks ago, no? That's why they were working on the script itself now.

"O-kay," Victor said slowly, hoping his annoyance at the sudden shift in his creative thinking remained in at least *audible* check. "What's the problem? And where? Where, *exactly?*"

Fortunately for both of them, Frank knew exactly where the problem lay. He wasn't vague the way virtually all the people Victor had ever worked for in film or TV tended to be, with their "feelings" and their "impressions" and their oh-so-vaunted sense of something being "not quite right," which was about as useful to a writer as a quart of lemonade was to an ocean. Didn't they realize how much contempt professional writers had for "feelings" and "intuitions" that weren't their own and thus immediately accessible?

Frank's problem had to do with exactly where in Anna-Marie's suddenly darkened apartment she and Theo would each be at that climatic moment near the end of the script when Theo would use the key stolen from her building's super to get inside.

Perfect! This Victor could deal with.

As he began explaining, Frank stood up from the desk and went behind the other large leather-covered club chair in the room, where he crouched down. "I'm Anna-Marie hiding. Now where does Theo enter?"

So they acted it out, the exact motions, the counted number of steps each would make in the darkness (in the "film-set darkness"—after all, the audience had to be able to *see* them) vis-a-vis each other, and where each of them were as the two characters gestured and said certain key words of their final dialogue.

Victor purposely stumbled about a bit, being Theo carrying a flashlight with a faulty battery connection. Frank only crawled around the big office, being the crazed and terrified young woman avoiding Victor's determined, night-blinded young man.

Thus, a kind of dance ensued, until both of them somehow ended up at the corner at the front door of Anna-Marie's apartment, where she was trying to escape and where he was trying to cut her off.

Still crawling, the captured Frank stopped and looked up at Victor standing above him only inches away. "Gosh. That works pretty well, doesn't it?"

Even so, Frank had them go back four positions and repeat their movements.

Once again their movements dovetailed so they collided at the front door.

"It worked again!" Frank was amazed.

Victor pointed up the obvious. "It'll *always* work."

Frank stood up. "I was sure it *wouldn't.*"

"I visualized it for the book, Frank.. And if it worked for the book, why wouldn't it work in the film?"

"You mapped out both apartments?" Frank was baffled.

"In detail. I had to. Theo already has the floor plan in his head from her downstairs neighbor, remember?" Victor said. "The witchy older refugee? The one you want a far-too-young Ellen Burstyn to play? So *we* know *Theo* knows what he's doing once he causes all the lights in the building to short out and goes upstairs."

"I guess we must," Frank said in a totally uncertain tone of voice. Then added, "Never mind, then. Let's go back to the opening lines of conversation in the script again."

They did precisely that for the next hour or more. But Victor now had more ammunition to add to his next conversation with Sam Allen Haddad about how Frank Perry was really beginning to "lose it."

That saddened Victor. Even as it convinced him further that he and Sam were definitely doing the right thing, lining up people like the Monster Girl Actress and the Agent-formerly-from-the-*maitre'd*'s-station on their side to help salvage Black Hawk Films—and Frank, too, if it came to that—from the Movie From Hell Perry was intent upon making. What he still wasn't sure he believed was why Perry was making the movie: that Frank was in love with this unknown woman. Mrs. Perry, a chic, sophisticated, and it turned out pretty famous biographer had shown up at the office twice, and Victor was sufficiently taken with her to wonder if Sam was making it all up.

"You know, she helped me and Eleanor. Financially," Frank said.

He meant Ellen Burstyn.

"She got back her investment, of course. Other people helped us. In the beginning the biggest help came from Rock Hudson. I guess he and Eleanor had worked together on a picture before I met her, and he was at this party when we began talking about our first production together, her writing, me co-writing and directing. Rock said it sounded like a good project and he'd happened to have a windfall and he'd like to invest in our new company. He's the nicest guy."

Victor wanted to tell Frank that he knew Rock Hudson, or rather Roy Sherer, Jr., but in a more personal and social way than from some infra dig Hollywood party. A mutual friend of theirs, another writer, had introduced them for a "semi-glamorous gay weekend" a few years back when Victor was in San Francisco just finishing a book tour.

The three of them had met for dinner—Roy's treat—in a Market Street restaurant where the actor, by now a middle-aged and somewhat stout man, was known by the staff. They'd moved from there to a glory-hole palace South of Market that the other writer had been visiting regularly: two floors of little slatted wooden cells with no ceiling, a door, and four-inch round holes carved in the walls for someone's genitals or face or ass to come at you for particular attention. After about forty minutes of that, Victor and his buddy had met at the metal fretwork bridge connecting the upper level of cells, both of them sexually sated.

Then Roy showed up in a grumpy mood that he couldn't hide. No surprise. Victor had wondered when the writer first announced this particular stop if the patrons would snub Roy because of his middle-age spread. While Roy went to take a piss, the friend said, "My error. And a big one. This is not a good sign for the rest of our night." Victor knew they were headed to the Top of the Mark at midnight to hear Barbara Cook, and then tomorrow at noon they would all be flying down to L.A. for parties. "Look, if worse comes to worse," Victor stage-whispered, "Steer Roy into one of the darker rooms, and I'll do him myself!"

Just then Roy came their way and was half-seriously cruised by a younger guy. While their mutual friend tried to persuade the reluctant actor to follow the lad, Victor cut him off by going around another way and was able to utter what in future telling of the anecdote became the classic line: "Psst. Hey kid. Wanna blow a movie star?"

Turned out the younger guy already knew Roy, but from TV. He'd regularly watched Roy's successful series, *McMillan and Wife*. So it worked out fine. Roy was in high spirits the rest of the night.

Some minion had left Roy's Rolls Corniche—pale yellow with fawn rag top—at the Van Nuys airport, and when they arrived there the next morning, it was driven up and they cruised, top down, in summery weather climbing off the 101 up to Roy's house in the Hollywood Hills.

The actor had been going on about how that particular November Sunday happened to be his birthday, and how he was certain there would be a special gift from his agent or manager or some combo of them and friends waiting for him at the house. He was excited, a little kid.

Sure enough, when they arrived, there were mylar balloons

everywhere and twenty pretty guys between the ages of eighteen and twenty-two in various colors of Speedos frolicking in the pool and upon the terrace.

"Who *are* they?" Victor had to ask.

Roy pulled the Rolls into his garage and without missing a beat turned to him and said "The blondes are called Scott and the dark haired ones are named Randy."

How could Victor possibly tell Frank this story about someone they knew in common, but whom Victor knew to be witty and unique and quite different from what most people in Hollywood, or even the world, thought?

Victor couldn't. Of course, Frank knew Victor was gay. There was no doubt about that because Sam knew it. Virtually all the people Victor met or saw through either of these two men must therefore know he was gay. Which was just the way Victor lived his life and how he wanted to. Except, well, no one in L.A. ever spoke of it, alluded to it, referred to it, mentioned it, breathed it, or thought it—*no one!*

It was as though Stonewall and the Gay Activists Alliance had never happened. As though gay plays, gay novels, gay poetry, gay Community Centers, gay newspapers, gay magazines, gay politics, and the entire network of intramural gay liberation and personal gay dirt and gay lit bickering that, let's be frank, had been the main features of most of Victor's lived and chatted-about life for the past decade in Manhattan and San Francisco and everywhere else but here, really simply *didn't exist!* All of it made suddenly invisible.

Thinking back, that actor/producer Noah What's-His-Name, was the only person Victor had met so far in all the cocktails, drinks, dinners, lunches and work-sessions out here this trip to ever even refer to anything gay at all. And then probably only because he had enough sense to "get" Victor in a slightly different way alongside Joel Edison—Joel, a man whose behavior was always just one eeny-weeny twig of kindling away from bursting into a raging inferno. Even then, Noah had probably thought, "Vic's a nice-looking straight guy. Joel's probably blowin' him on the sly, the way he did me."

No wonder Victor needed the grounding phone calls back East

so badly. There were two calls daily with Mark, who was increasingly frazzled and discombobulated (but just as loving) as the Bar exam loomed. The semi-weekly ones with Gilbert were less so. He was actively hiding something, probably a positive HIV diagnosis, and doubtless more and worse. The weekly calls with his agent, Marcie, were even more distant. Truth be told, she was less interested in Victor these days. Marcie seemed to have done a one-eighty turn: she had talked him into it and now she considered script writing to be a chore, not an art, even when doing so for someone as well-known and honored as Frank Perry. It was on the same level as cleaning out your garage every decade. And as such, about as serious for one's actual *literary* career as Victor having two small plays done in two gay theaters that sat sixty, tops, and with most of the cast on "Equity waivers, for Chrissakes." Especially when the film script under question was from a book that was—hold me, I'm choking here a little—*seven years old!* and might expect to have had most of its sales life comfortably behind it. Where was Victor's new hit novel? *That* was the unspoken undertone of all his and Marcie's conversations these days. *That* was the sixty-four thousand dollar question. Not what happens twenty minutes into Act Two. Didn't he have even a novel *idea* they could bat around, she all but begged whenever they spoke?

Victor's gay life in West Hollywood from his previous visit proved of no help with the Gay Silence Is Not That Golden Problem. There was Andy, the Voyeuristic Goat Boy. There were the rare dinners with Isherwood and Don Bachardy who, though sweet and intelligent, caring and intellectual as all get-out, weren't really very poofy themselves. And who else? The beautiful and fun Perfect Paul? Gone to pasture. Or at least, according to several people, back to Racine, Wisconsin. (And, Victor hoped, to lasting health, although he seriously doubted it and feared exactly the opposite.)

Victor's one foray into the vaguely Roman-esque Hollywood Spa last week had ended after less than twenty minutes when he entered the steam room and overheard, unseen, two persons dishing, one mentioning that *he* was there in the bathhouse. Victor had crept out, unseen (he hoped) through the mist.

Admittedly the Detour bar had astoundingly—given that ultra-dreary opening—survived and seemed to be thriving. As did a new place a mile away, Cuff's, smaller and more fun, which someone described as "Totally time-stuck in 1968. But, like, in a good way."

But coming from Benedict Canyon and Mulholland Drive, either bar was almost an hour's drive one way. And while the drive *there* would go fast because of the expectation, the sad reality was, in such back room "candy-stores" Victor never quite knew when to stop. He wouldn't come back until 4:00 a.m., half drunk, more than half drugged, and totally exhausted. Approaching home, going fifty miles per hour, he would doubtless miss one of the many curves and plow the Z into a bank of Lillies of the Nile or a ranch-style four-car garage, ending up in someone's kidney shaped pool, just like Roy's co-star, the divinely perky Doris Day, in—was it *That Touch of Mink* or *Move Over, Darling*?

No wonder, then, when Victor got wind one afternoon, through the overheard conversation of two not-at-all-uncute guys in a Melrose Boulevard Fern Bar Slash Lunch Place, that a glory-hole-style "private club" had opened not that far away, he leaned over sweetly, flirted like a hundred dollar whore, then bluntly asked for the address.

Even then, he went to purchase the twenty buck membership on a Wednesday night, wanting to keep as low a profile as possible. In *Nueva Jorck*, this would never happen. He'd go to the tubs any time, anywhere, from The Wall Street Sauna near the Battery, way uptown to the St. Nicholas Baths in Harlem. He'd hang out with anyone, joining George Stavrinos, whose Barney's ad drawings were splashed over four pages of every Sunday *Times*, and get into a four way with two Broadway gypsy dancers from *Mame*. Only the featured actors were at all circumspect in the Apple, and even they would cruise you off most any Manhattan street. Victor had made it with two genuine (and handsome) stars: Larry Kert and Brad Davis, both of whom lived a few blocks from his West Village duplex.

(And then there was that time in the pouring rain as he was walking home along a deserted post-midnight Hudson Street, when a chromed yacht of a poison-green 1961 Plymouth Fury station wagon had pulled up and he'd gotten in, only to discover that the driver was comedian Paul Lynde from *Hollywood Squares*. Victor would have let him blow him, really he would have, he was that horny. Except that Lynde kept trying to act butch, really butch, which, given a voice that could, unaided, rip the wrapping off a champagne bottle and uncork it—became simply too funny. Victor was kicked out into the water-up-to-your-ankles gutter—laughing all the way home.)

Wednesday night was pretty quiet at Basic Plumbing, as this new spot was cleverly named. But when Victor got into conversation with the bearded kid behind the entrance window (that is, they sat together and played with each other's joints while smoking weed), he found out that Sunday afternoons were by far the best times. "All the A-gays are all fucked-out from Saturday night, when we're open to 5:00 a.m. But on Sunday, we're open 2:00 p.m. to 7:00, so it's all family guys and your other Undercover Operators."

So that would be when Victor would go.

At times, when it was raining, the place was empty and he'd sit in a corner and watch porno tapes on the TV or read one of the three fat paperback volumes of Montaigne's *Essays* until someone showed up. Everyone who did show up was intent on getting off, and they seldom played around waiting for "Mr. Right." One Sunday afternoon, he went to a party and didn't get to Basic Plumbing until close to 5:00. The place was very active. There were two double-sized rooms for group activities with multiple glory holes and even built-in elbow rests. Above the open-work wooden cells, instead of a ceiling there was suspended Mylar sheeting. One could see what was going on simply by looking up.

Sunday after Sunday the place got better and hotter. Victor had only limited contact, having a lover back home, and doing what he and medical others had determined was "safe" sex. Even so the quality went up week after week as more guys from around the city found out about the place. And since there weren't any kind of physical requisites to entry (*just the opposite* of the Club 8709), he saw all races, all sizes, all shapes. It could get varied and hot, with Mexicanos who looked like Mayans straight off maize fields in the Yucatan, Jewish guys with *pais* yet, Farsis in skullcaps, sharkskin-suited Persians, ordinary-Joe Armenians, not to mention the taxi drivers and off duty truckers. Then there were the black security guys, still in uniform, headed home after a short stop for action. Best of all to Victor, those cutely rumpled nerds who pulled up in station wagons with "baby on board" bumper stickers and infant car seats still wedged in.

What in the world would Frank Perry say to those afternoons? Or even Sam, who was slowly loosening up, but if you scratched him hard was still pretty square? These afternoons were, *Come on admit it, Victor*, a come-down, a let-down, a total low. But what was "left to do" from the real high times, now alas vanished into ancient history?

In Manhattan during the 1970s, a typical night out for him meant dinner, say at some new Thai place (they had just begun to sprout up thanks to the U.S. government's bombing the shit out of their homes in Asia) eating "Golden Chicken in a Basket" or "Frog Legs in Hot Basil," then off to a fresh production of *Les Troyens aux Carthage* with Crespin, Norman, and Vickers, or *Ariadne Auf Naxos* with Tatyana Tee and Monsterfat Cee at the Met; or to some off-Broadway and Forty-Third Street play, virtually underground, that people were taking seriously. Victor would be all dolled up and with straights and/or gays. That would be followed at 11:30 p.m. by a nightcap at a bar, again straight or gay, depending, and really only if it was mid-week. If it was a Saturday, he was off to one of the private dance clubs—Paradise Garage, The Loft, or *Les Mouches* (if he felt like Euro-Trash)—and getting porked by an Saudi Oil Princeling, who'd take him back to a suite at the Waldorf or the Pierre. And maybe if he hadn't sex-connected by that late, it was off to some good After-Hours-Party peopled with disco and gay-bar employees and with a unplanned orgy at someone's Jones or Duane Street loft. Or perhaps he'd stumble into a cab headed off to the New Saint Mark's Baths or to one of the West Side Highway and Twenty-Something-Street "private" sex clubs for the final part of the night.

That had been the way to live. Not this. And it had taken Victor most of the decade to figure out how to dress for any such single evening, which—think about it—went clothingwise from tuxedo to jock strap with several distinct stages in between in a twelve hour period.

And yet. And yet. He had never felt an iota more dissolute than the next straphanger on the IRT Number Four train, no more decadent than those businessmen reading the *Wall Street Journal*'s stock tips, waiting at the Lexington Avenue's Rector Street Station. If asked, Victor would reply that he was merely interested in a variety of different things. But then, after all, it was *La Citta*, and wasn't everyone?

Evidently not. Because here was Frank Perry asking why their character, Theo, who was new in town, would want go to Studio Fifty-Four? Would he even know about it, Frank asked? What were the chances he'd even get in?

And for the first time, Victor did lose his patience, though he hoped it didn't show.

"By the time of the book—and the movie, Frank—Studio was, like, *totally* over. The only people going *would* be newly arrived out of towners like Theo Anderson!"

Lord, it really was a trial at times!

CHAPTER TWENTY-FOUR

It wouldn't have been quite so bad if it hadn't been quite so unexpected. What am I writing? *Of course,* it was expected. Just not at that particular moment. And it probably would have been equally bad no matter *when* it happened.

It was the ninth week into the *Justify My Sins* script writing sessions. Victor and Frank had spent two hours and a half of very detailed work so far that afternoon on the Act Two climax of the script. Which meant of course going back to the sixty-minute-in "Turn" of the script, which they'd already decided was not the news that Anna-Marie could "see" Theo while speaking to him on the phone, but instead was their truly accidental (if acceptably so since they were close neighbors) meeting at the corner delicatessen. Her total panic, and befuddlement. His attraction and interest. All that had led to their first date as Theo and "Marion," the name she'd made up on the spot so as to be anyone but Ann-Marie. If that was the "Turn," the Act Two climax, therefore, had to be the discovery that Anna-Marie, with whom Theo continued a phone relationship all the while physically dating "Marion," could see him, *had been* seeing him, spying on him really, from the very beginning: from in fact Act One, Scene One, Fade-in.

They'd acted out the two crucial scenes as written, Frank taking the woman's part. Always the woman's part. *Always!* Why *was* that? (Had he acted out Joan when he worked with Cheryl Crawford on their script together?) And Victor acted out Theo, whom Frank once or twice said, "Is, after all, you." To which Victor had corrected, "Who is me, had I *continued* the phone calls, which I did *not.*" And in this way they tried out phrases and intonations, moved words around, shortened lines, lengthened pauses, as well acting it all out physically.

It had been a fairly grueling, if fascinating, two and a half hours but now was coffee-break time, and on this break Victor was grateful for the large and strong Coffee and Tea Leaf French Roast special he'd ordered, black with sugar. He'd really needed it.

Frank usually drank tea alone in his office during these breaks, thinking (or, more likely, making phone calls), while Victor sipped and ate and schmoozed with Sam Alan Haddad.

Sam and he had come to enjoy these breaks. They discussed books, cars, films, and other things of interest (but *never* the girls or guys they were seeing), and the fairly extensive rewrites that Victor was doing on the script written by Miss Hot Pants Screen Writer and starring Monster Girl Actress. It was now in its first week of shooting and Victor was finding it to be ten times more difficult than *Justify*.

Sam had just read Victor's latest changes and approved them and promised another check to be quietly slid into a bank account that Victor had opened recently. That was the solution of course: he could still legally receive the money, and still would pay taxes on it, but Frank would see it, if at all, only as a "production expense" wired directly to a nameless account number, of which there were several already.

(The experience of opening the account was so different from the bank confrontations Victor was used to in Manhattan as to be of note. Here, it entailed excessive friendliness and unpretentiousness, mugs of coffee, and shared first names. All of which was in line with the down home red-tiled roof, adobe-wall architecture, and interior rife with cowboy motifs underscored by vast murals sporting actual purple mountains' majesty and spacious waves of grain.)

So he and Sam were about as relaxed as relaxed could be when the downstairs bell rang and someone was let in, which happened dozens of times per day and went unnoticed. Except, suddenly, someone was at Sam's office door, which he kept locked. Sam had to get up, saying, "We're not expecting anyone. Not even UPS, I don't *think*."

Victor recognized her immediately, even though she looked nothing like her flattering book jacket photo, nor in any way like anyone's idea of a fate-changing femme fatale.

"Didn't Frank tell you I'd be here?" she asked, blustering in and more nudging than bussing Sam's cheek.

The immediate impression she gave was of a heavy woman light on her feet, a little older than Victor, with a Farrah Fawcett tidal wave of honey-colored hair, a well-tended very bright smile, a nearly unnoticeable rhinoplasty, and sweet, cornflower blue eyes. Glancing at the bejeweled watch on her almost chubby wrist, she half-smiled, did something with her shoulders that might have been an attempt at a shrug, and added, "Only 4:00. Willikers! I didn't think I'd be *this* early. Well, I'll just say hello and back out."

So saying, she entered deeper into the office and plopped herself opposite where Victor sat on a loveseat at a coffee table, watching her unhook the fluffy wintry coat, remove the light gloves *(gloves* in El-Lay?!) finger by finger, hand by hand. As she thrust it all to one side, he couldn't help but be attacked by a little hurricane of perfumes and cosmetics cast into the local atmosphere, strong enough that his nostrils began to smart and his eyes water.

The hastily not-quite-kissed Sam remained standing nearby, too stunned to do more than watch her, muttering, "He's...He's..."

"In a meeting. On the phone, Busy. I know," she said, without a trace of rancor. "Let him know I'm here. I'll pop in for a 'Hi' then get out of you guys' hair." Said with a breeziness that undid the effects of the too strong, conflicting scents and which nearly made Victor like her.

"Okay, I'll try him," Sam groaned.

She then turned to Victor, one newly ungloved, childishly plump hand out to be taken, and introduced herself, as he was certain she would, as Miss Hot Pants Script Writer. He then introduced himself as Her Replacement.

"With the new movie?" she asked gaily, and he almost added, "Yes. And with *your* movie *too.*"

"I thought you'd be in there with Frank?"

"I was. Coffee break." He pointed to the sweets wrappers and tall cup. "Did I ever need it."

"I know what you mean. He can be relentlessly detailing. But...," peering over the irreparable damage Victor had already inflicted upon an innocent pineapple turnover, not to mention the tell-tale skid-mark fruit stain on plastic wrapper, the only sign remaining of a demolished apricot Danish, "Luckily, you have a metabolism to allow all this . . . refueling."

"Not really. What I have is a very"—he sought for the word, and settled on—"*active* sex partner. As in lots of chasing."

"She an athletic trainer?"

"Try, *he's* a construction worker. A roofer."

"Oh! Lucky *you*! That's even better than a good metabolism. Before I got married I had one of those. *Paisano*?"

"Southern White."

"Umm-mmm!" She put two fingers together and to her lips. "Purr-feck-see-ohn! If you're gonna go for the whiter meat—"

Just then Sam re-entered, "He'll be a few minutes. He and Victor weren't quite done and—"

She stood up. "I could just pop in. Then go shopping and come back?"

"I'm afraid it'll still be a minute or two," Sam said with a hang-dog expression.

She sat back down. "I'll wait." Then, to Victor, "So? I understand you're also from The Island?"

There was only one The Island: his old neighborhood. They began comparing notes. Of course, she would know someone Victor's sister had dated in High School, a guy she said who'd become a very successful mortician.

"He was in training even then," Victor said. "He used to come pick Cathy up in a 1949 Caddy hearse, right out of *The Munsters*. He always swore there were no corpses in the back, even though there always was a coffin or two. But she told me that one time he swung a corner too tight leaving Green Acres Mall, the back doors sprung open and a casket slid out onto Hillside Avenue. She had to help him lift it back in and she swore up and down that it was too heavy to be empty. That was their last date."

They talked about her neighborhood, a little to the north of where he had grown up

"Fitzgerald's 'West Egg' in *Gatsby*, right?" Victor asked.

Right.

It also turned out that she'd gone to the same synagogue and hair dresser as several girls he'd dated in high school. She gave a home address he was familiar with.

"I caddied the golf course down your street for a summer, my senior year. Real pain in the ass golfers on that course every weekend. But boy did they tip well. I made a bundle."

He decided to not add the fact that he'd received his first blow job inside the golf course locker room from the clubhouse manager, a good-looking guy ten years his senior with a reputation as "a ladies man," who managed to do him regularly until Victor went off to college, and who, of course, had arranged for the liberal tippers.

She and Victor were now discussing various doctors, dentists, and psychiatrists they and their friends knew, finding there were connections everywhere between them, not thick ones like family, but slighter, yet all told, forming a sort of encompassing social network. No wonder he was the one who was rewriting her script, set after all in their shared neighborhood, a kind of teen paradise in North Central Long Island in the 1960's, not at all dissimilar to George Lucas' Santa Rosa as he'd depicted it in *American Graiffiti*.

Frank's office door opened and he stepped out, looking for her.

Frank had changed shirts, put on a tie, and was wearing a sport coat. Victor saw Sam noticing and knew it was all for her, and he also now knew Sam hadn't been lying.

She bounced up from her chair and into Frank's arms, not quite towering, but totally taking charge of him. After a minute or so, Frank noticed Victor still there and apologetically said, "You wore me out, Vic. Too much to go on working. She's only an excuse." Then, to her, "He's worse than you were. Sometimes I feel like I've been *ravaged* in that office." Back to Victor, "You don't mind too much, do you, Vic, if I take off a little early?"

"No. No. You kids get the hell outta here." Victor held back the gratuitous grandfatherly chuckle, but it would have been missed by them anyway since they were already heading out the office door.

Seconds later, they were gone and Sam was such a mass of anger and resentment that he all but emitted black smoke.

"Did you see? Did you *see?*" he at last was able to utter.

"I saw that Frank was too smitten to even notice my parting

statement, which if I may so myself, contained so much irony it should have reversed the Earth's magnetic poles."

Sam put a cupped hand to his mouth and stared at the shut office door, probably at his own bleak future vanishing there.

The silence became so marked that at last Victor got his jacket and leather case of scripts and got ready to leave.

"Just remember," Victor tried, "it's always darkest before it gets pitch black. No? How about, the first hundred years are the hardest? No? Then, try 'Doom is dark and deeper than any sea dingle Upon which man it fall'?"

That last roused Sam from his stupor. "William Butler Yeats?"

"W.H. Auden. But Sam, I'm *proud* of you. Yeats was a *very* good guess. Really!"

CHAPTER TWENTY-FIVE

There had been no reason to go onto the set over at the studio where the film was being shot, so Victor hadn't. He and Sam were trying to downplay his involvement as much as possible to keep it unknown. Victor was surprised to discover that Frank wasn't there all day every day either. Sam explained that was because there were a variety of "easy" scenes he allowed his assistant director to do, usually with Sam nearby and everyone near a phone just in case problems arose.

Any scene involving The Principals (as the main actors in the cast were called), and especially the Monster Girl Actress, naturally Frank *had* to be there. After all, he was known in the Biz as an "actor's director," as opposed to those directors who specialized in crowd scenes, epic views, or multiple explosions on giant moving sets.

The arrival of Miss North Shore (as Victor now referred to Miss Hot Pants Script Writer) changed that. She'd allegedly come for a weekend but was still present seven days later. Sam had rescheduled most of the shooting to reflect Frank not being there a lot, or when there, being distracted. There was only so many scenes without the MGA however, and if Frank wouldn't be there, she wouldn't either.

"Unless, of course," Joel Edison temporized to Victor, "*you're* there. She trusts you implicitly," he added on the phone, the third call so far that day. "No clue why." He then asked, "What are you eating?"

Victor wanted to answer back, "Choice Georgian pecker," but it was only 11:25 a.m. and he wouldn't get to that morsel until after 3:30. It was becoming increasing clear that he was going to have to forego his afternoon treat today.

"She trusts me because I'm a fine and intelligent man. And I'll go if you insist, Joel."

"I insist."

"And so it shall read on your tombstone, Joel. Remember I'm only doing this for you."

Not to mention the extra weekly income.

So he got into the Z after shrugging elaborately in the general direction of the roofer, as though to say he had no idea when he'd return, and headed over the hill, enjoying the long death-spiral down Beverly Glen Boulevard's other side. He succeeded in achieving that daring drive using his brakes only four times—a record!

The MGA was in her dressing room, fully costumed and made up and supposedly prepped for her scene, Sam said.

Victor arrived wearing a navy turtle-neck over which he'd thrown a gray Irish tweed jacket with suede patch elbows. He'd stopped to buy a pipe, which he left empty, but held in his mouth as he entered the supposedly busy but actually dead-stopped set.

"Who are you supposed to be?" Sam asked, "David Niven?"

"Do I look like him?"

"Kind of."

"Or do I look like someone's shrink?"

"Ahh! Clever!" Sam pointed Victor to the MGA's dressing room.

"Thank God you're here!" she said, looking around to see if anyone were watching—they were all busily, pointedly, *not* watching—then pulling him into the big shallow mobile room. "No one understands the problem!" she all but wailed.

The "problem," as Victor saw it, was that Daddy—i.e., Frank—was off with another girl—i.e., Miss North Shore—and so couldn't give all of his time and attention to the MGA.

So he did. For thirty minutes straight.

He told her exactly what was wrong with her. She cared too much for other people; she cared too much what other people thought; she put herself out too much for other people. All lies of course. Yet she all but wept as she acknowledged these glaring personal faults.

He told her what she had to do now: show them all up; let them see she was strong and independent; make sure they knew who they were dealing with; give the performance of a lifetime. Everything he knew she was utterly incapable of doing.

Later on, with Mark, he'd describe the conversation and Mark would describe it back to Victor as "sounding highly testicular."

But— He did succeed in getting the MGA out of the dressing room and onto the set and into the scene, with the Assistant Director, Sam, and himself all there watching her do it, with cameras, sound people, lights, and etc. all taking it down on celluloid. In fact, the MGA was on such a roll she did a record-low twelve takes before the A.D. and Sam declared they were happy with the result and then she kissed them all before flouncing back to her dressing room to learn the next scene and think up another round of general *agita.*

To Victor's astonishment and instant mortification, once the scene was done, Frank and Miss North Shore were also revealed to have been on the set for at the last few takes, and they came over to the three younger men.

"Slumming?" Frank asked Victor.

"I invited him," Sam said as the A.D. skedaddled away lest he be caught in a lie.

"He might as well get used to a shooting set," Frank admitted. "We may need him next time around." Another unveiled reference to their own project, now already at Act Three, Scene Two, script wise.

"I never cared for it," Miss North Shore admitted. "Too cold and draughty on set," she explained, looking at Frank as though he were responsible for the forty foot ceilings. She was dressed in some kind of vaguely equestrian outfit today. Tam-like cap, pullover, boots, all in earth shades right down to her tan, under-the-boot fitted pants. She exuded a kind of Amazon glamour. Several of the grips and the middle-aged Best Boy Electrician were staring. Victor hoped she and Frank were finally doing it. He decided that if she once called Frank "snookums," he'd murder her on the spot.

Victor excused himself, and after a short talk with Frank, Sam walked him off the set. "They're not staying. He'll be back tomorrow. That was a real life-saver, Vic. God, she almost *acted* today."

"Yeah. Yeah. Yeah." Victor replied airily. "Blow me in the back of a limo when it premieres and I call it even!"

But driving back home through winding canyon roads that rose precipitously, twisting and turning as in some daft analogy to his stupid life, Victor kept thinking how he had earlier that week rewritten at least sixty percent of the dialogue in that scene shot today. How could they not notice? Not Frank? Not Miss North Shore? They were bound to someday. Soon. It was a dangerous game, and he had to wonder how long it could possibly last before they discovered it and crucified him.

He arrived home and fixed himself a mind-deadening triple-Stoli on the rocks and was done with it, staring at a strange and muted sunset, when the phone rang. It was Gilbert's boyfriend, Jeff.

"I spent all day getting him admitted to St. Luke's today. Pneumocystis carinii. He's on Keflex and a steroid and some other drips. But he's been in and out of what looks like a coma for several hours now and . . ."

From the background noises, it was clear Jeff was speaking from a hospital corridor pay phone.

A week ago, Victor would have predicted exactly this phone call; receiving it satisfied nothing in him.

"He said your name three times," Jeff addded. "He can't urinate. They've got him on some kind of . . . His kidneys are shutting down."

"Hang up the phone, Jeff, so I can get a plane."

"Wait. I've got to—"

"Hang up the phone, Jeff. I'll catch the first plane out of here and come right to the hospital."

"Can you do that? Won't it be—?"

"Hang up the phone, Jeff. Wait." He looked for and found Mark Chastain's schedule. "First, call my lover, Mark, at this number. Tell him you need him there and that it's a *legal situation.*"

"A what? Let me get a piece of paper."

"Use the admission sheet."

"Oh! Right!"

"Do what I said, Jeff. Call him. Do what I say, Jeff, now, or I'll hit you very hard when I see you. Which will be in about seven hours. Do you hear, Jeff?"

"Okay. Okay. It's just that I'm just kind of . . . you know. . . It's all so sudden and all so . . ."

"I know, Jeff. I know. Now hang up the phone. Call Mark, and wait for me at the hospital. It's Intensive Care, right?"

"Yes. Thanks. I thought I'd know how to handle it all when it came to us. But it's too much, Vic. It's just too much, waiting down there all day in that pit, while he got sicker and sicker and no one cared and . . . !" Jeff began crying and Victor told him to be strong and hung up the phone.

"Fuck. Fuck. Fuck. Fuck. Fuck. Fuck. Fuck. *Fuck!*"

At the airport, the V.I.P. lounge had free phones. Victor used them to leave messages for Frank, Sam, Joel Edison, the MGA, and Andy Grant, who'd known Gilbert when they were all boys together.

He arrived at the hospital at six a.m. the next morning.

Mark was splayed out with his law books on the ICU corridor floor, studying. Jeff was slumped napping against one shoulder.

"I'm sorry I made you come, Mark, but he was a complete mess when I spoke to him on the phone."

"He was when I arrived, too. You did exactly the right thing getting me here," Mark said. He extricated himself from Jeff and they went in to look at Gilbert.

"The intern said he passed some urine through a catheter and he's been hydrated again. He's doing a little better. So *that* crisis is passed."

"Hey, sleepy head." Victor kissed his friend's desiccated face. "You look like shit! If you're not careful I'm taking photos and blackmailing you for everything you're worth."

Gilbert didn't really wake up, but he said Victor's name so he somehow knew he was there. Victor held onto his hand until he began snoring again.

They found an empty cot for Jeff to sleep on, then went to sit in the waiting room, together watching the sunrise reflected in the downstairs windows. A few others were there sleeping, covered with coats. While breakfasting on coffee and crullers, Mark stared at him.

"What?" Victor asked.

"You're so tan!"

"Head to foot," Victor declared. He stood and modeled, pulling down his pants a few inches at the waist. "With *no* tan line."

"You're kidding!"

"I had a top floor deck. Lotsa privacy. *And* if a certain law student plays his cards right, he'll get to see every scrumptious inch of perfectly tanned epidermis."

Mark pulled him onto the waiting room sofa and they kissed. A Latina coming through the waiting room noticed them and laughed "Ay! *Hijos*. So early in the day!?"

CHAPTER TWENTY-SIX

"Is that you, Andy?"

Victor hadn't seen Andy Grant in what? Two months? Three? And Andy had changed. He'd dropped twenty pounds. He'd gone to a gym. He'd shorn the beard and clipped the hair to near normal. He was wearing recognizably gay male oriented clothing. His long front locks even looked frosted. No? Could they be sun-streaked? He looked great. As he should, even on a dull, rainy, Sunday afternoon at Basic Plumbing. He was also half staggering out of the place with another guy twisted around his body like ivy around a redwood.

"Hey!" Andy recognized him too. "You're back? I'm flying out Wednesday to the East to see Gilbee!"

"Good! He's better. But . . . I'm glad you're going."

"Yeah. Good. See you." Andy was being manipulated by his vine toward the front door. "Sorry! I got the last guy here!"

Then they were gone and the rain hammered down on the tin roof and the place seemed even colder and emptier than it actually was. The kid behind the front screen was sawing Z's like someone three times his age, and even trusty old "Michel de" wasn't helping today.

Victor had returned to Los Angeles some ten days ago, once Gilbert had been declared out of "immediate danger" and released from ICU to a double room at St. Luke's.

In the week and a half he was in Manhattan, Victor had managed to set up a strong support network for his friend that he could join when he returned. He'd also managed to have three "serious conversations" with his over-studied, sex-starved lover, who, after a lengthy and loving perusal of Victor's entire and entirely tanned body, would have agreed to almost anything. In turn, as a sign of his support, Victor promised Mark he'd be back in New York in less than a month, before the dreaded Law Boards.

He met half of the other studiers, seeing for himself that none of them was a threat. The three women, including the tardy Angelica, were all clearly head-over-heels infatuated with Mark, as any sensible woman would be. If any of the Law Board guys were gay, they hid it well.

Victor had many talks with Gilbert in the hospital. He spent so much time in the ICU with Gilbert, alternately harassing and making friends with the staff there, that his friend really had no choice but to be completely open with him. Victor was completely open with him right back.

At Victor's instigation, on the next to last hospital visit Mark dropped off Last Will and Testament papers as well as Medical and Financial Power of Attorney papers. Both Mark and Victor sternly instructed Gilbert to read them through and make needed changes.

The next day, the day before he enplaned for El Lay, Victor returned and demanded to see them all, adding, "And they'd better be filled out." Ever-practical, Gilbert had gone over and marked and signed them all exactly as he should have. An hour later, as Victor waited outside the room, the hospital social worker and notary inside witnessed the signing and made it all legal. Jeff, who was in the room, had done everything but black out.

Once Mr. Oversensitivity was shooed out of the room, Vic and Gilbert finally had a conversation like the ones they used to have: non-medical, non-nurse-like, and real! Victor began by saying, "So! Do you want a big or little funeral?"

"Let my parents do the funeral. You guys do a memorial service slash party."

"With a big cake and hats and balloons?"

"Sure. And silver paper crowns for the queens."

"Two hundred crowns coming up," Victor noted.

"And you know what would be fun?" Gilbert added, "Why not have a loop of a film going in the background?"

"One film. Titled?"

"*Funny Face.* Isn't that one where Dolores Gray does the big Vogue Magazine 'Think Pink' dance number as they travel to Paris?"

"That's the one," Victor said. "One movie loop. Real age on the cake? Or big lie?"

"What will I care?" Gilbert laughed and coughed. "Sure. Go ahead."

"What about what's his face? Miss Jeff? He was an Em-Ee-Ess-Ess until we arrived. Will he hold up?"

"I don't know. Dope him up for the party. Oh, and why not buy him that cute porn star he likes for the evening. The Italian American bottom?"

"Two Quaaludes!" Victor notated and looked at a dubious Gilbert. "Three? Okay. And one porn star named Joey Stephano."

"The real problem," Gilbert looked suddenly deeply concerned, "is what we do with my devastatingly important collection of twenty-four years of *Silver Screen* magazines, in pristine condition?"

"When I'm back in Aitch-Wood, I'll check around. Maybe the Academy of Motion Pictures Arts and Sciences wants them." When Gilbert didn't register what he was saying, he added, "The people who give out the Oscars? The Academy of 'Academy Awards'?"

Gilbert's eyes lit up, and suddenly he was star-struck seventeen years old and dewily newly gay again. "Wouldn't that be fabulous? I can see it now: 'The Gilbert Onager Collection.' Everyone will wonder who the fuck I was. Some great make-up artist. Or a deeply devoted yet unknown hair-dresser to the stars. You *are* the best friend in the world. How could I have gotten this far without you?"

"You couldn't have, Gillo. *Am-po-see-bluh.*"

"Now tell me all about the MGA again? What does she call Frank?" He had months of questions saved up dealing with the extraordinary excitement of his best friend actually being involved in making a movie, no matter how terrible Victor said it would end up being. This, in effect, closed the other conversation.

Victor got medical power of attorney with Jeff as a second when he wasn't available. The general prognosis—as far as one could be made with everything so topsy turvy in an immunologically defective body—was that Gilbert would have a few months before something equally horrible happened to toss him back into ICU again. Victor intended to be done with both scripts and back in Manhattan again well before that and he said so.

Easy to say in New York.

His "real life" consolidated, he flew back to California.

Once he arrived back on Mulholland Drive and checked the hundred and seventy-eight messages left on the machine (most of them repeats), he realized this would be a bit less easy to get out of, right here, on the spot.

He decided to brass it out.

Talking to Frank on the phone the first full day he was back, Victor said, "My closest friend is dying of AIDS. If he calls me again, I'm flying back. Period. I'll work from there, if need be."

Frank seemed subdued and vague and at last he admitted they only had two more work sessions anyway.

The MGA proved to be astonishingly compassionate. "You poor *thing!* And your poor *friend!* Yes, I'll definitely understand if you must rush to his bedside. But of course, you'll let me phone you there and bitch a little, won't you? Please! Please," she begged.

"Only if you do so while wearing a steel-ribbed brassiere and speak dirty with a Viennese accent."

"I'll miss you. You're such a card," she delightedly trilled the last word.

Sam Alan Haddad was a little less sweet. "We are this close to utter disaster, you know. These past ten days while you were gone, the Beast With Five Heads"—Miss North Shore, formerly Miss Hot Pants Script Writer—"also left. I had a drained, depressed, and energyless Frank on my hands to deal with."

All this while script pages had shot back and forth betwixt the two coasts via telex and overnight mail, Victor sometimes working next to Gilbert's bed, moaning in frustration at the thinness of the material he was supposed to tinker with.

"Sam, you're going to heaven with your shoes on."

"What are you talking about?"

"That's what my little old Italian grandmother used to tell us kids whenever we'd done some good and selfless deed. I guess having shoes was a big thing back then."

"I am so close to snapping, Vic. And you're talking about grandmothers and shoes?"

"Why don't I come right over there to—where is it you live? Westwood?—and give you a naked hot oil massage? Believe me, Sam, you'll be far less stressed afterward."

It took Sam a half a minute to understand what Victor had said.

"Ummm. Ummm. I've got someone coming over in about ten minutes."

"Great! Then let *her* do it," Victor said and hung up

Victor retold that little piece of dialogue to Joel Edison, who was next in line to be called back.

"That one will need more than *one* hot oil massage, believe me. He's a walking advertisement for 'Uptight.'" Then, "Listen, *she's* almost human. And it's all thanks to you."

"Diva Number Two?" Victor asked. "She's not a bad person. She's just in over her head. Unfortunately, she's just smart enough to realize it."

"I mean this flick isn't going to *totally* tank, is it?" the agent asked.

"No clue at all, Joel. I saw some rushes before I left. *She's* funny. And she's surrounded by some real pros. But—"

"*But* . . . the script still sucks."

"If Shakespeare was doctoring it, it would still suck."

"Don't say a word to anyone. Meanwhile I'll manipulate and finagle her into another project before this can open and be seen."

"Great idea!"

"And while we're speaking of real pro's, Victor Regina, you did step up and save the day. I will not forget this good deed."

"Just get me some options on my other books. That's my financial means for spending full summers at Fire Island Pines. I don't give a fuck if they intend to make movies of them or not."

"Good as done."

All well and good. But then Victor had gone to Black Hawk Pictures with his penultimate four pages of the *Justify* script, as per their schedule, and that's when it all began to unravel.

As always, Frank was in his inner office reading the pages Victor had written. But this time Sam had barely let Victor in the door when he had to leave to go to the set. He said sure the secret

204

pages had arrived and they looked good and another under-the-table check had been deposited. But there was this undeniable distance between them, as though he had an actual right to be upset and offended that Victor had left a goddamn lousy movie to tend a dying friend. Sam was so brusque as he left the office that Victor almost told him off.

Just then Frank came out and Victor, still fuming, said, "You know, Frank. I've beaten up straight boys before. If that one," pointing at the door where Sam had exited, "isn't careful, he's next."

Frank was astonished by Victor's aggressiveness. (Andy Grant had once told him, "For a faggot, you're a little too macho sometimes. I think you take your name a bit too seriously.") He apologized profusely for Sam, probably out of guilt knowing that he himself was responsible for his Production Assistant's case of Cosmic *agita.*

"These are good pages, Vic."

"No notes?" Victor asked.

"Tiny ones. But I think it's now time to talk about the ending."

So they sat down and discussed the ending of the script of *Justify My Sins.*

That was when weft and weave parted company.

As Victor might easily have predicted many moons ago, indeed, as he *had* predicted to Mark only last week, Frank suddenly performed a Hollywood-About-Face, compared to which a man falling from Mt. Everest and transforming into an eagle and flying away is but the slightest of variations.

He prefaced it by saying, "We're bringing the new shoot in at budget. More or less on time. Everyone's happy with it."

For a brief moment, Victor wondered if they were talking about the same film. This was like Frank saying "black is white, and always was white." But hey, Victor was a big boy, and he could accept bald faced lies as well as the next guy. "Everyone" being the key word, after all, and meaning, he guessed, the studio money men and administrators, who were, of course, co-financing the new production, and would doubtless also co-finance *Justify.*

"But . . . ?" Victor cautiously lifted a bare quarter-inch the lid of Pandora's box.

"*But* . . . while they loved the scenario, they found it ended a bit too starkly."

"Too darkly?"

"Well, that too."

I.e., it was not a "happy ending." Duh and double duh.

The appropriate response—and as a rule, only the Yiddish have an appropriate response for this kind of tumultuous and total disaster—would be: "*Oy, veys mir!*" But Frank's a goy, right? So, he wouldn't get it and sat there waiting for Victor's response.

Now let us review the previous four months as though it were bunched up into a flash-forward reel, speeded up four or five times, and I think you'll agree that Victor had very little to complain about. He'd lived like a king, in great weather, for free. He'd gotten Primo construction worker dick. He'd had various kinds of fun. He'd beached, sunned, and mostly he'd been overpaid for work he'd done, and better yet, for work he'd never signed on to do. He'd become friends with a big *macher* film director, a hot show biz agent, and a very famous TV actress. This was *not*—putting it all into context—chopped chicken liver

"So, what do we do now?" Victor said, as though he was nineteen years old and never been fucked up the rear and so was unaware that particular activity was at that moment about to occur (we're speaking metaphorically, natch).

"Well . . . let's try to find a"—Frank didn't say the dreaded phrase—but instead uttered "a finale more palatable to the studio. Not to mention one for the two actresses who've seen half the script and expressed interest."

From there on, our hero, Victor, was totally Missing In Action. Had Frank been queer, or known Victor better, or cared more, the key would have been that Victor didn't even bother to ask who the actresses were.

They spent the next three hours trying to work out a "palatable" ending.

Let's hear it for Frank. With the thirty pieces of silver all but weighing down his tweed trousers, he got up and gave a really good show. He had an idea for a final scene. They discussed it, wrote dialogue together, and acted it out. No go. They tried another tack and wrote more dialogue together. Not good. He came up with another possibility. It stank. And another, even more in-genious. Even worse.

Still, it seemed like work, and it seemed as though, if they kept at it, they actually might accomplish something. So when Sam re-turned and knocked on the door and stepped into the office, Victor attempted not to glare daggers at him, but instead smiled, even though he suddenly sensed strongly that Sam Alan Haddad was behind what they'd been wasting time on for the past few hours. Sam needed to talk to Frank, and Victor said he had to leave, and Frank followed him out saying, "Spend some time on it. Feel free to call me with whatever comes up. Anything at all. I've always got time for this."

Of course, Victor did foolishly spend some time on it—about an hour—then he phoned Mark who instantly said, "That lying fuck," and threatened to come out himself and deal with the turncoat. Then Victor phoned Marcie, who said, "What did you expect, Vic? They lie like rugs! You always knew that." Victor called Gilbert who said, "You mean you aren't going to play the building super-visor in the movie?" Vic had to let him down gently, saying that in case there actually was a movie (which was looking more dubious by the second), of course he'd be in it. He'd insist on being named Gilberto and wear a big Puerto Rican mustache. That mollified his sick friend who quickly wandered out of this misfortune and into some others which seemed of equally crucial importance to him although they involved blue rather than yellow plastic pudding cups at lunch, since minor dementia had definitely settled in for the duration.

By the following week, Victor handed in the last rewrites on the Disaster of the Decade, and subsequently saw the zeros rise in his savings account. He sunbathed a lot, and had more sex with Jared, and he even went to Basic Plumbing. He lunched twice and laughed a lot with the MGA, and once with Joel Edison. When Thursday came up, he was getting ready to drive downhill into the "Golden Triangle" when Sam called to say Frank had to cancel their script meeting as they were so close to wrapping up shoot-ing on the other film.

That went on a second week. And a third. Clearly, Frank hadn't come up with anything viable as an ending either.

One morning Victor received a piece of mail from a company he'd never heard of saying that the house lease would be up in nine days and he sighed in relief and instantly phoned and made plans to fly back to Manhattan without saying anything to anyone in La La, because why bother, it was all over, wasn't it? Why make a scene?

So here he was, a day before he was headed back East, with— to be ruthlessly, depressingly candid—yet another bigger, even more expensive, even more fabulous, potentially even great film project based on his second novel. And it was dead, dead, dead!

Which might explain why he'd come to Basic Plumbing having dropped a Quaalude and smoked a long joint of quite good Sinsemilla weed, hoping for a final total sex and drugs blow-out.

Alone in a nearly empty building, shaken by gusts of wind and rain, on an early May Sunday afternoon at 3:16 p.m.

At last, the front door was flung open, and the doorman almost fell off his chair with surprise. From where he was, Victor couldn't see who had entered. Then, a minute later, the inner door was flung open and he could see very well: a tall, auburn haired, rock-star handsome man of about thirty with an amazing body, followed by an African-American version of same with an even more astounding body.

In an instant Victor's gay brain did the math and the read-out was: Pro footballers, off season, looking for action on the down-low.

He leaped up, almost tripped, caught himself and headed out into the maze surrounding the little rooms.

The next ten minutes was like a bad joke. He did finally get face to face with the first guy, who looked back at him, as he turned a corner. Then the black guy who had a to-die-for two day beard caught Victor in his arms and said, "Hey, bay-bee. Where ya goin'?"

"You're together, right?" Victor asked. "Him and you?"

"Not necessarily." Seeing it was the wrong answer, he amended it to, "We could be."

"Since we three are the only ones in here," Victor said, "I suggest you find your friend we work something out for all of us to do."

This was sealed with a death-grip hug from "LaMarr" and a

tongue thrust which stopped roughly inside Victor's upper esophagus, which Victor took as an assent.

They ended up in the single long room, and in the (slightly altered) words of Edward Gorey's immortal tome, *The Curious Sofa,* after some poppers being opened and some pants being pulled down, "many were the moans, barks and giggles" that ensued over the next twenty minutes.

Evidently the two Offensive Rams had merely been the spearhead of a rush on the place and everyone else who had followed them in could see—via the Mylar ceiling, not to mention the many glory holes accessing the center space—exactly how hot the triple action was. Victor remembered at one moment being something like the bologna in a white bread and pumpernickel NFL-Pro sandwich, as others' hands suddenly came out every hole as though in a second rate Ingmar Bergman movie, reaching and grabbing and wanting some of the action. After he'd orgasmed twice, and had done pretty much every combination possible with the two Sport-Adonises, Victor staggered out of the room—two other guys squeezed their way in as he left—and, trying to get his clothing more or less back onto his body in the correct places, he stumbled his way over to the lounge.

He'd just managed to get more or less together, had even stepped into the excuse of a lavatory to wet down his hair, when he heard:

"Why Miz Vic-tor! I never 'spected to see you here!"

Joel Edison. Of course.

"What are you doing here?" Victor asked back.

"I heard there was a scene and a half going on with some major meat from the Sports World. Someone I know phoned from the Shell station across the street."

"Go right, then left, it's the third door."

"Directions from the very person who has just exited such a scene. As I might have guessed. And left *what* slim pickings?"

"The guys had about a tenth of load left each when I vamoosed."

They could hear a loud moan, which Victor recognized as coming from "Bart" quickly followed by another from "LaMarr."

"I'd guess the pickings have been picked clean by now."

"Just my luck." Joel said. Then, philosophically, "Well, one of them was probably a friend of my brother's, anyway."

They sat down and Joel opened a Thirties silver cigarette case that Flynn might have borrowed off Harlow and removed a joint that he tamped tight and lit up.

"I heard you're headed East soon."

"9:45 a.m.," Victor specified.

"Shame. We coulda done great things."

"Sure. Right."

"No, really. You were just with the wrong people."

"Then put me with the *right* people!"

"Gay-boy poontang," Joel said.

"Wha-at?

"That's what my older brother and his teammates call coming in places like here and getting off with fellows, or going to some bathhouse in Kansas City or Denver after a game." He was slurring a little. "'Hey lil' bro,' he'd say, 'We got us some first rate gay-boy poontang t'other day. And it was as good as gash poon!' And they'd all laugh, thinking to shock me, thinking I didn't know shit about what they were saying."

"You're kidding . . . You're *not* kidding?"

"*Not*. But I am now leaving here. You should too."

Out on the street it had stopped storming. The sidewalks were littered with blown down palm tree husks the size of a Vespa and about as sturdy.

"The very bad boy at Frank's office is going to call you and apologize. I have it on the best of words."

"Who cares anymore?" Victor said.

"You should. He's going places, that one. He'll count some day. You watch."

"Maybe. But he's the one who pretty much ended *my* film project."

"Come on. If the other's a hit, it's completely on again. Full blast. That's how it works. And anyway, you knew it had a shaky chance at the long run from the get-go. Admit it."

"I guess I always did. And you know why. Because it's just too good. Too smart. Too real."

"All of the above," Joel admitted.

Just then the two NFL Pros exited Basic Plumbing. LaMarr saw Victor first and they headed over.

When they reached him, Joel was gone.

"Hey man! We want your phone number." Bart said. Big smile. Big ass and dick too.

"I'm in New York."

"Well, we kinda' travel a lot," Bart said, and they both laughed.

"I got a lover."

"He hot as you?" La Marr asked.

"I think he's hotter."

"Well, then o-kay! Put that number right down here."

Victor wrote his phone number.

"We can't give you ours—" Bart began.

"I understand."

"We'll be out New York way by August at the latest. Got an exhibition game, right LaMarr? So check your newspapers and if you don't hear from us, call us anyway. Go through the Coach's office. Call and say you're my *cugino* Victor. You hear me, *ouaglio?*"

"I definitely will call!"

"Don't make me come find you!" Bart mock threatened.

Big hugs then and another taste of LaMarr's pythonesque tongue.

They split and as Victor started up the Z for the last time, Joel was at the driver's window.

"Not bad for a consolation prize," Edison said.

He held up his hand in the Vulcan greeting. Victor laughed and tried to do it back.

Suddenly a tiny tornado arose as another cell of the storm hit. Joel ran for his Merce.

Victor turned off Sunset Boulevard and headed uphill. Once safe and dry at the hilltop house, he looked back at the storm over the lower part of the city, lightning striking down around the basin area that he'd left not twenty minutes before. He was amazed to see the bolts were not only extremely theatrical-looking in their shapes, but also strangely, almost grotesquely, electrically *pink*.

"It's Hollywood," Victor said aloud. "Why *can't* the lightning be hot pink!"

ACT THREE

1999: RED LIGHT, GREEN LIGHT

We represent the lollypop guild,
The lollypop guild.
The lollypop guild!

                    --The Wizard of Oz

CHAPTER TWENTY-SEVEN

Spider webs covered every square foot of the shoulder-high Jade Tree hedges surrounding the half dozen Hollywood Boulevard houses down the hill on the other side of Laurel Canyon. It almost looked as though they'd been sprayed with those cans of fake gluey gunk sold around Hallowe'en to make everything look aged, long-abandoned, and "scary." But it was a week after New Year's, and Victor Regina knew the webbing was real, despite the industrious ministrations of weekly Mexican-born landscape minions and enthusiastic home gardeners: another bizarre response of southern California natural life to the meteorological madness that was El Nino.

That specific weather pattern had arrived early the previous Autumn, eliciting great fanfare from the SoCal media. And as Victor himself had arrived then himself, this time for good, he'd noted it without paying it proper attention. From his viewpoint as a Manhattanite, weather was something you endured momentarily from the subway to the movie theater, from the taxi to your front door. The occasional snow storm that stopped traffic and closed schools, the once-in-a-decade hurricane that came as a dramatic caesura, was something to talk about later, once it was over. It was seldom actually experienced, never mind important.

But here, weather was all around you, because in truth, and especially if you were like Victor, relocated fairly high in the hills above West Hollywood with enormous windows facing three directions, weather was an all-dominating factor. Not a problem as a rule, since the weather was ordinarily temperate, clear, and sunny by day, with mists in the mornings, some fogs at night, with rain from January through March, at the most.

But since this past November, and with increasingly serious weirdness, weather was becoming an unwelcome character in the narrative of his new life. Now he went out with an umbrella and raincoat in the car, no matter how sunny and clear it looked from his extensive view over the L.A. Basin. Who knew what he might possibly encounter an hour later? The ordinarily drab and pre-dictable weather that could as a rule be seen by satellite coming across the Pacific Ocean for five days in a row, and that could be described almost hour by hour by experts, was now transformed into pretty much totally-up-for-grabs. Every minute variation in the jet stream once it passed the Juan de Fuca Straits (Juan, the Straight Fucker, Victor called it) somewhere north of Seattle these days gave him much pause. This season drew unsuspected lines on the otherwise bland brows of the Weather Blonds of nightly television news, all those previously unfrazzled Fritzes and sunny Sonnys and undrummed upon Toms. Hell. Victor could hear the thread of semi-thrilled fear in their voices as they fore-omened all sorts of bizarre weather monstrosities headed toward him out of the skies. No wonder Victor felt like he'd wandered onto the set of some unreleased Spielberg movie.

This very noon's lunch meeting was in downtown Hollywood, inside a Hamburger Hamlet right across the street from Mann's Chinese Theater, and thus sure to possess a sort of over-the-hill glamour. And, being less than a two mile drive, what could possi-bly happen? Right?

Wrong! As Victor turned right off Hollywood Boulevard and onto Orange, searching for the entrance to the garage that Geoff Bax told him his company used and thus would validate parking for Victor, he suddenly heard and then saw hail. Hail the size of golf balls loudly crashing down all around him out of a sky nearly cloudless a minute ago.

He found himself in the middle of an action-scene from a hor-ror flick. Every car stopped in its tracks no matter the traffic-light color. The Iowan *turistas* in front of the row of movie theaters on both north and south sides of the streets screamed, panicked, and rapidly ducked for cover. The Supermans, Batmans, Darth Vaders,

Wonder Women and other colorful "personalities" working the street for tips from posed photos with said *turistas* stood utterly dazed, getting bonked on their bat-ears and bass-amplified helmets. Unbelieving SoCal motorists got right out of their cars to confirm what was happening, only to witness a double hail ball the size of their head crash into their tinted-for-only-$99.95-plus-tax windshield. As the hail doubled so did the noise and the breakage.

Victor saw a chance to maneuver through stopped cars and made a quick turn, illegally on red, and zipped over to the underground garage just as hail shattered down wildly, randomly, and three times as thick around his car. He didn't even stop to see if there was damage as he shot into the covered entry, stopped for a ticket, and watched the astounded ticket-taker check out five, count 'em!, five large balls of graying ice where his windshield met the car hood.

Luckily there was no damage. He drove to a spot a floor down, parked and got out. He crumpled a copy of the Calendar section of the *L.A. Times* to wipe the still-quite-hard ice-balls off the front and back windows of the car, counting twelve of the mothers.

As the elevator rose to the floor connecting to the office building, he could see that both ticket-takers were illegally and uncharacteristically outside their booths at the street entry, gawking at the amazing barrage. He entered the back of the building's lobby and noted people gathered in the Hollywood Boulevard entrance, clearly entranced by the pavement-thunking weirdness outdoors. Upstairs, he gave his name to the sweet-tempered Latina dyke at the desk and sat shaking his head as the clouds transformed rapidly into a fully sunny sky.

When Geoff Bax held out a welcoming hand for a shake a few minutes later, Victor was ready. Quickly unwrapping it from the newspaper, he clasped a still hard, if now melting, ice ball from his palm and into Bax's meaty palm.

"What the . . . ?!" Bax, another Midwesterner, recognized it but couldn't believe it. He dropped the hail onto the coffee table then picked it up again. "Where in hell did you get that?"

"Just outside your front door. A dozen more like that blitzed my car as I was parking."

Geoff went to look, but Victor said, "Its over, already." Geoff was unfazed however, which boded well if he was to be Victor's new editor. He dropped the ice ball into a vase of giant African daisies in the lobby. "Let's go eat. I'm starved."

Once in the leather booth, Victor ordered off-menu: "The guaca-burger with everything," he told the waiter, leaving Geoff to search for it on the big double list.

"You're only here a short time and you're already playing the 'off the menu game,'" Geoff said in admiration.

"Not really. I've been ordering these since I was a kid out here. All the chefs at Aitch-Aitch make 'em."

Five minutes of small talk and then the food arrived. After, Geoff sprung his surprise. "We've got a new marketing person. Don't worry. He won't interfere with me or with your books."

"Books in the plural," Victor picked it up, "Because . . . ?"

"Because your agent finally sent me the British Edition of *In-Sanity* and I read it and I've *got* to publish it here. So now refresh me on its background. Your American editor left after *Never Can Say Goodbye* came out at the other place and you didn't offer them this crazy-good book because why? Because you didn't want to stay, right?"

"Exactly. I had been orphaned at my first publisher in 1981 and it was such a Colonoscopy-Without-Benefit-of-Percodan that I vowed up and down that I'd never let it happen to me again. The new editor that time did mostly romance novels. The editing process resembled thirty-two root canals in a row. She even changed the title of the book to something utterly meaningless. The dust jacket ended up looking like a Daniele Steele reject. A com-plete dis-ass-ter. So with these guys, I decided to cut to the chase. I offered the so-called replacement to my irreplaceable-if-utterly-nuts-but-terrific-editor a collection of short stories as my next book, as per contract. And as I hoped he would, he passed on it."

"What an idiot! You'll send the stories to me too, right?" Bax asked. "And we'll do up a new two-book contract."

"Sure," Victor sad, surprised by how quickly and easily that had happened. "Meanwhile *Goodbye* topped all the charts in England and around the Commonwealth. So my really nice and cute editor there in London begged for the next work. *In-Sanity* was all but finished. It's a nice package." Victor pulled his own surprise out of his jacket pocket. "Don'cha think?"

"Nice, indeed," Geoff agreed, handling the hardcover. "Correct me, but this matches the UK cover of *Goodbye*, doesn't it?" Bax asked.

"Two peas in a pod. *Goodbye* is at twenty-five thousand copies already, which is a best-seller in the U.K."

"Can I have this copy long enough to bring to the editorial meeting on Friday where I'll present your stuff?"

"It's all yours. Keep it."

And so the business aspect of the lunch went better than Victor had dared expect. A two book contract: *In-Sanity and* the stories! Wow.

What pleased Victor even more than how easily this was all happening was that it severed another connection with the East Coast and his utterly painful and hopefully forgettable past. If he had a West Coast publisher, he reasoned, he didn't need to truck at all with New York-based ones. Not that he expected that Bax's group would be able to sell his titles with the sweeping ease of the corporately-owned megaliths in Manhattan. But who knew? They might do pretty well for him. The advances Bax mentioned were only about half of what he'd gotten for *Goodbye*, but that book had earned four times that advance and counting, now that he had foreign language editions out all over Europe. So it almost didn't matter.

What did matter was that Victor was a very big, possibly the biggest, fish in Geoff Bax's editorial pond. And for now that was enough.

Bax himself was an odd kind of guy: half lumbering former-football-halfback in physique, damned with the nimble mind of a soccer player, and, even worse, with the fertile but not yet much tested imagination of a dangerous world class hoaxster. His experience, he had confided to Victor at a recent upstate book conference dinner, effusing equal parts of irony and humor, ranged from working at a Southeastern U.S. purveyor of those plastic-covered grilling cookbooks you used outdoors alongside your half-ton all-chrome Weber, to a tony little shop of four located in a pre-Revolutionary War building in Cambridge, Massachusetts, where he irregularly issued foreign policy textbooks and diplomatic memoirs of such exacting topic discrimination that they were clearly intended for a grand total of eight hundred and twenty-six readers, most of them located deep within the D.C. Beltway. And now he'd arrived at this once-hippie-owned publisher, taken over a decade ago by an alternative magazine mini-empire owned by two elderly gay men and their straight sisters. He'd been recently hired to overhaul this small and rather sleepy press and goose it instantly into the Big-Time. His Midwestern origins (openness and even residual naiveté) had been neatly eroded away by years of Ultramontane Brahmin sophistication, with the lightest of Georgetown U. slash Big-City polishes.

Whenever Bax looked at the unfailingly hot and handsome guys who sauntered into the Hamburger Hamlet in twos and threes for lunch, his eyes all but rolled in their sockets, he was so intent on *not* looking at them. From this, and given the little he knew of Geoff's rather restricted East Coast personal life, again previously presented with wit and deprecation over too-strong Mojitos and deadly Appletinis, Victor could already predict for the editor two years of intense immersion in El Lay sex/drugs/rock'n'roll'/n'boys, with either a precipitous decline— ending in a police and hostage stand-off in a motel room littered with empty beer cans and pizza delivery boxes somewhere Coastal south of Capistrano—or a suddenly cleaned-up act, twelve-step program, and a bit of discreet cosmetic surgery as he skipped town. Something drastic was clearly in the wind; it wouldn't be easy for Bax. But then he was twenty years younger, and so Victor guessed Bax still had lots of time to make a few Truly Major Mistakes.

Two of those lovely young things just now entering the Hamlet swerved on their heels from where the *maitressse d'* had aimed them and instead ambled over to their booth. One was tall and Afro-American with expressive facial features, a swank style of dressing, sea-green eyes (or lenses?), and ultra-cool skin tone of lightly-stained oak. From his decades of visits to the West, Victor already knew this type as the Guy-in-the-Aitch-Wood-Know, working part-time for some less than top drawer pop music producer or film-maker, who partied more than he ever recorded or shot anything, but who nevertheless had the right kind of BMI or AMPAS credentials.

He now intro'ed himself as Lindsay Something-or-Other. His lunch companion (they'd probably gone home to screw one time and had ended up in giggles realizing they were both bottoms) was a Caucasian without any immediately identifiable ethnicity, just below medium height, thin without being in any way meager, with scarves tossed across the shoulder of what looked like a quite expensive custom-made sports jacket, and those designer jeans with pressed pleats that ordinarily made Victor gag. He had masses of thin, curly, perfectly charcoal-black hair framing a not handsome but rather distinctly "Aristo" head and face. This featured much nose-bone, distinctive brow ridges, cheekbones for days, sulky lips, and a very good though pallid complexion.

The latter approached the table, took Geoff Bax's unsuspecting hand, and spoke to Bax, reminding him that he was Dimitrios Juenger, and they'd met through Muffy-So-And-So at Scott-So-and-So's commitment ceremony to that awful boy, what was his name?

It took a few minutes for Geoff to mentally validate his credentials upon which a single question about their connection, Scotty, was asked, and Dimitrios then turned his semi-reptilian, washed-out blue eyes upon Victor.

"Of course, Lindsay and I both *instantly* knew who you were."

While Lindsay went on to talk about two of Victor's better known books that he adored in particular, Victor watched Juenger look upon him with that radiating interested benevolence typical of an alley tabby approaching a heedless golden oriole.

He was no longer surprised that in L.A. people whom you were certain had last actually picked up and read a book when Mrs. Soos was discussing *Return of the Native* in the seventh grade nevertheless somehow knew who he was, and that he was (in their own parlance) a "Marquee Name" writer. They knew a few titles of what he'd written, and even could tell him which ones had sold well. The Marquee Name business was, of course, the give-away. These folks seldom read books; the closest they came to any volume besides the *IMDb Annual* was *U.S.A. Today's* Thursday best-seller lists. Also they apparently memorized by heart any marquee they'd ever come across. Victor had long ago gotten over any annoyance at this phenomenon and now accepted it as his (questionable) due. Let 'em gush, even if their gush was nine-tenths spam.

However, once lover-boy was done talking and it was Juenger's turn, he didn't so much gush as say directly to Victor, "We should get together some time. Maybe we can figure out some sub-rights sales of your titles. I take it you don't have a film rights agent?"

"I don't have a film rights agent who actually wants to sell the film rights to any of my books," Victor replied candidly.

"Maybe I can. Here's my card."

After they'd sauntered off, the *maitresse'd* came by for a not-that-subtle "Now who was it who's famous that I missed" look-see at Victor while Geoff paid the bill.

"I have no idea how I met the guy or who this Muffy is," Bax admitted. "But I definitely was at Scotty and Ron's commitment ceremony."

Confirming for Victor that the two had stopped by the table because of him.

"Maybe the young man blew you behind the ice sculpture and you forgot?" Victor suggested.

From the silent, pained look that Geoff returned him, it was very, very possible that or worse had occurred, and was now being only spottily recalled

He and Geoff stepped outside four minutes later into another darkly threatening all-encompassing thunderhead, leading to yet another potential secretly-shot Spielberg flick filled with huge clouds moving far too fast, and all of it rumbling and sounding quite *sturm und drang.*

"Who knows what'll fall out of the sky now," Bax said.

"Rolex watches made in Taiwan?"

"Anything's possible." Geoff summed it up: "It is, after all, Holly-Weird."

"Canyon floods in rain" read a sign in place along Laurel Canyon Boulevard right before the intersection with Kirkwood. Victor always noted it, but wondered how that was possible since the street rose so high to Mulholland Drive.

Returning from lunch, he couldn't help but notice that the depressed sides of the road were indeed filled with swirling eddies of wildly flowing water. Stopped at the second uphill traffic light, he looked about and made out their source, the roads and lanes and dead-end streets on either side, all of which debouched into this central cut through the five mile wide band of Hollywood Hills. All this water must be from the same downpour he'd experienced an hour or so before that had brought on the Hollywood hail. And as he watched, the braiding, twisting, streamlets seemed to gain density and energy. Someone in a car behind beeped, and he accelerated.

Victor had joked about the road up to his house that it was "a good ten minutes up, and maybe three minutes down to Laurel Canyon again." The road twisted around itself a dozen times, swerving around every bluff and cliff whereupon property had been carved out and a house set, placed, leaned, or floated on stilts. Even though this was a relatively early built-up section, circa 1950 to 1975, newer homes had been added, and many of them seemed like one good wind would take them down. He knew that sewers had been installed and strengthened every time the road was upgraded, but still, given the steep angle, the water rushed down like Niagara after storms.

He was driving up now, approaching one such section of road half-way up to where he lived, a spot beyond which a solid enough looking bluff held three large architecturally modern houses, blocking the view of the road behind. The road widened here temporarily, and there were sewers on either side of the expanse. But with this much runoff, that only served to spread the water like a sheet across the entire road.

Victor must have sensed, intuited, or for less than an instant possibly even seen flashes through foliage of a vehicle coming down at him. It was mostly hidden from view, though, as he came to the wide section he stopped and idled the car, all the while feeling the wheels being tugged at, almost feeling the car being pulled by the water back along with the rapids on either side. He saw to his left and rather high up a silver SUV slew around the curve just past those houses, headed down right at him.

In a flash it was clear the car was out of control. The flooded road and the sheeting water had grabbed the big vehicle and it was now hydroplaning.

He could make out the driver—a male in a baseball cap — grabbing at the steering wheel and attempting to turn the wheels, to no avail. The SUV just kept coming, faster, headed right toward him, toward anything right here.

Thinking fast, Victor accelerated into the nearest driveway. As he arrived, he turned around in time to see the SUV slide past *exactly* where he'd just been stopped. The young man at the wheel had his mouth wide open and was clearly out of control.

Victor got out of his car and ran out to the road.

The SUV hydroplaned another seventy feet down into a curb at the next big curve, rebounded from it jerkily, and spun around completely, then halfway again. At last it came to a stop, facing opposite the direction it had been going, in fact now facing uphill.

Victor ran down to the car, slogging through the water, which at times was up to his ankles. The guy at the wheel had slumped back into the seat's headrest, his head back.

Victor rushed the driver's side door, which proved to be unlocked and opened it.

The young man stared up at the ceiling in horror. "Jesus! Jesus! Jesus!"

Victor jumped in far enough in to reach over and shut off the engine. He then reached over the guy's lower body and pulled up the emergency brake. He snapped off the seat belt restraints.

"Jesus! Jesus! Jesus!" The young man was saying over and over again.

"The car's stopped. Are you hurt?"

He looked at Victor, utterly appalled.

"It's okay. You're okay!" Victor assured him.

"Jesus!"

"It's all over. The car is stopped and shut off. You're okay."

"Jesus! I thought it was just going to keep turning round and round all the way down the hill till it fell over or—!"

He'd begun to tremble. He was going into shock.

"You're okay. Get out of the car. C'mon! Out!"

He half-stumbled, letting Victor half-pull him out, and leaned against the car. That immediately began to move. He quickly pulled away, frightened anew. The head and tail lights were still on.

"Come with me!" Victor commanded and grabbed at his jacket. The young man was taller than him and, even though the jacket, muscular. "Come!"

Victor led him to his own parked car, not sure what to do.

An elderly couple just then came out of the house where he'd so precipitously parked. They looked worried.

"Can we come in for a minute?" Victor asked. "I think he's in shock."

By now the other driver was shivering. Victor pulled him up the few stairs and indoors. The woman sat them down on an enclosed porch sofa and gave him a heavily crocheted blanket, which Victor arranged around the young man's chest and shoulders while he continued to try and failed to speak through his intense shivering, the words coming out broken, but similar to what he'd first said.

After a few minutes, he stopped shivering. He was extremely handsome, even *in extremis.* Young. Maybe twenty five. Looked like a kid. Thick butterscotch hair. Wonderful bone structure.

The woman was there with a cup of hot coffee.

Victor held it to him and the young man was able to sip as long as Victor held it to his lips. He looked up at Victor in horror. Pale gray eyes. Gorgeously flecked with green, blue, brown. He had just had a new thought.

"It's just sitting in the middle of the road. What if . . ."

Victor held the keys in his hand.

"If you want, I'll go move it."

"Be careful. Jesus! You saw what happened." He began telling the woman, "It just kept going around and around and I couldn't stop it no matter what I did."

Outside, down the hill, the SUV was where they'd left it.

Victor started it up and easily drove it across the now much decreased flow of water. He parked it alongside the house.

The woman met him at the door.

"I think he's a little better now. He's had a terrible shock."

The young man was on his cell phone, explaining something. His hand and the phone were still shaking.

"Two years ago," she added, conspiratorially, "a car did the same thing and then went over onto its roof and continued sliding down the road. It was this same kind of downpour. The girl inside became completely hysterical. We needed an ambulance to come get her."

The young driver was off the phone. Victor handed him the keys.

"Your car's okay. It's right here. But . . . look . . . how far do you have to go?"

"I just postponed it. I was going to an appointment in Beverly Hills."

"You live there? Or here?"

He pointed up the hill. "Twenty-six fourteen."

A house or so away from Victor's.

"Your car is fine parked here. Why don't I drive you home? You can pick it up later, when you feel a little . . . calmer. Okay?"

"You're in no shape to drive," the man of the couple assured the young man.

Ten minutes later in Victor's front passenger seat, the young man still seemed shaken. He couldn't leave it alone. "You saw the whole thing, didn't you?"

"I did. I saw the whole thing."

"I thought, Don, your life is all over. All over with, right here and now! And it would have been—if you hadn't moved your car . . . Why did you do that?"

"I saw you couldn't stop. Look, Don, is it? Take a little nap. Your car's fine there. Go get it later. Or tomorrow. Okay?"

Don clutched at him suddenly. "Dude! You saved my life."

"Don't worry about it," Victor laughed as he pried Don's hand off his arm.

"Both our lives," Don added.

It was as the very handsome, muscular young man shook his hand that Victor discovered his full name was Don Wright. He watched until Don got inside his house, waved, and closed the door.

"Done Right, huh!" Victor said to himself as he drove the seventy or so feet on to his own driveway. "I'll say. For once, Miss God, you seem to have made something *completely* right!"

CHAPTER TWENTY-EIGHT

"Well, if it's cold and rainy there, why not just come on out to the desert? It's perfectly dry and warm here," Andy Grant said, adding, "And it's midseason. Bathing suit weather. January is when everyone is here and when everything and I mean *everything* is happening."

He then mentioned half a dozen names of chantoozies so utterly over-the-hill that Victor had to restrain himself from asking, "You mean she's still *alive?* And *her?* And her *too?*" Obviously they were all alive and most of them were appearing at one desert *boite* or another, luckily in the weeks to come and not immediately, so Victor didn't have to actually commit to joining his childhood friend night after night as Andy idolized them from the front row, where loose neck-skin and drooping, over-cosmetized eyelids were sure to be the order of the day, no matter how good the voices still might be.

"It's been years since I've been to Palm Springs," Victor mused aloud.

"It's only a two hour-or-so drive. Given the variable traffic, of course. You can come during the day, which is best. C'mon down. It'll be fun. Lassiter Smith is here. And Alliger Munday. Everyone's down here, really."

Victor had no idea who the second person was. He did recall Lassiter: one of Andy's best buds, and, unexpectedly, a man from the previous generation, and according to Andy, a laid-back, semi-genius at tickling the ivories and singing Hoagy and Irving and George Gee slightly hoarsely. Until a few months before, he had lived high (in all ways) in an architectural marvel of wood, glass, stonework, and waterfalls(!) in a canyonette just off Wonderland Road in Laurel Canyon, not far from where Victor now resided.

There had been one particular dinner party at Lassiter's Laurel

Canyon home during the December holidays a few seasons back. Food was served alfresco until the winds suddenly rose. Inside, first Lassiter, and then even more surprisingly, Andy (who knew he had a voice?) and Lassiter together had regaled the guests with solos and duets from the 1930's in as effortless a manner as Victor assumed those standards had first been sung: usually back then by slender, high-Irish-tenors wearing bow ties and four-button suits in little nightclub dance floors on Wilshire Boulevard. That was a great memory, even if one of the tunes, Noel Coward's "You're the Top," had reminded Victor so bitterly of Mark Chastain, now gone, what was it, three years already?

That had kind of been Mark and Victor's song at the beginning of their love affair once they'd returned to Manhattan. Each of them would say to the other at any time of day out of nowhere, "You're the Mona Lisa," or "You're Garbo's salary," or the ultimate compliment from the song, "You're Cellophane!" Any time of day, any place at all, including the Intensive Care Unit at the very, very end.

"Get a pen," Andy now commanded, "I'm giving you the simplest possible directions." He then went on to do anything but, saying that the house was in "The Movie Colony," wherever that was, and just around the corner from Lucille Ball's old estate, "the one with Desi; you know, before the divorce," which was when and where, exactly? And other really unhelpful tips for someone who'd been in Palm Springs exactly once in his life and that maybe fifteen years previously.

All of it naturally uttered by Andy in his newly minted, totally throwaway, *soigne* tone of voice (hinting to anyone listening that he'd *lived, darling, lived!*), demanding that surely Victor had to know these places, since simply everyone did. Even so, Victor managed to get down the street name and the number and he guessed he would figure out where it was even if he had to go to the library and look it up on a street map. Palm Springs couldn't be that difficult anyway. Highway 111 ran down through it to the next town, and there were maybe ten perpendicular roads of note crossing the 111. Everything lay in a grid, even though some recalcitrant residential streets at times curved around and around, even looping.

From an earlier conversation with Andy, he'd gathered that Lassiter was in the desert because he had nowhere else to go. The fellow he had lived with for decades in the fabou house in the Aitch-Wood Hills had inconveniently upped and died. Andy was never too clear about what Lass's relationship to the man had been based on to begin with. Certainly it wasn't in any way "legal," and that was all that now seemed to count. The heir or heirs or their attorneys had eventually kicked Lass out on his proverbial piano-bench ass. Where was he to live? Surely not in that Sixty-Nine Seafoam-Green Thunderbird, which while stylish, could just about hold all his tuxedos and cummerbunds.

So Andy had drawn Lass down to the desert to Rancho Mirage, where he was house-sitting in some luxury for a friend of a friend of Andy's for a few months, surrounded by ex-U.S. Presidents, their henchmen, mistresses, and wives, until Andy could figure out what to do with him. Lass had never paid into Social Security, Andy explained, and at 75 years old or more (*That old!* Victor found himself thinking. *Gosh, large amounts of gin actually* did *pickle one marvelously*), Lass had lived off what he made tinkling the keys at parties and at a few San Fernando Valley bars two nights a week. Most of his pay arrived in the form of strong martinis placed within easy grasp upon the piano during the night. He didn't require money anyway: what for? To pay for the cup of black coffee and the ham-on-rye sandwich per day he ingested to keep reed-slim?

Meanwhile, from what Victor could make out, Andy was renting, sharing a place with another older fellow, one Tobey Hatch, who, according to Andy had "done hair on stage and in film, most recently, of course for his dear old friend, Ginger Rogers." Thus Victor could well believe that the place where Andy was living was "biggish" with a pool and multi-purpose outdoor decks as well as having several bedroom suites, one of which presumably he would stay in for the weekend. Since Andy hadn't referred to Tobey at all, Victor further guessed that the owner would be away all the time. Which would be great.

Why Andy was there and no longer in Topanga Canyon he did not explain. Why he was renting and sharing also went unexplained. Could IBM's stock, his legacy after all, have fallen so drastically? How would Victor know anyway? He had several mutual funds, an I.R.A., and a tax shelter. He was utterly naïve when it came to Modern Money: How to Make it Grow and How to Lose It a topic which seemed to utterly obsess the other four gay men his age he knew who were still alive.

The location info at last released into the telephone-atmosphere, Andy now began to moan and sigh, to whine and gripe about his life in minute, if strangely telling, detail, filled as it was with the most glamorous kinds of non-problematic *proble-mas* mostly concerning pool-drain-people and gardeners, fountain contractors and other such types: nothing Victor could take in any way seriously. All of which he nevertheless listened to mock-seriously and responded to at least sensibly: his apparent role these days in Andy's eternally turbulent life, filled as it seemed to be lately and especially in the Desert with theater people who were long on *panache* if rather short on practical solutions—"I know! We'll put on a show, and save the ranch that way!"—although Victor had a feeling that most ranches were long past saving.

Fifteen hours later, Victor was driving along what seemed to him a very much expanded Santa Monica Freeway, replete with cloverleafs several football fields in length connecting to other freeways whose numbers he'd never heard of. He barreled past one development after another, adobe and red tile roofed developments on either side, no matter how far he looked. The exit signs spoke of Cherry Avenues and Walnut Boulevards, of Citrus Streets and Lemon Grove Lanes and Mountain Forest Vistas, but like the freeway construction men, those once salient local attributes were long vanished. Too bad; he well recalled and had looked forward to once more seeing fogged-in fields of green onions stretching to the edges of the brown hills, and to peering backward as the car climbed the high road up to Redlands. He could even now recall the ghost of an orange flower attar filling the sunset air from square miles of valley orchards hidden under low mists below.

Just as he'd begun to feel peckish and was barely holding his small Rice-Rocket onto the tarmac along the high-wind corridor of the San Gorgonio Pass, he came upon a good-sized shopping mall, evidently new, and sure to contain a food area. It was wind-swept, breezy, and even somewhat cold, but amazingly desert-dry and thus really quite tonic after all that humidity he'd suffered through for the past few months.

Victor sipped his caffeinated pick-me-up and then even cruised the Armani F/X and Calvin Klein shops for ten minutes each. Somehow, looking through an amplitude of high-quality, over-priced, well-tailored leathers, silks, and wools, none of which he needed nor wanted, cheered Victor immeasurably.

A half hour later he was driving into Palm Springs town itself, and his library atlas directions proved perfect.

Of course it was impossible to tell if he'd actually arrived at the address given, except by painted numbers along the low curbstone, since every street was graced with ten-foot-high Oleander hedges out of which soared from behind an occasional, name-bestowing *Washingtonia filiara,* as well as huge fan palms, mixed in with tum-bling cascades in impossibly pastel hues of bougainvillea, all but hiding the wrought-iron gateways. Block after block looked like nearly solid hedges, or like large, dull, identical green sculpture. Until at last you stopped, got out of your by now flaming-hot-metal-fender car and peered in closely to what had to be an entrance.

At the number he'd been given, he did this and was immedi-ately greeted by the sharp yipping of several small Sheltie dogs, instantly followed by the voice of a very bored Andy Grant drawl-ing "Shut up Cassius! Portia, knock it off."

Seconds later, Andy's face appeared between matching, per-fectly cone-shaped, boxwood hedges. Or at least Victor assumed it was Andy, he looked so different: So thin, so clean shaven, and—let's be bone-breakingly honest—so old and gray!

"Oh! It is you." Andy's voice at least was still sixteen years old. "I thought for sure you'd driven further on to Sunny Dunes Road and been abducted by horny old queers there who'd dipped you in honey and eaten you whole."

Victor checked his watch which said he was maybe four min-utes late.

"Don't linger on the street like a fifty-dollar-a-night hooker," Andy instructed. "Come on in! Do you have a lot of luggage? I'll just bet you do. I'm sure this one," hefting a bag filled with CDs and books Victor had dropped on the first paving stone inside the gate, "is simply brimming with unguents and potions, with face-masks and creams and lotions! How else would you look so good, given what I know of your Decades of Deep Trampitude? Follow me! Cassius! Portia! Stop barking! Or I'll feed you to Ricardo the Pool Man."

The Shelties fled, yipping in terror, leading their cortege along the long, paved path into the ajar silvered ten-foot-high double doors of the entry.

If it was burning white hot outside, once indoors it was crepuscular and virtually frigid, an effect enhanced by the over-liberal use of reflective surfaces including entire wall-sized mirrors, while smaller looking-glasses hung at all levels as well as leaned along the floor boards, amid paintings so deeply set in glass one could barely make out the subject, all set against the highest gloss obtainable of silver, brass, gold, and copper paint on all the main living area walls.

Those lambent surfaces were further enlightened by varied water-features ranging from small, gurgling fountains indoors and out, to sofa-length, waist-high, rough-stone fish pools behind each of the two matching matte-silver couches, all of it leading to and starring, ta da!, the ten by eighteen foot wall of the dining room: entirely aquarium, in which only silver, gold and otherwise iridescent fish glided and swirled.

In the days of his visit to come, Victor would never enter these rooms by day or night without having to quickly grasp something solid so as to retain any inner-ear balance at all. *Mal de mer* was always a possibility. At times his arms automatically flew into the positions needed for doing the Australian Crawl.

"Tobey's a big believer in Feng Shui," Andy said, noticing Victor gawping about, and in a not quite sufficiently explanatory gesture, he added, "He's not having the easiest time lately and so he's dispersing bad *Chi* like mad."

Andy's flip-flops made an inordinate amount of rattling, as though they were made of slatted wood, as he led Victor past these various aquatic features. Suddenly they were in a differently decorated hallway, wall-papered in lattices and hatching, as though it was a jungle cottage with a tiny forest of Okapi horns along the crown molding, all simply dripping ferns.

"The bedroom suites," Andy quick-walked them past two closed doorways, adding, "The Master suite, and the Mistress suite," and thence into another corridor, this one all mirrors again. "And since I know you'll have sex every night you're here and scream like a stuck pig while doing so, I'm putting you way over here, where you can't possibly bother anyone."

He opened a door into a small, entirely carmine-painted room, cheerful with white accents: window shutters, Swiss-dotted curtains, polka-dotted leatherette bed headboard, painted little wooden desk, slatted matching desk chair, and even a white wicker faux-Windsor chair with red pillows piped in white, and, capping it all, set upon a white wicker lamp table late of some Alpine chalet, a monstrosity of a white wicker lamp maybe four feet high.

Andy dropped the bag he'd been carrying and Victor had to make an effort to shut his mouth.

"The Ginger Rogers Memorial Suite," Andy announced.

Only then did Victor see that each one of the pillows was embroidered and each chair-back pillow stitched with her signature, each silver framed photo and gold framed poster was signed by her, and pretty much half the knick-knackiana in which the room abounded was in direct reference to the perky blond movie star.

"It should be ghastly," Victor said. "But instead it's . . . kinda cute!"

"Well, I figured that your ego and hers were equally large, and so you'd fit well," Andy explained. "Settle in. And you'd better nap a bit because heaven knows you must require lots and lotsa beauty sleep. We'll meet for cocktails outside at the pool at five. Some people are coming. No one important. Don't dress."

Andy spun on a heel like Mrs. Danvers and was gone.

Victor scanned the over-themed room, thought he wanted to unpack and put everything away, wondered if he hadn't made a Huge Mistake in coming here in the first place as Andy was so envious, then found himself suddenly and totally drooping.

In seconds he was nestled among photo-stills from her RKO-era films, his head sinking into her stitched-name pillow, flat out upon a pink satin coverlet edged in miniature representations of silver stilettoed pumps—and if Victor didn't dream of her pirouetting backward in heels across a vast circular glass dance-floor, it surely wasn't Ginger's fault.

CHAPTER TWENTY-NINE

"Oh! It's you!" Dimitrios Juenger said, his mouth suddenly going all twisted with thought. He was wearing a Kimono-like outfit under which he was evidently clothingless and was barefoot. In the background, Cher was belting out her major hit anthem to the power of Belief.

"We confirmed yesterday morning by e-mail. Remember?" Victor asked. He was standing in the doorway of a large apartment with many wide windows—foolish Victor; he had assumed it would be an office—on the seventeenth floor of 9000 Sunset Boulevard, a great big black glass edifice that stabbed West Hollywood with Height and Night just as it was trying to quietly subside into posh residential Beverly Hills. Given Juenger's evident bafflement, a great deal must have happened since that cyberspace agreement was made at 10:23 a.m. yesterday morning.

"Well, come in then," he said. "I'm done with my ginko-biloba rub, and the ginger-root foot-massage can wait a sec." He gestured to a grand sofa. Victor assessed it as American Beidermeir, ca. 1846, with lion-paw feet on rollers and elaborately scrolled ends. The upholstery was wheat-gold and quite shiny. The back and sides fan-palm mahogany. Very rare. Yet it fit well in this super modern space, filled as it was with Beaux Arts shiny swag curtains and gilt footstools with rose chintz covers.

Juenger vanished into a doorway out of which a tall, wispy blond lad emerged to peek. "Are you the guy deep into Kabbalah?" he asked. The masseur. Victor thought for sure he would be Asian.

"Hindu Astrology," Victor glibly lied.

"Oh, right. Well, that's okay!" And he vanished.

The door bell rang and Dmitrios shouted "Would you mind getting that? And if its Jaecklin, tell him . . . Never mind," he added darkly. "I'll deal with him myself."

Victor opened the apartment door upon one of the loveliest young men he'd ever laid eyes on: tall, butter-haired, pale-green-eyed, clearly a model or . . .

He carried a medium-sized black leather portfolio case, and without even noticing Victor slumped over onto the other end of the sofa, propped his expensively shod feet onto the glass-topped, baroquely brass-legged coffee table, took out his cell-phone, and began checking his messages.

"Are you Jaecklin?" Victor asked when he was clearly done and not at all happy with the results.

"Why? Did he say I'm in trouble?"

Dmitrios chose that moment to enter the room, a bit more dressed with sporting pajamas beneath the robe he'd had on and gold-leafed flip-flops. He swanned over to his desk, making a big show of barely noticing Jaecklin, and ended up sitting before his large computer screen.

"Santa Monica Casting: twenty minutes late. Ventura Boulevard Casting: forty-five minutes late. Ginny Goldberg Casting: no show."

Jaecklin didn't seem to care about the litany. Then it came out in a torrent: "Ricky Sachs chased me around his desk for forty-five minutes trying to get into my skivvies. So, of course I'd be late at Ventura.

"I warned you he'd try that."

"You didn't warn me that he had the limbs of a giant squid. And that Almond woman at Dominguez Hills? I mean that was a hour's drive and all she did was wave me over to have five polaroid shots done by some sub-sub-assistant in two minutes while she spoke on the phone and totally ignored me."

"It's The Biz, Babe." Dmitrios had no sympathy. "And now you've got a two-thirty at the Gower Boulevard Studios. Eight lines. It's now one-twenty-four."

"I learned the lines. Dumb as they are. I'll be there."

"Leave in exactly three minutes. Take a magazine if you're early. Sit in the damn car and read. Here!"

Jaecklin and Victor glanced at the cover of what he'd tossed: *Freshmen*, featuring a nubile strawberry blond named Jon, shirt-less and slowly pulling down his sweat-pants to reveal more than half of his doubtless strawberry blond-covered glutes. Jaecklin dropped it onto the coffee table. "I'm straight. Remember?"

"Oh, right. I always forget. I wonder why? Well, you'll have to get your own *Penthouse*."

Jaecklin picked up a six month old copy of *Premiere* and began leafing through it.

"Do you know how many auditions I got for Buddy Gee, yesterday?" Dmitrios asked the air. "One. And for Tom Trithon? None. You get five in a day and screw them up."

"I appeared at three of them, eventually," Jaecklin said, now in a black mood which Dmitrios picked up as he instead turned to Victor and, changing tack in a headwind, expostulated, "Actors! Now Victor Regina here is a famous writer. And if Fate does right by us all, I'll be managing some of his books. Show Victor your portfolio! Maybe we'll do a film and he can hire you. Meanwhile, and excuse me Victor, thanks to Tom Cruise the Second here, I've got many, many fences to mend!"

The next fifteen minutes were spent with Victor and Jaecklin going through the younger man's five-page portfolio consisting almost entirely of photos, only two of them from roles he'd had, one in a college production of *Our Town* ("Every school on the planet does *Our Town*," he commented). The other still from a community theater production of *The Fantasticks*. ("Ditto with this play," he added.) Behind them, Victor heard Dmitrios on the phone in a voice too low to make out.

"Is there a role for me, Victor?" he handsomely asked.

"Sure, if we ever sell, *Never Can Say Goodbye*. You look just like how I describe Tim Brautigan in that book."

"Gosh," Jaecklin was all Candid Young Man and was even more winsome. "I *know* that book. Half the cast was reading it when we were doing *The Fantasticks*. Wow!" Suddenly he was thoughtful. "Gosh. You really are someone famous, aren't you? Wow!"

Victor suddenly remembered what Andy Grant had said to him the last visit before he'd moved here, when they'd gone to dinner at Spago. "I phoned and they said they had no tables open all night. Ten minutes later I phoned again, this time saying I was an assistant needing a table for my boss, the New York writer, Victor Regina, for two at the window. And here we are! Overlooking

Sunset Boulevard and Tower Records parking lot!"

"Meaning?" Victor had asked. Goldie Hawn, Kurt Russell, and her two gorgeous teenagers had just been seated at the next table.

"Meaning! If you want to live in El Lay you ought to possess at least one of the following: youth! looks! wealth! talent! fame! Having one, talent say, will just about get you in the door. Having two, talent and fame say, as we both saw tonight, *exponentially* increases the perks."

"And having them all . . . ?" Victor wondered aloud.

"Having two is plenty. Be content," Andy had said.

Handsome Jaecklin was now confirming that fact.

Dmitrios suddenly came swooping at them, shouting. "Time to go! Go! Go! Pose! Speak! Act! Make Mother proud of her baby!"

Jaecklin leaped up from the sofa, grabbed his portfolio and was out the door in seconds.

The masseur followed him a minute later.

"Now that the children are gone," Dmitrios declared, "let's have a civilized cup of tea and chat. Do you like Raspberry Zinger? We've got a half hour until more of the chickadees come flapping in with broken wings and flattened egos, all needing to be mended."

"How many actors do you manage?"

"Too many for any peace of mind. Not enough for a real income. Now I heard you talking about Tim Brautigan in *Goodbye* as a role for our little Blond Godlet. He'd be per-feck-shun!"

"But Brautigan is gay. I mean flamboyantly, wildly gay in the book."

"He will be in the flick too," Dmitrios confirmed.

"But Jaecklin is . . ."

"Gay for pay, honey. They all are. Show-Biz lesson number thirty-five: if you wanna work, you gotta play by no rules at all."

"But you don't really think anyone would want to turn *Never Can Say Goodbye* into a film, do you? I mean the one agent I talked to about it over at CAA when it first came out said it had a snowball's chance in hell."

"That's exactly why CAA is no longer Aitch-Oh-Tee!" Dmitrios said. "I don't see why not. It's a best seller, right?"

"In four languages."

"International market!"

"Who would we show it to? A producer? A director? I only

know one or two people in Hollywood any more," Victor said. "And I've not spoken to them in a while."

"Names?" Dmitrios was suddenly Ann Southern as Bob Cumming's secretary, his pretend pencil-nub wetted, his imaginary pad held high.

"Well, one was an agent. I'm not at all sure where he is now. Or even if he's still around, Ever hear of a fellow named Joel Edison?"

"Oh, he's definitely still around! He runs talent, I mean he absolutely *is* talent at William Morris! And the other?"

"Well, I could see Joel remaining on his feet," Victor admitted. "But I've totally lost sight of this guy I worked really closely with in the Eighties and I'll understand if you don't at all know of him. His name is Sam. Sam Alan Haddad?"

This time Dmitrios stood up and inadvertently knocked over his chair.

"S.A. Haddad?! You don't fool around, do you? Haddad took over the two Indy lines at Fox. His films grossed almost as much as Disney last year."

This was less than welcome news to Victor. "Maybe we should forget about Sam. He and I didn't end up all that terrifically. But Joel, he always wanted to get into my pants, so that must count for something."

"Well, now you've got me fascinated, and as the woman says in that old Bette Davis movie, a fascinating man is more than fascinating: he's *downright* fascinating! Victor, you've got eighteen and half minutes before the children come tumbling in and I want to hear everything and I do mean everything! Hold back nothing! And to prove it," he added, "Keep talking and I shall freshen up our teapot."

He'd decided that since he was only a few blocks away, he'd drop down into Boy's Town and stop in A Different Light Books and get that gay novel Ed White had blurbed (this month; he blurbed so many!) and then actually recommended by phone to Victor.

San Vicente Boulevard began at Sunset right here and swooped down to West Hollywood and then further on, and it didn't end until way past Mid-City.

Right on the sidewalk were two young men running down the

steep hill of the street. One had dark hair and wore Aviator sun glasses a bit too big for his face and looked kind of Nerdy-Cute, albeit he was a bit chunky. He wore close-fitting white shorts, and an oversized black wife-beater that read "Rio is Better," and was wearing what looked like two-hundred dollar running shoes.

The bigger surprise was the guy running next to him, speaking to him all the while, or maybe yelling at him, urging him on. It couldn't be, but it was, Don Wright.

Victor pulled up to Cynthia Street at the light, where the Big Dig for the new fire station was still a mess on the other side of San Vicente, and the two thundered down past and sure enough it was Don, wearing black basketball shorts, an A-shirt, and a silver sweat band around his handsome head.

Victor beeped twice and they turned. Don recognized him, and stopped, yelling to the other guy, "Go. Don't stop. I'll catch up."

"Hiya, neighbor!" Sweat trickled down his perfectly sculpted neck past his Audrey Hepburn collar-bones and down the sternum hidden by the shirt.

"You're a fitness trainer!" Victor said.

"Gotta' make a living somehow!"

"You're busy. I won't keep you."

Someone beeped from behind for Victor to move.

"Ciao!" Don Wright saluted and ran on.

Victor watched him in his side and rear view mirror all the way to Santa Monica Boulevard

"He's a fitness trainer," Victor repeated to himself. "Of course he is. What else would he be?"

CHAPTER THIRTY

Two cars were parked in the shadiest area under the gigantic rose oleander where Victor had parked previously. Rats! And there were two cars parked inside the gated driveway. He recognized Andy's "Lesb-mobile," a lime-green Subaru Forester four-wheel-drive wagon. But that gigunda chrome and purple Oldsmobile had to be Tobey Hatch's. Who else was here this weekend? He recalled the phone conversation with Andy three days back and decided that, of course! Those two unwashed beige Crown Vics must belong to the so-called Church People that Andy had spoken of. No one but the L.A.P.D. and the Religious Right was dense enough to buy a gas-guzzling V8 that weighed three tons anymore. Even straight guys with small weenies had switched to Hummers.

As he unpacked his own car, Victor tried to recall exactly how that phone conversation had gone.

To begin with, it had come as a surprise. Only a few weeks after his first visit to Palm Springs, his childhood friend had called and asked when he was coming to visit again. Given their track record over the decades, Victor had replied, "I thought . . . maybe . . . sometime next year?"

"No, no, no! You mustn't think that way," Andy had astonishingly replied. "That was the *old* Andy Grant. The Hermit-of-the-Canyon Andy Grant."

"Okay. When would you *like* me to come visit?"

This coming weekend it turned out, and Tobey would be there. Andy so wanted them to meet. Victor would love Tobey. A Munchkin. And adorable. And he knew so much about Old Hollywood and where so many corpses were buried. Why didn't Victor plan to come Friday by noon?

It meant rescheduling a Sunday brunch, and the weather was at last moderating so he *had* been looking forward to that rarity this year—some local sun in El Lay—but it wasn't, Victor admitted, actually "impossible."

"Great! We'll have such fun!"

That should have been the tip-off. The human person, Andy Grant, and the word "fun" didn't exist on the same plane. Victor had temporized, asking, "Did someone ask for me in particular?"

"No, it'll just be us three. Unless of course Tobey asks some of the folks from the Church to drop by."

"The Church of the Ever-kneeling Fellator?"

"I wish! No, unfortunately. Just the people from some church Tobey's gotten . . . *interested* in lately. They've been *awfully* kind to him. Visited him *regularly* during his radiation sessions and all. But he's feeling *much better* now that he can keep down solid food. So we'll have a barbecue! Just we three—and Cassius and Portia!"

Of course, all this was the very first hint Victor was hearing of Tobey and any even vaguely problematical health situation. *Nada* during the entire last visit here, nor in any phone calls. Piecing it all together now three days later, on the very doorstep of their shared domicile, Victor knew there was still some mystery involved. He sensed it and wondered if he really and truly wanted to get at that mystery's little black heart.

Andy was sitting on the side terrace looking depressed, an equally silent Sheltie on either side of him. He sucked for dear life on a woebegone joint of grass and contemplated what might have been lethal-to-the-planet fast-spreading algae on the surface of the pool. He barely noticed Victor walk up and drop his bags.

"Well! I'm here!" Victor declared. "I can see you're simply too thrilled to even respond."

At that moment the front door of the house swung open. The Shelties growled as low as such small animals are capable of. Andy quickly, surreptitiously, dropped the weed, stamped it out with a flip flop, and stood.

Two tall people came out of the house, he bald and washed-out looking, she wearing some kind of hair-net and a very long skirt with white socks and nurse-like shoes. Very 1954, Victor thought, if otherwise non-distinctive. They were followed by a leprechaun, an orange-haired elf, a . . . it must be Tobey!

"Good meeting, was it?" Andy asked, some unclear emotion apparent in his voice.

"We prayed together, Brother Andrew," the bald man said. The elf turned and noticed Victor and a bit of life came into his eyes.

"Prayed for our brother, Tobey," the drab woman added unnecessarily in a toneless voice.

The man looked at Victor with his own spark of interest, but Victor turned away so as to not encourage any possible introduction, never mind the humiliation of being "brother-ed" by a stranger.

The Tall Two said a few words very quietly to Tobey and were soon out the wrought-iron gate.

He waited until their cars had started up and taken off, then turned to Victor and almost squealed, "You must be the *boyhood pal!*"

"Everything Andy said about me is a lie."

"And to think I believed you." Tobey said. "But then, you must have heard I've had my mind surgically removed—Not! Come on in! Let's have a cocktail! I'm not supposed to. But my test results are the best in months, so we oughta celebrate."

From close up, Tobey Hatch was maybe sixty-eight or sixty-nine. He was also clearly sick or quite exhausted, and over the weekend he would tire easily, leaving the others alone. But at least the smallness of the dogs made total sense now. Against Andy they were like specks of color and motion. Sitting next to and licking various unclothed parts of Tobey's well-put-together little body, they were appropriately-sized pets.

The three had to be indoors most of the time because of the strong sun's effects on the chemo Tobey was still taking. Victor would never learn where the cancer had begun in him nor when. He was such a cheerful guy that Andy Grant's wild-sounding prediction came true. That whole weekend they had fun. Had fun indoors and out. Had fun driving around town in the oversized Olds 98, Tobey sitting on a specially upholstered seat, "So I can see over the dashboard and not mow anyone down—at least not *accidentally!*" he added with mischief in his green eyes.

That first night, when Tobey retired before the others, he said, "You're staying in Miss Roger's suite, right?"

"I don't have to," Victor said. "I could sleep out here," meaning one of the long living room sofas.

"No. She'd want it," Tobey declared with authority.

The following day, when they were alone, Tobey confided, "The first time I spent any time with Miss Rogers, I inadvertently walked away with one of her little pink stationery pads. It read 'From the Desk of . . . .' well, you know Who."

"Were you mortified?" Victor asked.

"For about a Baptist minute," Tobey giggled. "For the next six months I left messages all around the city, using her stationery."

Later that night, Victor commented to Andy about Tobey's using "Miss" so much about the actress.

"Well, he's completely inaccurate. She married three times, you know. Although the truth is she was slurping on Howard Hughes's pole long enough, hoping to become Mrs. Hughes. But after that first adolescent marriage and divorce, clever Howard played the field forever after, and never got hitched again."

"You know this how? A tell-all biography?"

"There are a few of those. No, I know his nephew. The one Howard turned queer when the boy was sixteen? Just like Hughes's gay movie director uncle turned him onto fellatio when young Howard was fourteen. Don't shake your head. It's a known fact that Hughes didn't have vaginal intercourse until he was forty."

"I'll believe all that when I hear the nephew tell it to me in person."

"It'll happen. I'll throw you two together some time. He's eighty-four or so. He lives up in one of those very old posh nabes in the Ess-Eff Valley." (San Fernando)

While Andy was at last cleaning the pool, Tobey drew Victor inside the very deliberately "cottage-y" kitchen with its cleverly cross-hatched-everything when not ceramic-everything-else. "Look at these Polaroids I found."

They were from about the year 1960 or so, and they showed a forty years younger and not much physically different Tobey Hatch wearing an "arty" too-big beret, tight, striped sailor's shirt, and body-hugging toreador pants with big Keds sneakers.

"Wasn't I a sight?"

"Are you kidding? Look how cute you were! I would have gone after you!"

"Gotten me too. I was so horny!"

He pulled out a dozen more, all from the same period, all showing himself among young men and a few young women.

"That's when I met Miss Rogers. I was a film chorine then. A dance gypsy. We all were. Well that lasted about a Protestant second for me. They just kept wanting to cast me in what they called 'novelty roles.' Because of my height. Or rather my lack thereof."

"Prejudiced bastards."

"Well, it is Show Biz," Tobey said in a tone of religious finality. "So while that lifelong dream was slowly strangling on the vine, I'd begun to fix some of the girls' hair in the companies. Some of those dizzy broads couldn't comb-out a shampoo or make a French Bun that didn't look like a dog's turd. But I could. Easy. Frosting hair was big then. Cut Italian-boy short in back. Gina Lollabridgida bangs in front. With blonde frosting. I learned how to do that in a cinch, and even the dance boys started to coming to me for what they called 'The Surfer Look.' Right. Surfing Selma Avenue for twenty bucks a suck! Well, after a while, I decided to charge money and they all paid, without even blinking. Then one film, where I had like about fifteen seconds onscreen, the hair lady left and all the gypsies said to the producer 'Hire Tobey. He redoes our hair after she does anyway.' So they did hire me."

"Wow!"

"Funny, huh? So there's Miss Rogers on the studio lot, two buildings down, and she sees all these frosted kids and she's perpetually worried about her hair. I mean, to look at it you'd think it's perfect, but take it from me, her hair was like another entire personality altogether. Yes, that much trouble! Not to mention that she's now En-El-Why."

"No Longer Young," Victor parsed it.

"Eggs-act-ly! So she has me come see her in make-up and she doesn't want 'frosting.' What she wants is 'touching up' because that perfect yellow helmet is beginning to go dark on her and not just at the roots. Uh-huh! I am telling you! And Miss Rogers is freaked about it as she believes her yellow hair is now her fortune. At least that's what *she* thinks.

"Well, I am so very nervous I almost spill my entire color tray all over her head the first time. But I take a good look at her hair and it's like ten different types of blonde. So, of course, it's going to darken in time, naturally.

"But not if *Miss Rogers* has any say-so in the matter. And she does. So I begin, quote, touching-her-up and the film-stock for whatever film she's in is some kind of new Mescal-Color. When the film premieres, everyone else's hair comes out yellow-green and yellow-red, except Miss Rogers, who is as blonde in 1960 as she was in *The Barkleys of Broadway*.

"The next day, I get out of bed and go to get my newspaper and what do I see but a shiny new cream and aqua Nash Metropolitan automobile parked on the curb in front, with a big satin bow on it and a card containing keys and from, you guessed who, Miss Rogers.

"It was the absolute perfect size for me. And the colors were my faves too," Tobey said.

Victor had to laugh, he could picture it so well.

"So, when The Movies got tired of her, and she began to go on the road in live shows, well, she hired me."

"To 'touch-up'?"

"And that's what I did, until several years ago. Traveled all over the country, all over the world, as part of her *Hello Dolly* stage company. I even did her mother's hair. Because you know that stage mother was around, I swear, almost to the very end. She simply would not up and die!"

Tobey giggled. They both giggled.

Then Tobey mused: "I guess it was . . . *some* sort of a life. Even though I never did become the new Fred Astaire like I wanted."

"It sounds like a perfectly fabulous life to me," Victor said in all sincerity. "People would *kill* to have had that life, and you very well know it, Tobey Hatch! Now we've only got fifteen minutes till dinner and I want to know who was she dating then? Year by year."

"Well, by then she'd gone through Hollywood—the last husband was Jacques Bergerac. Remember him? Utterly dreamy! But I swear, half her age! So she'd turned to *foreign* money! And I mean foreign. Cuban. Venezuelan. There was this Brazilian millionaire . . . " Tobey began. "Hung like a donkey.

"When she dumped him, he came after me! Can you believe it? A total bisexual! I can tell you that was one extremely carefully backdoor affair he and I had. But, what is it Greer Garson used to say? 'The only good thing about playing the "other woman" is that you always get to wear the best jewelry'!

"Of course some hustler boy got away with most of those baubles ten years later. Fucked me good, robbed me, and took off with my jewelry case. He probably pawned it all for gas money, thinking it was costume crap!"

Tobey Hatch almost fell over laughing at the memory.

CHAPTER THIRTY-ONE

"Today will be a 'Meet and Greet' at Warner Brothers," Dmitrios Juenger said when Victor met him at the glassy front lobby of 9000 Sunset. "And of course, you're dressed properly, casual yet businesslike. I can't tell you how bad these actor-children of mine are. I've got to literally go through their wardrobes and pick out what they can and cannot wear at auditions and meetings. But you're a Man of the World, so I knew you would instinctively know."

He nattered on as they dropped down to the underground parking, where Dmitrios's pale green current model year Mercedes Benz CLK-320 Coupe was waiting. When he'd first seen the expensive car—it cost what? five times the price of Victor's "Rice-Rocket"?—and whistled the younger man had stopped, made a mock serious face, and said, "When the Parking Valet brings it up, no matter what bullshit line I've just given them, I'm, like, totally vindicated."

"Them" meaning the various people Dmitrios had met one way or another, over the past year or more, with some connection to feature film or television, mostly encountered socially, or because one of his boys had auditioned well for them. Earlier this week, he'd put together a tentative list of several such people. All of them were "in a position to offer or buy," and they would be visiting them over the next several weeks in hopes of getting someone interested in the film or television rights to Victor's hit novel, *Never Can Say Goodbye*.

That there were so many was, according to his new Entertainment Rights Manager, a testament to the power of Victor's name as an author. Victor however was certain that few of them actually knew who he was or had read any of his books. It was more like they vaguely recalled his name from years of perusing airport paperback racks, where they would invariably see one of his and buy someone else's.

In some cases, Dmitrios admitted, they in all likelihood didn't even know that, but were instead open to anyone with his track record for turning out books and getting them published.

The younger man was certainly unstinting in his activity on Victor's behalf. In return, he'd asked Victor to do some work beforehand "on spec" (that is, without pay) on the book, making it easier for him to "pre-sell" or at least present it. This meant that for every fat copy of the trade paperback they would leave with someone, with its first four pages of fabulous quotes and its bright gold stripe across the top declaring it the winner of a literary prize Victor was sure they'd never heard of, they would also receive one of several new précis he'd prepared. One was as short as three pages of widely spaced text for the least lexic among them; the others ranged up to as many as ten more ordinarily spaced pages condensing the book's material. All of these spelled out the setting, time, and major characters, as well as a selling logline or instant description they could then present to their own superiors. No matter the length, each précis was laid out in three "acts," saving the prospective buyer from even doing this not-that-onerous task.

It was assumed, of course, that none of those meeting the duo would have actually *read* Victor's book, but would instead have farmed it out to an unemployed writer, a great enough number of which abounded in the city, some of whom made side-livings or even primary-livings out of doing such reports. But just in case even this short-cut was too much effort, Dmitrios had gotten a trade-off from a hopeful screen writer he'd done favors for, who had produced a perfectly professional "Reader's Report" on the novel. This, Dmitrios would quickly claim to any new contact "just came in" from some other, never named, source. "I couldn't possibly reveal who," Dmitrios would assure them, making sure they knew someone else was interested in the book. Because, after all, why else would anyone even *think* to buy it?

The several layers of inanity involved in playing this particular game did not too much bother Victor. As he'd told his editor, he didn't really have anything to do with himself these days and could easily enough waste the time while waiting for a new book to gel somewhere in his unconsciousness: a psychological area he seldom peered too closely into, fearing what might lurk in its depths; and worse, at other times, fearing nothing resembling depth lurked there at all.

In some ways, he was having fun doing all this—fun of an admittedly somewhat attenuated and unnatural kind—and Juenger had made enough contacts along the way and was enthusiastic enough so that it even at times seemed like they might actually be getting somewhere.

Seemed...

The Warner Brothers lot on the edge of Toluca Lake consisted of a half dozen giant buildings, each side of which boasted Herculean adverts of current television shows or upcoming films. But they weren't going into any of those buildings. Instead, they took a back route to a parking lot bigger than many Midwestern towns. There, cell phone conversations confirmed that they were indeed expected at the gate—an edifice which approximated what Victor thought surely must guard Area 51 where all the downed U.F.O. bodies were kept.

Parking took five minutes since they wanted to be within a half mile of their destination by foot. That destination ended up being amidst a row of tiny, shabby wooden shacks huddling below the grand sound stages, where Dmitrios assured Victor the best and brightest producers currently with the fabled studio resided by day and worked.

They found the number, but the door was locked. They knocked and the shack seemed to shiver with the impact. Maybe three minutes later, several locks opened and they were able to step in.

The decor inside was what you would expect of an unheated windowless wooden hut. One interior door was left open, another shut. The outer office held two fold-up canvas beach chairs and a tipped over orange crate splashed with movie magazines, pretending to be a coffee table. A spindly Ficus fought for dear life in an icy, under-illuminated corner. The only sign of the work done here was seven giant posters that literally covered the walls, in all likelihood put up for some heat-retention, all theater cards for films which Victor knew had premiered from five to twenty years ago.

"Sandy"—no last name was offered—was anorexic, or at least bird-thin, and she shivered here. Once they went into her office through one conspicuously open door, she all but perched atop a tiny electric heater.

She was, she told Victor, the producer's assistant, and said that she guarded his privacy and his time. She then admitted that she pretty much also took all of his meetings, as he was "a little Aspberger-ish, and the studio prefers that he not meet anyone directly."

"You mean Aspberger-ish as in Autistic?" Victor had the bad grace to ask.

She then went on to explain her boss, the actual film producer's, problems. The more he heard about them, the more Victor had to conclude that they added up to a bit more than that the man wasn't particularly social. He was downright weird around others, most likely sociopathic, and probably dangerous. "Still," Sandy concluded, "he can be a genius!" She gestured to get them to look up at the ten theater cards that wallpapered her office.

She was a pretty if exceptionally fidgety young woman. She spent most of the twenty-five minutes while Victor and Dmitrios pitched the book as a film filing her nails, and after that rummaging through a leather purse half the size of the room, in fact so large it often blocked her from their view.

Victor assumed Sandy was in search of some much needed prescription to calm the severe attention deficit disorder so evidently at the root of her personality. But what emerged at long last from that Saharan expanse of a pocket book was an eentsy packet of her personal professional cards, over-wrapped in red rubber bands. Upon them standing to leave, she distributed them with a face so serious they might have easily been vintage Liberty gold dollars.

Sandy said that she would look over what they left. Victor had chosen a smallish packet, but even so, he felt he was literally throwing away a perfectly good copy of his book since neither Sandy nor her producer appeared to be calm enough to read a prescription, never mind four hundred printed pages.

"Is it major or minor Bertolucci?" Dmitrios whispered loudly in the crowded and just beginning to quiet screening room, then half answered himself, "Actually even minor Bertolucci is worth seeing."

"Major, *major* Bertolucci. Up there with *The Conformist* and *Last Emperor of China!*" Victor whispered back. He could see from Dmitrios' eyes that he'd never even heard of the first film, but had heard, if not seen, the second. "This is the longest print ever available in the U.S. for *Nineteen Hundred*. It was badly cut for its American premiere and never shown in full before. I guess this screening came about because of the release of the VHS version."

Four hours later, a conspicuously pleased group loudly applauded the ending and sat through about a minute of the credits. The crew mostly being Italians, they were no one anyone on Santa Monica Boulevard and 26th Street would be expected to know or have worked with.

"I forgot how amazing Dominique Sanda is," Victor said aloud. "He certainly took a step down to Maria Schneider. Don't you think?"

His younger companion was clearly flummoxed. He had no idea who either actress was. Victor was about to explain, when from behind them a very distinctive voice said: "Maria Schneider was Marlon Brando's punching bag lover in *Last Tango in Paris*. And I'd recognize your voice anywhere, Mister Victor Regina, world famous novelist."

As Victor and Dmitrios turned to see who had spoken in the row behind them, the speaker added, "Whatcha doing back in El Lay, Hon? Slummin'?"

"I live here now," Victor said.

They all stood as people threaded around them and sure enough it was Joel Edison. Despite the perpetual and probably applied tan, and what must have been many, many spa treatments, he showed his age rather precisely. Of course he'd gained weight; they all had. On him it looked—well, *affluent* was the only word Victor could come up with.

"You live here? No shit! Where?"

"A minor street off Laurel Canyon."

"City view? Valley view?" the agent probed.

"City View. Well, most of downtown is blocked, but I've got a south-western view right to the airport. Sometimes I can see the ocean."

"Me, too. We must be facing the same way. I'm off Outpost."

"That's not far at all," Victor agreed. And since Joel was looking at, almost staring at, the younger man with that peculiar mixture of hunger and disinterest typical of a gay man of his years and station in The Biz, Victor added, "This is Dmitrios Juenger. He's got an entertainment company. And—"

"And I'm hoping to exploit some of Mr. Regina's literary works for the screen," the unfazed Dmitrios added, shaking the older man's hand. "I'm very honored to meet you, Mr. Edison."

"The honor happened when you met Victor," Joel pointed out. "He's the talent. I'm just a 'suit.'"

"Ah but *what* a suit!" Victor fingered the cuff. "Armani?"

"Yves St. Laurent."

Dmitrios cut in, "I was discussing with Mr. Regina how we could begin to arrange some meetings about that exploitation. Naturally, your name came up right away."

"In what capacity?" Joel asked, and as he did he revealed a slight twitching just below the left eye that Victor recognized as the result of a nerve-damaged facial condition known as Guilliam-Barre syndrome. "Oh, I know: it must have been as eye-witness to the truth of some of Victor's more debauched memoirs."

"Really?" Juenger's eyes went wide. "You mean you were *there?*"

"Well, I was there when it was Victor versus half of a particular National League football team."

"There were only two of them," Victor corrected.

"Both gargantuan. One the quarterback. The other the offensive captain. And it was at an extremely low-class joint named Basic Plumbing," Joel added, "Don't deny it," he warned. Then, "And the outcome was . . . well, iffy."

"'Iffy' my well-plowed rear end," Victor said. "I was like the mayo on a ham and cheese hero." All three of them laughed.

Joel quickly looked around to check that they were pretty much alone in the theater before adding, "The regulars at Basic Plumbing spoke about that evening for years afterwards. And especially, and I quote one of them, 'That pushy, lucky, New York queen!'" Turning to Dmitrios, he explained, "It was kind of like Woodstock. Everyone claimed they were there that night."

Dmitrios' eyes remained large with wonder. "You two must have had some terrific times before HIV came along! God, how I envy you!"

Victor felt he had to make an emendation to that. "That's certainly true. But then we also had to go through AIDS and all that too, for which we were *not* so lucky! Right, Joel?"

"Cor-rect-erooni, Victor! I ended up being HIV-Negative. And I must say, my diagnosis was to the general astonishment of the entire populace!"

"Me three," Victor admitted. "And there wasn't much fun in that, since everyone else died." To Joel he added, "It was after my life partner passed that I decided to come out here. We'd been talking about it for some years."

"So, I heard. And of course, I myself became quite cautious," Joel admitted.

"I'll say. I heard you'd married. A woman." Victor said. "That's cautious."

"It wasn't quite that drastic. We just lived together. We still sort of do," Joel added enigmatically. "But then, unlike you, I wasn't right in the thickest of it! How ever did you escape?"

"Well, you know what the Paulette Goddard character says in *The Women*? 'Where I spit, don't no grass grow ever'!"

They all laughed.

"Actually, I'm sort of not kidding. After the doctors and researchers nearly exsanguinated me, searching through my blood to find out why I never did get infected, they discovered I was in that small percentage who *can't* get infected. Because our T-cells are deformed. Yes, I am a mutant. I don't deny it. Which goes far to explain a great deal of my nefarious existence. But to change the subject, Joel, what did you think of this uncut version of the film?"

"Scrumptious. I wouldn't have missed it for the world," Joel said. "I remember how much I loved it when it first came out. I mean the star power alone! Sterling Hayden and Burt Lancaster as the fathers. DeNiro and Depardieu as the two sons! Even *I* would have never thought of that particular casting coup!"

"That homecoming scene in the barn between the two?" Victor said. "When they kissed in the hayloft, I thought Depardieu was going to buttfuck DeNiro, the way he lifted his legs up like that."

"I hoped! But then the scene with the whore in bed with the two of them? Jerking them off together?" Joel effused. "And of course Donald Sutherland and Laura Betti as fascist child killers. Priceless!"

"And Storaro's cinematography?" Victor asked.

"You could eat it with a spoon."

The screening-room staff had begun to come in carrying brooms and rolling vacuums, so the three moved into the aisle and began up toward the door.

"Of course with all the heroes being Communists, the film was sure to offend most Americans," Victor said.

"It did rather bomb here. But it delivered internationally. I believe it was Bertolucci's top grossing film, until *The Last Emperor* came along."

"Even beyond *Last Tango?*" Victor asked.

"I believe so. Remember, no one would screen that in much of the Mid East or even the Far East. Whereas this one . . . "

They'd reached the screening room lobby. A few smaller groups of people clustered, discussing the movie.

"Listen, this is great and I'd love to continue. But I've got a dinner thing I can't get out of," Joel said. "We've absolutely got to get together, Victor." He was all bonhomie. "I forgot how much I missed our cocktail sessions. Let's do one very soon."

"Okay. Sure. My schedule's pretty open."

Turning to Juenger, Joel said, "I'm sure Victor never told you any of this, because unlike every Hollywood writer I know he is modesty personified. But when Victor was out here working, he knew *all* the top directors."

"Hardly. Two, maybe. "

"And the *biggest* film stars, at their height of success."

"Oh, come on."

"Admit that Warren Beatty and Julie Christie were like your bosom buddies?"

"I met them twice."

"Victor virtually wrote the last decade of Frank Perry's *oeuvre.*

Not to mention being the only human actually able to speak without murdering Sh—"

Victor interrupted, "Yes, let's do have cocktails soon. You're at William Morris?"

"With yet another loser secretary! How do I pick them, Victor?"

"By their crotches?" Victor asked.

Joel laughed. "Call tomorrow. I'll warn Vlacheslav in advance so I don't have to yell at him when he screws up."

Out on the curb, it was dark and glittery with West L.A. evening traffic negotiating the slowly deepening West L.A. evening fog.

Naturally, a large charcoal gray Lincoln Town Car was idling just where Joel stepped out onto the curb.

"Can I give you a lift?" he asked.

"Our chariot's down there a bit," Victor pointed to the street.

"Call!" Joel insisted, got inside, and was gone.

As they were walking to Juenger's car, Victor could see the numbers being added up behind the younger man's mind.

"Don't get your hopes up, kiddo. Joel Edison talks the talk, and walks the walk, and we *will* have cocktails together. But he's never *really* delivered for me."

CHAPTER THIRTY-TWO

Victor was using the hose to water the potted plants on the deck and trying to recall exactly what the hard-faced transsexual in the gardening department at the Sunset Boulevard Home Depot had told him about gardenias. Did they like morning sun and hate afternoon sun? Or was it the opposite? And what had "Mara" said about wind? It was pretty windy on this deck, no matter what Victor did. He was shielding the gardenia somewhat, using a wall of the house. The roses, of course, loved the sun and the heat and the wind: they were such sluts! They were already over-filling their pots. But the gardenia . . . ! If only he'd not tried to *not* pay attention to Mara's face, which resembled Patrick Swazyze's taken apart and put back together again by a cosmetic surgeon with macular degeneration. Or Mara's voice, which was several full tones below Victor's. Maybe he was watering them too much? But then the leaves would turn brown, right? What did it mean that they were turning yellow? He'd gotten a gardenia-positive potting soil for them. He'd raised the pH factor for them. Maybe he should have lowered it? Christ, but these plants were more of a pain than raising a child!

"So, hello there, neighbor!"

Victor was so startled he all but hosed down the person suddenly standing on his deck. How had the guy even gotten there? It was twenty steps from anything even resembling an entry from the street.

"Didn't mean to startle you!"

He had truly startled Victor. Primarily because of who he was: Don Wright, Mr. Totally Gorgeous Physical Fitness Trainer from next door. Well, actually, next door and down the hill about seventy feet. This close, he looked even taller, maybe six-two, and handsomer: perfect butterscotch hair, straight, good sized, obviously whitened teeth, Midwestern American face. He was wearing a vaguely silver A-shirt, which barely covered his large and perfectly muscled torso, and a pair of black running slacks with a single silver line down the side made of some kind of ultra-sheer material—solidified jizz, probably. Like the top, the slacks revealed as much as they hid. And flip flops. Big bony feet. *Be still my heart*, Victor thought.

"I'd better put this away before I get us all soaked," Victor said, recalling that it had a quirk of giving one last, unprepared for spurt—much like a Cubano married lover he'd known years ago in Cocoanut Grove. He moved the hose over to the side of the deck before totally shutting it off. "There!" he said, but it spurted once more when he least expected it—just like Gustavo—and he got splashed.

Don Wright: "So I've been meaning to come say hello. You're here what? Two or three months?"

Six. "Something like that."

Don: "But you know how it gets. Busy, busy, busy."

If he'd ever thought to glance at this deck he would have seen that Victor was anything but busy, busy, busy. "Right!"

"And we *will* get together. I have these like monthly cocktail parties for my clients."

Victor had heard the last one. It had gone on till after midnight.

"Some of them you really should meet. You're a famous writer, I found out, and you'd all get along fine. But the reason I came is that house there!"

He pointed to the house between theirs, if above them both by about sixty feet. Two cute gay guys, maybe thirty-five or so, lived there. One red headed and kind of solid, the other leaner with tight black hair and seductive eyes. Victor guessed him to be some Mediterranean combo, half Lebanese, half Greek, maybe. Red drove a new smoke-gray Porsche Carerra, and Charcoal tooled around in a late model tan Tundra.

"What about it?" Victor asked.

"Well, their dog is like the size of a pony. The black one?"

Jeremy, he remembered Red calling it once. "I've seem them walk it."

"Well, here's the thing," and suddenly Mr. Midwestern Muscles was very intense. Victor could tell because, despite clothing, he was more or less unclothed and suddenly all his muscles sort of clenched: those around his neck, along his arms and even on his shoulders. "That dog barks constantly. Especially at night. And it wakes me up at like 5:00 a.m. You must hear it. It must wake you up too."

"My bedroom windows face this way." Victor walked Don along the deck and pointed. "Totally facing the other direction. In fact, they're blocked from the house that's annoying you by that hilly hummock. I can barely even see their place from here."

"Well, you're lucky. It's really loud and it's not right."

"It's certainly not good for you to be awakened a 5:00 a.m.," Victor agreed.

"I mean I get up early anyway. Eight. But at five?"

He was so sincere that Victor wondered what a penis would look like sort of angled thirty five degrees out of the left side of his mouth.

"So I was hoping you would say something to them. I mean back me up a little."

"I never hear the dog."

"Never!?"

"Well, when they're walking it past the house and maybe sometimes late at night."

"It's got that real deep voice because it's so big. Woof. Woof." Don actually imitated it pretty accurately: a diverting party trick. "They keep it outside all night. Is that humane?"

"I'm not a dog owner. I'm the totally wrong person to ask."

"And then, when they were away for ten days last month? Man! That was when it was the worst."

Victor had actually heard the dog during that time. He said so.

"They should have put it in a kennel," the fitness trainer said. "Wouldn't you have done that?"

Victor said he knew there were two schools of thought on that topic. Some people felt that kennels were a bad influence on dogs. Unduly toughening them up. Others thought kennels socialized dogs better. He didn't know which was right.

This was not a subject Don wanted to hear about nor consider in any depth.

"So, will you agree to back me up? To say something to them and back me up?"

He was so tense, so muscle-clenched, so annoyed that Victor said, "Sure. Next time I see them, I'll—"

"Sooner, please! I mean, I can't take another night being awakened at five . . . !"

"I don't know what effect I can have," Victor said candidly. "They get home around six. Why don't I arrange to get my mail at that time and 'bump into' one of them?"

"I'd really appreciate it. Really!"

He awkwardly came forward and sort of half hugged Victor, leaving a strong and clear body odor, part salt, part sweat, probably mixed with anger and free-floating testosterone molecules, and a little Calvin Klein *Obsession for Men*. It was all a little too *potento* for Victor's lizard-like sense of smell, but he could certainly grasp its attraction.

Don: "Thanks. You're a good neighbor. Come over and get a session. On the house."

A fitness session he meant. Fitness, Victor. Focus!

Victor was about to say, "I do yoga," when suddenly Don was jogging up the twenty steps to the parking area, his square buttocks pumping like pistons in an engine.

Victor realized he had a chubby.

"Down boy. With that b.o., he's *gotta* be a top. *C'mon!*"

259

CHAPTER THIRTY-THREE

He'd overslept, and now heard voices outside: doubtless Andy's company.

Victor dashed cool water on his face, dashed warm water on his hair, then, only slightly awakened, he changed into something that was still shorts and t-shirt, if a smidgen more night-like and formal.

While he could hear and even, at times, see them, it seemed difficult to actually get directly *to* them. Certainly not from his little suite, and, it turned out, not from either of the other bedroom suites, although allegedly all of those opened to the outdoors. At last, Victor steeled himself to potential sea-sickness and exited through the icthyphilic dining room.

A tall, middle-aged queen with lacquered black hair in a loose fitting Hawaiian-knockoff shirt and very long canvas shorts with so many side pockets he might be a plumber's assistant, turned to face Victor and all but glared, which made his hound-like face and expression even more hangdog.

"Esteban Barshai," Andy announced, "meet my house guest, Victor Regina. And yes, before you ask, he is *the* Victor Regina!"

"The writer, right?" Esteban asked in the flattest, most Midwestern accent, one utterly at odds with his exotically European name and South American appearance.

"Dat be me. What's to drink?" he asked Andy.

"Stebie is here with his partner, Elmer Radicchio the Turd."

"Bitch!" A short fireplug of a fellow, closely resembling the larger of Tobey's Shelties, pushed himself forward now and dropped a surprisingly small, well-manicured hand onto Victor's elbow.

"Elmore Raddizzi the Third," he said with a tight smile. He was dressed similarly to Esteban if in somewhat dulled colors. His hair was both sleekly gray and dark blonde in seemingly alternating sheeted patches, kinda like little Portia's head fur. The name meant something: wasn't he the Raddizzi dried-pasta heir or something?

"You've met The Light of My Loins, I see," Elmore all but curt-seyed. "And this is . . ." turning about and not seeing someone, "Well, I guess she's at the bar, to no one's astonishment."

The other men turned as one to the outside bar behind them, which Victor guessed (and later had confirmed) was a portion of the original second backroom bar from Ciro's on Sunset Boulevard, and thus even more glamorously out of place on this side patio than it appeared. There, hoisting a giant green-glass bottle of what looked like Scotch, was a fake-ly blonde-haired harridan wearing a mint-green sheath and straw-yellow low-heeled sandals. She spun partly around, revealing beneath a stage-turban a face halfway be-tween the aged Lillian Hellman and George Washington in the Gilbert Stuart painting. She winked at Victor—not the prettiest sight—and took a sip and then an even longer sip.

"Carol Bruce," Elmore finished. "C'mere, Care, and meet Victor. He's a famous writer from *Nueva Jorck*!" In a lower voice, he added with no little awe, "Carol's an actress in L.A who still gets work in the Biz!"

She more or less ambled in their direction; some pleasantries were exchanged. Victor half kept up with the conversation, more or less ruing that he'd awakened himself and changed to meet this particularly fashion-challenged crew.

He managed to keep away from the film star as much as possible and he only vaguely listened to Elmore and Esteban going on at ex-cruciating length about their trip to "gorgeously tropical" North Western Australia. It seemed that they took some pride in being a long-term if famously tempestuous couple. Even after having downed a tall vodka tonic, it took Victor a long time to wake up enough and figure out that Esteban was actually the younger and the more beloved of the two. Victor was constantly amazed in meeting new couples which of the two would end up being the prettier and thus supposedly the more sexually active one, over whom the other boyfriend suffered untold personal anxieties and burning agonies of jealousy. He was constantly being put in mind of what Thomas Mann had written in *Joseph and His Brothers*, "Who is to say who can be loved; and who cannot?" Not Victor, for sure.

After a longish time and several cocktails each, Victor realized that they were suddenly all in motion, from which he assumed they were headed out to dinner. He joined Elmore and Esteban in their aged posh dove-gray Bentley drop-head coupe, sitting up front while Esteban rolled a joint in the back seat. Andy and Carol had already departed.

Elmore drove, sitting ramrod-straight and reminding Victor even more of Portia the dog, especially when she was "begging" for bacon-bits. Esteban meanwhile nosed around the right front window in the guise of handing Victor the grass and began whispering low-voiced, quite filthy propositions into Victor's ear. He was unheard by his lover, who, while staring straight ahead as he drove, was expatiating unbidden upon the subtle differences between the Bentley convertible, coupe, and drop-head coupe models of this peculiar vintage, all the while inhaling the weed whenever it came his way like a drug-starved addict.

"It's not just the rimming you'll dig," Esteban was now going into some detail, himself low and close into Victor's other ear, "but especially, you know, that long muscle between the scrotum and the ass. Let me tell you, I like to lunch on that baby until you're ready to . . ."

Victor was happy to flee those two once they'd arrived at the over-awninged swirled-adobe-façade restaurant, a series of gray cubes stuffed between two fat stands of Fan-Palms. Luckily, they'd left the car windows open, otherwise the parking valet would have been stoned in a trice.

Inside, Antonio's (or whatever it was called) looked as though it had last been decorated by a Sinatra henchman circa 1956: heavy on the burgundy velvet, gold-scrolled woodwork, sharp-enough-to-cut-your-lips white linen, and sheepskin menus the same size and color-coding as an illuminated Twelfth Century missal.

"I'm treating you," Andy said, placing Victor next to the actress as he took the head of the table.

Carol was smoking what looked like unfiltered Benson & Hedges yet again. Even when she wasn't, smoke seemed to drift out of her lower lip as she ate or spoke. Halfway through dinner, after having utterly ignored him, she uttered *sotto-voce* to him, "You're queer, natch," in her smoke and liquor-cracked voice.

"As a three dollar bill," he confirmed.

"But you like to party, right?"

"Who doesn't?"

"Got a tux?"

"Matter of fact, I do."

He was wondering where all this was headed. After a while, she said, "I'm part of this group of over the hill actresses who party heavy around the Oscars. We call ourselves 'The Brassy Old Dames.' And we get dolled up and usually watch the ceremony over a good catered meal in one of our houses, then go out to the parties. Since we're all Academy members, we're invited everywhere. Miramax. Disney. Sony. Even Morton's."

"Me and my tux enter into this idyllic picture how, exactly?"

"We need guys to drive us to the parties. We especially need more or less presentable escorts in tuxedos. You've got enough looks to tickle one of those old vaginas. We feed you, you drive us and escort us. So? You in?"

"With an invitation as gracious as that, how could I possibly refuse?"

She burst into a torrent of J&B-laced laughter that ended in a coughing fit, requiring half a glass of water and another unmixed drink.

His *Mozzarella in Carrozze* appeared and Victor lit into it with gusto. Carol ate sparingly. Carol spoke sparingly. Always to the point, not a word more; as a rule, answering someone's question. She offered little herself and often carefully watched the others interact. Instead, she smoked, drank, and picked clean her *trout meuniere* with the precision of a brain surgeon—explaining her not-bad figure, given her age.

During the rest of the dinner, Victor was treated to the unexpected spectacle of his old pal Andy Grant being dapper, sophisticated, witty, and knowledgeable about oddly urbane topics such as the best vintage year of a Pomeroy, or the sad, complicated history of Julie Wilson's piano accompanists, or the travels of the 18th Century *doyenne,* Lady Mary Wortley Montague, and exactly how to order perilous *Fugu*—blowfish to you—within the borders of Japan.

Not only was Andy now one hundred and eighty degrees away

from the back-to-the-earth Topanga Canyonette Hippie he'd been in the 1980's—the guy who knew more about Klinger's TV haberdashery than any one else on the planet—he was also—was it geometrically possible?—equally a hundred and eighty degrees away from the dirty-old-man young gay sleazoid he'd been in the 1970's. In fact—*in fact!*—Victor recalled a High-Fag dinner at someone's manse in Bel-Air filled with men who had been their age now, back around then. He recalled Andy's disgust at their interests and their talk and how after dropping not very subtle hints about what a-holes he thought they all were, he had ended up doing something outrageous, one step from defecating on the carpets, and so they were forced to leave, never of course to return. Driving off, Andy had then blathered at some length about what loser-jerk-phony-queers the older guys had all been. Possibly true, but he would fit right into that *Haut-French* decor and pretension today.

As they were getting up to leave the Italianesque dive, Victor going in Andy's car, Carol with the others, she edged Victor against a wall. "It's coming up in April. I'll get your number from Baldy." Meaning Andy.

"Nice meeting you, too," he said.

"Little . . . prick!" She laughed at his insolence. Then repeated, "I *will* call you."

"I *will* answer!" he dared back.

Later that evening when they were alone again at the house having a nightcap with their feet dangling in the still sun-heated pool, Andy, in a suspiciously mellow mood, said, "You made *quite* the conquest tonight."

"I *did?* With which? Cassius or Portia?"

"Carol, of course. That's the most in a decade any of us has heard her speak to someone she's just met."

"She's just after my body," Victor joshed.

"Of course she's after your body. She's hornier than a fag half her age. But she'll settle for far less than that. You know, you could do worse. Knowing her, I mean. She's been everywhere. She's seen everything. And she's *done* everyone!"

Victor checked his boyhood friend's profile, which looked youthfully noble in this oh-so-ambivalent desert night light, fuzzed over as it was by the pool's underwater lamps. He remembered how startlingly handsome and how utterly desirable to Victor and almost everyone they knew Andy Grant had been, aged thirteen or so: the young Poseidon of the suburbs. Andy turned an inch, and the memory or illusion was gone.

"Are you saying I should take Carol up on her offer?"

"*I* certainly would! But then, she's never *asked* me. Or El. Or Es, for that matter."

The pool lights went out, and all of a sudden, in the northern edge of the moonless, starry sky, Victor noticed a long bright streak covering a third of the area, just a hand's height above the mountains.

"Is *that* . . . ? Can that be . . . ? No! It *can't* be!"

"The Comet Kohoutek," Andy assured him. "On its return journey from around the sun."

No wonder it had been hailing in Hollywood.

"It's so big! So far away. But huge. No wonder it scared the shit out of ancient people!"

"It boded the fall of kings," Andy said, musingly. "And queens."

CHAPTER THIRTY-FOUR

"Please don't tell me we're going back to see Sandy the Lameoid?" Victor begged.

Dmitrios had just pulled off Barham Drive and onto the back lot of Warner Brother's immense parking lot.

"No, this is someone new. Gil Dittersdorf. He works for—" He named someone vaguely familiar to Victor. "I met him last week at a pool party atop the Mondrian. He's a huge reader and I'm sure you guys will get along just great."

Again they found a parking spot within sight of the wooden shacks. Again the interior office was under-decorated and wall-papered with theater cards. But this at least held real furniture, albeit it was done in aluminum and glass. Unlike the other hut, this one was warm. Perhaps too warm, which might have explained the overabundant botanical life: the Boston ferns and fishtail palms sitting, hanging and all but falling out of their giant ceramic pots around the rooms seemed amazingly healthy. In the outer office, they drooped into your eyes and their branches all but nudged you while you were seated.

The producer himself was on the phone in his office with hiss door enough ajar that Victor could make out that he faced away, and was tossing a smaller than regulation-sized basketball into the far corner hoop.

Gil was tall with far too much badly cut yellow hair. He was also effusive.

"Hi, you guys! Glad you could make it. C'mon into my den of antiquity. Har-de-har. Watch out for the books. They're everywhere."

Indeed they were. Hundreds of them stacked in piles on the floor rising shakily to maybe four or five feet and partly blocking out the omnipresent wall art. They were all about, stacked edge to edge as high as his desk, as though defending it from outsiders. Victor and Dmitrios found themselves having to be careful crossing their legs, otherwise five volumes would come crashing down. And of course, books were all over the desk, standing, leaning, flat down, and crossed like building blocks.

"Didya ever read this?" Gil thrust a copy of *Captain Corelli's Mandolin* at them. "Terrific read, but the French got the rights in like two days after its European publication."

On one wall were maybe a half dozen photos of Gil's favorite authors, the classic book cover photos you always saw of Truman Capote (gamine), Eudora Welty (ugly), John Steinbeck (nautical), William Faulkner (sober), and Henry James (snooty). Center of them all was his idol of idols, author Tom Wolfe, pictured in 1978, and it was clear that for better or worse, Gil patterned himself totally after it, sartorially speaking.

This might not have been too distracting were it not that Gil had gained substantial girth in the intervening decade. His pale-pink button-down shirt bulged inappropriately. Its buttons, where present, hung on literally by a thread, while the candy-striped seersucker trousers were by now too short and worn quite below any hint of a waist. The jacket fit not at all and had been decoratively abandoned, flung over a chair-back. The once brilliant, now food- and drink-stained silver-foil tie was pinned down to various areas of shirt-like material by who knew what combination of perspiration and ketchup. But Gil's face was clean and bright and his oversized tortoise shell glasses, while patched over the bridge of his nose by what looked like four or five Band-Aids, were polished, allowing his merry brown eyes to glow intelligently as he managed to spout the names and titles of virtually every book he must have read in his life, attempting to make Victor feel at home as a fellow *litterateur.*

"Gunter Grass's *Cat and Mouse*? As great as his *Tin Drum*, in my humble opinion. But German TV snatched it before we could. And here's Baalshevis Singer's *Shosha*. Could have been as great a film as *Sophie's Choice*. But he's dead and the estate threw up so many obstacles it might as well have not been for sale. J.G. Ballard's *Terminal Beach*. You know the collection? I was all ready to send an option agreement, when *Crash* came out of Canada. I loved it, but it was felt to be far too harsh, and a box office dud, so no deal.

Iain Banks *Wasp Factory*! Tell me it's not a movie? By the time I'd read it, BBC had an option sewn up."

On and on, Gil recited the list of books that he'd almost bought, never quite been able to buy, just missed buying through a "fixed-in-advance phone auction," or that he'd gotten to a day too late. Not to mention those that were mired in contractual restraints, or that a bit of research had revealed to possess unclear copyrights, or that had far too many ownership problems. And so on and so forth.

From Alan Ginsberg's *Howl* to Lady Murasaki's *The Tale of the Genji* to Beatrix Potter's *Peter Cottontail*, Gil Dittersdorf had tried to obtain the rights; only to be thwarted at the last minute by a nefarious conspiracy of International Law, executor's whims, Warner Brothers' front office shenanigans, authorial paranoia, agenting idiocy, and just plain bad stars. It was an unparalleled tale of woe.

When he was done with the tragic litany, Dmitrios said: "*Never Can Say Goodbye* has no problems. Victor Regina, right here before you, is the owner and sole copyright holder, and he's ready to deal."

To which Gil Dittersdorf, that devoted reader and long-suffering, much-frustrated option-obtainer, replied, "Guys, we're always looking for fine material, but I gotta tell you I've just recently been put on a strict diet by you know who," gesturing to where they heard another thunk of a basketball onto the floor, "of only the tackiest of genre-stuff: horror-Sci-Fi, action thrillers, and mystery/courtroom dramas."

Needless to say, his candor, his correct pronunciation of Polish *auteur* Krzysztof Kieslowski's name, and his much-advertised though never proven love of reading earned Gil the largest and wordiest packet of stuff they'd brought along with the book itself, which Victor was talked into autographing, and which they later on in the car driving away agreed he might actually use as more than a doorstop, all the while explaining to the next person to walk into the office how this masterpiece, too, had somehow or other "gotten away."

"You call this 'cocktails'!" Victor asked. "The Palm is hardly a Normandie Avenue hangout."

"So? I can't buy you a nice dinner? Anyway, you're just a little too thin and a little too toned for what I really know to be your age. I intend to change that."

Their drinks arrived: two very fat-glassed Martinis. The middle-aged man in a so-crisp-it-hurt white shirt and black tie with black leatherette apron attempted to place black, embossed menus the size of the obelisk in *2001: A Space Odyssey* on the table.

Joel Edison waved them off as though they bore the anthrax virus.

"We already know what we want!"

"We do?" Victor asked.

The waiter had already snatched up the menus and was giving a hundred and two percent of his attention to the agent. Edison was clearly a valued diner here. Victor could have set his hair on fire and it wouldn't have done any good, attention-wise.

"The Prime Ribs the way I like, Reggie. The lower set. Medium rare. Baked potato with the works. Creamed spinach. Caesar Salad to begin. Dutch Apple Pie with Cheddar and Decaf coffee to end."

Reg wrote and vanished.

"That sound okay?" Joel asked.

"Heaven," Victor admitted.

"What'll we toast?" Joel hoisted his chalice. "Survival? No we've done more than survive."

"Any toast we make is sure to be premature. And sure to be undone soon enough. Instead, let's toast the twenty-seven year old male beauty of Mr. Don Wright, my next door neighbor, whom I refer to as Mr. Totally Gorgeous Fitness Trainer."

"To Don Wright." They sipped. "So tell me about Demetrius."

"My so-called manager, Dmitrios? You make him sound like a spoiled gladiator in a toga and sandal epic."

"He isn't?"

"He's all business as far as I'm concerned."

"Rightly so," Joel admitted. "What did you think of Vlacheslav?"

"He reminded me of who was it before, Boris? *Vid dee distingveshed acksent?* You always take on these Russian immigrant types who are a half step away from either ballet school or a life of crime. It's clearly the so-far untapped but brimming-over altruism at work that your life requires. It's the Social Worker in you coming out."

Joel laughed. "That's certainly one way of putting it. Other people would say you're out of your mind. That I'm bad through and through."

"Ahhhh!" Victor admitted. "But they haven't known you as long as I have."

"True . . . So, you're really trying to break back into The Biz?"

"Meetings, meetings, meetings! One more ghastly than the other. But there I am, ever fresh, the perpetual New Kid in Town. That's me." Victor said brightly. "Truth is, I'm a little bored. I've got a hit book out here and in England and The Commonwealth. It's being translated into French and German and I expect it'll do well there too. I've got the next one already written and already in the pipeline. It's equally good, but kind of intellectual in comparison, so it'll get great notices and sell about a fifth of this one. And right now, I've got nothing else to do." He twiddled his thumbs to illustrate. "Besides which, I'm not the only one who thinks that *Never Can Say Goodbye* has a shot."

"As a six-hour movie with a cast of four thousand?"

"You skimmed it?" Victor was surprised. "No. Wait. You got a reader's report on it! I'm touched."

"I read the whole damn book. I read most of your books, Victor. I kind of have to. To keep my chips in, in this town. And it's terrific. Truth is, I caught the kids in the mailroom weeping over the ending, so I confiscated it. But seriously, Victor? We have to film the Student Siege of Columbia University? The first Gay Pride Parade? The '91 March on Washington? Even I choked on the dollar signs. I don't choke that easily."

"From what I've heard, you don't at all. What about a miniseries?"

"Is that how Demetrius is positioning the property?"

"Dmitrios wants the six-hour movie. That's how *I'm* positioning it. Trying to be a little more realistic."

"Not much more realistic. You about ready for another 'tini?"

"Shoot! If you're trying to discourage Dmitri, why build me up so much with all that 'buddies with Warren Beatty' crap?"

"These kids should know who they're dealing with. They're far too arrogant and act totally entitled for no reason I can figure. Reggie. Hit us again. I mean after all, he's no one. No one. Whereas you—"

"Are known to six people in this business at the moment," Victor said.

"Ah but when the other five find out you're back in town, they'll get all sentimental and give you all kinds of regards and kudos."

"We shall see. In fact we shall see in April because that's when I'll be escorting an aging Academy member to various parties around town after the Ceremony at the Shrine."

Victor began telling Joel about "The Brassy Old Dames Club."

Joel, a true Old Hollywood fan, was mesmerized, and began asking for details, more than Victor could provide.

"I just don't know, Joel. Ask the women yourself. I'm assuming you'll be hanging around after the ceremony."

"I usually go to the Governors' shindig, then drop in at Morton's. But this year I'll look for you and your 'date.' Do you know who you'll be with?"

"Maybe Carol Bruce. Maybe Marie Windsor. Or Jan Sterling or . . . I'll know in a few weeks, I guess."

"Leave it to you to locate the very soul of this town. I mean really, Victor, I couldn't ever have gotten into that."

"You couldn't because you're gainfully employed and otherwise engaged. Not an obvious bum, like me."

They sipped. Victor said, "Since you were making us such close pals the other day, want to hear a funny story about me and Warren Beatty?"

"Are you kidding? Let me pretend to adjust my undies and in reality start up my tape recorder. Okay, shoot!" Joel puts his "I'm listening" face on.

"This is in New York. Some years after he and Julie have split and she's back in England being a socialist. I'm at one of these rich kids fund-raising parties to make an Indy Prod movie in some oversized loft way down south of Soho in Manhattan. Garbage on the street and maybe a wino in the gutter and not much else to be seen. But twenty big black limos with drivers parked all around the place. One for me and my literary agent, Marcie. You two never met, but I believe you talked on the phone."

"Marcie. We talked, yes. Lots of fun."

"Lots of fun. She retired agenting to do competitive dressage.

With horses. Don't ask. So we're at this party, noshing, drinking, and occasionally getting hits off a three foot high mountain of coke—this is the mid-70's, right? sitting right out there on a table in the main room!—we're at this party, where we pick up the late and great Mark Chastain. He's helping cater this affair. He's not yet officially my lover, but we've already begun dating. At midnight, he's getting off and joining Marcie and me going to Flamingo for The Black Party. There, Mark will be working again, being a statue of a man in black leather high on a plinth. He's working his way through Law School."

"I heard about those Black Parties!" Joel shook one hand in a "Va Voom!" gesture.

"Every sordid rumor you heard is true. They were as fabulously down and dirty as you could get. So we're all three dressed in black, natch, for the party. Marcie has on a black bra, jodhpurs and a riding crop. Very Venus in Furs. And this very tall, pretty girl comes over to us and asks what's the occasion. So we tell her.

"Two minutes later, she drags over Warren, who's her date at this shindig, and she begins needling him, saying that Farrah Fawcett and Liza Minnelli always go to Flamingo, which is not completely untrue, and how she wants to go to the Black Party.

"Now, I'm certain the very last thing Warren wants is to go to this dance club filled with eight hundred gay guys and like six women. So he tries to weasel out of it. No deal. Clearly, she makes it that No Black Party equals No Nookie. So he gives in, and says to me, 'Okay, "Comp" us in.'

"At which point I have to say, 'It's a private club and I think the party is sold out. I'll have to call the club and see what I can do."

"This," Joel adds, "to Warren Beatty, who's has never, but *never*, been told he can't get in anywhere?"

"At least not since he was sixteen. Right. You've got the picture. At which news, I receive a look . . . Well, I won't describe it except to say friendly it wasn't. At any rate, Marcie stays with him and the model, Angelica or whatever, because after all it's Warren Beatty and he's got a reputation, while I go call. I finally get club owner Michael Fesco on the phone, he says, 'Victor! If you're bullshitting me . . . !' Then he reminds me that Warren and Roberta, or whatever her name is, have got to come in the door with us on my membership card or it's no go. So I've got to go back to Warren and report that to him, too.

"Well, he is not at all happy. I'm guessing he was hoping I'd say they couldn't get in at all. But we leave and they leave, their limo follows ours across downtown Manhattan to lower Broadway and we're all jammed together with a dozen dance queens in full black leather regalia in that little entrance hall, getting in. And even Marcie can't distract Warren from this bad choice he's allowed himself to get into.

"Once upstairs, with luckily no coats to have to check since it's Spring and anyway we have limos, I figure Warren wants to be on his own with the model. So I make sure we lose them fast."

"Wow!" Joel is suitable impressed. "I'm picturing Warren Beatty at a Flamingo Black Party."

"I'm not done. It gets better! Given all the drugs and ex-tricks and ex-boyfriends of mine who are there, not to mention the ex-treme crowdedness of the place which is like a study in Homosexual Brownian Motion, in two hours or so I've lost Marcie, and Mark is off his plinth and who knows where. I'm distinctly over-Quaaluded at this moment, and quite happy. I decide to wander to the back lounge, where I can get away from the crowds and the loudest noise and kind of contemplate my very pleasant high. Except it's all sex back there. So I have to find an unoccupied spot and I lean against the wall to groove on the drugs and on Riche Vasquez' mixing.

"Two minutes later, it's Guess-Who at my side? Right, Warren. He's lost Becky, or whatever her name is. Have I seen her? No. He leans up against the wall as I'm smoking a joint and shares it, and he begins talking about the break up with Julie as though I knew her like a sister. Defending himself. Saying how she just wouldn't let him get away with anything. How she was intellectually de-manding and exasperatingly rigorous and after a while he just wanted a rest. Then he begins in on Ed Trefethern, the producer who had introduced us, about how they were doing a project to-gether and why it fell through and all just kinds of stuff, like we're long lost buddies . . . Like I actually would care.

"Suddenly Warren leans over to me, right close, and he whis-pers something in my ear. I ask him to repeat it, and he says, 'I think someone is trying to open my fly.' I look down and sure enough, we both have guys kneeling in front of us."

"No!"

"Yes. After all it is the darkened back lounge of Flamingo in the midst of the annual Black Party."

"Oh, my God!"

"Mind you, I'm so deeply stoned at this point I could have Dumbo the Elephant down there and I wouldn't really notice. I can barely focus, and this actor's demands upon my attention are seriously bringing me down. I just wish he would go away.

"Then he leans in even closer and says 'Do you think he's trying to suck my cock?'

"No, he's taking a semen-sample for Biology class! So I say, 'Push him away!' I push my guy away and he falls over and is nearly trampled. But I can see that isn't going to work with Warren. The guy has like a total hold on his lower body and he will not be daunted."

Joel Edison is now cracking up.

"So I grab Warren and forcefully turn him around. The guy in front of him falls to one side. I yell in Warren's ear, 'Zip up!' I give him five seconds to do so, then push him forward out of the dark room and into the flashing lights, crowd, and absolute mayhem of the Flamingo dance floor, filled with six hundred dancers on drugs. His shirt is wide open. He's utterly dazed and confused, and I've got my arms on his shoulders and still can barely hold on. The crowd in front of us is packed so tight that it takes all of 'Ring My Bell' and 'Disco Inferno' and half of a Jackson Five hit to boogie him through and out the other side. Of course people continually stop us to snap poppers under our noses, to stuff ethyl chloride rags into our mouths while tweaking our nipples in greeting. One or two people recognize Warren but shake their heads, *No, it can't be.* Must be the drugs they're on."

Joel can't stop laughing.

"After what seems to little old stoned me like forever, we finally reach the main lounge, and there, miracle of miracles, we immediately spot Antonia the model, or whatever her name was. I'm relieved. He's relieved. They hug and he's all over her, he's so turned on now. I see them leave the club and figure they'll probably screw in the limo."

Joel is stricken. "No! And that was it?"

"Never saw or heard from him or her again."

"He could have written!" Joel is enjoying himself. "He could have called! You two had something 'special' together."

"In retrospect, I'm glad he didn't."

At that very moment, someone in the restaurant passing by stopped, turned, and suddenly slid into the booth, right onto the banquette next to Victor. Before he could even register who it was, the man grabbed Victor's head in his hands and planted a kiss on his lips.

When he pulled away, Victor saw it was . . .

"Sam? Sam Haddad?!"

Sam to Joel. "You were right. He's still much too young-looking. Wanna be my Boy Toy, Vic?"

Victor didn't know what to say.

Sam slid a snaky arm across his shoulders and hugged him.

"Now, *this* is why I come to the Palm," Sam said. "To render *this one* speechless."

Sam had gained weight and heft, but it was Sam all right. His head was squarer and his face was definitely lined, his hairline way back now, and he was dressed superbly.

"You didn't just happen in, right?" Victor guessed.

"In fact, I was going out somewhere to celebrate with the wife and my two daughters, one of whom is fifteen today and a total carnivore!" He pointed to a booth ahead of them. "And then Joel said you would be out, too. So . . . So you're here in L.A. now?"

"A little late, no?" Victor admitted. "Laurel Canyon. Tiny little house with a view."

"Ah, *La Boheme!* For me it's Crescent Drive, Beverly Hills. Stockbroker's Tudor. Three car garage. Exactly as banal as you'd expect." Then, "I would ask if you've seen anyone. But who is there to see anymore from the old days, huh?"

"You stuck with Frank till the end?" Victor said.

"No. I couldn't. After the fiasco that you predicted and worked so hard to avert, Frank gave up. You were a trooper, Vic. I was a slave driver and a louse. But you did what you could to keep the production afloat. And that's how we were able to finish it."

"*Now* you tell me! All these years I was certain you hated me."

"What? *No!* You were a *prince!* I happened to be *insane* at the time and couldn't recognize it. So after it opened and tanked big time, Frank moved to the East Coast. He got cancer. He made one last film, about having cancer . . ." Sam waved an open hand back and forth to indicate its questionable quality. "And boom! He died. I offered but he didn't want me to join him there. He set me up here instead, in some little development department at Fox. I was sure it was a dead-end he'd placed me in, like putting me out to pasture. But it became an independent unit. Six of us in it. First we produced an Irish movie about an ugly horse that everyone in town had passed on. We took it to Venice and Berlin and Cannes, gathering awards. A hit! Next we took on a French-Vietnamese 'Co-Pro' about a gang-lord and three plucky kids. More awards. And a German movie about a crazy house-party. They all struck international gold. We shot in Mongolia and in the Po valley. In the Amazon jungles of Peru and in the Carpathian Alps. I loved the travel. I met Luce," he nodded to the table ahead at his wife, "the former Lucinda Carpenter, track and field star, on a shoot in the Caribbean. She was with a gang of Euro-Trash, scuba diving a hundred feet down in the Caicos Trench. We were shooting locales on shore. She came out of the water and we nearly killed her with falling sound equipment. I took her out to apologize and the rest is history."

"I'm happy for you, Sam." Then, "You don't happen to still have that Porsche?"

Sam's face lit up. "You *remember!* My first and most bitterly lost love. Nah. In 1989 the brakes died all of a sudden as I was coming down Sunset Boulevard onto the Pacific Coast Highway. You must know that hill." He made slalom gestures with a hand. "I was going ninety miles per hour when I hit. Luckily, it was at 4:15 a.m. and I was the only car anywhere in sight. But I ended up three feet deep in the Santa Monica Bay surf before I could stop. Good thing it was low tide or I would've drowned! Nothing was really wrong with the car. But it was never any good after that." He reached over and kissed Victor's cheek. "I missed you. We both did. Especially when we heard that you had some really hard knocks."

Victor laughed ruefully. "Everyone died, Sam. My family. My

partner. All my friends. Everyone. Everyone died but me. What the hell is that all about!"

"We're glad you're still around, aren't we Joel? See? That's one little reason for it."

Victor felt strange discussing what had happened since he'd last seen the two. He knew AIDS had hit Hollywood and hit it hard. Both of them must have been affected. But he still felt singled out somehow. It was as though no one who had not undergone the decade or more of illnesses and deaths, one after the other, could possibly get it. Never mind the immense personal and social problems those deaths brought, including dealing with mean, greedy, and bigoted relatives. Mark filed lawsuits on behalf of the stricken, but he no sooner got his degree and the high paying job of his dreams than he, too, began showing symptoms and ultimately needed all that help himself. Could these folks living and working in their Golden Triangle, living in their Golden State, with their golden everything around them possibly comprehend how dark the world had become for Victor—and if they did, could they care?

"Some day I'll tell you all about it, Sam."

"That's a promise. But right now I gotta go to *my* family before my wife comes here and *I* die. You guys work out a date to come see me at the office and check with my assistant."

"Great. A week or so," Joel said.

"Sounds good."

"You don't want to wait until after the Oscars?" Joel said. "You're gonna pick up what, four? Five?"

"From your mouth to God's ear. Two, if we're lucky!"

Sam stood up, stroking Victor's chin, lovingly. "You look good. Despite everything bad."

He was about to leave when Victor reached out a hand to stop him. "Sam, why are we coming to your office in a week or so?"

"I thought he told you already? I want to make *Justify My Sins* into a movie. Your second book? Remember?" He seemed to be addressing the air: "I'm *there!* I'm *coming!* See? I've stood up and *left their table!*" Victor now saw he was addressing his daughter, who'd gotten up to come fetch him. She now tenderly dragged him off.

Their Caesar Salads arrived and Victor was still too shocked to wave off the extra grindings of white pepper.

Some four minutes later, Joel looked up from his salad and said, "So, right now, Victor Regina is thinking what?"

"You don't want to know."

"What do you mean? Of course I want to know!"

Victor stared at him and said, "What I'm really thinking, Joel, is, 'Please God, let me have a ten-inch cock for one hour so I can fuck the hell out of Mr. Totally Gorgeous Fitness Trainer.' Because right after that I can die in peace."

"But . . . no movie business. Why not?"

"Not with that book, and you already know why, Joel."

Joel laughed. But he looked at Victor carefully. "Don't be foolish, Victor. Both Sam and I have very good reasons to want to make that particular movie. It's nothing personal. And you know that, nowadays, we *can* make it."

"What you've got to understand, Joel, is my history with that book."

"I know already. Twice optioned, twice never-made."

"Twice!? *Justify My Sins* has been under one option or another since the month it was published until, I think, the current option ended, maybe a week ago. That's twenty-two years under about twenty options. Twenty! During that time it's been optioned for television movie of the week and for feature films, for stage plays and for musicals. It's been optioned for everything but a board game! Well-known producers have optioned it. Famous film directors have optioned it, and it was more people than just Frank, believe me, who optioned it. Movie actors like Sissy Spacek optioned it. Television stars like the woman who played Wonder Woman did. Theatre divas like Julie Harris optioned it. Two corporations of gay men and two consortiums of straight women have optioned it. The blind, the halt, and the lame have optioned it. The Japanese optioned it for non-exclusive rights. Truth is, Joel, I'm waiting one day to be abducted by aliens at some abandoned crossroads in the Sierra Nevadas so *they* can option it for who knows what kind of non-carbon-based entertainment venues they have in the Andromeda Galaxy."

"Are you done? Listen, with a track record like that?" Joel said admiringly, "It's just *got* to be made into a movie."

"With a track record like that—" Victor began to say, and never quite completed his sentence which would have ended, "it will *never* be made into a movie." Instead he said, "It is clearly jinxed in some way."

"Come on, you don't believe that."

"I have *twelve* other books. Option one of those. They're just as good. Many of them are better."

"Don't fight it, Victor. Sam wants it because he couldn't make it with Frank. I want it because I couldn't be part of your great team back then. He's optioning the book. I'm handling the paperwork. It's a done deal. You've got no say in the matter. You sign the papers and you take the money. Ahhh! Here's the Prime Rib. Dig in."

CHAPTER THIRTY-FIVE

"My friend Lindsay says this producer sees absolutely no one!" Dmitrios assured Victor. "He only involves himself in a very few special projects every year, and each one is a gem."

They were attempting to get past the 405 freeway traffic jam, which evidently happened at all hours of the day at Wilshire Boulevard

Dmitrios went on to mention three movies that Gaspar Gustavsson had put his very rare imprimatur upon, although it wasn't at all clear to Victor in what capacity he'd done so. Had he been producer, co-producer, executive producer, or what? The films themselves were solid middle of the road products—no Adam Sandler comedies, thankfully. Was Lindsay the good looking black guy Dmitrios had been with when they first met?

"So, this Gustavsson is seeing us because of Lindsay? Or because he's gay and looking for a gay project? Or why?"

"From what Lindsay said—and he was whispering into his cell during a meeting in his office at the time so I couldn't really make it out clearly—Gustavsson needs a new project. He's been busy with some other matters and hasn't really presented any new product to any of the bigger places, and it's getting to be time to do so."

Victor guessed he could live with being the purveyor of "product."

"So he's quirky, but like genius-quality," Dmitrios offhandedly assured him.

"Quirky" would adequately describe the three pics he'd mentioned; "genius" wouldn't.

They'd finally cleared the mess and were moving again, making a semi-circle around the V.A. Hospital's extensive grounds, and suddenly were back in the midst of tall buildings.

Victor had been dubious until the very moment that Dmitrios pulled the CLK-320 into the parking garage of one of these newer skyscrapers

On the lower level where they located "Guest Parking" there was a glassed-in elevator shaft. Chic.

It was glassed-in on the fifteen floor too when they arrived. Very chic.

The office was easily accessible from the high-ceilinged lobby; not off in some side corridor. *Tres* chic!

A not-too-attractive gay man in his late twenties let them in, sat them down in real chairs at a real coffee table with manicured plants, and popped in to the other door to announce they'd arrived. He popped back out again, said, "A minute or two," then sat down at his desk and began pecking away at a computer keyboard.

Given the previous two meetings, it all seemed to Victor refreshingly professional.

However, a lot more than a minute or two elapsed while they flipped through recent copies of *The Hollywood Reporter* and tried not to be too bored.

At last something buzzed at the assistant's desk. He looked up and smiled. They stood up and walked in.

This office was tall and narrow. A desk filled the far end. Three tall windows behind it gave a view down Wilshire Blvd toward the ocean.

To say the room was stark would be an understatement. No shelves, no pictures, no plants. Two leather director chairs and the big bare desk with its own leather director chair. The far half-wall below the far windows held a blond wood credenza with one door open enough to see it contained scripts. Lots and lots of scripts. All this was reassuring.

Gustavsson was small with an oddly shaped body and a bald head. His face reminded Victor of those characters who flit in and out of Ingmar Bergman films, where they might be janitors or court jesters, or they might easily be—Death! Come to life! His eyes were red and runny looking, his face gaunt with a hint of a rictus about his pulled-back mouth, his nose bony and large, his ears gargantuan, almost gargoylesque. He wore a black turtle neck, black canvas belt, black levis, black rubber-soled plimsolls. When he greeted them with several large florid gestures inviting them to sit down, the hands he displayed were gaunt, bony, and enormous.

By now, of course, Dmitrios and Victor had honed their *spiel* to an efficacious, information-rich, twenty minute-long pitch. His manager would "Intro" Victor and his *ouevre* and then discuss the "social changes in the world" that Victor allegedly represented and wrote about.

Victor would then step in and explain why he'd written the novel *Never Can Say Goodbye* and what he had hoped to accomplish with it. Dmitrios would rapidly follow up with the novel's literary reception, its great reviews, its terrific sales, its many readers who were sorry the book ever ended, and the many nominations and awards it had been graced with. Victor would mention the British sales, the German and French translations just coming out, and then he would tell the story.

He was halfway through this last, penultimate portion of what he was increasingly beginning to think of as "Their Act," in fact just about to begin the wrap-up segment, when Gustavsson held up his huge paw and said, "Wait just one moment! This sounds familiar."

Before they could slip a word in, he spun around in his chair, facing the window and the credenza.

"Yes. Very familiar. Extremely so."

He almost fell off the chair and onto his knobby knees so that he could get into the over-filled shelves, rummaging through them, all the while speaking in an unending flow of words: "Now I remember, I was reading this book. No wait, someone sent me a reader's report on this book, and I swear it was just like what you were talking about, about these two cousins and how they had a love-hate relationship over the decades, but they were still bound inextricably and always came together and could never stay apart, no matter where they went or what happened to each of them. But somehow or other it always ended badly for one of them, while the other one always did well, or at least gained while the other one lost. Who would have thought that two stories would be so alike, but then people will tell you that it happens all the time. Take for example," and he went on to give them two lame examples, all the while faced away from them, hunting amid his piles of manuscripts and books in the credenza, among the stuff which had by now risen into tottering piles all around him, before shouting, "Only I know that it isn't *happenstance*. It's *theft. Intellectual theft.* And if you *think* that I'm going to for a second believe you that it's a coincidence, you've got another thing coming. It's a good thing for you, there is no actual *law* against this, or you would be *nabbed* the minute you left my office for this quackery! This forgery! This theft!" he thundered. "Ah! Here it is!" he screeched at them.

He turned and faced them, demonic in his appearance, accusatory in his stance, one huge hand gripping the desk edge, while the other paw easily held out the book he'd been searching for.

"And before you two *miscreants* and *fakers* say another word I must warn you this book, unlike your silly pseudo-production, received a glowing reader's report!"

He said it with such venom, the words were accompanied by such a spurt of spittle, that Victor, at least, fell back, to avoid the worst of the drool ruining his good shirt.

"Do you *see? Do you see now!*" he shouted at them so angrily, so bitterly, and so loudly that the walls shook around them.

"But, Mister Gustavsson," his manager bravely dared to say, after at least a minute, and quaking all the while. "That's *Victor's* book you're holding."

Dmitrios pulled out a copy from their packet, and held it alongside the other one, showing him it was the same.

The wet, watering, running eyes glanced askew at the two identical book covers side by side, in horror.

The man then slid backward, dropping the books, grasping at the bare top of the desk. He slumped backwards onto the floor where he huddled until he'd spun into a fetal position.

Victor looked at Dmitrios, who looked back and put his index finger between his teeth, and spun it around.

Gustavsson was gibbering on the floor, perhaps headed into some sort of convulsive fit.

They exited, looking for a second at his assistant outside.

Without them having to more than "Ummmm . . . ," he got the message. He stood up and peeked into the office and then closed the door. He handed them a copy of what he'd been typing and said, "Bye."

They heard him dialing 911 and saying. "It's me—again."

In the elevator down, Dmitrios glanced at the paper, bunched it up, and tossed it.

"What was that, anyway?" Victor asked when they'd gotten back to West Hollywood.

"Whaddya think? His resume."

Page four hundred and seventy-five of the seven hundred and fifteen page Japanese multi-generational saga appeared to repeat. Sure enough, there was page four hundred and seventy-six some five pages on ahead. Victor decided to check to see if other pages repeated or if that were the only one. His heart had skipped a beat. What if it all repeated, and he'd never reach the end?

After all, he was by now highly invested in time and interest in the Inamori clan with its lower than plebian tide pool-clamming origins in Yokohama, its eventual if by no means assured mercantile successes in old-time Edo, the varied social-climbing missteps of the third generation and those nearly disastrous Imperial court *faux pas* of the fourth one, not to mention some of the more *outré* sexual proclivities of this newest, seventh generation of increasingly effete, wealthy, if apparently doomed, young Inamori men coming of age under Hirohito and the super militarism of Tokyo in the 1930's—when Victor noticed the cat again.

This time it was gingerly tight-walking alongside the inch or two of brick wall and settling itself onto the top pillowed portion of an adjacent chaise longue.

He'd seen the cat a half dozen times before, though it had never come anything like this close, and had always seemed skittish to a fault. Probably a rescued animal, beaten daily by a previous owner.

He knew that it was a ceaseless hunter of the many birds that abounded in the Hollywood Hills. He had come upon evidence of its work before, the headless corpse of a pale gray house-dove among his rhododendrons.

Victor had no idea whose cat it was. Surely not the two guys with the big black dog. And definitely not the household further up the hill from him which seemed to be occupied by ten, maybe a dozen twenty-something dudes living in seven rooms intent on working as little and partying as much as humanly possible. Then again, *their* pet would likely have to hunt its own food. The old man and his invalid wife down below Don Wright? Possibly? The cat looked well tended, black with white paws and a white bib, sleek, and, at least from twelve feet distant, well cared for.

He was just dipping back into the sordid tale of Genjuri's latest conquest, a peasant woman in an otherwise empty cable-car half way up a scenic mountain, who had just accepted his money in return for a taste of her dirty left foot, when he heard someone calling, "Ellll-vis. Elll-vis!"

The black cat looked up. It—he thought it was a she—must be Elvis. It smooched its eyes at the sound of its name but was unmoved and continued sitting where it was, Sphyinx-like.

"Ellll-vis! Ellll-vis!"

Victor put down his chunky paperback and quietly stood. Sure enough, down there, on his largest terrace was Done Right (Don Wright) wearing even less than usual—a pair of silvery gym shorts and nothing else—and turning about and calling. "Ellll-vis! Ellll-vis!"

Slowly, Victor gently slid the living room screen door open and gingerly stepped inside. There, among several other cards and slips of paper numbers within his antique ceramic bowl next to the phone was Don's. He dialed and watched Done Right stop calling, look around and go indoors.

"This is your neighbor up the hill . . . Victor? The writer."

No response on the other end.

"You came to me about the other neighbor's dog woofing."

"Ye-ah?"

"Your cat is Elvis? A black cat with white paws and bib? Well, your cat's visiting me at this moment. In fact, your cat visits me daily. I would bring Elvis down to you, except Elvis seems really skittish and I've never gotten closer than ten feet."

"I'll be right there." Phone hung up.

A half hour later Don still had not arrived. Then he was there on the deck, again arriving quite silently. Maybe it was his shoes, which looked like the kind gymnasts wore at the Olympics. He wore an ink black Guinea Tee and the silver shorts, which up close looked like the kind of material NASA used on the moon.

Elvis sauntered up to him and allowed itself to be picked up and loosely held.

"Any relief with the big dog?" Victor asked.

"They moved it to the other side of their back yard. I still hear it barking. But not as badly."

"I'm not sure why you thought I'd be of any help."

Victor's own phone began ringing. He let the answering machine take the call. He could clearly hear Vlacheslav from the William Morris Agency setting up an appointment for next week.

"I told you they wouldn't pay attention—" Victor began, and was instantly hushed by Done Right.

"You know Joel Edison!" Don said. It wasn't a question.

Victor smiled to himself: what an interesting development.

"Sure. We go way back."

He could see emotion of some sort break out on the trainer's handsome face. The cat felt it too and pushed itself out of his grip, dropped to the terrace, and sped off into the bushes.

"I ... really ... *really* ... need ... to ... meet ... him!"

Said with such strain and such a total clenching of his upper torso, neck, and head that Victor couldn't believe it. He was going to ask why, but he already suspected why. Done Right wanted to do a television show or be a fitness guru in a movie or, hell, be a movie star himself, or something of the sort.

"Real ... ly ... need to!" Don repeated.

What's in it for me? would have been the true Hollywood rejoinder. But the more Victor saw and heard of his neighbor, the more unsure he was of what he wanted to do with him, despite his stellar looks and overpowering emittance of testosterone. And he was almost half Victor's age.

"We're just old friends. We're not doing business together or anything like that," Victor said, not exactly lying. They had nothing signed, did they?

"Can I leave something with you? Would you give it to him? It would be a *really big favor,* if you did."

This could go so many ways, right now, Victor thought. It could be a real future, or it could be a real can of worms. *Above all,* he thought, *be casual*. What did Krishnamurti write? Wanting is the root of all evil. Ah, but Krishmamurti hadn't met nor stood in the testosterone-drenched presence of Done Right, had he?

"Sure. Why not? I'll be seeing him sometime this coming week, anyway."

Victor returned to his chaise, sat down and picked up his novel, the very picture of *soigne*-tude.

When he looked up a minute later, the trainer was gone as soundlessly as he'd arrived.

Two hours later, when Victor went to check his mail in the box along the twisting road, he found in it a twelve by fifteen mailer containing Don Wright's professional photos, variously clothed and almost naked, as well as a labeled video, and some ten pages of closely printed information. All very professionally done. He didn't look at any of it beyond a glance, but he had to wonder if everyone but himself in these Hills had such a publicity-packet on hand, ready to be handed out just in case s/he was discovered.

When he got back to the house he noticed a yellow Post-it attached to one side of the envelope that read, "You're a prince."

"No, "Victor said aloud, "Taboru Inamori is a prince. Or at least the youngest son of the clan is *about* to be one—just as soon as he marries the Emperor's niece."

CHAPTER THIRTY-SIX

Even from this far away in the Ginger Rogers Memorial suite he could hear their voices.

Victor sat up in bed, lifted the red satin sleepy-eye-patches Tobey had thoughtfully provided against the late March sun, and listened.

Andy Grant and Tobey's voices rose to some kind of a crescendo, high pitched, each saying one, final, frustratingly indistinguishable word. Then silence.

Maybe he was still asleep. He pinched his lower arm. No. Yet now it was all quiet.

Suddenly he heard the sound of a car revving up and taking off. From the depth of it, it was the Oldsmobile. Tobey had left.

Of course, Victor was half expecting something like this. Ever since he'd arrived back in Palm Springs yesterday mid-afternoon, he'd sensed tension in the house: Tobey skulking about and rather surprisingly being ginger about being in the same room whenever Andy was there. Andy had been gloomier than usual. Curt and unwilling to talk. Stomping about when he did get up to move.

Even the dogs had come to stay with Victor when he'd gone out to the pool with a copy of *The Married Man*, a big glass of iced tea, and a towel. Cassius and Portia hung around him all afternoon— around *him*, whom they usually barely tolerated and had certainly never gathered this closely to before!

Dinner last night had been the only bit of relief in the dour atmosphere, and it was a comic relief. Es and El (Esteban and Ellmore) had come over early and had been in rare form. Undistracted by two weeks of fun in the sun in North Africa, their relationship had been reconstituted and its excesses re-infused to its core by fourteen days of Ellmore's unceasing jealousy as Esteban was approached by one Maghrebi cutie after another. "This was no surprise," Elmore was philosophical if digging, "since Stebie wore virtually nothing all the time we were there and took off whatever he had on at any possible two degree rise in the temperature. Those agog lads have seldom seem so much unsoiled, light tan flesh in their poor, deprived lives." For his own part, Esteban remained unconcerned, not to mention unabashed by these fanciful recountings of his possible infidelities. Whenever they were alone, he continued his low voiced verbal assault upon Victor with statements such as, "I'll fill your anus with whipped cream and eat it all out," and other such alleged titillations, more colorful in the contemplation than in the "it's-too-#$#@^*-cold!" reality.

Then Lassiter walked in the door, suave as ever, his ancient shorts a perfect tartan, along with high white socks and loafers. But the shirt was as ever crisp and clean as a whistle. He came for desserts, he said, which consisted of a pitcher of Martinis he made up himself. He regaled them with tales of Kaye Starr and Mary Martin, and all but repeated verbatim their shows he'd accompanied at Stars and Bars, the little club at the top of Radio City in Manhattan.

Despite this wonderful distraction, clearly something was up among the hosts. When he left, Lass took Victor aside and said, "Whatever's going on with those two, stay out of it!"

Victor hoped to hell he could stay out and not be drawn in. No sooner was he up then he quietly snuck into the aquarium dining room. Food was spread upon the table: French toast, bacon, cream cheese, coffee, marmalade. But only one setting had an empty plate. They'd eaten and already dropped their plates into the sink. So Victor settled down and looked over the local paper, *The Desert Sun*, which Andy had spoken of as "Slightly to the right of *The Wall Street Journal*. It advocates the skinning alive, if *not* the drawing and quartering, of illegal immigrants," making gagging motions with his finger and mouth. But at least it reprinted day-old *New York Times* crossword puzzles, and Victor began one.

The Shelties came clambering in, astoundingly clumsy and noisy given their tiny size, and huddled under the table around his unshod feet. As a token of gratitude, he dropped tidbits for them while he hummed away in satisfaction as he planned out his day. There was a used bookstore he could visit; he'd passed it on Sunrise. Maybe he'd take a hike in one of the Indian Canyon trails later this afternoon. An Italian film said to be rather good was playing at the Camelot Cinema on Baristo. (It had played for about a minute in El Lay, so naturally he'd missed it.) If no plans for dinner were announced, he just might take in an evening show, then go to Johns on Palm Canyon Drive for a cheap burrito dinner; stay out and check out the Rainbow Café and Bar; leave tomorrow early.

He'd just gotten comfortable when the phone rang and was picked up. Two minutes later, Andy stomped into the room looking sleep-deprived.

"It's for you," he reported.

"For me?" He told no one he was coming here. Who was there to tell, anyway? Who was there to call him? He, who had easily fielded thirteen calls on any given day in New York City only a few years ago, half of them from Mark, now got at most two phone calls a week, and one of those was usually a wrong number for someone named—as far as he could figure out, given the various accents—Lebchuck Vermacularis.

"You've got to do a big favor," Andy said tonelessly. "When are you driving back?"

"Depends." Victor answered with the utmost delicacy. "I was thinking tomorrow, around 10:00 a.m."

"Perfect. She has to be home by two. That's plenty of time. She'll give you the address and directions. Go. Take the phone. She's waiting."

Andy vanished.

Victor slowly got up, wondering what he was getting into. The iridescent Princess phone lay open on one of the sofas. Outside he heard buzzing and saw though the filmy curtains that Andy was trimming the hedges with a gas-powered clippers.

"Hello?" he tried into the receiver.

"Hello." A woman's voice. Small, clear as a bell, precise. Possibly elderly. "Are you the young man who's going to drive to Los Angeles tomorrow?" Yes, elderly.

"Yes, Ma'am."

"I was going to call a limo to take me. I don't drive anymore."

"That would cost a couple of hundred dollars. I'll take you. Where are you going?"

She gave him an address he didn't know and said it was off Bundy Drive in Brentwood. She was afraid it was out of his way.

Victor almost asked, "The famous Bundy Drive? Like in the O. J. murder trial?" Instead he acted grown up, "*No problema!*"

After she had given him her address and directions, she added, "Carol said you're a published author. Would I know any of your books? I mostly read mysteries. Sometimes romances. And of course, biographies. Carol said you write literary fiction."

"That's right." So this must be one of Carol's "Brassy Old Dames." He just wished he knew who she was. From various visits out here, he knew he wasn't as up on them as the other guys were. "I'll tell you all about my writing tomorrow, and maybe you'll tell me a little about yourself, since we'll have a longish drive."

"Oh, I'm long-retired. There's nothing to tell about my life," she assured him.

"Anyway, it'll be fun having company," he told her before replacing the receiver.

Outside, Andy was furiously trimming away. The path was already littered up to his ankles and yet the endless Oleander hedge looked barely clipped. Victor waited until Andy noticed him and shut off the machine.

"It's all settled! I'll get her at ten."

"I would do it myself . . . "

"Why? I'm going back anyway." Long pause. "It'll be fun."

Andy turned the machine back on and went back to his anger-management intensive-labor.

Victor soon left and didn't return to the house until nearly midnight. Tobey had gone to bed. But Andy was still up. He was by the pool smoking a joint. Clouds enfolded most of hulking San Jacinto Mountain as though it was a Chinese scroll, and the night sky was flecked with clouds that played hide and seek with the stars. The Shelties were nowhere to be seen.

"Don't go in yet," Andy said. "I apologize. I invited you out here and then I was a lousy host."

"Not a problem."

"Here!" The joint as a peace-offering.

Victor went closer and sat and toked on the joint.

"The Fundies want this house." Andy said. "They've made that clear. I don't know what they're prepared to do to get it. I'm guessing they'll do just about anything."

"Tobey's not that sick. It could be years."

"They'll wait. And Tobey's a lot sicker than he looks. He's got half a year at most, more likely a month or two."

Victor wanted to commiserate and at the same time ask why this was so important to Andy.

"It's not just the principle involved," Andy said. Then admitted, "Although that *is* a big part of it."

"The principle being that you're opposed to these Angels of Death. Whereas Tobey—"

"Whereas Tobey grew up with this kind of shit happening all the time in Asswipe, Missouri, and he considers it business as usual."

"And so the lines are drawn."

"We're refusing to bring anyone else in on it," Andy said. "At least so far. Who knows what'll happen down the line."

"If you do, I'll stop coming."

"I know that."

"I like Tobey," Victor said.

"I love Tobey like a brother. We've known each other most of my adult life. He was like my mentor when I came out here. My tiny gay mother. This is all so utterly out of character for him. I can't believe he'd stoop to it."

"Oh. I get it. He's betraying you."

"He's betraying everything *he* stood for and said for decades. Everything I bought. Yes, a simple case of betrayal."

They passed the joint back and forth in silence.

"You're totally objective about this, right?" Andy asked. "So now, you've got to tell me what I should do. As *you* see it."

"Nothing. Nothing until Tobey does something."

"You mean like changing his will?"

"Did he will the house to you before?"

"This house? No. To some cousin in Asswipe."

"Then just monitor the situation. He may never do anything."

"Come on! They're vultures. More come every time. You saw them!"

"Do nothing until you know for certain that he's changed his will in their favor."

"Okay," Andy said. "Then what?"

"Then, as soon as you know that fact, you move out."

"Abandon him to them? No way!"

"You're shrieking, Andy. If Tobey's made that decision, then Tobey knows what your reaction will be. You have to leave and never see him again."

"I can't do *that.*"

He was really shrieking, albeit in a whisper.

"What about your principle? How else can you uphold it?" Victor argued. And when he didn't answer: "An-dy?"

"Of course you're a hundred percent right . . ."

Andy was silent a long while, then asked:

"But that's not the only solution, is it, Victor?"

"No. The other is that you love Tobey unconditionally and you help him die and you don't argue with him. And you quietly leave when it's all over. You don't trash the house. You don't burn it down. You do nothing."

"That would be the other Andrew Grant . . . *Saint* Andrew Grant."

"Well, you fucking *asked!*"

"And you fucking *told* me!"

"And now I'm going to bed and I'm going to forget this conversation happened, and instead I'm going to remember the to-die-for handsome Italian actors I saw in that movie tonight and I'm going to jerk off till my dick falls off."

CHAPTER THIRTY-SEVEN

She was small and she was old. Eighty-five? Ninety? Who could tell? Her hair was white and curly. Sort of wrapped about with a colorful scarf, but not as a kerchief, more as a headband. Her clothing too, seemed a little Hippy-Dippy to him, which was exceptional here in Ultra-Republican-for-anyone-over-fifty Palm Springs. She wore a colorful vest over a pale pink silk blouse and a wide skirt with colored panels in it. Her shoes were deep red, flat, strappy, and they reminded him of a ten-year-old's patent leathers.

She was waiting for him in the high-ceilinged foyer of the big old Spanish Style house, seated like a little girl with her bags at her feet, as though she were going off on her first vacation without her parents and family. She was sitting in profile, as though in thought, or in reverie—and he didn't want to disturb her. But after a minute or two, he tapped lightly on the glass separating them.

She almost leaped up and opened the door for him, amazingly spry.

"I'm so glad you didn't ring," she stage-whispered. Adding, "I think she's taking a nap." Speaking of her hostess. "Poor thing! I probably wore her out. Let me get my bags."

There were only two of them and they were light enough. Victor got them easily into the trunk along with his own multiple bags— he never traveled lightly in his own car if he could help it. He opened the door of his low-slung Japanese coupe for her, concerned about her age and flexibility, and showed how the seat belt just folded over her once she was seated.

She slid right in. "Comfortable?" he asked before he went around to his side.

"I used to have an Alfa-Romeo Spider," she said, gleefully. "Not that long ago, either. I like small, fast cars."

"I drive fast but carefully," he assured her.

Once they were on Palm Canyon Drive, headed out of town, he sped up to sixty. She seemed unfazed.

"I love the desert!" Her eyes were bright and her complexion clear, her skin not all crepey, and her arms and legs looked pretty solid. She was in fact, lovely. Yet she had played a woman about a hundred in *Titanic*, hadn't she? At the beginning and at the end of the movie? "It's so wild and so—clean. I really ought to come out here more often. But I get so busy," she confided.

"I've begun visiting people who live in the higher desert, two, three thousand feet higher," Victor nodded northerly, in the direction they were headed just before they would turn onto the freeway. "Morongo Valley. Yucca Valley. Joshua Tree. It's so amazingly filled with wild life. You almost trip over it, there is so much."

"Calling it a desert is a real misnomer," she agreed. "You may have noticed one of my bags was filled with my paint supplies. I'm usually a water-colorist. But out here, I layer one color slapdash over another, because it's all so intense and bright!"

She began telling him about her painting, how she'd begun it as a hobby, and how eventually she'd ended up doing it all the time, shown in galleries and sold substantial amounts.

"Of course that was an outgrowth of another craft that I'd been doing for some years," she said, "making books. Well, mostly little art and poetry books. From the bottom up. Making my own paper and book covers out of rag and all."

By the time they'd passed Banning and were headed down into the first of the enormous valleys they would pass through, Victor and Gloria Stuart were chatting like old friends.

By the time they'd reached the next one, the San Gabriel Valley, he felt comfortable enough to say, "You must get this question all the time, but weren't you in old-time black and white movies in the 1930's? Or was that someone else? I remember growing up watching this 4:00 p.m. movie program called *Million Dollar Movies*. It showed all these Thirties, Forties and Fifties films. So, in a sense, I was able to grow up with Lon Chaney and Bela Lugosi, with Abbot and Costello, Laurel and Hardy, Ginger Rogers and Fred Astaire, Bette Davis and Barbara

Stanwyck, and all the rest of them. Occasionally, silent stars like Chaplin and Arbuckle and Buster Keaton, too.

"We would watch those movies over and over. They never played in movie theaters, the way they sometimes do now, you know, at repertory houses and festivals and the like. And there were no film classes in schools then, either. Cinema was considered merely a popular art. But lucky us got to know these movies pretty well because they played them twice a year or so. And even though it's difficult to say for sure now, I recall a very pretty young blonde woman named Gloria Stuart in two of my favorites, *The Old Dark House*, and *The Invisible Man*."

"That was me," she said, without any false modesty or boasting. "I began young and made maybe twenty movies in those years, before the war. Then I became interested in the U.S.O. and helping our enlisted men at The Old Garden of Allah, which used to be on Sunset Boulevard not far from where you live now."

"I can't believe it. This is so exciting!" he said.

"Virtually no one ever talks about all that," she admitted. "Oh, of course when *Titanic* came out, they mentioned it a little during all the publicity. Right now, they're completing a documentary about the making of that movie, which should be out in the summer or fall, and in that I talk a little about my past in films. But no one knew, really."

"So . . ." Victor didn't know how to phrase it. "So, if I may ask, what happened? I mean between, what was it? 1939 and 1997. It's a pretty big gap."

"Isn't it? I did some TV, and my one speech was cut from *My Favorite Year* when I danced with Peter O'Toole. Still it's sort of a miracle that I was chosen for this role. I don't know if it will lead to anything, beyond the documentary, of course, but if so I'm ready for it."

She took a breath then said, "What happened, Victor, to be perfectly frank, was that I met a young man. Isn't that what always happens? This young man came to Hollywood from New York. He was a young theater critic for several papers there and his reviews were syndicated elsewhere in the country.

"Well, the Marx Brothers had their plays on in Chicago, written by them, and, of course, starring themselves, and he reviewed the plays. It wasn't just that he reviewed them well, Groucho later said. It was that he reviewed them intelligently, with complete understanding of their madcap brand of humor. So Groucho asked to meet him and they met and soon they discovered that they shared that same zany sense of humor. So after their last show closed in Chicago, the Marx Brothers brought him out to Hollywood to be their writer on the film versions of the plays: *Coconuts* and then *Duck Soup* and then other movies, too."

"His name was Arthur Sheekman, and he and Groucho remained lifelong friends. They died only a month or so apart, you know. That's about twenty years ago, and from the same cause, believe it or not. I met him doing a Broadway show called *Roman Scandals* with Eddie Cantor. Are you old enough to remember him? Then Arthur was the screenwriter on the movie *The Invisible Man*. I was the very visible girlfriend of the Invisible Man. I married Arthur, and in effect I married the Marx brothers, too! Mostly Groucho, because Arthur and he were so close. Groucho found us a house to live in where our back yard connected to his back yard. So they were in and out and we were in and out and the house was filled with them and with their family all the time.

"Being in that situation and raising children and all, it was like . . . unending pandemonium. But of a good kind. I was certainly never for one instant bored. Arthur worked with Groucho and the other brothers on their books, and helped write their touring shows, and he wrote their radio shows, and he also wrote some other movies. Oh, a lot of those! He always made a wonderful living."

Victor discovered that, as Gloria's career failed to go big-time in the late 1930's, unlike many Hollywood actresses she found being a wife and mother satisfying and also discovered her own creative pursuits away from film and television. First, decoupage when they were living in Italy. Then oil-painting, and she showed in major American galleries and sold well. Later on, she became fascinated with the art of making fine and rare books. She still had a studio and worked most days, and so remained open to new things.

She had evidently asked around a little about Victor, and so she knew he'd been involved in various kinds of gay rights issues and she spoke very positively about it. She told him about some of her own involvement in women's rights during the 1930s and 40s, and how she and other women had made demands on the studios for equal pay and equal rights. They had won several important victories, way before the 1970s when it became, in her words, "So popular and fashionable to do that."

At one point, as they passed downtown Los Angeles on their right, he asked her for more succinct directions to her house and she gave them. The address sounded suspiciously close to what he recalled had been Nicole Brown's address, site of the sensational murder case.

"Are you near Dutton's bookstore?" he cautiously asked.

"Victor, where I am is right across the street from the scene of the so-called 'Crime of the Century,'" she admitted.

So he'd been right. "What's that like?"

"Just awful! It was bad enough when it happened. So terrible! Those two nice young people! And all the police people all over the neighborhood for weeks, asking questions over and over again. But once the trial began, and it dragged on for months, you'll remember, well, it got so bad with strange people visiting all over the neighborhood, gawking, stomping on lawns, looking into my windows, that I had to leave the house. I moved into a hotel on the beach until it was all over."

"That really stinks."

"I felt I had no choice."

He got off the 10 at the Bundy ramp and drove north. Approaching her area, he said, "When I lived here in L.A. in '83, I would take Sunset and turn down Bundy to San Vicente to drive out to the beach near the Santa Monica Pier at least once a week, maybe more. And there I was, living in Berlin, Germany, on Schiller Strasse in the Charlottenburg area, in '94, getting the trial on CNN News Nightly, an hour of it at a time. It was weird. Especially hearing O. J.'s lawyers saying that he couldn't have made the drive from Nicole's house back to his own in fifteen minutes late at night. I used to do in eight minutes or less during the day, and so could anyone, except maybe during rush-hour traffic."

The area was quiet enough when he dropped her off. After its flurry of attention, it had sunk back into suburban quietude. Gloria's street had large trees with leaf-dappled lawns and sidewalks. Her house was a rambling story-and-a-half cottage guarded by mature roses and other foliage. It wouldn't have looked out of place in southern Connecticut. "Not the big place we lived in for years in Beverly Hills. But I'm all alone now, except when the grandkids visit."

They promised to keep in touch.

Driving home to Laurel Canyon, Victor remembered, when he'd specifically asked her about sacrificing her movie star career for marriage, Gloria had replied: "I didn't ever think that was what I was doing. I thought I could return at any time. And I did. Well, anyway, I was kept laughing all those years. It seems like a fair trade."

CHAPTER THIRTY-EIGHT

Producer number four was located in Pacific Palisades, a pleasant drive on a spring afternoon, right across Sunset Boulevard from the Yogi Paranamansha Self-Realization Center, and so was at least scenically situated amidst towering eucalyptus and pine trees.

Five little cottages had been painted dove gray and trimmed bone white with severely stripped pale-ash floors and maybe two pieces of furniture assigned to each. The only decor in this office of any excess was a single floor-placed earth-tone ceramic vase holding a six foot high stalk topped by a single, thorny, pale-purple thistle-flower—it looked like what the monster in *Alien* would sport should it happen to require a *buttoniere*.

Amid all this extreme "taste," the producer wore nothing but white: white suit, white t-shirt, all-white track shoes—only once flashing an unanticipated charcoal gray ankle-sock when he crossed a leg—the latter matching his *odalisque* eyes and his expensively snipped helmet of jet hair.

Middle-Eastern and of recent provenance. Unlike the others, he was clean and perfectly, almost astoundingly, courteous.

However he said at most six words altogether in the entire half hour, including "Hello," and when the phone rang, even his taped message was a terse, "Yes?!"

Unspeaking, unresponsive, adamantine in his politeness, he sat: a nice looking Persian or Armenian or Syrian or Turkesmani guy clad in overpriced white material upon an overpriced matte dove gray sofa and listened to them talk about the novel and what a great film it would become. At no time did he respond in any way that could be humanly interpreted as interest.

Within ten minutes, his utter passivity, his lack of any signs of life save for a barely audible, occasional *hmm*, led Victor to—

correctly—assume that he wasn't in any way interested in them or their project.

More than that, it led Victor to fantasize about coming back after hours, grabbing him unawares, tying him up, slowly stripping him, and having his way with the man—if only to elicit some, *any*, reaction!

By the time the more avid, or more unnoticing, Dmitrios was asking Victor which packet of material they ought to leave with the book, Victor was caught wondering why it was they hadn't left hours before, since their interlocutor had been mentally out of the room at least that long.

Joel Edison spread out the photos on his lap and popped the video into the entertainment center TV that took up most of the back of the driver's seat in his Lincoln. "Well! Well! Well!" he said after about five minutes. "And what's Don Wright like in person? Please don't tell me he's five-two."

"Six-two and so butch it hurts. From close up, he smells like he's about to orgasm or just has."

"Gosh All Mighty, Miss Scarlett. You do say the *nicest* things!"

"What if he's straight?" Victor asked.

Joel stifled a laugh. "That's *his* problem!"

"You're going to call him, aren't you?"

"Puh-leeze, I can taste him from here! If you weren't about to make some big money, I'd offer you a finder's fee."

A few minutes later they were at Sam Haddad's office.

In the lobby, two dark, wiry, curly-haired young men met them. Joel introduced them around, but Victor didn't quite get their names nor figure out who they were and why they were going inside with him and Joel.

The double doors opened and in they went.

For a minute Victor thought, "Wait! I've been here before!"

But when? And where?

When he realized both when and where, he also realized that the view, while *almost* the same, wasn't, couldn't *possibly* be the same. Because wasn't that one building away? On the *other* side of Constellation Boulevard, in Century City? That had been 1977, NBC, Brandon Tartikoff's office.

So, Victor hadn't been the only young man to be impressed on that day.

The office was large and the windows were on three sides, with the huge main one behind Sam's desk, which was an antique cherrywood partner's desk from the 1920's with old brass fittings, all of it shined to a dull gleam.

Two other people came in and sat down with notebooks, both evidently from Sam's staff. One was a sexy dark blonde mid-thirties woman, very tightly dressed yet formally, too. Her Peter Pan collar even enclosed a necktie the same color as the blouse. She was officious and crisp down to her slitted gray eyes and somewhat kick-ass attitude, and was named Jamie Drexler. The guy was mid-forties and had a sluggish British, more likely Commonwealth accent. Very nice looking, with dark blue eyes, rugged face, brighter than hers blond hair that he wore long on the sides and back, casually dressed in Dockers and a black Izod that showed a nice torso. He was intro'ed as Colin Renfrew, and based on the shards remaining of Victor's gaydar, he was queer. Sam had just joked that both Jamie and Colin were his "right hand men." Victor wasn't at all surprised to see that Haddad had become one of those executives who always kept a gay man close by at work, whether for contrast, loyalty, or some other unconscious reason.

When Sam shook his hand, Victor murmured, "I remember it like it was yesterday."

Sam gave him a conspiratorial half-smile. Then sobered up to meet the others.

From there on, the meeting was so professional, so succinct, so fast moving, that Victor found he missed a great deal of what was proposed, discussed, thought necessary, added, eliminated, and figured out.

Later on, discussing it with Joel to ensure that he'd gotten it right, Victor came to understand it all in detail. But even during the meeting he had realized that the two dark-haired young men they'd met were Joel's clients, "hot young screenwriters" who would actually be writing the script for *Justify My Sins*. Both liked the story, but each had plot revisions to suggest to update it, and both foresaw technical problems to be gotten around.

When Victor asked the group why they couldn't just go back to the script he and Frank Perry had worked so hard on, Sam stepped in.

"Black Hawk Pictures still owns that script. And yes, the company still exists as some sort of legal entity. Even though Frank is dead, his last wife is still alive as are other relatives and heirs, and even though everything involved with the company is probably embroiled in a variety of suits and countersuits as well as unresolved tax situations, it still owns your script. And while we're on that topic, we can't even use the scenario that you first did for Silver Screen—remember that one, two decades ago? It was pretty good. Why not? Because, again, that company is still existent as a legal entity in some form, and it owns that scenario."

"Explaining why Scott and Evan here will do the story and script," Joel explained. "If you do it, both other parties might get wind of it, step in, and hold up or even legally stop the process at the onset or at any point along the way."

"It will still say 'From the novel by Victor Regina' won't it?" Victor wondered.

Sam, conciliatory: "Naturally! Naturally! It'll say that in the biggest type we can get for it. You know . . . what's not already co-opted by the actors or the director above the title in their own contracts."

Joel: "How about a consultancy for Victor? A co-producer credit?"

Sam: "We'll have to see about that. Jamie," to the younger of his colleagues, with whom one of the screenwriters was flirting, "look into that possibility. And, Colin," addressing the man, "what about those diagrams that I showed you that I'm hoping for us to use as the basis of our production's sets? Those were *never* purchased by Black Hawk. So, Victor and Joel, we'll include them in whatever agreement is drawn up, and refer to them as 'collateral intellectual property.' Will that cover their sale and use, Colin? Good."

Victor was going to ask what diagrams when he saw photocopies being handed around and took them. They were the two drawings he had done on the spot for Frank at Frank's desk in his office: one of the street layout from the book, the other of how the two apartments lined up facing each other, to clarify the script's action.

Seeing them, remembering that day and Frank's exultant excitement over how he'd already done so much of the work for them, Victor suddenly felt the loss of the older man with a jolt that he'd not experienced since hearing the news of his death. Frank had really liked Victor. And the feeling had been mutual.

Sam and Colin, Jamie and Joel were now all discussing other details. He wasn't even sure what details since it had become even more technical, having to do with "most favored nations clauses" and "graduated clauses for sequels and prequels," and he found his mind drifting back to one day when he and Frank had been working out a scene in his office, acting it out. He couldn't even recall what scene, but suddenly they'd both fallen to their hands and knees, Victor hiding behind Frank's giant can of popcorn, Frank behind a stuffed chair, and had begun pretend-shooting at each other like nine-year-olds, using their outstretched hands as guns, until Frank mimed being fatally shot and did an elaborate death scene and they ended up laughing on the carpet.

He remained sitting there, looking out the windows, half hearing the others discussing, wrangling, suddenly stopping and agreeing to discuss whatever it was later, and he found himself thinking it was all so different now: the technical-technological issues were now so hugely complicated for such a simple plot, such an easy-to-make film with its two or three sets and half dozen locations. The financial issues were now equally dauntingly complex for such a simple film with such a small cast. There would have to be dozens more meetings like this, with or most likely without him, or even without Joel, possibly without even Sam, before anything would even begin to happen to launch the project.

He was pulled back into the here and now by Joel at his sleeve and Sam saying, "This is of the utmost importance and will either make or break the project. Casting. We need everyone's input now. Colin has a list of people we want to approach for the two main roles. Go on."

Colin rattled off a series of names of young actors and actresses, only one or two of whom Victor had ever heard of. Colin, often Joel, even the two writers and Jamie all knew these actors, however. They knew their upcoming roles, what roles they'd recently shot, what they already had in cans waiting for release at which studios, and what the "buzz" around each unfinished, sometimes still being shot, or still in post-production, or unreleased film and performance was believed, said, or thought to be.

Victor was about to stop them all and remind them that in the book, the girl was dark, ethnic, Mediterranean, while the boy was fair, Nordic, Midwestern, and the contrast between the two of them was absolutely needed—that is, the same speech he'd made to Frank and Sam sixteen years before.

Then he thought, *Why bother? These people know what they're doing.* Good-looking Colin here, Joel's casting people, the make-up folk, the advertising people, the marketing and publicity people: they are who will select the actors, based not on how they look, or whether they fit the roles or if they can act, that's all assumed or can be rearranged. It'll be because of many other factors, beyond mere availability and the career building programs in place for each, but also on how the actor "tracks" in name recognition and general likeability among film viewers of different ages, according to surveys handed in at screenings in cinemas in Westwood and Pacoima and Simi Valley. *So, anything I say will just be utterly retro and lame and ... old fashioned.*

Lame and old fashioned!

Colin had done some pre-assessments of the production costs under three separate probabilities, dealing with well known stars, actors and director combos, as well as lesser-known and on-the-rise talent combos, and he now began laying those out for everyone in the room. Again utterly losing Victor.

Before he knew it, the meeting was over, people were congratulating each other all around, including him, as though he had actually said or done anything useful or been anything more than merely a presence in the room while it all happened around him.

"I wanted to say what a huge fan I am of your work." Colin took him aside. From close up he was even better looking, strong jaw, facial skin smooth and tanned, the eyebrows intriguingly multi-colored blond. From his rather sluggish first impression he'd become more vivid when speaking at the meeting, and now he was completely alive, his eyes dancing as though with little lights in them.

"When Sam said we were prepping and then meeting about one of your novels, I was totally stoked. I'd not known this one. But I'd picked up *Nights in Black Leather* at Heathrow on my way back home after University one year and read it the entire twenty hour trip, only stopping to eat and use the loo."

"We had the paper chemically treated so you couldn't put it down."

"I couldn't. And I've read everything since. Or, most of them, I believe. It's going to be great working with you. And as you also write screenplays, which I only just discovered ten minutes ago, I'm wondering if we couldn't at some point talk about a project I've got the rights to and am interested in. It's a bit arcane for these folks and will need a literary touch."

"Sam has my number and e-mail."

"Oops! That's His Nibs now," Colin said turning and seeing Haddad and Jamie together, discussing something, "With something not quite so pleasant. We have to hire someone none of us like for a project. I'd better go."

In the Lincoln driving back to Joel's office, the agent was on the phone virtually all the time, excitedly talking to various people in his office or in other offices. Leaving Victor to think about the meeting and, even a little, Colin. He'd not noticed a ring on any finger. Was he perhaps unattached? Unlikely. He was too much of a catch for that. Dream on, Victor.

Only when they were separating at Victor's car in the building's underground garage, did Victor ask Joel, "So . . . We are where? Exactly?"

"They'll do more work on it, then in a few weeks Sam and his people will present it to the larger group there."

"Meaning no offer has even been made yet to option the book?"

"No. But I'm on top of it, Victor. Trust me. Everything will happen in time. Item after item. Everything in the proper order. It's a process. Believe me. Formal as a Japanese tea ceremony. I do this all the time. And today! Today this was a *great* meeting! And I've been to more than a few, so I know," Joel concluded and took another call as he headed toward the elevator, blowing a kiss to Victor.

CHAPTER THIRTY-NINE

"This guy's the real deal. He's aligned with Fox. Worked with them before and they want to work with him again," Dmitrios said as they drove along Beverly Boulevard

He added that Jonathon Dembrowski had done "several big international projects based on the classics, working with people like De Laurentis and Cubby Broccoli making features in Europe. Over here, of course, they'd been major events on television. Miniseries and the like. Very prestigious!"

When Victor heard what they were, he had to agree.

So Dembrowski had actually himself produced long and good movies, although the past tense on that verb was growing ever longer.

And they weren't meeting him at Fox, as Victor had hoped. Instead Dembrowski was treating them to an early dinner at a nice Italian place located in the "Golden Triangle" of Beverly Hills right on Canon Drive where they could all be seen together, this being a big deal, according to Dmitrios.

For the first time Dembrowski actually seemed to fit the role: he was an ordinary looking, middle-aged Jewish man of substantial heft, wearing a good summer-weight Italian wool suit, good shirt and shoes, and he drove a late model Mercedes S-Class sedan to be valet parked. And so he might actually be assumed to still be a "player."

Not much conversation allowed them to learn that he lived on Rancho Road in Encino. While Victor knew this might be posh as all get out, it was rather far from the center of things, Beverly Hills-West Hollywood. But at least he was easy-going and he ordered them all cocktails as well as a bottle of wine for the table.

Dmitrios began with a revised (because it would be broken up by eating and talking convivially) version of his and Victor's pre-arranged "act."

Dembrowski seemed completely unfazed by the allegedly hot-topic nature of the material. In fact, by his own admission he was "fascinated by all this gay business," and he instantly began asking when the younger and cuter Dmitrios (but not Victor) knew he was gay and what he did about it. And with whom.

Juenger was instantly taken in by this candor, and spoke at some length. Their appetizers arrived and Dembrowski kept asking for more details, which Dmitrios continued to supply, the two of them getting chattier and chummier.

Two men Dembrowski knew strode past their table, spotted him, and said hello. The producer eagerly stood and introduced everyone around, explaining to the others that Victor and Dmitrios were "an interesting new development I'm considering." Of course this would allow the others—probably also in The Biz—to assume that Dembrowski was at least tilting back into it via some hot new project. They either bought it whole or pretended to and so it was all extremely cool.

No sooner had the two guys left for their own table and the three sat down again than Dembrowski all but shoulder blocked Victor, facing Dmitrios, and the conversation became increasingly personal and two-sided again.

Sometime after their pasta had been served, Victor concluded that Dembrowski had a case of the hots for Dmitrios, despite having a wife back in the Valley and two grown children in college. Doubtless he was playing this particular game based on physical attraction and was looking in return for physical action.

Victor wondered if this was even worth signaling the younger man about, not to say taking him aside to give warning. Then he figured that Dmitrios was no child, and after all he sure seemed to know what he was doing over there.

Dembrowski had begun to delve into his own past and brought up a certain early morning in a fraternity house when he'd awakened entwined with two other frat brothers, all of them passed out from excessive mixed liquor the night before. Victor realized that he was bored and that the subject of his book and any subsequent film or TV miniseries based on it would probably never come up again tonight. Or if it did, would do so only glancingly and *post-coitus.*

Unseen by the others, he arranged to have his cell phone dial itself, and he took the call loudly.

The other two were only momentarily distracted and hardly at all disturbed when he said he had to leave and did so, just before Dembrowski's *specialite de maison* dessert arrived: the "Volcanic Tiramasu." Instead, Victor ate sliced cantaloupe for dessert at home while watching *Star Trek: Enterprise* on the tube, which, despite good looking and kinda game guys and girls, was a little ho-hum even for someone as over the hill as he apparently was.

He never later asked which packet of material his manager left with Jon Dembrowski. And naturally he never heard Dmitrios mention the name again.

Probably the most exciting thing about the party was being able to see where he lived from a totally different angle, from below—from, in fact, Don Wright's point of view.

It helped that the sun had been smothered early today in an untypical April excess of marine layer. Early fog had settled in, burnishing everything in the canyon in a generous misting-over. The occasionally visible streetlights that wound about the hilly road might have been night traveler's lanterns or gatherings of fireflies. His own place, with its few dim lamps on, its balconies and decks thrust over the hillside above, resembled some fabled Taoist temple, or at least a late Spring pavilion where Mandarins gathered to pen ink-stone poetry about the delights of imbibing rice wine. The entire hillside looked like nothing so much as one of those Sung Dynasty scrolls suspended two stories down at LACMA's Asian Pavilion.

"What a night, huh?" someone said near by.

"It's enchanted!" Victor replied before turning and seeing the other speaker was the Once Famous Actor, the alleged star of the party and Don Wright's big "catch."

"I was going to say *depressing!*" the actor (Victor couldn't recall his name) said. "But yeah, I guess it's also kind of enchanted. Don-Boy tells me you're a writer, so I guess I should listen to what you have to say."

"Don't!" Victor warned. "You're entitled to your own opinion."

"That's true. But even so, we go to writers to tell us something

new, or maybe something more about what we think we're seeing, don't we?"

That was a refreshing way to put it.

"I guess we do," Victor admitted.

His own unwritten experience so far this evening had been to
arrive kind of late, since he was unsure he'd even come, and then
be introduced by his host to others as a "writer," which received
about as much interest as if he'd been introduced as a local car-
pet-layer. When Don went on to say, "No. No, you guys don't get it!
Victor's a *real* writer. He's published like, what was it, Vic? Fifteen
books?," that received a bit more response. Nothing special. Writers, after all, unlike directors and producers and money-men,
didn't hire actors, actresses, make-up people, set-designers, or the
other occupations, which apparently abounded at the party.

True, one dark haired woman who looked like she'd divorced
and then had cosmetic surgery and then done lipo-surgery and
then started Pilates "seriously," did come to him with a mini-tray
of canapés looking for a date, or to fuck, or who knew what. Victor
was polite and vanished at the first opportunity. Now he was
alone on the top terrace in the slightly weepy weather, trying to
remember what he knew about the Once Famous Actor.

"Don mentioned something about how you've returned from
abroad recently," Victor uttered, he hoped politically. "For a new
role, was it?"

"Yeah. I mean I actually came because of some family trouble.
Dad's got prostate cancer and could use support during treatment."

"I hope that works out for him."

"Thanks."

"You've been working abroad all this while?"

The actor laughed and took a sip.

"That's pretty much the official line being given out. The reality is,
I was unofficially eighty-sixed from Hollywood some nine years ago
after a series of what my publicity guy calls 'unsavory incidents.'"

Now it was coming back to Victor. The headlines. The pics of
the actor kickboxing a paparazzo's camera out his hands. Drink,
drugs, and wasn't there also a teenage girl in the picture, hidden
in an SUV somewhere?

"Welcome back."

"Hey, thanks. I did do a few pictures there. But they were all standard stuff. You know." He drew back and swung his body into Kung Fu attitudes and even did a few sudden jabs near Victor's left ear and another with a foot aimed at his groin. "Paid the bills till the Rich Bitches came along. After that, it was just relaxing and Riding the Pussy Popsicle!"

"That sounds sweet," Victor said. He'd not flinched at the hand and footwork and so felt he could say, "if you like pussy."

"I like it well enough. Although, when I come across someone like your pal, Don-Boy inside, well, then I suppose the attractions of the other side become more clear. He's a total package like I *never* was."

"No, you were." Since he'd already been pegged for queer, it was easy for Victor to then say, "The attraction of someone like Don-Boy is that you can have the dick. Then, if you're lucky, and/or play your cards right, you can turn him over and he can have yours. All in that same package."

"You think so?" The actor laughed, and from close up and even in the bad light, he looked less than the thirty-eight years old he surely had to be by now, having been discovered almost two decades ago. Even the bad skin around his chin, from what must have been a torrid acne, was kind of sexy.

"So now," the Once Famous Actor said, "I naturally enough wonder if you said that because you've had him already? Or if I've got to do all the work myself?"

"Don and I are strictly neighbors."

"Even though he talks like you're every Baskin Robbins flavor rolled into one? Saved his life and all that shit."

Once Famous Actor *could* be insistent. And not uncharming.

"Strictly neighbors. The other was . . . unintentional. But I don't think it would take that much work," Victor flirted back, "for *you*, at least! So if you don't see any special female around tonight, you might . . ."

"I might . . . . ?"

"You might get 'a little too drunk to drive home.'"

The actor laughed. "You may be right. He *has* been trying to get me to these monthly parties of his since I got back from Hong Kong."

"There you go!"

He could it see it now. This older, very solid guy, pinning Don Wright to the sheets like one of Nabokov's specimens to a stippled page. The cursory struggle. A few bites. Maybe a knock, forehead to forehead, and then . . . .

"He's just signed with my agent." The Once Famous Actor was thinking it all through aloud. "On top of which, he's looking to get into my very own special project . . ." He finished his drink and set it down. "It would be minor role." He laughed again. "Poor fucker doesn't seem to have a chance, does he?" He nodded. "Know what? You've put it all into real perspective for me! I'm going in for another one of these guys," hoisting the drink, "so I can get convincingly tanked. You coming?"

Some forty minutes later people were splitting. Victor didn't find the Once Famous Actor among their number and suspected he might have already staked out a claim in a bedroom below.

A much older woman with a German accent was speaking to Don and a few others, and when Victor went up to his host to say goodbye, Don grabbed his arm excitedly and pulled him very near, shoulder to shoulder, whispering into his ear, "Magda. My acting coach."

Magda was charming, answering some of the younger guests' questions about how she found Central Europe now, after the Soviet puppet governments had been kicked out. She'd not been there since the 1950s. What she had to say was witty and accurate.

"Victor lived in Berlin a few years ago," Don offered.

"My godmother was German," Victor explained. "Even though she died when I was young, I learned enough German to be comfortable there. But all the educated people speak English."

"Better than we do," Magda put in. "*Wo bleibt Sie im Berlin?*" she asked Victor.

"I lived in the old Western section. Charlottenburg," he answered. "But of course I went all over the city. By subway and by bicycle: *Fahrraden*. One friend had a car and we drove outside the city to the lakes. *Die Heiligen See.* The enchanted forest and all."

"For me it was so fascinating returning, having been there as a girl." Magda said. "But for you it was brand new, yes?"

"Except what I knew about the city and the air-lift and the dividing wall and all. I had friends there, too, that I met in

Manhattan. Also, you could see the past and present side by side all around you in Berlin. It's not hidden."

"A lot like Los Angeles, *nu?*" she asked. "On two blocks of Santa Monica Boulevard you have the old RKO Pictures buildings, turn the corner and there's Charlie Chaplin's Studios, and the old Formosa restaurant, and the Yukon Trading Company, all being used the same or being reused, and it all works together. It all fits. No wonder they are sister cities, Berlin and El Lay."

The others moved away. She and he continued to talk about Germany, and she about what she'd seen of Prague and Budapest. It was a great chat, the one he'd so far missed tonight. And a great contact, like the ones Victor found he made so easily here. Unlike New York or D.C., here people of all pasts, all occupations, came together instantly, fluidly, and easily mixed without needing rigid hierarchies of professional status and income-earning capacity to define their selves and boost their morale.

It was some twenty minutes later, once they had all left the party and he was distantly following three younger men, who were walking uphill in the fog now turned white as milk to where they had parked the car they'd arrived in, that Victor heard his name spoken.

"I'm *sure* it's the same guy. Maybe that's why they were here together. Victor Regina and ____." Naming the Once Famous Actor.

"And Don Wright!" another said.

They couldn't know he was behind them in this fog, Victor lingered out of sight but within hearing.

"Don's aiming for the role of the guy's sidekick or something, in the new film."

"I heard the whole thing is like his big comeback vehicle," the first speaker said. "All the Big Guns are like giving him 'one more chance' and this is 'it.'"

They meant the Once Famous Actor.

The third asked, "And the script is what? Boy-girl?"

"With some twists. Scotty Burns and Evan Dolfmann are writing it. Scotty's girlfriend told my regular squeeze about it. They're adapting some old novel, and like, seriously updating it."

Scotty. Evan. The two screen writers at the meeting at Sam Haddad's office. They were talking about *Justify My Sins*!

"As a vehicle for him?"

"His big comeback vehicle . . ."

"And Don Wright's first film role," the third one added.

"Lucky Don."

"Lucky both of them."

They'd stopped at the car and the driver dropped his keys and Victor walked past on the other side of the road. Even with the fog he knew they knew it was him, since one said after he'd passed, "That was the writer guy, wasn't it?"

"Don said he was a neighbor. Are we getting into the car? It's beginning to seriously *rain*."

In the remaining twenty feet or so to his house, Victor figured out what role Don Wright would be playing, the one he and Frank had taken *out* of their version of the movie. He also understood what role the Once Famous Actor would play: the twenty-two-year-old *naif*, just arrived in Manhattan from the Midwest. Because, of course, he was signed up with Joel Edison. Meaning that he must be the "personal reason" Joel had for doing the film in the first place.

Indoors, Victor shook off the wet jacket and even dried his hair, hearing the rain begin to pour down onto that small section of copper sheathing upstairs, roaring like horses' hooves.

He was baffled and upset by all this news.

Or was he pleased and unsure?

Or was he angry and insecure?

Or . . . ?

It used to be that he could call someone and ask what he was thinking, what he was feeling. His hand had instinctively gone to the phone and begun to dial Mark. But there was no Mark to patiently listen to him and talk it through. No Mark, no Gilbert, no Jeff. No adoring lover, no trusted friends.

No one, in fact, any more. All of them were dead. He was alone. Alone in the rain in an empty, dimly lit house, in a milk-white fog, on the side of a tall hill, in a city he didn't really know and couldn't even see, at the very edge of the continent.

He sat in the dim light of the house with the rain thundering down all around him. For a moment, Victor pictured Done Right and the Once Famous Actor having sex not that far away, just down the hill.

But no matter how he fantasized it, he still felt un-turned-on. And worse, in his gut he felt unrelentingly out of place, with no way to turn back.

CHAPTER FORTY

"It was good of you to arrange to meet me, way out here," Carol said. She was looking a lot more sober; her eyes had an oddly more life-like appearance, although her mascara application had been hit or miss that morning. Still, she'd tried. The rest of the make-up was almost subtle. She was dressed conservatively in a pale blue outfit with a cream sweater over the shoulders, knotted at the throat, apt for her age.

"You look well," he said, then remembered she'd told Andy she hated compliments. "That's *not* a compliment."

"Not taken as one. I'm off the sauce. I'm working too much lately. Or at any rate going in regularly. It's daytime-drama," she specified. "They're all twelve or thirteen years old on the set. I was in a hospital bed scene, right? And the director kept fidgeting with the scene which I thought me and the girl were doing okay. Finally he said, 'The old bag's gotta go!' I thought he meant me." She laughed. "Turned out he meant an ice-pack, some prop on the bed I wasn't even aware of."

She looked down at the menu through very svelte and narrow reading glasses. "I recall the egg salad sandwich being edible."

"I'll take the Pastrami on Rye," Victor said to the waitress in the delicatessen they'd met at. "And a Cel-Ray." To Carol he said, "I like living dangerously."

Carol ordered a coffee, changed it to a decaf, then to a cream soda. After all, they were at Solly's in Van Nuys.

"This is a fun place! Reminds me of *Nueva Jorck.*"

"It's okay." She looked around. "I'm locating places near the Nearly Dead Stars Home where I can be taken out during my declining years, which are approaching fast."

"Is that near here?"

"Woodland Hills." She pointed. "Just up the yellow brick road."

The Oscars were Monday, a week off. Victor figured Carol had called him so they would discuss details about the parties and cars and whatever. Instead she talked about everything else.

A long-retired musical actress her age had just had her memoir published and it had been recently reviewed. Lots of discreet scandal in the book, including that humpy Jeff Chandler—one of the *primo* shirtless "Indian-chiefs" of the 1950s and '60s movies of Victor's lost-in-a-movie-theater youth—had allegedly gotten himself up in drag.

"What a load of bull!" was Carol's assessment of that factoid.

"He didn't get into dresses?" Victor asked.

"He got into *my* dress," Carol said and laughed. "And hers. And plenty of the other half-wits too. But he wasn't into travesty or anything like that. Problem is, she's hit the diving board a few too many times, so who knows what got knocked into or outta her head."

"So some of these guys were real studs, huh?" he asked, all innocence.

"Some of them wouldn't leave you alone. When I first came out to El Lay, Johnnie Weismuller had stopped making films. He was living off his residuals from worldwide serials and from real estate, as he'd bought up a good section of the valley. But he'd make sure he came by and introduced himself. And if he liked you—he liked me—he'd invite you over to his place for a dip in the pool. Great house and what would you expect? Jungle-like pool, with lianas and elephant ears and all that shit. Of course, you'd feel safe with Weismuller in the pool. Guy was like a porpoise. Really in his element . . . Only underwater rapist I've ever met." She laughed. "Smooth as glass. You scarcely knew what was happening until he had that thing in you, and it was pretty noticeable too."

"Underwater? Wow!"

"I asked around—carefully, of course. He did it to everyone. Sort of 'Welcome to Hollywood,' where you're screwed before you know what's happening."

They toasted each other with their delicatessen soft drinks.

"So, about next week?" Victor began. "I'm taking you, yes?"

"No chance, squirt. Bobby always squires me around. How about, wait a minute, Loretta Young said she was peeking her head outta her shell this year. She's not exactly one of the group, and I talk far too blue for her exalted company, but how'd you like to take her around?"

Loretta Young! With the huge blue eyes and porcelain face and long page-boy! God, he sure remembered her! His Mom used to watch her TV show all the time. That would be something to write about in his journals, no?

"That would be great."

"Course, you'll be done in an hour or so. With one of the rest of us, it could be all night. But that's your look-out."

"I'm at your command."

"I'm not putting her down, you understand," Carol said. "She's a nice enough woman. Only, you know, some of us had brains. We stood up for ourselves. And some of us didn't."

"Women, you mean?"

"Women. Queers. Coloreds. Anyone, really. The men with the cigars ran the show from their office, and the guys around them ran us. Or tried to. A few of us rebelled. Bette Davis is the big example. Burt Lancaster also went out on his own early. And Cary Grant later in life. As for me, I came here from New York, and it was after the Big War, hoop de doo! After ten years of Abbott and Costello movies I wanted to do something different."

"They said no?"

She had opened up the egg salad sandwich as soon as it arrived, and she picked at it with her fork and spoon, cutting up the bread into little triangles and eating them last. Her potato salad and pickles landed on Vic's plate, where he gobbled them up as he listened.

"They pretended they never heard. Then some lawyer arrives and tells me I'm under contact, and I can't work for any other studio, and Lah-di-dah. So I left."

"No kidding?"

"They shit a brick! I went back to Broadway and did a few things there. Made a name for myself. They'd never been smart enough to include a theater clause in their contract, so I did theater. Then I did some television. No TV in their contract, either. They never thought that was important. Shows you how much brains they all had. More Broadway, and by then I was the

Mother, not the Girl, so I was scrambling. I had a daughter and no husband. I'll explain later. And TV moved out here and I moved back and I did—"

"*WKRP in Cincinnati!* I loved that show!"

"Where big-boobed Loni was the Girl, and so I was free to be the Rich Old Lady, which was fine by me by then because I needed the work and that's what I'd become anyway. Except for the rich part."

"It's a classic show." Victor said. "You're TV history."

"Hoop-di-doo. I'm not going to eat this half. How's yours?"

"Try some," he offered.

She dipped a fork into it, made a face.

"I didn't mean to go on about that."

"Someone else would have told me, anyway," Victor said. "At least I got the story right."

After a while, he said: "So! Jeff Chandler and Weismuller. Anyone else?"

"Fernando Lamas. Always stepping out on his sweet wife. She let it just go over her head. I would'a killed him. What am I talking about. I was no better."

"You mean the daughter and no husband? The daughter's father?"

"I married someone for a while so she'd have a last name. But no, it was Gene Krupa's kid. Krupa was my guy. Only, stupid me, I hung in there, year after year, believing him when he said he'd divorce his wife . . . He never divorced his wife."

"You're kidding! The great drummer?"

"One of those guys told me you lost someone recently."

"The love of my life," Victor said.

"Then you understand. I mean, it wasn't at all rational on my part. At first it was because the sex was so good. But then . . . and of course I had to know . . . And then he never acknowledged her and all that, and so she's all screwed up, naturally, and of course it's 'all my fault!' Except I don't know how I would do it any different."

"Right."

She looked away at the corner or at some lower heaven where the great drummer must be, and her eyes were young again, briefly.

"Okay, enough of all that horse crap. You call Bobby and he'll tell you what has to be done for next Monday."

"Monday. I'll even vacuum my car."

"Get the tux Saturday, so that you're sure—"

"I own one, remember?"

"Best. And we meet at 4:00 p.m. Sounds too early, I know. He'll give the details because I don't remember."

As they were leaving he said, "You know, Carol, you should write your memoirs."

"They'd need asbestos to print it on," she assured him. And laughed.

Dmitrios had okayed two more not-quite-official-meetings re: *Never Can Say Goodbye*. However, he would not be attending as they were completely Victor's contacts, not his.

The first one took place in the commissary on Disney's "campus" in Burbank, through which a particularly stream-like portion of the Los Angeles River ran—thus the Riverside Boulevard address—and even more surprisingly, horse trails, upon which riders from various local stables passed anywhere you looked, providing a disconcertingly rural aspect.

This informal lunch had been arranged by the lover of a friend of Geoff Bax, Victor's new book editor. They'd all met each other at some shindig or other and spoken briefly. Geoff had done the leg-work. Victor expected little or nothing to come of it. Still, he was tickled to be in the midst of the famous movie studio with its bizarre architecture of Witch Hats and Dumbo-like winged roofs in what was otherwise laid out like a suburban high school with a large and quite fun cafeteria.

There wasn't really much chance that the family-oriented, if gay-friendly, studio chiefs would sanction anything resembling his book into a movie, but he'd mentioned it at the shindig anyway. Via Geoff, he'd mailed out a book and requisite packet with the shortest possible version of the précis: virtually a paint-by-numbers in three pages with lots of white space. This had been read, and, according to Zeb, the guy he had lunch with in the whimsical cafeteria, it had been passed from his unlikely source (The Department of Merchandising: Paper Products) to someone in Film Development.

Victor walked away from the campus an hour later with a full tummy on Zeb's dime and his own unique Disney memento: a black and blue rubber loose-leaf telephone book. It's only sign of origin was the subtle, virtually abstract black-rubber mouse head on the front cover.

For a minute, he actually thought it was this Zeb character calling him back two days later when he took the call. It turned out to be Sam Haddad's assistant, a person of not-aurally-determinable-gender named Leonie, who said. "Oh good, you're there! Hold for Mr. Haddad."

Interference from what sounded like the asteroid belt ensued, followed by the very hollow-sounding if jovial voice of Sam Haddad. "We're having lunch and your name came up. It's close to where you live. Why not join us?"

It was such a surprise that Victor first thought, *He's going to say yes to the film*. Then he realized it was less of a request than a demand.

"Okay, sure. Where are you?"

"Orso! Do you know it? It's on Third between Robertson and San Vicente. We'll only order appetizers. What do you drink? White wine?"

"Fine."

"Don't dress. Come as you are. It'll be fifteen minutes."

It was seventeen minutes because while he did change he also stopped and called Joel Edison's line. Joel was out and Vlacheslav semi-explained, "He kennnt be gontackted nauw."

The directions had seemed familiar to Victor. All the more of a surprise when he pulled up and left his Rice Rocket in the hands of a fourteen-year-old parking valet and peered across the street.

Yes! That very doorway to some medical offices connected to the octopus of Cedars-Sinai Hospital had, for a decade or so, been the entrance to the Club 8709, once the hottest bathhouse in the Continental U.S. So, this must be . . . ?! There were the red brick interior walls, intact, although the rest of the building had been gutted and redecorated to within an inch of its life, including the addition of a big cheery outside dining patio surrounded by obscuring ficus trees and other potted "walls" of foliage. Orso had been Joe Allens! Where twenty-two years ago he had allowed himself to be quote entertained unquote by Joe Whats-his-face, the Schlong Ranger himself.

There was no possible way that Sam Haddad had known about that. He would never have told Sam that story, would he? No, never. Nor Frank either.

Victor had wondered while driving who the "we" that Sam referred to having lunch actually were. He and Joel perhaps? He and the screen writers?

He found them outside on the patio, already having gone through one bottle of Valpolcella and enjoying their *calamari fritti* and *fritti misti.* "They" were his colleagues, Jamie Drexler and Colin Renfrew. With them was a very pretty red-haired young woman, who, from the way she stared on first meeting Victor, he guessed had to be an actress.

So it was a "family" situation. Fine with Victor. Less hassle than if it were all business. Sam was seated between the two women and so Victor took the other side of the table next to Colin, who couldn't have been jollier and more friendly.

"I know this place is very old-fashioned 'The Biz,'" Sam defended himself. "But we were tired of the usual joints. And Tina," obviously the actress, "is new to it all so she doesn't mind. Do you, hon?"

"I love it!" she declared in an unexpectedly smoky alto voice.

Ah! So that's how she'd be in the running for *Justify My Sins*: because of that seductive phone voice!

"Me too," Victor admitted. "In fact, way before *any* of your time, I used to come here. When it was Joe Allen's."

"This was Joe Allen's?" Sam asked. "I always wondered. Frank spoke of it."

"It was Joe Allen's and it was perfectly disgraceful. Except for the cheeseburgers and onion rings, which were sublime."

This led to a general conversation about who made the best contemporary burgers in El Lay, with votes going to In-'n-Out, Fat-Burger, The Silver Spoon, and Hamburger Hamlet—with a preference to the one on Sunset off Doheny. At least among "places where all of us could go," according to Colin, who evidently knew some seedier ones.

He was looking exceptionally good. His hair was naturally

feathered beyond his temples and tucked behind his ears, and in this strong early Spring sunlight, it looked ten shades of blond, all of them good. His face was as tan as a week before and his eyes somehow brighter. Whenever the talk moved away from their side, he began telling Victor about his project, a film based on the life of two elderly British women who, according to him, had lived together alone for decades as proto-feminists and equal-sexers and probably dykes too, in the 1900s in Wales. He went on at great length about them and their biography, which he'd obtained film rights to, and discussed how he could turn it into a film someday. "With some real writing talent," he added. "Not teenagers whose idea of literature is a Green Arrow comic strip!"

Several people came by the table and Colin or Jamie or Sam or sometimes all three would stand to meet them, and then Victor and Tina would be introduced, too. The lively eye contact all around during these moments suggested that some of the meeters would rush right back to their offices and get on the phone where they night hawked as paid sources to *Variety* or *The Hollywood Reporter.* (Why else would Jamie spell names?)

As Victor's *Pappardelle alla Coniglio* arrived and was being eaten, he reconfigured the meeting as an informal-very-early-publicity-on-the-run kind of affair combined with a casual meet-and-greet of a potential actress: a type of lunch highly unlikely anywhere else in the known universe.

While he remained as clued-in as possible to what Sam was saying and to what Colin, closer to him, was saying, even so he missed the significance of the arrival—or perhaps semi-arrival, as he didn't stay—of another fellow. He barely came up to them but stood for a while at the next table over to get attention. First Jamie, then Sam, then at last Colin looked, and the last got up and went over to him. Victor could see through a scrim of yellow hibiscus the two of them greeting with European cheek kisses. The older fellow was very European-looking, bull-chested, solid, with the sneering lips, prow nose, porcine eyes, and thoroughly sculpted head of one of the more dissolute post-Antonine emperors.

"That's Rudolf!" Sam said, seeing Victor looking, and dropped back to his veal *piccata.*

"We're not very fond of Rudolf!" Jamie added, taking a sip of wine.

"That's not so," Sam corrected. "We're not very fond of how Rudolf treats our beloved colleague, Colin."

"We're not at *all* fond of that," she added, giving it even more darkness of tone.

"We think Rudolf is . . . Well, I hesitate to use the word evil unless it's immediately followed by a film agent's name or one of several actors' names," Sam said. "But he's not at all a good influence upon our beloved colleague's personal life."

"He cheats?" Tina asked.

"If it were only that *simple*." Jamie was theatrical.

He makes him do what? Victor wondered. *Be beaten till he's bloody? Eat the flesh of Gentile children? Spit on the Cross? Kite bad checks?*

"We, on the other hand," Sam said, "very much like and very much appreciate one Victor Regina!"

"Who is only *months* away from official Beatification," Victor joked. "No idea why the Lateran Council hasn't called back."

Colin came back to his seat somewhat downcast but cheered up quickly to their laughter.

As they were waiting for their cars to arrive from the hands of one of the Olympic-sprinter valets in front of the restaurant, Sam took Victor by the arm and walked him away from the others.

"Colin is a very busy man," he said. "I keep them all busy. And he's got his own projects. But he's a hundred and twenty percent behind *Justify My Sins*. He'll be the point man in the general meeting. And I heard you two talking about the Ladies of Wherever-it-is project?"

"Llangowen, yes. It would be interesting."

"It really needs a writer's hand in it. *Your* hand, maybe. What do you think? Could you work with him closely?"

Oy, these straight men! Could he be any more transparent?

"I don't know, Sam. He's *so* good looking. I'd be tempted to—"

"Let yourself be tempted," Sam interrupted in a stage-whisper. "Wasn't it you who told me what Oscar Wilde said about temptation?"

"It's a sin to resist temptation!" they said together.

Sam hugged and kissed his cheek and took off in his sparkling chrome and sky-blue classic BMW 702 two-seater convertible.

Driving back home, Victor found himself thinking: Sam isn't even Jewish. He's like, the opposite. What? Jordanian? Egyptian? And look at him, trying to make a *shiddoch*!

CHAPTER FORTY-ONE

He could hear music from the party long before he got near Tobey's house. Then when he did get near, there was no parking anywhere. Cars, most of which he'd never seen before, several of which he recognized, were parked all about the house with no regard to how hot it had been earlier. Among them he spotted the Bentley, signifying that Es and El were there; also several beige Crown Victorias, meaning the Religious were putting in a forceful appearance.

"Hold onto your hairpieces, Girls, it's going to be a stormy night," Victor announced as he opened the gate and entered.

Two tall, nearly naked men clad in what looked like the remnants of silvery togas fled backward in front of him, totally oblivious of him, and then flew up together in the air, where one caught what looked like a sequin-studded Frisbee. The other caught the guy with the Frisbee and they fell in a heap on the lawn just as Portia and Cassius joined them underfoot.

Many were the barks and the giggles that ensued.

Closer to the entry, unusually ajar for this time of day, stood Esteban in a diaphanous tunic, dripping fake diamonds on twenty chains worn against faux-silver shorts. He held crystalware filled with some concoction.

"He walks in beauty! Like the night."

"More like he stumbles in dog-poo," Victor corrected.

The music, which had been loud, got louder as several people began singing at once, "Hell-lo Doll--y!"

Esteban offered a glass. And removed four or five chains to put around Victor's neck, trying to lick his ear or kiss his lips with every one.

"Hemlock?" Victor asked.

"Cosmos. We've got a small lake of the stuff here. That and

Long Island Iced Tea. Tobey wants to use up all the hooch in the house. Leave your bags at the door. You're staying with *us* tonight."

Victor dropped the bag and followed Esteban into the living room. Two elderly tiara-wearing although not otherwise overdressed men were perched on the sofas with fishing rods aimed at opposite aquaria. They shouted "Hi ya!" and hoisted their own cosmos in salutation. One of them was Andy's old pal, the cocktail pianist/showman Lassiter, and the other Alliger Munday. Victor bussed Lass and shook hands with Alliger who said in the unmistakable Scotch brogue, "I've heard so much about you that I took you to be entirely mythical."

"Not from me, he didn't," Lassiter quickly clarified. He went on to tell a story about how he was touring the country with Sally Kellerman impersonating Greta Garbo, of all people, the two of them singing and playing piano, in effect doing a cabaret act. "It was headed for Broadway," Lass said, then sipped. "But it closed in Hamatramack!" He laughed a big, throaty, unbitter laugh, and they joined him.

In the dining room, at least three people appeared to be necking on the ten foot long table. Chips and dips, including guacamole, had been moved to the side.

They ambled into the kitchen, where strange collies and dalmatians were dry humping each other while leaning against the cabinetry.

Victor took a big glass full of cosmo.

"So remind me again what this party is about?"

"It's Tobey's seventy-fifth birthday. His Diamond Jubilee. Thus!" Esteban motioned toward his outfit and the various silver, gold, and sequin-sprinkled decorations.

"That's odd. I thought Andy told me to come because Tobey was dying and wanted to say good-bye."

"Well, you know what, hon? That's happening too," Esteban said brightly. "Both! A birthday and a deathday! Together! Now, if you've got a moment, I wanted to show you what really feels nice with two guys when one has a very fuzzy tongue."

He almost fell into the wall-sized aquarium, just missing by an inch as Victor scooted out of the way, out the French doors and onto the terrace, and almost immediately into a Blue-Point Angora dyed pink. It squalled at him and turned and hissed, claws far out on one paw, but otherwise resembled a dropped, mobile, heap of cotton candy.

"You met Stravinsky!" Elmore picked up the cat, which subsided into a purring ball of fluff. "Have you seen my better half?" He stage-whispered. "We had a big fight."

"No!"

"It was terrible. China went smashing. The cats were all tossed in different directions. Stravinsky here, Schoenberg, *and* Sibelius. Igor-puss is the only one that socializes at all well. So the other two are moping in the Ginger Rogers Memorial Suite."

"Evidently, I'm coming home with you," Victor said.

"You and Miss Grant both. His stuff is already mostly moved in. We'll have a grand time."

As they walked around the garden a bit, Victor asked, "Was this really Tobey's idea? The party? All these . . . people?"

He was being kind with his noun. They peered into the kitchen, where three overweight middle-aged bearded men wearing *pret-a-porter* sequined frocks far too small and far too sheer for them, only partially redeemed by ropes of fake jewels, were standing on the table with arms around each other, singing and kick-dancing "Aint We Got Fun?" Outside, the pool was filled with silver- and gold-foil balloons and was crisscrossed with sequined "Happy Diamond Jubilee" banners strung from the eaves to the oleander bushes. It featured a half dozen muscularly nubile young men in silver lamé Speedos frolicking in the water, punching balloons at each other or necking in side-by-side lounges.

"Yes indeedy!" Elmore giggled. "Tobey picked them all out his very own dear little self! This crew, for example is the entire cast of last year's Coachella Valley hit theater piece. You've heard of *Naked Boys Singing* and *Naked Boys Dancing*? Well, ours was more literary—*Naked Boys Reading Marcel Proust*. Also, Tobey alone knows the secret of exactly what combination of *drogas* are in that ten-gallon garden canister holding the cosmo mixture. He swore Miss Grant to secrecy. And, by the way, you have to go and get your gift. Each one of us gets a departing present."

"Shirley, you jest!"

"I don't. But you can call me Shirley any day of the week."

They'd arrived at the door leading into the master bedroom suite, which was opened but covered with silver and gold curtains.

"Go on!" Elmore shoved him through the material.

Victor was instantly inside the jungly thatched corridor where a half dozen tall dull people in drab clothing were seated or kneeling and loudly praying. It was like being suddenly thrust through a rift in the *Twilight Zone* directly onto Planet Boredom. One looked up at him briefly and smiled, perhaps because he wasn't offensively naked and had only about six sets of glittery beads around his neck. The door to Tobey's bedroom was ajar.

Victor set his drink on a teak table with upended turtle-shell candy dishes, and in seconds the same tall man who'd been there when Victor visited before stuck his head out of the doorway and motioned him to come inside.

Four more people, including the woman from before, were kneeling or seated and far less loudly praying. The room was dim and very cool. Tobey was under a light cover with a fake diamond tiara set on the pillow just above his head. He was very shrunken, and his red hair had finally lost its flame and was settling into recalcitrant embers.

Across from where he lay was the settee with another Happy Birthday banner. On it were dozens of silver and gold-foil wrapped packages, bound in sequined chains.

"Is he conscious?" Victor asked, church-quiet.

"At times," the man answered. "We're not certain when. You are . . . ?"

Victor told him his name and the man went over to the pile of gifts, searching.

Victor knelt at the bedside and leaned over, lightly touching one of Tobey's shrunken little hands. "Hey, cutie!" he stage-whispered. "Happy Birthday! You made it to Seventy-Five."

He felt an inkling of a response in the fingers, but not an iota of Tobey's face moved.

"So . . . do you have your number planned?" Victor asked.

Another tiny, double response, as though in question.

"It'll be your biggest audition ever when you get up there.

You've got to dance like you never danced before. Remember, they'll be filming it all. And you know what, Tobey?" The doubled response in question. "You can dance as long as you want, because it won't just be a novelty act. And no one will ever yell, 'Okay, cut!'"

The fingers responded by holding his pinky. Tobey had gotten the message.

After a minute or two, his finger was released. Toby was sleeping or out of it again due to morphine.

Victor stood and was handed a package and walked out into the corridor again, into the loud praying.

He wasn't going to, but he was so curious that he tore the paper off in front of all the Fundies and then he had to laugh.

He was holding a copy of the 1943 book that had been in the guest suite. It was titled *Ginger Rogers and the Mystery of the Ghostly Ranch.*

"What a guy!" he said loud enough to be heard over the praying.

Outside again he ran into Andy Grant, who was bedecked with tiara, necklaces, and silver lamé, right down to his silver-painted sneakers. He was drunk and he was carrying two glasses of cosmos.

"Look what Tobey gave me!" Victor had to share. "How cool is that?" He took the offered drink and steered Andy to the pool area, where they sat at a table.

"Do you still have the wrapping?" Andy asked.

Victor had bunched it up and stuck in his shorts pocket. He pulled it out and laid it on the table, where Andy picked through the fake beads and pulled out an antique gold watch.

Victor inspected it. "It looks like real gold."

"It's worth about five thou'."

"I can't take this!"

"Maybe you can't *wear* it, since it's so small! But you can certainly *sell* it."

"But . . . why?"

"Tobey said you always supported and encouraged him." Andy sighed. "Unlike stupid me."

Victor thought about what he'd said. "I did again, in there."

"See?"

The party continued madcap around them. After a while Victor asked, "So now what? For you, I mean?"

"I'm moving into Es and El's place. And they're going away to Asia, for like a month. So I'll house-sit the cats and dogs. They're taking Claudius and Portia, too. Then I'll hang with Lassiter awhile at the place he's house sitting, as those people are staying in Bonaire forever! I've already gotten offers from five or six people here at the party to house or pet-sit for them. Others asked me to visit for shorter or longer periods of time. That might take me through a year or two."

"You ought to take this watch," Victor insisted. "You need it more than—"

"It's not the money, although I'm not affluent any more. Tobey left me a lot of things I can sell. The Olds. Another car. He had stocks and bonds, too, stashed away. Who knew? It's just— I don't know what to *do* with myself, Vic! I need to be loose and free and unattached to anyone or anything for a while to . . . I don't know, maybe find out what's important. I know you went through it big time, but Tobey and all this really shook me up."

Taking time out sounded like a good plan to Victor.

"When you run out of those places to stay, I've got a little upstairs sleeping area. It's just a mattress on a floor. Good for maybe a week. Anyway, here's to Tobey!" Victor said. "He came through, in the end."

"He sure did. Look at this party!"

Just then Es and El appeared with a giant severely overdecorated silver- and gold-frosted sheet cake and set it on the table, forcing them to vacate.

Esteban rang a bell while Elmore called out, "Time to sing Happy Birthday!"

When they'd all gathered, Andy parted the silver and gold curtains and Victor went in and asked the Religious to cease their praying for a few minutes. Then he stood looking in both directions, right at the bedroom door lintel.

Yes! From here, if he were at all conscious, Tobey could hear them singing "Happy Birthday Dear Tobey!"

CHAPTER FORTY-TWO

She flung open one of the tall front doors and stood on the blood-red tiled floor wearing a simple cobalt sheath that rose high on her neck, where a double string of globular, obviously authentic pearls glowed. Her hair was long and white and only slightly page-boy. Her eyes were a luminous blue, two shades lighter than the silk dress.

"I love doing that," she said. "You know it took me weeks to learn to do it on the sound-stage because the door they'd put up for the set was so flimsy. It was just pasteboard or fake boards or something. And I kept flinging it too hard. It broke twice!"

"I'm really honored to meet you. I've seen several of your films and my mom was your biggest fan."

"That's lovely . . . Victor, is it?"

He saw her into the car, wondering if it was too low for her to enter, but she was agile and so small.

As he took off, she was quiet. Fifteen minutes later, as he was turning into the *porte cochere* of the house on Carthay Square, she said, "Do you mind if we decide on a few signals for the evening?"

"In fact I'm relieved. I didn't know how to bring it up, myself."

They worked out a half dozen, which amounted to variations on "Get me away from her!" or "Get me outta here!"

"Just one word of warning. Some of these ladies take these awards a bit seriously, if you know what I mean. So no funnin' allowed on the topic of Oscars."

"Including you?" Victor asked.

"*Excluding* me. But I would like to meet several people later, so I've got the few parties I want to go to on this list."

He read two names. Governor's Ball. Mortons. She also handed him the invitations to be held in his tux jacket's inner pocket.

"Take a deep breath and ring the bell," she said.

Carol and Bobby opened the door with loud greetings of "They're finally here!" The evening had begun.

"This fellow is what people in Hollywood who aren't refer to as a, quote, A Class-Act, unquote," a slightly tipsy Sam Alan Haddad said to his wife, Lucinda, who Victor was meeting for the first time. "Did you see who he walked in the door with? A total legend! What befits a legend most? *Another* legend!"

"She's gorgeous!" Lucinda asked. "At what, eighty-something?"

"If it's in the genes," Victor said, "it doesn't ever have to go away. She's very nice too."

"*C*ome sit here with us a minute," Sam instructed, "while she's busy talking to those *alte kockers.* Colin Renfrew is out and about somewhere," he said in a confiding voice. "I understand you two have exchanged e-mails and phone calls."

"Guilty as charged. All business, unfortunately. Scott and Evan's scenario."

"Which everyone has signed off on. Good. Well, you'll get the chance to be far more guilty very soon, as Evil Rudolf has flown the coop."

"Colin left *him,*" Lucinda clarified.

"Oh! Right! When did I become the Ann Landers for El Lay's gay set, anyway? I'm not very good at it."

"Nor me, although I did see Joel Edison chumming about here earlier with ____ ____," Victor named the Once Famous Actor who was the Actor Now Clearly On The Return, "and my neighbor, the former fitness trainer, Mr. Done Right. I've got to take credit for him, at least."

Always quick on the uptake, Sam got the joke. "Is that what you call him?" He laughed. "Did you hear, Luce?"

"Heard and saw both of Joel's clients mobbed by other guys' wives and daughters. Mucho testosteron-i-o!"

"So, you know Joel's set-up, already?" Sam asked. "I get two of those guys more or less for the price of one."

"Because one is untested and the other is damaged goods?" Victor asked.

"Damaged or not, he's insurable again. That's all that matters."

"And I assume contrite, too. Tina too? The young woman we met with the . . ." he went basso for a second ". . . deep, sexy, voice?"

"Do you like her? Colin does. Ask him. I don't know. He'll be line producer. I'd only be Exec."

"Only?"

"Meanwhile I'm finagling the consultancy for you, but it'll have to be a shared credit. That okay?""

"Sounds fine."

"See all I do for you?"

"Next, we'll all watch you walk atop the surface of the reflecting pool without getting wet!"

"There's Jamie and Colin, now," Lucinda alerted them.

Victor followed her direction and saw them. Jamie was oddly all-girl and flouncy in a puffy peach frock. Colin was in a classic summer-white tux with a tartan bow tie and matching cummerbund. He looked as though he'd just stepped off the sound-set of *The Philadelphia Story.*

"Go!" Sam said, pushing Victor out of his seat. "Go make goo-goo eyes with him. In return, you'll get a wonderful man *and* a grade-A film made from your book. Go!"

"I'm going! I'm going! Sheesh!"

It turned out to be Jamie's first Oscar evening, and she was flushed with excitement. She'd championed the costumer who won the Oscar that night for their film, and she'd been more thrilled than the more *soigné* French couturier himself. Colin had been to a few ceremonies before. Even so, he almost choked on his champagne when Victor mentioned who his date was. The two men remained together, more or less saying nothing of any importance, until Lucinda came—doubtless, under Sam's direction—and dragged Jamie away from them and over to their table.

Conversation changed immediately to Joel Edison's "new" talent and their potential connection, which Colin confirmed by saying, "We do this for him, and I'm confident they'll work out fine. Joel Edison didn't get where he is today by handling his clients long-distance."

"You mean he's really hands-on?"

Colin began blushing. "What I meant to say was—"

It was then that Victor saw Loretta making a signal, which, if he recalled correctly meant "Not right away, but in a few minutes, come get me."

"My date's about to take me outta here," Victor said. "I suppose it's an early night for the Virtuous."

"And I. Though I've got one more hoe-down to face. I'd much rather Jamie and Sam and Lucinda went on without me."

It was then that a very awkward, nearly abstract, sentence questioning why both should have to be alone later, emerged from out of Victor's mouth unbidden. And it was taken up equally awkwardly by Colin, who stammered cutely while trying to think up a few especially dumb excuses for both of them going home separately and alone, which included working-out to make up for earlier wretched food and alcohol excesses; catching and answering all the congratulatory e-mails and phone calls that were sure to arrive; and something having to do with laying out fresh newspaper for budgerigars, whatever they might be—small caged birds, possibly, Victor thought.

Then, more hopefully, Colin appended to all that malarkey this statement: "Of course, I still have the printed-out e-mail directions to your place from—what was it, earlier this week?"

Equally more hopeful, if equally dim, Victor asked, "And who's to stop you from using those directions?"

This rhetorical query went unanswered, as it deserved to be, as several people Victor didn't know came up to them in their exposed position and grabbed at and cheered Colin, who seemed to know them all pretty well, and who was all but borne aloft by them to the other end of the party to meet some people he knew from some other film they'd all worked on together some time ago. *Oh well,* Victor figured, *maybe Sam will get his wish another time.*

Then he glanced at Loretta, who was much more clearly signaling, "Get me outta here!"

So he did.

As they got into the car, Loretta was thoughtful. She sat back in the passenger seat of the Rice Rocket and Victor thought for the first time since he'd met her that she did not appear completely serene and peaceful.

"Events like these must bring back all kinds of memories for you," he suggested.

"Yes," she said, and the luminous eyes were fully on him, even in the dark, as he pulled away from the parking lot on South Crescent Heights Boulevard. "They really do!" She seemed a little surprised to admit it. "One in particular, oh, forty-odd years ago."

Victor drove on through the tangle of side streets until he'd reached Third and could move freely.

"Want to talk about it?"

"Not really. Well, why not?" She answered herself. "It was a studio date, put together by the Fox publicity department to boost both myself and the young man. We were about to open together in a comedy, *Love is News*, I believe was its awful title. He was the serious young reporter, I was the snobbish heiress in the news all the time. I guess you can figure out where that script went."

"And . . . ?"

"And I was thinking how blue he was. I don't mean just that festive Oscar evening. I meant in life. How nothing could surprise him, or therefore, really please him. Most young actors would have thrilled by it all. But not him . . . Ten years later, when I saw him in the film they made of Somerset Maugham's *The Razor's Edge*, it seemed to me for the first time that he was playing himself. You know, that finally all of us were seeing the *real* Tyrone. But even at the beginning he was unsatisfiable, somehow . . . And then he died so young!"

"Didn't I read somewhere that the action he saw in the Pacific Theater during the war turned him into a nihilist?" Victor asked.

"That's just it, Victor. I think he was one from the beginning."

They'd gone a few minutes when she suddenly turned her entire little body toward Victor and said, "It must be fascinating to an observant person like a writer to see all *that* going on around you, including me having my memories."

"It is."

"Won't you want to write about it some day? To write your very own 'Hollywood Novel'?"

"I've never given thought to anything like that. I don't know . . . Maybe . . . Someday . . . " Victor wavered. Then, thinking about what had happened to him that evening, "But if I ever do, I've already got a title for it." He'd stopped for a red light, and looked at her, "I'll call it, *No More Happy Endings*."

"Oh! *That's* too bad. I *love* happy endings," she said.

"Me too," he confessed. Then he added, "And you got a happy ending yourself, at long last."

"You mean with my daughter? Yes. At long last, the truth came out!"

He wondered if she was one of the actresses Carol didn't respect because they'd let their private lives be dictated to by studio bosses. But he was afraid to ask, so they didn't speak again.

When they arrived at the house where she was staying, he got out and saw her to the door.

She'd still been thinking.

"I'm sorry," she now said, seemingly out of nowhere, "that you got bad news this evening about your movie!"

"In fact," he replied, "it was more like good news. A green-light, as they say in the Biz. The problem is, I don't know how much I want to involve myself with people whose motives seem so . . . I don't know. I want to say harebrained, but that's not true. Just . . . weird. At least to me. Am I being too judgmental? What do you think?"

"You must aim for the happy ending," she instructed.

"Got it! Still, in my gut, I believe the movie will never be made."

"You say that with such finality! If you're so certain, you can't be disappointed, can you?"

"Should I take the money and whatever other goodies and run?"

"No. Take the money and whatever other goodies and stay!"

She had to reach way up to kiss Victor on the cheek. He could see she was on her tippy toes, just as she must have had to stand when she kissed John Wayne and Tyrone Power.

"Whatever happens," Victor said, with a deep-voiced, fake Bogart accent, "I'll always have this memory!"

"Oh! You big *tease!*" she laughed and went inside.

It was only ten o'clock; early, as Carol had predicted. At home fifteen minutes later, Victor changed into a close fitting sweat shirt and black workout pants and sat drinking out of a bottle of cold Semillon he'd kept in the fridge. He sat for a long time sipping, trying not to think about the evening, trying not to think about the past.

Fog had begun to settle over the L.A. basin, and it was coming on so quickly that it was affecting all those revolving klieg lights from all those Oscar parties along Sunset, Hollywood Boulevard, and upper La Cienaga—from all around town, softening their light and at the same time extending their bright cones almost limitlessly on all sides, so that now they were filling the entire sky and softly brushing edges with each other, colliding, drawing all together. It was kind of lovely, Victor was musing, when the phone rang.

Carol checking up on him? Or her date, the evening's organizer, checking to see that he'd gotten Miss Young home?

"I'm on Laurel Canyon driving north and the fog is dropping like a stone. I know I turn off ____. Then what?"

It was neither Carol nor her date. The Commonwealth accent was unmistakable.

"Is that you, Colin? You're headed here?"

"You invited me, remember? Should I not? Here's the turn! Quick! What do I do?"

"*Left!* Turn left!"

"Okay, left. It's a sweeping ess-turn upward. Now what?"

"Keep going. Make a right at the first stop-sign."

"Here we go! You did want me to come, didn't you? I thought I detected an actual invite."

"Yes. Of course. *Yes.*"

Victor went to the balcony and looked down. Only one car was moving, seemingly led by its headlights amid the maze of streets and houses below

"I can see your head-lamps from here!" Victor reported.

"That's reassuring. You see, I'm a bit tanked. Actually a bit more than tanked. I haven't a clue what I'm doing."

"I'll guide you. I can see you from here."

"All right. But I meant that about something else, you know. About more than just driving."

Victor kept silent.

"You're still there?"

"I'm still here. You're telling me that you're not responsible for your actions because of what you've just been through."

"No, of course not. That's all over with."

"I can see you're one big ess-curve away."

"Here it is. The ess-curve."

"Are people pressuring you?" *You, too?* Victor had almost asked. He answered himself aloud. "Of course, they're pressuring you."

"They mean it for the best, you understand. They think I'm ruining my life. I'm passing a white house with a solid red door. I can't completely say they're wrong," Colin added. "I see numbers on the curbside." Colin gave out the numbers. He was at Don Wright's house.

"I'm the next driveway up the hill," Victor said. "The real question is, what do *you* think?"

"Here I am, at your driveway. Obviously I'm beyond knowing *what* to think! I'm acting completely on impulse! . . . Okay, I'm here and I'm driving in."

Victor left the balcony and went to the entry. When he opened the door, Colin was just arriving down the steps from the parking area, walking rather carefully and then forward along the path. He had a bottle of champagne in one jacket pocket—Victor could see the Moët label—and two champagne flutes in the other pocket. His cell phone was still up to his ear.

"There you are! I've made it!" Colin reported into the phone and then closed it and put in into his pants pocket.

He didn't look drunk, although his bow tie was loosened and his cummerbund missing and his shirt front was open four buttons down, revealing blond chest hair.

A tall handsome blond man in a white tuxedo with champagne and glasses in his pockets? *Where have I seen this astonishingly inviting image before?* Victor asked himself. Then answered himself: *Bill Holden! In* Sabrina! *Look how everything conspires to rope me in so I take the jump and I'm back riding the Wheel of Fortune again,* he thought. *Look! How everything conspires!*

"I look a fright, do I?" Colin asked.

"You look terrific!" Victor said. Like a movie star at his handsomest, he could have added, but didn't.

"I was right to come, was I?"

"You were right to come!" Victor let him inside and turned to see Colin holding out the champagne and glasses, then setting them down and taking off his jacket.

Colin barely looked around the dim room, but went—almost as though drawn—past the open glass doorway to the balcony sharply overhanging the hillside.

The klieg lights now spun gigantic misted cones through an ever-deepening charcoal gray fog. They completely filled the night sky with their lunatic gyrations.

"Now *that's* something one doesn't see every day! I always wondered why people would want to live way up here!"

Victor joined him on the balcony in the oddly illuminated night. Colin took one arm familiarly.

"Doesn't that pretty fellow we met tonight whom Edison wants in our film live somewhere nearby?"

"Right down there." Victor pointed to the dimly lit, temporarily unoccupied house.

"I thought for certain you'd be interested in him."

"Too young. Also, to my knowledge, he *never* carries champagne in his tux pockets."

"I can't possibly drive back down that unbelievable road, you understand," Colin said with total seriousness. "You must be Mario Andretti or some gymkhana whiz to do it daily. I made it up on sheer nerve!"

"So you'll have to stay the night."

Colin faced him and put both arms around his shoulders.

"You understand, of course, that you're letting yourself in for a *world* of trouble, having anything at all to do with me?"

Everything conspired. And I even got the warning, Victor thought. *How kind.*

"I understand, yes."

"I felt it my bounden duty to warn you. But if you're that far gone into equal madness, I suppose it's okay," Colin said rather recklessly.

He had to lift Victor by the shoulders till their faces met and he could kiss him.

Look at me, Victor thought. *I'm on a balcony in the Hollywood Hills, kissing a lovable foreigner, and I'm up on tippy toes. Just like Loretta Young!*

340

FADE TO BLACK

Acknowledgments

None of the previous story would have happened if I hadn't in the first place been invited by people in the film and television industries to adapt my novel into their media—several times! When possible, they are named. Similarly, if I had not moved to Los Angeles in 1995, I wouldn't have encountered and been befriended by the many talented men and especially women who worked in classic Hollywood films and TV. They are also named. Of equal importance, my thanks to those fiction anthology editors who published excerpts from this novel-in-progress over the years, in effect convincing me that it had some merit: Steve Soucy in *90069*, Timothy Lambert in *Fool For Love*, and Torstjen Hoejer in *Speak My Language.* Last, not least, I thank Louis Flint Ceci who read the manuscript closely many times without losing consciousness and who actually helped get it into its current condition.

About the Author

Despite his Bachelor's Degree and evident visual and draughting skills, no one wanted to hire Felice Picano as an artist or even as an art director after college. Instead he was roped into a series of moderately entertaining, barely paid, minimally creative editorial and writing jobs. These led nowhere important, and Picano ended up alternately book selling on the outskirts of the Warhol Factory among hangers-on, and at minimal pay occupations too embarrassing to recount. Somehow, one or other of these led to Rizzoli Bookstore, where eventually someone on staff thought him too pretentious for even that high falutin' store. They found him a literary agent who was beginning her own agency. She was desperate for anyone knowing the rudiments of the English language to flog to corporate-publishers, who should have known better. That madness led to repeated publication, a prestigious award nomination, book club and foreign language sales, and eventually best sellers. Everything since then—and it wasn't far to go—has been downhill.

Until this book, which has been one of the most rational, pleasant, and easy experiences he can recall.

CPSIA information can be obtained
at www.ICGtesting.com
Printed in the USA
LVHW110804291019
635678LV00001B/3/P

9 780998 126289